TIME BENDERS
AND THE LONG ROAD HOME
BOOK III

JB YANNI

authorHOUSE®

AuthorHouse™
1663 Liberty Drive
Bloomington, IN 47403
www.authorhouse.com
Phone: 833-262-8899

Published by AuthorHouse   07/12/2021

ISBN: 978-1-6655-2910-5 (sc)
ISBN: 978-1-6655-2908-2 (hc)
ISBN: 978-1-6655-2909-9 (e)

Library of Congress Control Number: 2021911951

Print information available on the last page.

This book is printed on acid-free paper.

FOR MY GRANDMA FLOYE and Nany. Two of the strongest women I've ever known, and where I learned everything from painting, to fashion rules, to sewing, to cooking. More importantly, it is from them I learned about strength of character and devotion to family. In their quiet strength, I have found two of the best heroes and examples of how to live. Though they are both gone now, they continue to be in my thoughts and in my heart. Every day there is something I wish I could share with them.

1

MARY AND THE OTHERS looked expectantly at Mr. Brewster, waiting for him to reply. Deb didn't understand what was taking so long, so she said again, "Mr. Brewster, of course, we want to know about your trips and how the machine was and everything, but really, we need to know what you learned about Mary's future."

After a few minutes where Mr. Brewster looked around at the kids and then at Thomas, he found he couldn't say a word. He couldn't tell them the news as it would break Mary's heart. Thankfully, Thomas stepped in. "I saw the report, Mary, before the nurse pulled it back when you left the office, and you do have the marker. I'm sorry to be so blunt, but there is no easy way to say this."

Mary looked down. No one said a word for several minutes and then Deb recovered. "What exactly does that mean, Thomas?"

"Truthfully, all it means is that she has the marker that was discovered in the mid-1980s and came into diagnostic use regularly a few years later. It doesn't mean that she is guaranteed to get breast cancer, and it certainly doesn't mean she is going to die from it. Advancements were already well underway for treatments when we went to the last date in the future."

"So, she could go her whole life with this marker and never get cancer, right?" Becky asked, hopefully.

"That's right. I was reading in studies that had been completed when we visited Mary the last time on our trips. Researchers were finding many more people had the marker than had developed breast cancer. With those findings, it would be safe to say she only has about a thirty percent chance of developing cancer."

"But you don't know that for sure, do you, Thomas?" Mary asked, still looking down at her lap because she was unable to look at any of them for fear of crying.

"No, Mary, I can't say for sure if you will or will not develop breast cancer later in your life, or if treatments will be discovered and made ready to treat you if you do develop it. There is no way to know for sure," Thomas replied as calmly as he could.

"Thank you, Thomas, and you too, Mr. Brewster, for doing this for me. Thanks to all of you, really, for helping me to discover what's in store for me. If it's ok, though, I just need a little time alone to process this, so I might skip the review of the trips. If that's ok with you all," Mary said as she climbed off the stool.

"Can I come with you, Mary?" Deb asked. "I don't think you should be alone actually."

"No, Deb. I need a little time. Maybe we can talk later?"

"Are you sure, Mary?"

"Yes, I'm sure. I'll come find you later."

At that, Mary left the barn. The rest of them sat very quietly for a few minutes and then Joe said, "Ok, why don't you start from the beginning and tell us everything. I think Deb is going to need to be prepared for when Mary does want to talk."

Mr. Brewster began to relay to the kids the events of the three trips they made in the machine. He told them that the machine performed beautifully, and the settings were nearly exact on the locations they picked. They discussed the logistics for a few minutes and determined they would check the logs, with the theory being that Joe's new programming language may have had a considerable impact on the performance of the machine. Then Thomas relayed the information they learned from the second and third trips. Together he and Mr. Brewster talked through going to Mary's apartment, setting up her blood test, and then meeting her at the hospital to see the results. They explained that Mary suddenly left before seeing the results when Ken showed up at the hospital. Apparently, he had called Mary at work and discovered that she was there, having some tests. He became agitated and went to see her. Thomas explained that while the nurse was asking about their relationship to Mary, he saw the results that showed her being positive for the marker.

"Well, I know this is not turning out to be a celebration, but this does mean the machine can go into the future without too many adverse effects, doesn't it, Joe?" Becky asked.

"I don't feel any differently, but I don't know about anybody else. Deb, Kim, did you feel any differently this morning or yesterday when they got back? Did you remember anything that seemed strange?" Joe asked.

"No," Deb said.

Kim agreed and so did Ryan.

"I realized this morning when I got up, Joe, that it might be possible that Thomas and I would forget the trips because of the jump into the future, but, because they happened in my present, I still have full memory of everything. I think that might be why you all don't feel differently, because you didn't make the trips, but it happened in your present as well. This seems to match what happened when any of us went to the past, so I expected it here as well," Mr. Brewster pondered.

"That makes sense. Since we didn't go, we wouldn't feel any different. And because you went to the future, we won't know yet if you changed anything inadvertently."

"How could we change something?" Thomas asked. "We barely spoke to anyone but Mary."

"Not true, Thomas. We talked to the truck driver that gave us a ride, the waitresses in several restaurants, the building manager at Mary's apartment building, several people at the hotel where we stayed, then finally, the nurse," Mr. Brewster replied.

"Any one of them could have heard you say something about the machine, time-traveling, or even something more mundane and be changed by it," Joe said.

"Yeah, like what if some young lady saw you, Thomas, on the street, and decided she wanted to meet you. Perhaps she searched for you for days and days and even broke off her engagement with the man she had planned to marry. That would change generations to come in her family," Kim added somewhat earnestly.

"That seems a little far-fetched, Kim, but a compliment anyway, I think," Thomas said laughing.

Everyone seemed to slump back on their stools, relaxing for the first time since they sat down.

"But Kim's right. We have no way to know what your interactions may have done. That is going to be a big problem with travel into the future.

We won't know, and we won't be able to just jump back into the machine and fix things," Joe added, more seriously.

"Can you imagine a future where we have to keep coming back and getting into the machine to fix an issue we realize was created by our time travel?" Becky asked no one in particular.

"We would be doing nothing but jumping back and forth in the time machine, each time potentially changing something else," Kim speculated.

"Or could it be that our future required the time travel to make it happen the way it should? I mean these questions could fry your brain if you start down this rabbit hole!" Ryan added, throwing up his arms

"I believe there are few novels that deal with these very questions, Ryan. So, at least authors have contemplated these questions. I'm not sure if the scientists have come up with anything meaningful yet," Mr. Brewster commented.

"Books about time travel? I want to read one. What are these books called, Mr. Brewster?" Kim asked, excitedly.

"*The Time Machine,* by H.G. Wells. It is the quintessential novel on time travel," Mr. Brewster said.

"Maybe we're getting a little off task here," Ryan suggested.

Joe got up at that point, went into the machine, and started the process for it to print out logs of the trips. He came back to the table as Kim said, "How are we going to help Mary?"

"I'm not sure," Deb said.

"Well, I don't have any ideas, but having you with her will have to help. She's going to need someone to listen," Becky said.

"Let's head back to campus then," Ryan offered.

They all got up to leave. Mr. Brewster said he would put the printouts on the table for when Joe was ready to go over them. After they shut down the lights, Mr. Brewster and Thomas went into his house.

"I feel terrible, Dad. We just brought this terrible news to Mary, and I can't do anything about it. Are you feeling that way too?" Thomas asked his father as they sat at his kitchen table.

"Yes, I do. She seemed so lost, and I feel so powerless."

"Should we not have done this?"

"I don't know. I've come to care about these kids so much. It's like they're my kids too—as much as you are my son. I felt compelled to do this to help one of them, and now I feel we have done everything but help her. This is one of the fears of time travel to the future that I've read about."

"What do you mean?"

"Well, if you know what's in store for you, what will happen to you? Why would you try anymore? It's like finding out there's going to be a war. Why work hard to build a nice new house if you know a bomb is going to be dropped on it in ten years. Knowing what is in your future might make you lose hope, and at the very least, it changes your behavior."

"I think I understand. Knowing what's in store changes your outlook. I can see how you would lose hope."

"Exactly."

"Is that how you felt when you went to meet your father?"

"No", his father answered, smiling at the memory of that day, "that was so totally different. I felt so good about doing that. Even that little bit of time I had to talk with him made me feel, finally, like I knew him. He became a part of my life. This is totally different."

"Well, I hate to leave you now, what with the kids in such a difficult position, but I've got to get back or Brittany will worry."

"Yes, I know you do. I'll be fine. Will you be ok?"

"I think so. Do you think I should tell Brittany about this?"

"That's going to be up to you, Son. I can tell you that Ken, Deb, and Joe all wrestled with telling the person they were involved with about the time-traveling they had been doing, in the same way I wrestled with telling you about it. The important thing to consider is that this is Joe's discovery, and if it gets out to the wider public, it needs to be because Joe wants it to. If you tell Brittany, you have to be sure she understands she can't talk about it to anyone but you."

"I can do that. I just don't want to keep this from her. If feels too important."

They talked a while longer and then prepared dinner before Thomas got ready to head home the next morning.

Back at the dorms, Deb went directly to Mary's room. When Mary didn't answer, she went back to the lobby area and told the others that she didn't think Mary was in her room. Kim ran out the main door, coming back a minute later and saying Mary's car was gone. Joe and Becky said they were going to go meet some friends in the Main Hall, and Kim went to go play games with her friends. Ryan left to get some homework and then came back to wait with Deb. He and Deb sat in the lobby area waiting for Mary to return and attempted to concentrate on homework.

Mary had left almost as soon as she got back to the dorm. She needed to think, without anyone bothering her. She got in the car and drove, ending up at the church. She entered and headed up to the front row of the chapel. Kneeling, she began to pray. Reverend Patrick saw Mary with her head down in prayer and waited to see if she needed any help. When he heard her start to cry, he approached and sat down.

"Mary, you're clearly troubled. Can I help?" Reverend Patrick asked.

"Oh, Reverend Patrick, I don't think anyone can help!"

"I heard about your grandmother from Deborah. I'm so sorry for your loss. Is that what's troubling you?"

"It's partly that. I don't know how much Deb told you, but she died of cancer. She was sick for a long time, and no one could figure out what was wrong with her. My parents finally found a doctor that figured it out, but by then it was too late. She had so much cancer inside her there was nothing they could do. But really, what's troubling me is that I just found out this cancer is genetic, and I probably will get it too."

"Dear, I know the doctors are doing amazing things to advance the treatments and tests for all kinds of diseases. Just because you might have a family history for something, it doesn't mean you will get it, and it certainly doesn't mean that it will take you, like it took your grandmother. Also, as you came here for comfort and to pray, you know that prayer is a powerful thing. And more powerful is the Lord's love for us and our Savior's power over everything, including death. Have you considered that? Your grandmother is with our Savior now. That doesn't have to be something to fear."

"Yes, that's why I'm here. But there's more. There's Ken. What am I going to do about Ken?"

"I'm not sure I understand what needs to be done about Ken?"

"I can't ask him to commit his life to me if I'm going to end up very sick and die from this. It would be so wrong. To put him through all that, asking him to put his life on hold while he has to take care of me. And it was so awful. My grandmother was so sick, and so pale and looked like she could be blown over by a light breeze. I don't want him to ever see me like that!"

"Mary, every day people get married in churches across the country, committing their lives to one another, with full knowledge that someday, some moment in the future, they could be called upon to care for that other person in sickness, to hold their hand in their last moments on Earth. This is, in fact, part of the vows. If you and Ken really love one another, even having some advanced knowledge that there might be trouble ahead shouldn't change that commitment."

"It's because I love him that I want to protect him from this."

"Yes, everyone wants to protect those we love from trouble, but facing trouble is part of being in a marriage or a relationship with someone."

"I just don't think I can do that to him. You didn't see her—my grandmother—she was so frail... so white. She had dwindled down to just skin and bones. It was scary to see," Mary said as she put her head down again, with tears running down her cheeks.

"I'm sure it was. Were you with her at the end?"

"Yeah. She looked at me, and in her eyes, I saw all the memories of the time she spent with me. She said to find happiness and love and give happiness and love whenever I could, then she closed her eyes and took several last painful, shattered breaths, and then she was gone."

Reverend Patrick put his hand on Mary's shoulder as he said, "See, Mary, she understood. We need to love one another and share life with others. She was trying to tell you it was going to be alright. She was telling you she was ready to go to her Lord."

"How does that help?"

"I know you're in pain, and you're scared, but, Mary, her soul leaving was her soul going to heaven and settling in your heart when you are ready to see that."

"I feel her with me. I have since that moment she closed her eyes. But here's the thing, how can I stand at the altar and promise to give myself to Ken and commit to making him happy knowing that my end may already be determined?"

"With faith. Everyone has an end that is determined, by the Lord. And you really don't know when yours will be or what circumstances you'll find yourself in."

"It's hard, you know, to have faith. At the very moment in your life when you need it most, it seems hardest to find."

"That's probably why they call it faith." Reverend Patrick got up and left Mary to her prayers. She sat there for a long time. Eventually, she got up, and returned to her car. Mary pulled a tissue out of her purse and wiped her tears and nose, and drove back to campus.

Deb jumped up when she saw Mary come into the dorm. She went over to Mary and hugged her. Ryan got up and packed up his books and things and Deb's too. He left, and Mary and Deb went up to Mary's room.

"Where did you go?" Deb asked, as they sat on Mary's bed.

"I ended up at the church. I talked to Reverend Patrick for a while and prayed."

"What did you talk about?"

"About faith, my grandmother, how I don't want to make Ken watch me die from cancer, and how every married couple promises to love in sickness and health. The only difference here is that I might already know my fate."

"Oh, Mary. Kenny loves you. He wouldn't look at this the way you're thinking he would, I know it."

"I know you're right. That's part of the problem, you see. He would stay with me, even if I told him today that I will probably get cancer. He would stick with me and care for me through it all. But what kind of life would that be for him?"

"One that includes the girl he loves—and I'm sure a lot of happiness."

"I want so much more for him. He deserves to be happy, with a woman who will be there to grow old with him and give him children, and all the things he wants."

"What on earth makes you think that with this marker, you wouldn't be able to have kids or grow old? Your grandmother had your father with it, and she was older when she died from this, remember? I'm sure if we go back, right now in the machine, and have your grandmother tested when she was your age, we will find she had this marker too."

"I don't know. It's just something I feel I can't do, or maybe that I'm afraid of, I just don't know!"

"I was reading while Mr. Brewster and Thomas were gone, and we talked a little about it after you left the barn, about how psychologically, if we know our fate, what will happen to us, we stop trying to better ourselves, learn, and have hope."

"What're you saying?"

"I'm saying that maybe what you're feeling today, is just that. Maybe learning you have this marker has instantly made you lose hope."

They sat there for a long time not talking, each thinking things through, then Mary said, "Listen, Deb, you have to make sure the others don't tell Ken about this. You can't tell Ken about this— at least, not until I'm ready."

"I'll agree to do this for you, Mary, so long as you don't do anything foolish until you have really thought this through, and we've had time to talk more. Deal?"

"Deal."

The next few days seemed to pass in a blur for Deb. Mary was doing her best to isolate herself from everyone and looked like she barely slept. Deb kept asking her if she needed to talk again, but she declined. That weekend, Ken announced that he was spending the next two weeks on Harvard's campus to finish his final papers and prepare for his finals. Mary was fine with his plan because she was not ready to face him. Deb was glad on the one hand, as she totally didn't think she could keep Mary's secret if he came to Choate right now, but on the other, she felt like she needed her brother's help. They spent the weekend close to campus, partaking in the scheduled movies, games, and events. Joe spent the weekend with Becky at the barn going over the printouts and talking with Mr. Brewster, but returned to campus for Saturday night activities.

"Where's Mary?" Becky asked as they found Deb and Ryan watching the younger kids compete in their Ping-Pong tournament held each weekend.

"She's talking with some of the other girls over by the refreshments," Ryan said.

"I don't even know what to say to her. I haven't known all week. I feel so helpless," Becky replied.

"Yeah, that's how we all feel," Deb said. "I think I'm going to push her to talk again tomorrow and see what happens."

"Can I help?"

"I don't see why not. At this point, I'm ready to try anything."

"She seems like she's withdrawn from everything," Joe said.

"I was reading while Mr. Brewster and Thomas were doing the traveling, and I told Mary about this—that psychologically, when you know what your fate is, you lose all hope. That's what she looks like to me," Deb said to no one in particular.

"I read about that too," Joe said.

"You'd think if you knew what's coming, and you didn't like it, you'd be working to see if you could change it," Becky added.

"That's what I thought when I read about it, but it seems the experts think if we know what's ahead, we just stop trying," Deb replied.

"I think it's because we suddenly realize the path is set, and you don't have control anymore. Why would you think you could change it, if there was some way to know exactly what happens already?" Ryan said.

"This sounds a lot like the arguments we had before the first time we used the machine. Remember when we talked about how each of us has a plan from God, and we can't change it? Then we decided that we could change it, a little, at least, but parts of it might be set, like when we die. Now, we have this new side of the argument. If you know what will happen in the future, do you have the means or the desire to change it? Or do you just give up and let it happen, thinking maybe the higher power has control?" Joe postured.

"I don't know, Joe, but we're clearly going to play this new dimension of the argument out with Mary. It's making me wonder if we should have done this trip at all."

"Oh, come on, Deb, you know Mary was not going to give up. Could you have told her no?" Joe asked.

"You're right. When she begged me, I couldn't refuse her, even though I was afraid of what would happen."

"And now it has. All we can do is try to help her... and Ken," Ryan said.

With that, the four of them finished watching the games and then went and watched the movie that was playing.

The next day after church, Deb and Becky went to Mary's room and knocked.

"Come in," came the reply from inside the room.

"Are you busy?" Deb asked.

"I'm doing homework, but it's ok," Mary replied.

Becky and Deb sat down on Mary's bed, and then Becky said, "Mary, I know you and I aren't like best friends, but I'm really worried about you. You seem so out of touch, and we want to help."

"I'm ok."

"Nice try, Mary, but we know you're not," Deb said, shaking her head.

"What do you want me to say? I'm trying to be alright."

"I think you should call Ken and tell him everything," Becky said.

"I can't. He'll do exactly what you all say he'll do, and he'll rush over here and try to help me. He will promise to always be there for me, and it will kill me. He will waste his life taking care of someone with cancer, and he will never find happiness."

As Mary said this, she turned back to the desk and put her head down into her hands and sighed heavily.

"Isn't that what you need though? Someone to promise to be there no matter what?" Becky asked, as she reached over to touch Mary's arm in an attempt to bring her back.

"No, I can't burden him that way," Mary said, as she stood up and started pacing back and forth in front of the bed where Deb and Becky sat.

"Mary, I understand why you feel this way, but I have to ask, and this is going to come off a little mean, but if it were anything else, any other threat to your life with Ken, wouldn't you want to face it with him? And furthermore, how can you hurt him that way?" Deb asked.

"What do you mean?" She asked as she stopped pacing and faced Deb.

"I mean, first of all, if you knew you were going to face moving across the country or having him travel a lot for work or any other big thing you two might face, wouldn't you feel better knowing you were facing it together?"

"That's not what I meant. I meant about hurting him."

"Well, if you're ending things with him, without fully explaining why, it's going to hurt him so badly, he may never come back from it. You will sentence him to a life without happiness—a long road without you, anyway. You might consider that he would choose to be happy with you as long as he can. Also, I would like to point out, you are not yet on your deathbed from cancer, so stop acting like it."

"You're right, that was mean," Mary said as she turned away from Deb.

"I'm sorry. You're my best friend. He's my brother, and I want you two to be happy together."

""Then I have some bad news," she said, turning back to face Deb and Becky, "because I'm pretty sure, well, mostly sure, that I'm going to break up with Ken as soon as his finals are over."

"Why?" Becky asked.

"Because I love him."

"That makes no sense at all."

"I think it's what I have to do."

"Mary, you can't," Deb pleaded with her, as she also stood up and grabbed Mary's hands. "It will tear him apart, and I'm pretty sure it will tear you apart too. Also, I think you should know that when Thomas and Mr. Brewster were in your future, and you all met at the hospital to receive the test results, Ken showed up. They said you were still in contact with him and were seeing each other."

"What do you mean?"

"They said that when they got to your apartment in New York, you all decided they would go to a hotel because Ken might come over. The next day when they met you at the hospital, you ran out of the room before finding out the results of your test because a nurse came in and asked you to come out and talk to Ken who was agitated in the lobby area. He had called your work and found out from someone that you were at the hospital having tests."

"That doesn't mean it will happen that way. We know something now from the future, and Joe said that knowing something would forever change the course of our lives. I think I need to change the course of my life—and Ken's life—to save him."

"How can it be that knowing something changes your future when you are holding so tightly to the idea that you're about to die of cancer? You can't have it both ways, Mary. If it's set in stone, you're going to die a gruesome death from cancer, and there's no hope that can change, you can't say that you can change something else like what happens with Ken."

They all sat in thought for a minute before Becky added, "Mary, it might mean you're destined to be with Ken, and doing this might make it worse, not better."

"I know this is what I have to do—for him and for me."

"Oh, Mary," Deb said with all the helplessness she felt as she plopped back onto the bed.

"Have you thought about the idea that Thomas proposed?" Becky asked. "He said that along with the tests that were developed, treatments had been developed. That would mean that even if you actually got cancer, there would be options that your grandmother didn't have. And, knowing now, you could stay on top of all the research and go to the doctor early and get tested before your cancer got as advanced as your grandmother's. Have you considered that?"

"I have been thinking about that. I just don't think it's enough to change my mind about this."

"I think you need to think this through some more," Becky added.

Mary got back up from the desk chair she had sat down in, and again paced across her room. She finally stopped in front of Deb and Becky and said, "Listen, I need you both to promise me. And, Deb, you need to convince Joe, Ryan, and Kim to keep this from Ken. I don't want him to know anything about this."

"Mary, do you know what you're asking of us?" Deb asked.

"Remember last fall, when we had all those arguments about trust, and you were keeping things from Ken. Why was it ok for you to keep things from Ken, but now it's not ok for me?"

Deb looked down at the floor for a minute before she responded. "You're right. If you want us to keep this from Ken, I will do my best to make that happen. You're my best friend, and I will keep your secret."

The next Saturday afternoon, Deb was just leaving the dorm to go to the library to finish research for a paper when she was told she had a phone call. Picking up the phone, she said, "Hello?"

"Hey, Deb, it's Ken. How are you doing?"

"I'm ok. How's your studying going? Ready for your finals this week?"

"I think so, but I'm just taking a short break to check on things."

"We're all fine. We have another week before we start to prep for finals. Kim is on a last camping trip this weekend, and I was headed to the library to finish up research for a last paper."

"Is Joe doing ok?"

"Yeah, he had a long call with Mr. Davis yesterday. Said that the computer sales are picking up and MIT had developed some cool new program to analyze data. He's busy with Becky looking that over today I think."

"I heard from Mr. Davis as well yesterday. It's great news for Joe."

"Yeah."

"And how is Ryan?"

"He's good. I think he's off playing baseball with some guys this afternoon. He's done with his paper."

"Well, you always needed to do just a bit more research, my bookworm sister." They laughed, and then he added, "So, listen, I've been calling Mary all week and haven't connected with her, what's up?"

"She's been busy on her end-of-year papers and projects too, I'm pretty sure. I'm sure there's nothing wrong." Although at that moment, Deb knew she was totally avoiding Ken, and she wondered if she was going to be able to keep this up all summer.

"You sure? We never go this long without talking."

"She mentioned that she didn't want to distract you from studying for your finals. I'm sure she's just sensitive to what happened last semester when you argued and then she had problems with finals."

"Yeah, maybe. Well, I've got to get back to it. I'll call you later in the week when my tests are over, ok?"

"Sure. Good luck on your tests, too," Deb said.

"Thanks. See ya."

"Bye."

Deb went to the library but struggled to concentrate. She finally abandoned the research and just wrote the rest of her paper. When she finished, she left the library and was walking back to the dorm when Ryan found her.

"Hey, there's my girl. I was just headed to the library to find you."

"Finished up." She smiled as Ryan approached her on the walkway.

"That's good. Feel like heading into town today for dinner and a movie?"

"I'm not sure it's a good idea to leave Mary alone."

"I'm more thinking about you. You've been sad all week. What can I do?" At that, Ryan pulled Deb's hand to stop their progress, and turned her to face him.

"I don't think there's anything anyone can do. She's made up her mind, and now it's just a matter of time before she breaks Ken's heart—and probably her own."

"Maybe she'll change her mind?"

"I doubt it. I talked to Ken before I went to the library. He called me. He asked about everyone, but he said that he and Mary haven't talked all week. He was really calling to find out what was up with her, I'm sure. I didn't tell him."

"Oh," Ryan replied, unsure what else to say.

They walked the rest of the way back to the girls' dorm in silence, holding hands.

Deb and Ryan decided to stay on campus and have dinner with Mary, Becky, and Joe and then went with them to the skating party that the school had planned for that night's activities. The next day, Deb gathered them all together in the main hall after Kim returned from the camping trip and explained what Mary told her. She told them all they had to promise to not tell Ken about the trip forward in time that Mr. Brewster and Thomas made and what they learned about Mary. Kim cried and said she was afraid Ken would never recover from this. Deb agreed but said they had to respect Mary's wishes.

Later, when Deb talked to Aunt Alicia, she went over their final schedules and planned for their return to New York after school was out for the summer. Aunt Alicia told Deb that she had spoken to Amy's mother and they had arranged for Kim to stay with them from after the wedding until just after July 4th. They were headed on a camping trip out west, and Kim was going with them. Deb thought that was a good idea, given Kim's response to the news about Mary earlier, but she didn't mention that to Aunt Alicia. They discussed the final dress fitting for Kim and Deb for the wedding, and once they were all done with arrangements, Aunt Alicia wished Deb good luck with finals and said to pass that along to the others, and then they ended their weekly call.

2

FINALS FOR DEB, JOE, and Kim were to be done on Thursday, so Ken showed up that afternoon to help them get ready, prior to Michael's arrival to drive all their belongings to the city. He found Mary just returning to the dorm from a last test and ran to her and picked her up.

"I've missed you so much, Mary! Let's go get some lunch before I have to help my sisters and brother, ok?"

"Ken, we need to talk. Maybe just a drive?"

He set Mary down as he said, "Ok."

They got into Ken's car and drove to Wharton Brook State Park, where they had many talks in the past, including the argument last winter. Mary didn't say much and wouldn't even look at Ken on the drive over. He was getting nervous about this talk, but he kept his cool until they got out of the car and started to walk.

"So, you wanted to talk, remember?" he asked.

"Ken, I'm trying to figure out how to say this. I've been planning it all week in my mind, and now I'm not sure anything I planned is appropriate."

He stopped walking, and she turned after taking a few steps farther. He just looked at her. She finally said, "I really care about you, I do, but I'm wondering if maybe we need some time apart. Some time to make sure this is what we really want. You need to fully experience Harvard, and I don't think you've had a chance to since you've been constantly coming back here for me. I think I need to have a chance to experience college too."

"Did your father put you up to this?"

"No, this is something I've been thinking about."

"Is there someone else?"

"No, no. I just want us both to be sure. You know you're the first person I really dated, and you started dating me after you just broke up with a girlfriend you had back in Cambridge. Maybe we should try to see other people and see if what we have is real."

"I don't need to see anyone else to know what I feel for you is real, Mary."

"You're just saying that."

"You don't love me anymore, is that it?" He asked, but he had slightly turned away from her so she couldn't see his face.

"No, Ken, that's not it. I just want to be sure, is all. I don't have any experience to compare this to, so I just want to be sure." She tried to say in a reassuring way, as she touched his sleeve.

"What is it that you're not sure of? Your feelings for me, or whether you want to be with me anymore, or what?"

"I just want to be sure this is the right thing for both of us before we commit our lives to one another. I know you love me, and I love you too."

"Why do we need to stop seeing each other and see other people for you to be sure about this? Why can't we continue as we are, and just let things happen during your four years of college and the rest of my college years? Why do we have to break it off for you to be sure?"

"I don't know, I just know this feels like the right way to do this."

"There's nothing I can say to change your mind is there?"

"I don't think so."

Ken turned around and started walking back to the car. After a few minutes, Mary followed. When she got to the car, he was standing by the passenger side, holding the door open for her.

"What are you doing?" She asked, perplexed at his actions.

"Well, if there's nothing I can say or do to change your mind, I presumed you wanted to return to campus. I'm not going to leave you here. I'm more of a gentleman than that. I'd like to think you knew that about me, but maybe not. Anyway, I have to go help my sisters and Joe."

Mary got into the car and they drove back to campus in silence. Mary got out the car right away and ran up the dorm steps and up to her room. Deb heard her door slam and went to her.

"Mary, are you ok?" She asked as she quietly knocked on Mary's door.

"No. I just broke up with Ken." The words were muffled by the door, but Deb could tell Mary was crying.

Deb entered her room without having received permission when she heard Mary sobbing. She asked, "Mary, are sure about this?"

"Yes. I have to do this. And remember you promised!" Mary had sat up on her bed when Deb came in and pulled her knees up under her chin.

"I know, I'll keep my promise. But you need to know, I think you're making a terrible mistake."

"Just go away!" Mary pulled her pillow into her hands and up to her face. She was sobbing to the point her whole body was shaking. Deb tried to reach out to her, but Mary shrank away and laid face down on the pillow. In a muffled voice she again said, "I mean it Deb, just go away!"

Deb left her room just as Kim came up the stairs to tell her that Ken was downstairs. Deb brought her boxes and luggage downstairs and then helped Kim get her things. Michael had arrived, and they loaded everything up. They went to the boys' dorm and did the same with Joe's things, and then Ken waited while Joe and Becky and Deb and Ryan said their goodbyes. Both Becky and Ryan were going to be there next week for Aunt Alicia and Uncle Darrick's wedding.

Joe, Deb, and Kim got into Ken's car, and they headed out of campus and toward New York.

Ken was quiet for a long time. Deb was first to speak, "Mary told me what happened."

"She had time for all that while you packed?"

"No, Kenny, she just told me what she did."

"Oh."

"Do you want to talk about it?"

"Not now."

The rest of the trip was taken up with Kim talking about her camping trip and all the chatter about the upcoming wedding. Ken barely participated, but they kept the chatter up anyway because they all knew he needed it.

Later that night, after they had gotten all their things moved into the apartment, had dinner, and everyone had gone to bed, Deb found Ken in the kitchen with no lights on, his head in his hands. She turned on the lights and startled him.

"Sorry, I didn't see you sitting there."

"It's ok."

Deb got something to drink and sat opposite Ken at the big kitchen table. She just looked at him for a minute.

"So, did you know she was going to do this?" he asked from inside his hands that still covered his face.

"Ken, Mary did tell me she was concerned about her relationship with you. I tried to talk her out of doing what she did. I told her breaking up with you was a terrible idea."

"She told me she just wanted to be sure about us before she committed and that we both needed time to fully experience college. That can't really be the reason for this."

Deb didn't say anything. Ken continued, "She was so worked up about how serious you and Ryan were becoming with the promise ring and everything. Now she wants to slow down with me? And actually, she doesn't want to slow down, she wants to take a break and see other people!"

Deb still didn't say anything. Ken looked up, tears running down his face as he asked, "Why did she do this? I know you know the real reason. Tell me, please, Deb." He put his head back down into his hands.

"I can't," Deb said in a tortured voice.

"What do you mean you can't?" Ken looked up as he asked.

"I mean she's my best friend, and she made me promise not to tell you about what she told me."

"I am your brother, aren't I? Doesn't that count more than a best friend?"

"Ken, I know you're hurting and you're mad, and you have every right to be, but for a minute, remember what happened last fall when she got upset about you and me talking and keeping secrets and trust. If she told you something she didn't want anyone else to know, would you break that trust?"

Ken put his head down again and whispered that no, he wouldn't break Mary's trust. He started crying harder, and Deb got up and walked over to him, putting her hand on his back and her head on his shoulder. He whispered again, pleading with her to tell him so he could understand. She did her best to comfort him, but he was inconsolable. After more than an hour, he finally looked up and said they should try to get some sleep, and without another word, he slumped off to his room.

Over the next few days, as they did the last few things for the wedding, Ken barely spoke and spent most of his time in his room. It was obvious he had been crying a lot, and nothing anyone said could make him smile.

Uncle Darrick asked Deb and Joe what was going on, and Deb explained that Mary had suddenly broken up with Ken right before they left campus, which was all the explanation necessary.

Two days before the wedding, Uncle Darrick took Ken and Joe for the final fitting of their tuxedos and then out to dinner. It was his bachelor party, he said. As they were changing in and out of the tuxedos, Uncle Darrick said to Ken, "I heard about Mary. I'm sorry, Ken."

"Yeah, I guess the word is out."

"Well, it's clear you haven't been yourself all week. I noticed and I asked Deb what was going on yesterday."

"Did Deb happen to mention what was really going on?"

"What do mean by that?"

"Apparently, Mary has told Deb some things about this break up that she didn't share with me, and Deb won't tell me either."

"I see. Well, they're friends, aren't they?"

"Yeah, best friends."

"You wouldn't want Deb to break that trust, would you? I know you're hurting, but this is not the man you've become. Don't lose track of that while you try to navigate your way back from this break up."

"No, I don't want Deb to break her friend's trust. It's just terrible knowing there is more going on here than what Mary told me and not being in on the secret. And I know if I knew what was really going on, I could probably fix this."

"I'm sure this has put Deb in a very awkward position."

"That isn't helping my broken heart."

"No, probably not. Is there anything I can do?"

"No, Darrick. Either I'm going to have to figure out what's really going on or figure out how to get over the love of my life. I think those are my choices—or at least they're all I came up with as options this week."

"Here's hoping you figure it out then. I wouldn't want you to lose the love of your life, but at some point, you might want to consider that although you love Mary deeply, she might not be the one."

"I don't know, but it doesn't look like it's going to be up to me either way."

Joe came out of the dressing room at that point, and Ken had enough of sharing his feelings, so he changed the subject. Somehow, he sensed that everyone knew what was behind this, and no one was telling. He didn't want to show them how much this was upsetting him if they wouldn't tell him what they knew.

The day of the wedding finally arrived, and it was beautiful. Flowers everywhere, and so many people. Deb thought that everyone—literally everyone from both the fashion world and the financial world—was at the church and at the Hampton house for the reception that followed. Aunt Alicia was so happy and totally in her element mingling with all the people. Deb and Ryan laughed about her flitting about as they watched her from the dance floor. Kim looked so grown-up in her floral dress, and she loved being fawned over by the guests and photographer. Ken left the party just after the dinner was finished, ignoring the dancing and the laughter from the crowd and his siblings that followed. Despite being invited, Mary did not come out for the wedding. Ken had called and left a message, but she didn't even call him back.

The next day, Michael took Kim to meet the McGowan's for their camping trip, while Aunt Alicia and Uncle Darrick left for a week in Hawaii. Deb, Ken, and Joe returned later in the day to the New York apartment.

3

KEN, AS HAD BECOME his habit, was closed off in his room for most of the week Aunt Alicia and Uncle Darrick were gone. He had called Mary every evening during the past week, trying to talk to her and get the full story about her decision to break up with him. She had refused each time. After the last call, he had confronted Joe while Deb was out with Ryan.

"Ok, Joe, it's time for you to come clean about what you know."

"I'm not sure what you're talking about."

"You know exactly what I'm talking about. I'm talking about Mary."

"Ken, Mary doesn't talk to me—you should know that. She talks to Deb. I don't know what is going on with her, and if you ask Becky this week, you'll see that I have no idea what goes on with women at all, in fact. We had some issues this week, and I've been trying to fix things for days. So, clearly, I'm no expert in girls, and that makes me totally the wrong person to be asking about what's going on with Mary."

"I know something happened at Choate. The week before I started studying for finals, something happened, and I know you all know what it is."

"You've got this all wrong, Brother. Nothing happened."

"I'm trying to get why Deb won't tell me, but why in blazes won't you tell me? I'm your brother!"

"I'd tell you if there was something I knew that might help in any way. Mary told Deb she made up her mind. Deb and Becky both spent two weeks trying to talk her out of this. Kim even said something to Mary about this breaking your heart."

"Our insightful little sister. Boy was she right."

"I'm sorry, man, I wish I had something I could say that would help you get over this, but I don't."

"I doubt that, I really do. I know if I knew whatever it is you're all keeping a secret, I'd be able to fix this with Mary."

"You think you'd just be able to go to Mary and fix it if you knew what you think is the big secret? Like you're some god or something? Listen to yourself! You might not be able to fix this. You might have come up against something you couldn't just make right, Ken. Have you thought of that?"

"Way to hit a guy when he's down."

"I'm not trying to make this harder, Ken. I wish Mary hadn't done this, but maybe you should concentrate on moving on, rather than trying to figure out what you think we're all hiding from you."

"I can't. Joe, I know I'm supposed to be with her. I can't let it go."

When Deb and Ryan were with Becky and Joe at the museum, Joe relayed this conversation to them. He said he was uncomfortable with not telling Ken everything. Deb said the same thing and that she was going to call Mary that night and try again to talk her out of it.

When they arrived home, Uncle Darrick and Aunt Alicia had returned. Deb and Becky sat with Aunt Alicia while she regaled them with stories of Hawaii, showing them all kinds of clothes and passing out all the gifts she had selected for everyone. While this was going on, Joe and Uncle Darrick had retreated to the room where Joe had all the computer equipment that he now referred to as his workroom. Joe had made some modifications to the personal computer and was showing them to Uncle Darrick. Ken, again, was hiding in his room.

After Aunt Alicia had finished and wound down from all the excitement, Deb went into the office and called Mary.

"Hello?" Mary said on the other end of the call.

"Hi, Mary, it's Deb."

"Oh hi, Deb. I was wondering if I was going to hear from you."

"Well, I've been busy. Busy comforting Ken."

"He's called me every day."

"I know. I have to ask you something."

"What?"

"Well, is this bothering you as much as it's bothering him? Or have you already gotten over him?"

"Of course, I'm not over him. Deb, how could you say that? I love him. I will probably always love him."

"You have a funny way of showing it."

"Clearly you're mad at me now. What happened?"

"Well, Mary, I told you I thought you were making a terrible mistake, and this was going to hurt both you and Ken for a long time. Sure enough, that's what's happening."

"I can't help it, Deb. I feel like this is the right thing. I went yesterday and talked to my Pastor for a long time. We talked about sacrifice and trust and how you can't commit yourself to someone if you know something terrible is going to happen."

"What did the pastor say?"

"Well, he said that I should follow my heart, and I should not be afraid of the future."

"See."

"I can't, Deb. I have to try to stay strong and save Ken from a lifetime of heartache."

"You mean more heartache than he feels right now?"

"I can't hear that and stay strong."

"What do you want me to do? Not tell you that he is in a terrible place, and he's angry at both Joe and me because he knows something is up? He's my brother, Mary, and I care about him deeply. We have become very close, and I know this might be hard for you to understand, as an only child, but I can't keep doing this."

"You promised not to tell him."

"I know, and I will, but you are totally putting me in the middle here. So now I have to choose between my friend or my brother."

"I'm sorry, I don't mean to do this to you. Should you and I not talk? Is that what you want?"

"I don't know. I just wish you'd reconsider. If it ends up as bad as you think it might, why would you not want to have whatever happiness you can and spend it with Ken? Why do you want to deny yourself someone who is willing to take care of you?"

"I don't think it's fair to condemn him to a life he knows will end badly."

"But that's the thing, Mary, you don't know if it will end that way. You are tossing away your chance at happiness because of a fear you have that we already know will not be as bad as you think. The test already showed you have the marker. Just take care and see doctors early and often, and there will be better treatments by the time you get to that point in your future."

"I can't. I just can't. It's so much more than you realize."

"I'm sorry for you. I'm sorry you can't see what the rest of us all see. And right now, I'm sorry we ever agreed to send Thomas and Mr. Brewster into the machine for you. It only meant this will end badly for Ken."

"Wow, that was mean."

"Maybe it's something you need to hear. The choice you're making is not just causing you trouble, it's also causing Ken trouble. You're deciding his future as well—you know that, don't you?"

"I think I'm going to make it better for him in the long run. I just didn't think it would mean I'd lose my best friend."

"I'm not ready to lose you as a friend, but I don't know how to be your friend while my brother is in so much pain."

A week went by and Deb hadn't heard back from Mary after that call.

Deb went to NYU to take some placement tests and to register for classes. She found out who her roommate was and started buying things with Aunt Alicia's help. Ken spent his days at Fitzgerald & Davis on his summer work program, and Joe spent some days there as well. At the end of June, Deb left with Ryan to go and spend several weeks with his family in North Carolina.

With only Joe and Ken in the apartment along with Aunt Alicia and Uncle Darrick, they spent most of their time talking about business. Aunt Alicia had to go on several trips, and while she was gone, the boys went out for dinner and spent their weekends going to ball games and again, talking about business.

Joe and Ken spent the 4th of July in Central Park, watching the activities and eating. They stayed for the fireworks and then went home. A few days later, just before Joe was leaving to go and spend the next couple of weeks with his friend from school and Deb and Kim were due back home, Joe was in the office on the phone with Mr. Brewster. They were discussing the trips he and Thomas made, had been refining some calculations on the time-lapse, and were discussing the anomaly found when Mr. Brewster programmed the machine to go one year into the future to the same location but changed the time. It was late in the afternoon, and Joe didn't hear Ken return from his work at Fitzgerald & Davis. However, Ken overheard enough of the conversation and stalked off to his room to change clothes and came back just as Joe was getting off the phone.

"So, nothing to tell me about those last couple of weeks at Choate, huh?" Ken looked at Joe menacingly with his hands on his hips.

"Wha- what are you talking about?"

"I heard you, Joe. Talking to Mr. Brewster. I heard you say that you figured out the anomaly of the trip he made where the location stayed the same, but the time changed, and they jumped one year into the future. I'm tired of finding out that trips are being made in that machine that I don't know about until well after they happened. I'm even more tired of you all thinking it's a good idea to keep these trips from me!"

Joe looked down. He knew he'd been caught, and he knew there was no way to keep this from Ken anymore. He wasn't even sure he was upset about that, actually, as he said, "Ok, I'll tell you, but we should probably go for a walk so Aunt Alicia and Uncle Darrick don't overhear this. This discussion is going to be hard enough, without having to explain it all to them."

They walked out of the building and headed for the park. They found a place to sit, and Ken said, "Start from the beginning, and don't leave anything out!"

Joe told Ken about the timeline where he went to Cambridge and caused all the issues with his parents—and how he, Deb, and Ryan decided to fix it. How Deb and Ryan went to Cambridge and met him in the neighbor's backyard. How Ryan got thrown from the machine, and how sick Deb was. He told Ken about their theories of jumping to the future and that Mr. Brewster and Thomas went forward to look into medical research. He explained that they jumped one year to the same location but a different time and how the machine registered some anomalies with Mr. Brewster's monitoring and the logs.

Joe said he discovered that the machine had issues going to the exact same location in the future for some reason, and his theory was that while in transition, the machine was both not present in any time, while still present in a shadowy way where it started and where it was going, and that being the same exact location, it was creating an issue resolving the two machines in the same location.

Ken listened carefully to all that Joe said, and when he was finished with everything, Ken said, "Why didn't you tell me about the trip to Cambridge? I understand why you wanted to do it, but didn't we go over this when you took the machine to Las Vegas and didn't tell me, that you weren't going to do this in secret anymore?"

"Deb was the one that wanted to minimize who knew about the Cambridge trip. She thought it would be most helpful to you and Kim, who were having such a hard time about Mom and Dad separating in the old timeline, and if we told you, you would have a memory of that timeline. She wanted to help you both. You know, that's what she does, she tries to take on things for us and help."

"Yeah, I know that's my sister. She takes on all the hurt and tries to make it better. I've been so mad at her all summer about Mary, and now this."

"Well, it turned out ok. We reset everything to our old timeline."

"But she was so sick. It sounds like she almost died. Is that true?"

"I don't think it was that close to death actually, but she was unconscious, and I was pretty scared there for about an hour. What we know for sure is that it's a bad idea to go to a space and time where you already exist, and it gets worse if more than one of you is in space and time together."

"Hey, wait a minute, were the trips into the future about Mary? Is that what this is all about?"

"Ok, so here's the thing, Ken. When I said I would tell you everything, I meant I would tell you about the machine trips we made that we didn't tell you about. What is going on with Mary is not something I can talk about."

"Why not?"

"Well, to start with, we all promised her that we wouldn't talk about her issues. But more importantly, I seriously don't know what's going on with her. Deb spent days talking to her, and outside of that, she was pretty closed off for the last three weeks of school."

"Just tell me what you know."

"Ken, you have always been the one we looked up to. The strongest, the wisest, the one that was clear about his values—what was right and what was wrong. Stop for a minute and think about what you're asking. You're asking me to betray a promise I made."

"How am I supposed to deal with this, Joe? When you all know something you aren't telling me. I know I'm asking you all to break promises, but come on, what about family?"

"You're right, we're family. I know that I'm going to regret opening this can of worms, but I've been bugged since the trips to the future and making this promise. I knew I was going to have to keep something from you. So, here it is, we made the trips because of Mary. She asked us to go forward to help her find out something she thinks she might have to face later in life."

"Did you figure it out?"

"I would say, and so would Mr. Brewster and Thomas, that the answer to that is no. We didn't find the answer."

"What do you mean?"

"Well, I guess what I mean is we answered one question, but in doing so, we probably created several more that are not yet answered."

"Thanks, Joe. I will not push you any further. Thanks for telling me what happened. I'm not sure I get your cryptic final comment about more questions, but I'm ready to cut you some slack."

"Yeah, I feel better. I hated doing all of this. Are we good?"

"Yeah."

They walked back to the apartment and found Aunt Alicia and Uncle Darrick just arriving. They went out for dinner as it was Joe's last day there and no one wanted to cook after the long day they had. It was becoming more of a habit, this going out for dinner, but after their cook left, neither Aunt Alicia nor Uncle Darrick had any time to interview new cooks. So, they just went out for dinner. Everyone noticed, apparently, because as they returned from dinner, Aunt Alicia commented that they would have to find a new cook because it was getting way too easy to just go out for dinner.

Joe was leaving the next day to go and spend three weeks with his friend, and Deb was due back the day after Joe left. That transition went smoothly, but shortly after Deb got her things unpacked, Ken arrived home from the office and went directly to Deb's room. With no greeting and no preamble, he said, "We need to talk. Right now, Deb."

"That's fine. I was just about finished up, and then Aunt Alicia called and said we were going out for dinner."

"I'm going to go change out of this suit, and then I want to go for a walk. I'll be right back."

"Ok. But can't this wait until after dinner?"

"No, it can't."

He left to go change, and Deb wondered what was going on. She had talked to him a few times while she was gone. She was still very worried about him, but he seemed kind of angry. She hurried up putting things away and met him in the hall. They walked in silence back to the same bench that Ken had sat at while he talked to Joe a few days earlier. Before Deb had sat down, Ken said, "I talked to Joe. He told me about your trip to Cambridge, how sick you got, and about the trips to the future by Mr. Brewster and Thomas. Now I want to know what this has to do with Mary, and what question she needed answered."

"When did Joe tell you all of this?" Deb asked as she sat down on the bench. Ken remained standing, almost looming over Deb, which only increased her worry.

"Does that matter? It was two days ago, right before he left to go spend time with his friend. I caught him on the phone with Mr. Brewster, and I overheard them talking about the anomaly on the jump forward in time to the exact location."

"Oh."

"Oh, is right! I've been upset all summer, and you've all known what's going on, and none of you thought it was a good idea to share any of this with me! How could you?"

Ken turned away from Deb and started crying, either out of sadness over Mary again or anger, he couldn't tell. Deb sat for a minute and then got up and walked around to face Ken and hugged him.

"I'm so sorry. I wanted so much to tell you, and I've been trying to get Mary to be honest with you, and I hate the fact that I'm part of what's hurting you," she said into the front of his shirt as she started crying too.

"Please, Deb! Please tell me what Mary needed to have answered in the future and why she really broke up with me. I can't live without her, and I know, deep down I know, if I knew the truth, I could get through to her and fix this," he said as he pulled away from her and sat down.

"What did Joe tell you about the trips Mr. Brewster and Thomas made?"

"He told me they went to the future to figure out something for Mary. Why does it matter what he told me? You just need to tell me everything you know, now."

"The day Mary got back to campus after her grandmother died, she came to me and asked for my help. She was scared because she had found out that the cancer her grandmother died from had some hereditary component, and so she could potentially get it in the future. She wanted us to use the machine to go forward and find out if she gets cancer."

"What! The girl that didn't want us to mess with God's plan—that believed that the Lord has a course set for us, and we should not change it or even know about it—wanted you to jump into the future to see if she gets cancer later in life?"

"Yes. She said she finally understood why we wanted to use the machine to try to fix things with our parents, and she understood what we were all talking about. She wanted to know."

Deb nodded in agreement with what Ken said and then raised her eyebrows at him in question of whether of he wanted her to continue.

"What happened?"

"Well, we were at the barn talking about it. Joe and Mr. Brewster were trying to sort through the theories about future travel—how we might know where to go and how to find Mary and about the issues that happened—when we went to Cambridge, and Thomas showed up a day early for a visit with his father and overheard us. So, Mr. Brewster told Thomas everything, and we decided that in order to avoid meeting ourselves in the future, Mr. Brewster and Thomas would go. Thomas could check the medical research, and Mr. Brewster could manage the machine, and they would see if they could get to a time when a test or something would show Mary if she had it or not."

"How did they know where Mary would be?"

"It was wild. We were talking about this theory that if you had this idea in mind today, that you were going to need to find someone in the future, you could ask them each year in the future because you planned to do that today, then each year you write it down and put it somewhere. It was wild because we found it in the barn! A listing of her addresses starting after she finished college!" Deb said excitedly.

"I'm not sure I get that, but I can ask more about that later. Go on."

"Well, Mr. Brewster and Thomas went first to the year that Mary graduated from college and went near Wellesley. Thomas went somewhere and figure out that the research was making strides, but there was no fully developed test ready. So, they went a few years into the future, and Mary was working in New York, and they researched again, but still, the tests weren't quite ready, so they went one more year into the future. When they found Mary a year later, she had the blood test. They all met at the hospital where Mary went for the test to see the results, but you showed up, and Mary ran out of the room so only Thomas saw the results."

"What kind of test was it?"

"It was a blood test to see if she had the genetic marker for breast cancer."

"I'm guessing she does, right?"

"Yes, but Thomas was clear that just having the marker didn't mean she would definitely get cancer, and even if she got cancer, it would likely not be as deadly as it had been for her grandmother."

"And this is why she broke up with me, to save me from having to care for her with cancer?"

"Yes, that's exactly why—and the only reason, really. There isn't anyone else, and it isn't about the fact that she wants to be sure or anything like that. We tried to make her see all that Thomas told us, and I tried to make her see that you wouldn't give up on her even if she got sick. I said that she probably had a lot of life before she would need to deal with it anyway, and Thomas tried to explain about his mother, and how she said she wouldn't trade anything for the time she had with him and Mr. Brewster, but Mary wouldn't see it. She couldn't get past this idea that she had to save you from a wasted life with no happiness, only dealing with a sick girl. She once even said that she had to save you so you could have kids and a life at all."

"Yes, when she's decided something, she's decided something."

"The last time I talked to her, it was just after Aunt Alicia and Uncle Darrick got back from Hawaii. I told her that I was sorry we went on these trips at all. That all it did was bring you and her heartache. I'm so sorry, Kenny. She made me promise because she was so sure this was the right way to deal with this, and I know I've been hurting you."

"It's ok, Deb. I know you made a promise, and it should mean something when you do that. Did you think about taking her to the reverend or anything? She is very committed to her faith; it might have helped."

"She went that first day when we found out at Choate, and I know she has talked to her Pastor at home, and they both said that married people and those in a relationship do commit to be with each other in sickness and in health and should go into it knowing that someday they might have to care for the other one. She just had it in her mind that she had to save you from all of that."

"What has she been saying to you lately?"

"We haven't talked since that call where I told her I was sorry we did the trips. I probably lost my best friend that day."

Deb looked down and started to cry again. Ken put his arm on her shoulder as he said, "Well, I'm going to fix this. You will have your friend back, and I will have my girlfriend back."

4

KIM ARRIVED HOME THAT Friday morning. Ken had tried to call Mary several more times, but he found that she had gone out west to visit an aunt and would not be back for another week. He was busy making plans on how he was going to approach her and what he was going to say, but he was at least smiling a bit. They all decided that a long weekend in the Hamptons was in order to celebrate Kim's arrival home and her birthday, so Ken, Aunt Alicia, and Uncle Darrick all surprised Kim by arriving home at lunchtime and packing them all up to head out to the Hampton house. They had a special dinner planned that cook was preparing for them, and then they went into town and stopped off for cupcakes at a new bakery. When they got home, Kim opened her gifts. She got roller skates from Joe and Becky, art supplies galore from Ken, Deb and Ryan, and a beautiful necklace from Aunt Alicia and Uncle Darrick.

That Saturday, they went out on a boat and sailed and laughed and had a wonderful day, while Kim spent the day regaling them with her camping adventures. When they returned to the city, it was decided that Aunt Alicia, Deb, and Kim would spend the next couple of days shopping for school supplies and all the things Deb would need—along with clothes and things Kim would need. Toward the end of the week, Deb visited Aunt Alicia at Vogue and was again taken to the clothing room where she picked out a whole new wardrobe for her first year in college.

That weekend, Ken took off right after work and went to Mary's house. She was back from her trip but wouldn't see him or listen to a thing he had to say. Ken was distraught when he got back later that night. He spent most of Saturday in his room, while Ryan and Deb took Kim to the Central Park Zoo and Joe, who had returned from his trip, went shopping with Uncle Darrick for his clothes and school supplies. On Sunday, Ken asked Deb if she would come to his room.

"What's up, Kenny?"

"I need you to read over this letter. I've been working on it basically all weekend, and I want you to read it over and tell me what you think?"

"Who's it for?"

"Mary, of course. She wouldn't see me, so I have to do something to get through to her enough so she will talk to me."

"Ok, let me see it."

Ken handed Deb the four-page letter he had written, and she read it over. She looked up a couple of times a little misty-eyed but didn't say anything until she was finished reading.

"Are you sure you want to pour all this out in a letter? If the goal is to get her to listen, perhaps you should simply say you found out about what Mr. Brewster and Thomas did, and you know about the test and suspect this is why she broke up with you. Then ask if she is willing to at least listen to you one more time."

"Why shouldn't I tell her all the rest—that I wouldn't give up on her, and I will be there for her no matter what?"

"Well, I've said all that to her, and it didn't change her mind at all. Maybe you should make it seem like she can still make the same decision if she just agrees to listen to you. Then pour on the charm and make her see that you love her, and she loves you, and you can face this no matter what it ends up being. Maybe all that needs to be said directly to her."

"You're probably right. I need to think about it some more, maybe."

"Sure. Did you want me to try to call her again and see if I can work on her?"

"No. I want her to see what it would be like without us all in her life a little. I know that sounds mean, but I want her to feel it, then make my appeal. I think she will see how this is a bad decision if she feels what it will be like without both you and me in her life."

"Ok."

While Ken pondered the right approach, Deb got ready to head to the dorms at NYU, and Joe and Kim prepared to go back to Choate. The next couple of weeks flew by, and move-in day arrived for Deb. Everyone went with her, which embarrassed Deb a little bit, but it made the others feel better about her being away from them. Ken was headed back to Harvard in a few days, and then it would be just Joe and Kim for two weeks until move-in day at Choate. Kim was starting to cry when Aunt

Alicia announced it was time to head home, but Deb promised her she would call every night.

When Ken arrived at Harvard and got settled, he called Deb to see how she was doing.

"Ok, I guess. My roommate is nice, and we're getting along pretty well. I see Ryan every day, and classes start on Monday."

"How did all the orientation events go?"

"Good. I met some of the history and archeology professors and found out about some projects I might be able to get involved in next summer."

"That's cool."

"So, did you mail the letter to Mary?"

"Yeah, last week."

"Heard anything yet?"

"Nope, and I don't know how to reach her at Wellesley. I didn't think about that."

"I'll call her parents and get a number for her. I'm pretty sure they'll give it to me."

"Thanks. Keep me posted."

"Ok, got to run—dinner at the cafeteria, you know."

"Yeah, I know!"

"Bye."

"Talk to you soon."

Deb called Mary's parents later that night and got a number to reach her at Wellesley. The next day, she called her.

"Hello?"

"Mary?"

"Yes, is this Deb?"

"Yes."

"I figured I was never going to hear from you again."

"You never called me either."

"No, I've had a hard time."

"Me too."

"I'm sorry. I know I've caused most of this with my request. I know you're sorry you helped me too."

"Oh, Mary, I'm not sorry we helped you, I'm just sorry about where that help has led us all!"

"Me too."

"How have you been? What did you do all summer? How is Wellesley?"

"I've been pretty terrible. I did almost nothing all summer, but I did go out to Colorado to see my aunt. Wellesley is nice, but I feel so lost without my best friend and Kenny."

"He's feeling lost too, if that matters."

"Of course, it matters! I love him."

"So now what?"

"Are we friends again?"

"Mary, I never stopped being your friend."

"But you did tell Ken, didn't you?"

"Actually, the news got out because Ken caught Joe on the phone with Mr. Brewster, and then I told Ken everything. He had basically figured it out anyway from Joe telling him only about the trips in the machine."

"I got a letter from him just before I left for Wellesley."

"I know. He told me he was sending you a letter. What are you going to do?"

"I don't know. I want to see him, but I know if I do, I won't be able to stick with my decision."

"Don't you think you owe him a little bit? Shouldn't you listen to him at least? Then you can decide if you want to stick with this foolish decision."

"I probably owe him that much."

"Can I give him this number then, so he can call you?"

"Can you give me his number instead? I want to think about it for a day or so and then call him."

"Ok." Deb agreed.

Deb gave Mary the number for Ken's dorm at Harvard, and then after she and Mary hung up, she called Ken right away and told him she had talked to Mary and that she was probably going to call him. He was excited to be able to talk to her, but he asked for her number from Deb. He said he wanted it in case she chickened out and didn't call him. Deb agreed, and they arranged to talk the next weekend.

Ken didn't have to call Mary. She called him the next day, but he was in class and missed her call. She called again the next day, and he was there.

"Hey, this is Ken."

"Hi, Ken, it's Mary."

"Mary! I'm so glad you called. I was just getting back from class and was going to try to reach you. Got your message yesterday. Sorry, I wasn't here."

"It's ok. I don't have any idea what your schedule is this year, so I was just trying to catch you."

"I'm so glad. It's so good to hear your voice."

"I got your letter. And I talked to Deb earlier this week."

"Can I ask why you waited so long to call?"

"What do you mean?"

"Well, I sent the letter so that it got to your house before you left for school. That was two weeks ago."

"Oh... well, I've been thinking."

"It's ok if it was Deb that convinced you to call. I'm just glad you did."

"I have to be honest; it was partly Deb that convinced me. But the truth is, I wanted to talk to you."

"I'm glad."

"So, you said in the letter you found out everything."

"Yes, Mary. You sound so strange. Are you ok?"

"I'm just not sure what you meant by you found out everything."

"I came home one day in late July and heard Joe on the phone with Mr. Brewster. They were talking about some anomaly that Joe thought he figured out from the jump forward to the exact place in New York. I confronted him, and he told me all about the trips from last year."

"All of them?"

"Yes, he told me about Deb and Ryan going to Cambridge, and the trips Mr. Brewster and Thomas made to help you."

"Oh."

"Mary, can I come and see you? I really want to have this discussion face to face."

"I'm not sure that's a great idea."

"Why not?"

"Well, I made up my mind about this, and I don't want you to waste time coming here."

"Are you sure that's it?"

"What do you mean?"

"I talked to Deb too, after you did, and she told me you still love me, Mary."

"That doesn't have an impact on my decision."

"Maybe not, but I think it's why you don't want to see me because that might impact your decision."

"Can't you just say what you have to say over the phone?"

"No, Mary, we need to sit together and talk this over."

"I don't know."

"Well, it's Wednesday. Why don't you think it over and call me tomorrow? Or better yet, how about you give me your address at Wellesley, and I'll just come there Friday after my classes are over."

"I have to think about it. I'll call you tomorrow, ok?"

"If that's the way you want, Mary, ok."

"Thanks."

"Thanks for calling. I'll talk to you tomorrow."

As soon as Ken got off the phone, he called Deb. He thanked her for whatever she did to convince Mary to call him, and he told Deb that Mary was avoiding seeing him. He needed her address. Deb called Mary a little later that night and asked for her address so she could write to Mary. Mary gave it to her without thinking, and Deb immediately gave it to Ken.

That Friday, as soon as Ken was done with classes, he tossed a bag into his car and left Harvard for the drive to Wellesley college. He arrived and was walking into the dorm building that Mary lived in when she started walking out of it with another girl.

"Ken! What are you doing here?"

"Well, you didn't call on Thursday, like you said you were going to, so I decided to take a chance."

Mary looked panicked but she recovered and looked over at her roommate, who was looking at her with eyes as big as saucers.

"Ken, this is Ashley, my roommate. Ashley, this is Ken, my friend from Choate."

Ashley shook Ken's hand and then smiled at Mary as she said, "Listen, I'll tell Kate and Sue that you won't be at dinner or the party later, ok."

"Wait!"

"No, it looks like you need to visit with Ken here. He drove a long way, and since you didn't call him yesterday, I think you should buy him some dinner!"

Ashley started to walk off, but Ken said, "Thanks, Ashley. It was nice meeting you."

"Sure, Ken. I hope we'll be seeing a lot more of you."

Ken looked back up at Mary. "Where's a good place for dinner? And I'll pay."

Mary came down the stairs and started walking to Ken's car. As they walked, Ken said, "I really like your roommate."

Mary looked at Ken and he was grinning widely at her. They both laughed, clearing some of the tension away. They got in the car, and Mary directed him into town to a pizza parlor. They ordered, and as they waited, Mary asked Ken to tell him everything Joe and Deb told him. Ken repeated everything, noting that both Joe and Deb had repeatedly refused to give up Mary's secret, but they both said they were glad once they had.

"Why were they glad?"

"Well, I think because they didn't like keeping things from me, but mostly, as Deb said, they thought we should be together, and keeping the promise was preventing that."

"Oh."

"I also called Thomas. Well, I called Mr. Brewster, and then I called Thomas. He told me all kinds of things. About how breast cancer gets detected now, or should I say, how it gets ignored by so many doctors now, and about the test he found that you had in the future. He told me about the research and testing he found on treatments in the future too. He said that some revolutionary things happen in the next decade. Didn't he tell you all of this?"

"He mentioned it. But truthfully, I wasn't paying much attention."

"I understand. You were facing something terrifying, so why would you be focusing on details."

"Yeah, it's been hard. My mother doesn't want to even talk about any of it. All Deb wants to talk about is how I'm making a big mistake, and I've been kind of lost."

"I bet."

"You understand now why I did what I did? Why I want you to find someone else?"

"Truth? I don't understand at all. Let me ask you something. If I was out in the quad at school playing football and got hit hard, and say, I ended up in a wheelchair because of a spinal injury, would you want to leave me?"

"Of course not."

"Then why do you think I would want to leave you?"

"I don't think you'd want to leave me; I don't want you to have to take care of me, and I think it's the right thing for us. I don't want to burden you with taking care of me while I get sick and dwindle down to nothing like my grandmother did!"

"I know what happened to your grandmother scared you. I wasn't at the hospital, but you told me. But, sweetheart, that isn't going to happen to you. Not even close. You know you might have it, all you have to do is find the right doctors early enough and find a good treatment, and that's only if you actually end up with cancer—which Thomas assured me is barely even a thirty percent chance."

"See, you're already doing it. Making me feel like you'll take care of me, and then what kind of life will you have?"

"Mary, I will have a life with the woman I love, and I'll get to do what I know I need to do—take care of her the best I can."

"I don't want to make you lose out on anything because I'm sick."

"The point is, sweetheart, you aren't sick yet, and knowing it might happen, doesn't mean it will happen, and by the way, it makes it remarkably easy for us to prepare for it—if and when it does happen."

"I don't know."

Their pizza arrived then, and Mary tried to change the subject by asking about his classes and his internship this past summer. Ken allowed her to shift them for a little bit, and they talked about summer and classes at Wellesley and kept it light. After dinner, they walked around town, and Ken asked, "So now what, Mary? I don't want to lose you, and I think we can tackle this together. Let me make you happy, please?"

"I'm not sure, Ken. I'm just not sure."

"Well, will you let me at least be your friend and help you get past some of this fear? Let's talk with Thomas, do some research of our own, and see if that doesn't help make you surer? Can you do that?"

"I can do that."

Ken returned Mary to her dorm and told her he was going to check into a hotel so he could see her the next day. He went to his room and called Thomas right away. Thomas agreed to come to Wellesley on Saturday as it was only a short drive from Boston. Ken then called Deb, but she was out.

The next day, Ken met Thomas and Brittany, and they had some breakfast and went to Mary's dorm. After all their greetings, they decided to find a study room at the library to talk. Once they were all situated, Ken said, "Mary, please listen to what Thomas and Brittany have to say. Keep an open mind and know that we're all just trying to make sure you're prepared."

"Ok," she agreed.

Thomas and Brittany went through the way breast cancer was detected right now, describing how it could only be confirmed by a mammogram, and then, only after it had grown large enough to be seen by x-ray technology. They talked about how doctors had no way of identifying or determining any early symptoms that might make the diagnosis come earlier and that treatments were limited, but because of this later diagnosis, most treatments were rudimentary and didn't help much. Then Thomas produced the article he printed from the research he did in the future. He talked about the blood test Mary had and how it noted the marker, which would categorize a person as higher risk and allow for more tests and earlier detection. Then they talked about the newer treatment programs, how they worked, and what they did. Mary listened carefully, asking many questions, and after a couple of hours, it seemed like they had exhausted the topic. Mary said so and suggested they all go and get some lunch. After lunch, Thomas and Brittany left all the papers and articles with Mary and departed Wellesley.

"Well, what do you think now?" Ken asked Mary as they sat outside her dorm.

"I don't know. I feel a little overwhelmed."

"Yeah, I do too, a little. But, Mary, that's my role here, as your friend, and because I love you so much, I'm going to keep the details straight and be the one you can depend on."

"Even if I don't change my mind?"

"Even if you don't change your mind, but, sweetheart, I know you want to. I'm going to be right here when you decide you can."

"You're really a sweet person, Ken. It's why this has been hard. I don't want you to sacrifice yourself for my illness."

"I don't see it as a sacrifice at all. You shouldn't either. I see it as being supportive and loving the person that I have come to love so much. Why don't you go get some sleep? You seem tired."

"What are you going to do?"

"I'm going to head back to Harvard. But I'll call you tomorrow, ok?"

"Thanks, Ken."

"Any time, sweetheart."

At that, Ken walked Mary to the door and left to head back to Harvard. He felt better than he had in months, and he was glad he did what he did. He learned so much from Thomas and Brittany, and now he felt like he had some control over the situation.

5

WHILE KEN WAS TRYING to repair his relationship with Mary, Joe and Kim were getting settled into their dorm rooms at Choate. Joe was happy to have gotten to the point that he had his own room in the boys' dorm, now that he was a junior in high school, and Kim was happy as she could be that she was again rooming with her best friend, Amy. After Aunt Alicia and Uncle Darrick had gotten them both settled and left to go back to New York, Kim and Joe got ready for their new year to start.

Kim was starting eighth grade this year, which meant she was taking her first true literature course. A week into class, she was excited to report to Joe at dinner that they had their first book assignment, and she was reading *Little Women*—a novel written by Louisa May Alcott about her siblings and her growing up. Kim thought it was perfect in that the girls in the book were so close and did so much together, just like she, Deb, Joe, and Ken had been doing for the last two years since their parents died. Becky added that she loved the book, and it was going to be one of her lifetime favorites. Becky had, for Kim, become the support she had from Deb for the past two years, and she was excited that they shared the love of this book. Along with the literature class, Kim was also taking her first dedicated United States history class. She had discovered a love of US history that she shared with Deb, and they talked about it pretty regularly when Deb called Kim.

Joe kept busy with the updates he had made to the personal computer—which went into general release early in the fall—and in finally doing some detailed documentation on the machine with Mr. Brewster. On weekends, Joe and Becky would do things with Kim, when she wasn't busy with Girl Scouts, and hang out with Mr. Brewster in the barn while he worked on his old car and they did their documentation.

On one such Saturday, Becky was working on some documentation for Joe, while Joe and Mr. Brewster were debating their open questions.

"Joe, it appears we are left with only two questions. First, from the first trips, mine to Iowa, yours to Dallas, Cambridge, and Las Vegas, can the machine return to the exact space and time it left from. When we moved the machine back and forth to the shed after the Las Vegas and Cambridge trips, we determined that we can, in fact, leave from a space and time and return to that space and time. Now in each case, it was a single trip out and single trip in and in all the trips, it was not to the same exact time, but a few seconds off."

"Agreed, but on your trips forward, we have an anomaly. There were some conflicting readings of the machine and on your monitor, but oddly they were not on Thomas's monitor. The readings showed issues when there is a trip into a space and time, out of the same space and exact time and back into that same space and time. We have determined, partly through our evidence of the second Cambridge trip by Deb and Ryan, that there is a shadowy knowledge of the machine and those who traveled tied to the space and time continuum that has a delay in fully registering the single final copy of it."

"Yes. We also had an open question on the movement both back in time and forward in time, and we have now set that to rest, in that we know the machine can go both back and forward, however, we have not tested the machine moving forward and then back farther than the present it started from. Nor have we moved it back in time and again, moved it forward beyond its present, but we see no reason to believe that it will not handle such activity," Mr. Brewster added.

"It looks like the only other open question then is that we know there is some more granular level or wider level of the space and time continuum, and we know that a person cannot exist more than once in that unit, but we do not know how granular it is or how wide it is, nor what the universe will ultimately do to that person if they remain in a space and time unit while already existing there," Joe postulated as he put notes down to make sure that appeared in the documentation.

"You're right. We don't know how close is too close, nor do we know what happens as more people are in a space and time more than once. We are presuming, because your symptoms were worse—and Deb's symptoms were considerably worse—when the two of you were in Cambridge twice, but at that time you traveled back there, neither of you were at your home at the time, or with your other selves. That would imply the granular level has to be wider than three to five miles yours and Deb's original selves were during that Cambridge trip," Mr. Brewster added.

"Right. But no so wide as to capture New York City or Choate because that is where Ryan's other self would have been on that day and he had no symptoms," Joe added.

Becky looked up from her pile of papers and added, "The only other item we have no clear way to document yet, is what happens when you go to another time and space and take any action. We know that you met your father, right, but he died shortly after you met him, so we have no way of knowing if there would have been some impact. When they all went to Dallas, they did several things, including talking to people, sending letters to people, and being in places where they may have been photographed, but we have not yet found any impact other than the one they went there to accomplish—namely, thwarting an assassination attempt. So, we know from this that travelers can impact a timeline, but we don't know what sort of impact the smaller events might have caused."

"Good point, Becky. That sounds like it, Joe, but if you think of anything else, make a note, and we can always add it after we compile all of these sections of the documentation. This has been a great day putting this all together!" Mr. Brewster exclaimed.

"This is such a huge discovery, Joe. What do you think you're going to do? I mean, now that you're so well recognized from the personal computer and language, I'm sure the scientific community would take you seriously," Becky said as she piled all the papers she had completed together.

"I'm not sure the scientific community will think this is anything more than science fiction, even if they see what I've done. Plus, given how much damage my small trip to Cambridge made, do we seriously want it out in the public? Also, with us not clear about the vague memory of the machine in a time and space, if we open this up, there might be hundreds of machines jumping in and out of time. We never really talked about the implication of that, but just saying it out loud sounds scary."

"I'm afraid you might be right, Joe. I'm not sure if the public is ready for this machine to go mainstream, but at least you have it all documented, and it will be waiting here if we ever find a need again," Mr. Brewster said.

As Becky and Joe walked back to campus that afternoon, they talked about how it felt like there wasn't going to be any more trips in the machine, and perhaps Joe might want to separate the theory of time-bending from the machine and consider that release. That way, the scientific community could argue about the theory for a long time before anyone tried to make a machine.

As it turned out, they were soon to find a reason to use the machine again. Shortly after the fall festival and dance, Kim returned from a final camping trip and found Joe and Becky in the main hall. She regaled them with the latest camping story and the girls that got frightened on the night hike, but then she diverted the conversation to her literary project, history class, and their link.

"We're studying the Civil War right now in history. And I learned something really cool late last week, Becky. Did you know that the Alcott's helped the underground railroad? They had some escaped slaves staying with them right before and at the beginning of the war."

"I didn't know that," Becky replied.

"Yeah, I'm doing my paper on Louisa May and her life, instead of a position on the book. Mrs. Sullivan told me I could do that, so Thursday I was in the library researching it. I found this book that printed letters between Mrs. Alcott and someone about the railroad traveler that stayed with them. Also, did you know that she knew Henry David Thoreau?" Kim excitedly said in nearly one breath.

"I did know that. Did you know that she secretly had a lifelong crush on him?"

"No, I totally didn't know that!" Kim exclaimed.

"Yeah, she never married."

"Even though she does in the book?" Kim asked.

"No, the book is based on their lives, but it is not completely true to life. I've read that she liked *Little Women* the least of all her works, too," Becky said.

"That's strange since that's the one she is most known for."

"My hunch is—given her ideas on things like suffrage, slavery, and how her parents supported her education—she was kind of out of place. She probably would have belonged better in our time when women were really able to fight for their rights."

"So, she was a feminist?" Joe asked, now slightly interested in what the girls had been discussing.

"Yeah, she was one of the first feminists before they were given the name," Becky said.

"Like, I'm all for women having the same rights as men, getting to vote, and do whatever job they want and get the same education and stuff, but I think that group takes it too far. Plus, aren't they the same ones taking men to task for not being more open about their feelings and more in touch with their feminine side?"

"What in the world are you talking about, Joe?" Kim asked.

"Well, don't the women's lib organizations now focus on men being in touch with their feminine sides? I mean what else do they have to talk about now that you have the vote, sports of your own, and can have careers?" Joe said smiling.

"Oh, Joe, maybe you should go with Kim the next time she goes to the library and do some research of your own! You really don't understand what women have gone through at all. It's so much more than the vote, jobs, and sports," Becky said as she shoved him in the shoulder.

"Joe, you need to read a little more I think!" Kim said, laughing at him.

They continued talking about Kim's new interest in the history of the 1800s until it was time for dinner. About a week later, Becky commented to Joe as they were walking back from class that she thought Kim was acting more grown-up, and it was fun having her around. Joe agreed, grudgingly, saying he never imaged he'd want to spend time with his youngest sister.

While the fall marched on at Choate, Ken kept up his pursuit of Mary by calling her each week, sending her notes and flowers and things, and doing massive amounts of research on cancer treatments and studies. She enjoyed talking to him as he wasn't pressuring her, and when they were all preparing for Thanksgiving break, she said to Deb on the phone, "He's been so nice to me, and I'd really missed him all summer. Maybe this is enough?"

"Mary, he's being so nice because he loves you. Isn't it time for you to just admit you love him too and let him totally back into your life?"

"I don't know. I feel like keeping him at arm's length might be a way to have him in my life and not totally ruin his."

"I think you just went from the frying pan to the fire! And you're not being very fair to him either."

"What do you mean by that, Deb?"

"Well, first you wanted to break up with him, now you want to kind of have him back, but not really, and you're not really letting him into your life. The end result of that is that neither of you ever gets to be happy. And, your kind of using him, don't you think?"

"You're being kind of dramatic, aren't you?"

"No, I think in the end, this will hurt just as much as you breaking up with him. And I would like to add that he's being awfully persistent, so you better be ready for that. Plus, he's never failed at anything he tried to do; you know?"

"Maybe we'll have to have another talk over break?"

"If you're not ready to give in to his efforts, you probably better make that clear soon."

"Ok, well, I'll see you on Friday, right?"

"Yeah, shopping trip with Kim—it ought to be fun. Joe says she's getting so grown-up, we probably won't recognize her."

"Can't wait to see you all!"

"Bye."

That Friday, after all the Thanksgiving Day feasting, Mary showed up at the New York apartment, and she, Deb, Kim, and Becky all went shopping. While they were out, Ken, Ryan, Joe, and Uncle Darrick looked over the newest model of the personal computer and played computer games all afternoon. That night, Uncle Darrick and Aunt Alicia went out to a big party, and the kids all had a pizza and movie night. On Saturday, Kim went with Amy and Amy's parents to an art museum, and the other six went to Central Park and the zoo. They walked and talked, and Ken spent the day trying to separate Mary from the rest of them so they could talk. When he was unsuccessful, he enlisted Deb's help to orchestrate something for that evening. When they got back to the apartment, Deb asked everyone if they wanted to go see a scary movie. Joe, Becky, and Ryan said sure, but Mary said she wasn't interested. Deb knew that would be her reaction as she knew that Mary didn't like scary movies. Also, the movie Deb wanted to see was The Omen, and she knew Mary had no interest because she had said that she thought it was bad for people of faith. Deb's plan worked, and Ken and Mary decided to stay at home and watch something on TV.

While Ken and Mary watched TV, Ken finally got a chance to talk to her. "Mary, I know you told me you wanted to take this slow, but really, what else do I need to do to show you I'm not going anywhere?"

"Kenny, it's not that I need to know you won't go anywhere, I know that. I've always known that," she replied. "It's about the fact that I don't want to put you through this. Don't you see that?"

Ken turned off the television as he said, "The only thing you're putting me through is this pain and anguish over your keeping me at arm's length. Why are you doing this? Have your feelings for me changed? Are you seeing someone else now, is that it?"

"You know better than that."

"I thought so, but, honey, I don't understand why you keep fighting this, and why you think you're saving me. You can only save me one way—let me fully back in your life and start being my girlfriend again. If you do get cancer at some time later in life, and if it is hard for you, you're going to need people that love and support you near you. You're going to need me. And I need you. You keep me at a distance, and you think you're helping me somehow, but all this does is hurt me. Every time I see you, I want to reach out to you, to hold you, kiss you, and tell you I love you. It hurts every time when I can't."

"I'm not trying to hurt you."

"I don't know how else to say this, but please, let me come home."

Mary sat for a long time not saying anything. She knew in her heart that she wanted to give in to him and she wanted so much to be held by Ken. She missed that so much. *Was she doing the right thing?* She didn't know, so she said, "Listen Ken. I'm just not sure. You have been very convincing, and I'll admit, I've missed you so much. I just need some more time. Is that ok?"

"I guess it's going to have to be, but I'll admit, I'm disappointed, again."

"I'm sorry. I'm going to just go to bed then, is that ok?"

"Goodnight, Mary."

"Goodnight."

When the others got home from the movie, Ken was sitting at the kitchen table with his head in his hands again. Joe and Becky went into the living room, but Ryan and Deb went to sit with Ken. When Deb asked where Mary was, Ken told her she had gone to bed. Ryan asked what happened, and Ken replayed the conversation he had with Mary to them. Deb suggested that Ken give Mary a little more time but not to let up calling her and writing her and making sure he conveyed his message to her. The next morning, Mary left on the train to go back to Wellesley, Michael took Joe, Becky, and Kim back to Choate, and Ryan went home to his parent's apartment in the city.

Back at Choate, with only a few weeks of classes before finals, everyone was very busy working on final papers and projects. Kim was finishing up her first big paper on Louisa May Alcott, and Joe and Becky were finishing their own projects. The Sunday before Deb's finals at NYU, she talked to Kim, focusing on this paper more than anything. Kim learned a lot about the writers during this historical time period—the transcendental movement, the underground railroad, and the plight of slaves trying to escape the south. She said she wished she could meet Louisa May and wished she had been there during that time so she could help the slaves and teach people about how bad slavery was. Deb pointed out that her perspective gave her insights that people of the late 1800s didn't have, and that perhaps if Kim had been alive during that time, she might not have felt the same way, but Kim would have none of it.

As they got off the phone, Deb wondered for a minute if Kim, Joe, and Becky might be planning a trip in the machine, but then she dismissed it. That seemed farfetched, and she hoped that if they learned nothing else last year, it was that they must not take trips without the others knowing.

At the end of Choate's finals week, Deb went with Michael to retrieve Joe and Kim and stopped in to see Mr. Brewster at his office.

"Hi, Mr. Brewster!"

"Well hello, Deb, it's so good to see you!"

He got up from the desk and came around and gave Deb a quick hug and then sat on the end of the desk while she sat down.

"So, tell me about your first semester of college," he asked.

"It's been busy but so much fun! I'm meeting so many people and learning some great new things."

"Sounds good. What stands out for you?"

"I'm taking my first archeology course, and it has been so great. The professor is great, and I might even get a chance to help out on a dig next summer."

"That sounds wonderful. How is Ryan doing?"

"He's great. He really enjoyed his classes this semester too. He struggled with the economics class, but we got grades today, and he called me and said he got an "A" in it anyway."

"Well, of course. I'm sure you both did well. You seem so grown-up."

"I don't know about that," she said laughing. "How have Joe, Becky, and Kim been? I talk to Kim every week, and Joe every once in a while, but I wondered what you thought."

"There's the old Deb, worrying about the others. They're doing well. I see Joe and Becky almost every Saturday. They come over and work on homework, or we sit around and go over theories and follow up on the machine. It's been a real pleasure having them. Kim comes over every once in a while. In fact, a couple of weeks ago she came over here and asked if I could read a paper she wrote. Said she needed someone to proofread it. When I asked, she said you had always done that for her, but I said I was glad to help, even if literature wasn't my area of expertise. It was a good paper. She did a lot of research—like her big sister. I told her, and she was happy about that reference."

"Well, I'm glad they still get a chance to spend time with you. Any talk about using the machine again?"

"Not with me. Our talk about the machine has centered on the theories of the time and space unit and the risks to anyone going to a time and space unit they have or are in via the machine. I think we might be on to a larger scientific breakthrough, but proving it would mean going public with the time travel, and I really don't think Joe wants to do that."

"I agree with him. After what happened in Cambridge last year, I'm not sure I want to have all kinds of people hopping through time. It could be a disaster."

"Yes. So, are you all off for break today?"

"Yes, I came with Michael to pick Kim and Joe up. But I brought you something. Merry Christmas—a little early." At that, Deb handed Mr. Brewster a box.

"How about if I wait to open it, would that be ok?"

"Sure, if you want. Are you seeing Thomas and Brittany for Christmas?"

"Yes, I am. I'm heading out tomorrow to go to Boston to spend the entire break with them. He is busy with med school but taking a short break like you all are, and we are going to finalize their wedding plans and celebrate together. I can't wait!"

"I'm glad you get to do that. I'm sure Thomas will be happy having you with him too. Please tell them both I said Merry Christmas and good luck with medical school."

"I will. He asks about you all every time we talk on the phone."

"Well, I better get back and help Kim get packed up. I'm sure she's out of class by now."

"Thanks for stopping by, and have a wonderful holiday."

"Bye, Mr. Brewster."

"Bye."

The Christmas holidays began with decorating the New York apartment and completing all the shopping. Along the way, they shared tales from Choate, Harvard, and NYU and all the happenings with Aunt Alicia's new job as Trend Editor and Uncle Darrick's job—which had changed a little bit, with several new, very large accounts he managed. Ryan and Becky were over frequently, but they did not see Mary at all. Her parents seemed to think that Mary's sad mood was because things were not going well with Ken, and so they whisked her away for a month-long trip. Ken was very disappointed. He and Deb spoke of it often. He felt his resolve to show Mary he was not going to let her down slipping, and Deb seemed to always be able to pull him back. Christmas Eve was similar to last year, in that Aunt Alicia and Uncle Darrick had another gathering to go to, but Christmas Day was so much better than last year with the bumpy proposal. Uncle Darrick was feeling particularly generous and lavished many gifts on everyone. They had an amazing meal together, as a new cook had finally been hired, and enjoyed the remaining days of the break, though Kim seemed a bit distant toward the end of break and spent a lot of time reading in her room. Deb couldn't get it out of her and shared her concerns with Ken, but they did not have a good plan when Joe and Kim headed back to Choate. They were going to alternate calling Kim for the first few weeks of classes to be sure she had someone to pour out her feelings to—should she decide she was ready. Deb was also going to enlist Becky to check in on Kim and report back to her.

6

A FEW DAYS AFTER classes started, Kim found Joe heading into the boys' dorm after his afternoon classes and called out to him.

"Can we talk?"

"Sure, let me put my stuff inside, and let's walk over to the main hall."

"I'll wait here."

When they arrived at the main hall, there were no free tables, and it was getting very noisy. Kim suggested they go downstairs to the music practice rooms. When they found a quiet room, Joe said, "Well, what's up, little sister?"

"Well, I've been thinking."

"I've noticed. Everyone's noticed actually. I heard from Deb yesterday, asking me to keep an eye on you."

"What for?"

"She said you seemed a little down over break, and she's worried about you."

"Oh. Is that why I've been hearing from her and Ken a lot more?"

"I'm sure it is. So, what have you been thinking about?"

"Well, you know last year when we used the machine to help Mr. Brewster?"

"Yes, I remember."

"What would you say if I said I want to use the machine to help some people?"

"I would say, who, and help how?"

"I want to go back to the 1850s, meet Louisa May Alcott, and help escaped slaves on the underground railroad. I've been reading about a few of them, and I want to help. Let's you, me, and Becky use the machine to help people."

When Joe didn't say anything, Kim continued, "Why can't we think about doing this, Joe? We helped Mr. Brewster, and it worked out. Why can't we help these people that help the slaves escape?"

Finally, Joe said, "I wasn't expecting this to be what you wanted to talk about. I'm not sure about doing this, though. It seems a bit more dangerous than anything we've tried to do before. You know, Kim, there's a big difference between meeting a nice lady at a book fair and talking to her and helping fugitive slaves escape to freedom. Also, this is not like taking a walk in Dallas a decade or so before we were born. You're talking about going more than a hundred years into the past and working in a society and culture we don't understand, to help people, and if we're caught, we could go to jail. There were laws back then that made it a crime to help slaves escape."

"I know. I've been doing a lot of research on the time period and practicing all the things Deb taught me about learning the culture and details to help us survive. I know this sounds a bit crazy, but, Joe, I want to do something for these people. I want to help in a way that only using the machine will allow us to."

"How about if we talk to Becky, bring her in on this, and sort through what you want to do here before we go too much further? Would that be ok?"

"Yeah, that sounds good. When can we do it?"

"We can ask her at dinner what she has going on tomorrow, check and see about all the homework, and then we can meet in the library?"

"Thanks, Joe," Kim said smiling.

"Sure."

They compared notes on what they each had at dinner that night and decided they all had time the next day to meet at the library after class. When they were all settled around a table in one of the study rooms at the library, Joe said, "Well, at Kim's request, we're meeting to go over her idea to use the machine."

Kim looked at both of them and started to explain her research and what she wanted to do. Becky waited for a break and asked, "Kim, why do you want to do this? I mean really, why is this important to you?"

"You're the youngest in your family, right? I'm the youngest too, and it's hard. It's hard to fit in. Ken is this superstar athlete that seems to be breezing through college on his way to being a master engineer and taking over our Dad's company. Deb is going to be this huge scholar and discover something great buried in the dirt. Joe invented these computers and things, and he is going to be famous. And then there's me."

"Kim, you're 12. You have so much time to figure out what you're going to be great at," Joe said.

"Didn't you ever wish you could just do something cool to catch up to Ken? Ever?"

"Well, as a matter of fact, when we first got here to Choate, I was struggling a bit. I didn't feel like I fit in here, and I didn't feel like I fit into the family. When our parents died, I felt lost. When they were here, I felt like I fit in with Mom. Then when we got here, I had to find a new place to fit in."

"Wasn't that part of why you pushed so hard to use the machine to try to save our parents? Didn't you want to either fit back in with Mom or do something spectacular to fit in with Ken?"

"I suppose. Maybe it was part of why I was pushing to use the machine."

"So, you see what I mean, right? I don't want to wait five years to fit in."

"I know what you mean, Kim. As the youngest in the family, it's hard sometimes to not want to hurry up and grow to catch up with your older siblings. But think of the things you'd miss if you could do that?" Becky said.

"I'm not trying to wish I was older all of a sudden. I just want to do something good for someone else and feel like I have accomplished something."

"Ok, I think I get it, but this is way different from the other trips you've made in the machine, isn't it, Joe?" Becky asked.

"Yeah, this would be different in a lot of ways. First, it would be the farthest back in time we went. We've only gone back to the 1940s when Mr. Brewster went to meet his father. This is more than a hundred years we're talking about. Also, I suspect we wouldn't be able to accomplish what you want, Kim, in only a few days, and we've never been gone longer than that."

"I thought you could program the machine so that it returned to the same date and time it left? Why couldn't we do that now? It would be like we were never even gone, no matter how long we're away," Kim asked.

"I'm not sure that would work in this case because of the way time moves for those that traveled and those that stayed. I would have to look into that and see if it would even be possible to be gone say two weeks and then return to the same date and time you left, even though time had advanced here in the present while you were gone on the trip."

"That's probably not the only issue. We'd have to have resources to be able to stay somewhere for a longer time, right? Like money and clothes and things. In the eighteen hundreds, kids didn't just get in a car and drive from town to town. So, we'd also need ways to travel," Becky pointed out.

"I think we can manage that. I noticed in the theater rooms they have all kinds of costumes from past plays. I saw some that might work. And we have money, remember, Joe. Last summer we took care of setting us each up with bank accounts and putting the money Mom and Dad left us in them." Kim said, looking at them both and trying to convince them.

"I suppose we do have money," Joe mused.

"The problem is that we have money from 1977, not 1853," Becky said.

"That's a problem. I don't know how we can solve that. It's not like we can go to the bank and ask for money from the eighteen hundreds," Joe said.

"We could buy coins from a coin dealer, couldn't we?" Kim asked.

"Well, if I remember my history from last year, we could get the money converted to gold. That was the underlying basis for the United States currency prior to the turn of the century. Then we could go to a bank there and get it converted to banknotes. That's what they called dollars back then," Becky speculated.

"So, we have clothes, and we have money. What else do we need?" Kim asked.

"Wait a minute, Kim. Just because you saw what you think might be correct time period clothing, doesn't mean it for sure is, and furthermore, we can't just waltz into the theater department and walk out with all those clothes and not be noticed," Joe cautioned.

"And then there is all the research Deb did when you went to Las Vegas. What about where we will land the machine, how will we make contact with whomever we're trying to help, and what they are doing on any given day during that time period, and all that," Becky added.

"I will do the research, and I helped in deciding the landing navigation, so I can do that too. Then I can research more about Robert Purvis, and we can set a date and work out how to find him," Kim said, somewhat pleadingly.

"One more thing. If this Robert Purvis was in Philadelphia and Louisa May Alcott is in Concord, Massachusetts, you do understand that it will take us two weeks to get between the two cities and two weeks to get back. Our only options for travel are likely carriage or train. I don't think you can plan on both things, Kim. We either would have to go meet Louisa or stay near Philadelphia and help this Mr. Purvis," Becky said.

"I hadn't thought of that. If there are trains, why would it take two weeks?" Kim asked.

"Well, there are trains, but I'm not sure about routes. I know for sure, they wouldn't run between cities multiple times a day like they do now. Also, I'm not sure we should plan to do both of these things. It just seems like too much to take on considering all the other big considerations of this trip you're suggesting," Becky answered.

"I agree with Becky here, Kim. We can't plan on landing in either place, taking a train and seeing the other person on your list, then getting back to the machine. I think that will keep us there too long. You're going to have to decide; do you want to meet Louisa May Alcott, or do you want to help escaped slaves with Robert Purvis?" Joe said.

"I guess I'll have to think about it. Is that ok?"

"Sure. Keep in mind, if you want to just meet Louisa May Alcott, we wouldn't be there as long too. That might make that choice easier all the way around," Joe added.

"Let's meet here again on Sunday to talk some more. Does that sound like a plan?" Becky asked.

They agreed and got up to leave the library. Kim had a lot to think about. She was glad Joe and Becky were taking her seriously and were considering it, but deciding whether to help the escaped slaves or to meet this person she really wanted to meet was going to be hard.

Joe and Becky talked later and they actually were both hoping that Kim would decide to meet Louisa May Alcott and not go to Philadelphia. They thought that would be a much safer plan, but secretly Joe was hoping all the roadblocks would make Kim decide not to do this at all. He was really nervous about going that far back into history and it only being the three of them. As he was walking with Becky back to the library that Sunday, he relayed his concerns and said he hoped if she wanted to go through with this, he could convince her to include Deb and Ryan.

Sunday—after church and the phone calls with Aunt Alicia, Uncle Darrick, and Deb—the three met again in the library study room. Joe and Becky looked expectantly at Kim and waited for her to start the discussion. Kim said, "I thought about what you both said about the purpose of the trip, and although I wanted to meet Louisa May Alcott, I want to do some good in the world, so I've decided to just go to Philadelphia."

"Are you sure, Kim? That does make the trip harder you know," Joe said.

"I know. But I want this trip to be about helping others, not just my infatuation with meeting this author."

"That's pretty mature of you, Kim. You would rather help some escaped slaves you never met than meet someone you've come to admire. You're way more grown-up than you think," Becky said.

"So now what?" Kim asked, smiling at Becky.

"Now I think we need to talk to Mr. Brewster—and probably Deb and Ken or Deb and Ryan," Joe said.

"I was thinking we wouldn't tell Ken and Deb about this," Kim offered.

"What? Didn't we learn last year with my trip to Cambridge, our trip to Las Vegas, and the future trips we're still dealing with, that it isn't a good idea to keep these trips from the others?" Joe asked more than a little incredulously.

"I know about last year, but this is really something I want us to do. I want it to be my idea and our plans, and I know if we tell Deb and Ken about this, they will either want to stop me or insist they come along and run everything," Kim said.

"I'm not sure I agree with you, but I'll respect your wishes while we do some research and talk to Mr. Brewster. We have to talk to him, Kim. I need his help to determine the math if we are going to be gone longer than three days," Joe said.

"Can we go talk to Mr. Brewster today?" Kim asked.

"No, he's busy with something at the church. He talked about it in class last week. I will talk to him tomorrow about when we can go over there. Besides, I have a big paper to work on," Joe said.

"Me too," Becky added.

"Ok, well, then I'm going to start on the research," Kim said as they got up and headed out of the study room. Kim stayed at the library, looking through books and maps, and Joe and Becky went to the main hall to finish papers together.

The next day, Joe told Becky and Kim at lunch that Mr. Brewster was available after classes that day, and they all went over to the barn after dropping off some books. As they sat around the table, Mr. Brewster brought in some juice and snacks.

"Thanks for taking some time for us, Mr. Brewster," Kim said.

"Don't be ridiculous, I love these little discussions and have come to depend on this barn table for some of my best moments."

"We need to take a look at some of the data, Mr. Brewster. Kim has suggested that we do some traveling in the machine to help people, and it will mean we will be at a place longer than a couple of hours or days even," Joe offered.

"It sounds like you three have been cooking this up for a little while now. Why don't you start at the beginning?" Mr. Brewster said.

"Well, it started last fall, Mr. Brewster, when I was doing projects for my literature and history classes. We were learning about the Civil War and slavery, and I was reading *Little Women*, by Louisa May Alcott. I decided that what I wanted to do was use the machine to help people. It worked so well when we went to Las Vegas to help you and Mrs. Brewster, right? So, I told Joe and Becky about this and have done a bunch of research, and we want to go to 1853 and help a man named Robert Purvis, who was a free black man—well, he's really mixed race—help escaped slaves," Kim said, a bit excitedly.

"I see. This is a bit different than anything you've talked about doing before. You know that, don't you?" Mr. Brewster said as he looked at the three of them.

"Yes, we do," Joe admitted.

However, Kim jumped in, saying, "It's not that different from when we went to Dallas. We were trying to change something about history to affect our parents—so they wouldn't die. What I'm talking about is going to a time period and trying to help a man that already was helping escaped slaves. I don't want to change what he was doing; I want to help him."

"But it is different in that we are going back farther than we've ever gone, and we likely will be there more than a couple of days, so the elapsed time is going to increase while we're gone," Joe pointed out.

"As I see it, there are two significant parts to this. The idea of going to this time and place, and the logistics of whether it can even be done. Which one do you want to discuss first?" Mr. Brewster asked.

"Well, if we find out we can't do it, does it even matter why we want to do it and if we should?" Becky asked.

"You're right, Becky, so let's start by focusing on whether we think the machine can do it, what the elapsed time is going to mean, and any other mathematical issues that might arise. Then we can focus on if we should go and plans to make it happen," Joe said.

"Ok, so let's start with the obvious—the machine going more than one hundred years into the past," Mr. Brewster offered.

"I've been thinking a lot about this question this week. I looked over the original mathematical formula, and the data that Joe showed me, and I don't think there's a reason the machine can't handle it. I mean, the power source for the field generation is derived from the mechanical parts spinning in the machine, so we don't need a power source we won't find in eighteen fifty-three," Becky said.

"Ok, but what about the scientific theory about time and space. Do we think we can go to any time and space forward or backward and not have any degradation in the space-time continuum?" Joe asked.

"If there is this space-time continuum thing, why does it care about any actual date and time?" Kim asked.

"Kim, it doesn't really work like that. Space and math are finite. There is a finite amount of energy in the universe. Any time we use the machine, we disrupt that a little bit," Joe said, trying to patient.

"Actually, why doesn't the finite nature of the space-time allow for this? Like in your computers, Joe? Does the machine care what you write and program, or does it care only that you live within the confines of the hardware, the wiring, and such?" Mr. Brewster postured.

"I think that rings true, Joe," Becky added.

"Let's see if we can make the math prove that out," Joe said as he took out some paper, and he and Mr. Brewster went over to the chalkboard they had near the table. They worked on the math formula for a short time and found they couldn't break it with a trip that far back. Joe and Mr. Brewster sat back down.

"On to the elapsed time question then?" Mr. Brewster asked.

"I've worked on this formula the past week. It looks like as the trip in the machine goes on for a longer period, the time passage here in its present slows down, and the longer the trip, the longer the slow down here. Let me show you the math," Joe said as he got up again, wiped off the chalkboard, and started over. They talked over the math and saw a point where a change was required in the calculations that might mean time wouldn't pass in a straight line in the present to what was going on with the machine. They found on Mr. Brewster's trip into the future, which lasted for five days, the elapsed time was only just over two days here. They couldn't find a reason why that would be tied to simply going into the future, so they recalculated and determined there was a variable to the formula that had seemed to impact the elapsed time every three or four days of the machine's trip.

"It looks like if we allow for this variable, we would be able to presume that if the machine trip is four days, the elapsed time is fifty-two hours. If the machine trip is five days, the elapsed time is sixty-eight hours, but if the machine time is ten days, the elapsed time six days," Mr. Brewster said after completing the calculations on the board.

Joe, looking at his watch, noticed that they barely had time to get back for dinner, so he said they would have to go. They all decided to resume the discussion that Saturday since they knew the logistics discussion would take much longer. When they got back together, Joe started by explaining what Kim had told him about why she wanted to do this.

"Kim, this is admirable, but you know you do have plenty of time to make your mark—both on your family and in the world," Mr. Brewster said kindly.

"I know, but I also just know I need to do this."

"Ok, for a minute, let's assume we agree with your desire to do this. What plans do we need to make?" Becky asked.

"I've done a lot of research on Robert Purvis, where he lived, when he moved to Philadelphia, and when he started helping runaway slaves. He was most active in this between eighteen fifty-one and eighteen fifty-seven."

"What else can you tell us about him?" Mr. Brewster asked.

"He was mixed race, born of a Scottish father and colored mother. He was very attached to his colored grandmother who was brought to Charleston as a slave. This is why he preferred to identify with his black heritage. He married a black free woman, and they had eight children. He used his house in Byberry, outside of Philadelphia, to house runaway slaves on their way farther north. He was involved in abolitionist movements most of his life."

"What about the fugitive slave acts, Kim? Didn't that make it a big risk for people like this Robert Purvis to harbor and help runaway slaves?" Becky asked.

"It did make it risky for some, and I'm sure that what I read in books today is colored by the fact that we did eventually abolish slavery here. I'm sure it made it hard to help these people, but he still did it. Harriett Tubman still did it. Also, because Philadelphia was originally settled by Quakers, there was a bigger abolitionist presence and acceptance there. They often disregarded the fugitive slave act and the courts more often than not sided with the fugitive."

"All of that is true, but Becky's point is valid. There will be some risk to this. Much more risk even than meeting a would-be assassin in the book depository of Dallas, Texas," Mr. Brewster said, smiling at Joe.

"Ok, so logistically we do have this risk of helping people that were in eighteen fifty-three clearly breaking laws to help fugitive slaves. But I'd like to talk about more detailed logistics, like where will we land the machine, and how will we manage clothing and money and lodging and all of that," Joe said, trying to redirect the discussion.

"They do have the clothes we need at the theater department. I got the research information from Kim and talked to one of my friends, Annie, and she checked. She thinks we might be able to borrow the clothes from the theater department because of two projects in the history classes going on soon involve some presentations, and we could coordinate and ask to use the clothing," Becky said.

"And I called the bank yesterday and we can, in fact, ask for gold in place of money in our accounts. It would come in the form of small bars, I guess. Then we would have to take those to a bank in the eighteen fifties and get that converted into currency," Joe added.

"That was a good catch. You can't just take our current currency into eighteen fifty-three and use it to rent rooms. With gold being the standard in this country then, you should be able to convert money easily, but as you said, Joe, only at a bank there. Pick the bank carefully. Remember there was no protection on your deposits back then. If the bank got robbed or they didn't manage it well, you lost money. It might be better to hold some of the gold back and change it a bit at a time," Mr. Brewster cautioned.

"Then lodging and a story about who we are and what we're doing there are all we have left, right?" Joe asked.

"The simpler the better," Mr. Brewster cautioned again. "You don't want to get caught in a lie."

"But we won't need identification and such, right? They didn't have social security cards or driver's licenses then, so we can just say we are from somewhere and it doesn't get verified much right?" Kim asked.

"That's right. But we will have to have a believable story, especially when we start changing gold around, and we have to be able to explain why two teenagers and a pre-teen are traveling together with no adult," Becky said.

"That is going to be easier than you think. A hundred years ago, only boys went to school for very long, but even then, they were usually done by fifteen. Your parents could have easily died from common illness, and you could have taken your fortune and your younger siblings on to make a fortune somewhere else," Mr. Brewster commented.

"That's true. People got married younger and rarely went to college. They just started working," Becky said.

"I know! We could say we were from near Charleston. That would give us a reason to seek out Mr. Purvis, to make contact with someone from the same place. We could say our parents died, and we came north because of our anti-slavery ideas," Kim said excitedly.

"That should work. Simple, yet plausible," Joe said, smiling at Kim.

"As far as lodging, I've found reference to a hotel called Girard House. It is located on Chestnut Street. I brought a map I found and copied in the library," Kim said as she laid the map out on the barn table. They all looked at it, then Joe asked, "Did you happen to find any references to banks?"

"As a matter of fact, I did. Not because of it being a bank, but because of its architecture. There is a Merchant's Exchange Bank on Chestnut Street, here." Kim pointed to a place not far from the hotel. "We could go there. With a name like Merchant's Exchange, maybe you could store the gold in a safety deposit box or something. It sounds like they do a lot of exchanging of money, so our request would not seem strange."

"Banks wouldn't have had safety deposit boxes, they would have vault storage of some kind," Mr. Brewster added. "But this would work nicely for your plan."

"Did Mr. Purvis have some business in Philadelphia, or are we going to have to travel to where he is?" Becky asked.

"He did have some business interests, and his wife was from a family that made sails and such for the naval industry. They were mostly just wealthy because Mr. Purvis's father left them a huge inheritance. They were activists in anti-slavery movements."

"How will we find him then?" Joe asked.

"By attending a meeting for one of these organizations," Becky answered.

"Yes. I don't have dates or anything like that, but I have a list of those organizations he was involved in, and we can probably locate meeting times from that. Also, with Philadelphia being a Quaker city, we won't be looked at suspiciously if we say we are there to contact an abolitionist," Kim said.

"We just can't be too obvious, though. We have to carefully ask and carefully explain that we want to help. There will be just as many people that don't want to disrupt the slavery and are willing to turn others in," Becky said cautiously.

"One thing I was thinking about, while doing some of my research, the language was much more formal then," Kim added.

"That's right. They used formal names for everyone, and had very little slang," Becky said, "We'll have to be really careful when we speak to anyone."

"I think they might have had slang terms then, but likely, you would have more trouble trying to remember these terms and using them, so

I would stick to the formal language as much as possible. That would include no contractions. So, you'll have to stop using those too," Mr. Brewster said.

"This might be harder than we think. And, by the way, how are we going to explain our different last names? Me and Becky I mean," Joe asked.

"I think you should be engaged to each other." Kim said, smiling at Joe.

"At sixteen years old?" Joe asked incredulously.

"That was probably more typical than you think. Plus, it would take one thing out of the confusing column. You could use your real names," Mr. Brewster explained, chuckling at Joe's reaction.

"I like it!" Kim exclaimed.

"All questions answered, I think," Mr. Brewster mused. "When are you planning to bring Ken and Deb into this?"

"Well… we're not sure we're going to," Kim said hesitantly.

"Didn't we learn this lesson last year?" Mr. Brewster asked.

"Here's the thing. I know Ken will tell us not to do this, that I'm too young and all that. And if Deb is here, she'll want to run everything. I want to do this, Mr. Brewster, me," Kim said pleadingly.

"Mr. Brewster, we already went through this with Kim. She's pretty convincing on this point, actually. Both Joe and I understand what she means, and we want to support her," Becky added, in defense of Kim.

"I do understand your desire to find your place, Kim. But I'd like you all to think about this a bit more," Mr. Brewster asked. Then he added, "I could possibly go with you, that might make this easier for me to support."

"Mr. Brewster, I thought of that too, but I think it might be a good idea for someone to be here that knows what we've done, just in case," Joe pointed out.

"Good point."

The three of them agreed to put some more thought into bringing Ken and Deb into this trip planning over the next week or so. By the end of January, they had decided to go ahead without telling anyone, and Mr. Brewster reluctantly agreed to keep their secret. He didn't really agree with them, but he understood Kim's desire to make this her own effort. She had made a very compelling case to all of them, in fact. There was a very long weekend coming up with days off from classes, so they set the date for their trip and finalized all the navigational and programming plans. Becky requested the clothing for a class project and was granted access to the wardrobe room where she, Kim, and Annie found three outfits for each of them and accessories that would be date-appropriate. The plan was to leave on Wednesday after dinner and be back by Monday evening. Joe's calculations meant they could be in 1853 for nine days during that elapsed time.

7

ON TUESDAY AFTERNOON, BECKY and Kim went to the theater department, picked up the clothing and accessories, and took everything to the barn. While they were lugging everything, Joe went into town to the bank and pulled out money from his account, returning with a bag full of gold bars to take to the barn. They programmed the machine and went back to campus for dinner. Kim could barely sleep that night; she was nervously excited about the trip and just couldn't settle down. She had to lie to Amy—as they all had to with their friends—by saying that they were meeting Ken and spending the weekend at Harvard during the long weekend.

Wednesday after classes, they made their way to the barn. Mr. Brewster was there, and he helped Joe confirm all the machine settings and pack their bags and things into the machine's storage compartments. They had managed to get three or four dresses for both Becky and Kim and several suits for Joe from the theater department since no one else was working on a project from this historical period. Becky convinced the theater director they hadn't decided for sure which of the costumes they were using, so he said they could have them all for the weekend. It was a real challenge to get all the strange clothing on under the dresses for the girls, and Joe commented that dressing would take an hour for him every day if he had regularly worn all the things men wore during the 1850s. After they had all changed into their appropriate attire, they bid Mr. Brewster farewell and climbed into the machine.

When the machine stopped and Joe looked out, he saw they were, in fact, right where they planned on the maps Kim had found. They had landed on Petty's Island, which sat in the Delaware River, with Philadelphia to its west and New Jersey to its east. It was owned by a Quaker family but was not inhabited regularly in 1853. There was a farmhouse, a barn and various outbuildings, and fortunately, a dock with a small skiff. They took the skiff and rowed down to the harbor in Philadelphia. When they arrived at the harbor, they pulled into a small shipyard and asked the man there if they could leave their skiff for a week or so. He said he could for a small fee, and Joe indicated that he had to make some monetary arrangements with the Merchant's Exchange Bank the next day, and he would bring payment to him. The man agreed. He also arranged for a carriage to take them all to the Girard House. On the way, Joe marveled at how trusting people were in this time.

"I wasn't asked for identification or anything. The man wrote down my name and said tomorrow would be fine to bring payment for storage. I can't believe it!"

"You know, with such a smaller population, no automobiles and such, the economy ran in a very different way here than it does in our time," Becky said. "I'm glad. It will surely work in our favor. People will just believe what we tell them about why we're here and won't be able to check our story or anything."

"Yeah, that's going to make it easier to be here longer and not mess up so much," Kim added.

"Except we will have to watch how we speak here. Remember, it's much more formal than we're used to. Everyone is called by their surname here, and there aren't as many contractions and slang. We all have to be careful about that," Becky cautioned as they pulled up to the hotel.

There Joe registered them for two rooms, and again, he indicated that he had to make some arrangements at the Merchant's Exchange Bank and was told he could bring payment for the first week the next day. Joe asked if the hotel could extend him some credit for meals until the next day, and the hotel manager, seeing one of Joe's gold bars he intended to exchange for banknotes, agreed. They ate dinner in the hotel dining room and settled into their rooms.

The next day, after enjoying breakfast in the courtyard behind the hotel, they walked down the street to the bank. There Joe spoke to the bank manager and obtained vault storage for his case of gold and exchanged enough to provide them with money for a week of lodging and food—and to pay the gentleman for the boat storage. The girls waited in the hotel lobby while Joe took the carriage ride back to the harbor, paid the shipyard man, and returned to the hotel. They then decided to take a walk down Chestnut Street and strolled through shops and began to talk to people.

In the early afternoon, they strolled over to Walnut Street and enjoyed a lovely meal at a place called City Tavern. This was a local restaurant that had several dining rooms, a bar, and limited lodging. In the eighteen hundreds, Kim found, the biggest meal of the day was this early afternoon meal called dinner. While they ate, they listened to the people around them talking. Becky noted that several of the men left their tables and went to the bar after eating, while the women stayed and had dessert. She suggested that Joe do that to see if he could learn anything.

Joe went down to the street level of the tavern where the bar was and walked up to the bar. He asked what the specialty of the house was and was told it was a house-made ale. Joe ordered a glass and looked around. Several men were seated at a table near the bar discussing abolitionist topics, so Joe turned toward them to listen.

After a few minutes, one of the younger men sitting at the table looked at Joe and said, "We have not seen you in here before. What is your name, sir?"

"My name is Joseph Fitzgerald. I arrived in Philadelphia only yesterday with my fiancé and younger sister. Your name, sir?"

"I am Henry Bennett. You seem rather interested in our topic of discussion today. Would you like to sit down and join us?"

"Sure, I would be delighted to join you."

Joe took a seat at the table and listened to the four men talk about several meetings being held that week. One of the other men turned to Joe and asked why he was in Philadelphia and where he was from.

"Well, my family is from North Carolina. My folks recently died from the fever and left me to care for my younger sister. We have traveled here so that I can make a living and marry my gal. My people knew the Purvis family. I heard Robert was here in Philadelphia and was hoping to make his acquaintance."

"Sorry to hear about your folks. You are in luck though; Mr. Purvis will be at the meeting on Friday, over at the Bishop's barn at 7. My name is George Gannet. Pleased to meet you."

Joe held out his hand, and they shook as Joe said, "Well, this was fortuitous. Meeting you all today."

"You one of those slave owners down there in North Carolina?" another of the men asked.

"No, sir. Never owned another human being. I do not think it is right to do so."

"Good. I'm glad to hear it. Here in Philadelphia, we outlawed slavery."

"That is another reason we came here. More like-minded folks."

They talked for another few minutes, and then Joe said he needed to retrieve his fiancé and sister from the dining room. He shook hands with the gentlemen, and as he walked away, Henry asked, "Where are you and your ladies staying?"

"At Girard House."

"Good lodging there. You must be a gentleman," George said.

"Trying to be, sir. Hoping to take care of my sister and fiancé."

"What is your situation? Education?" Mr. Smith asked.

"Mathematics. Studied at the University of North Carolina."

"Mr. Purvis should be able to help you out. He knows several important businessmen always in need of accounting help," Henry said.

"Good to know. Good day, gentlemen," Joe replied as he headed for the stairs.

While Joe was downstairs, Becky and Kim enjoyed the desserts and were approached by a matronly woman who introduced herself as Mrs. Rebecca Fairchild. The girls introduced themselves and invited Mrs. Fairchild to sit down. Which she did.

"Where are you ladies from?" she asked.

"We are from North Carolina, ma'am. We recently came to Philadelphia with my fiancé," Becky replied.

"What is his situation?"

"He is a graduate of university. We recently lost both his parents to the fever, and we have come to Philadelphia to resettle here."

"I am so sorry to hear. I lost several friends and distant family to the fever as well. Devastating at the end, I hear. You must be devasted, Kimberly."

"I am, ma'am, but my brother and his fiancé have been so good to me," Kim replied politely.

"Where are you staying?" she asked.

"At Girard House."

"So, you have means, then?"

"Yes, ma'am. My family left my brother a substantial inheritance, and he is a mathematical genius," Kim answered.

Just then, Joe returned to the dining room and came to the table. Becky introduced Mrs. Fairchild to Joe, and then Joe said they had best get back so Kimberly could do her reading. Mrs. Fairchild invited both girls to tea at her home on Friday, and handed Becky her card, bearing her address.

"I will see you on Friday, at two," she said as Joe helped them from their seats, and they departed the dining room.

On the way back to the hotel, Joe told them of the men he met, and how he had already discovered a meeting where Robert Purvis was going to be. Kim and Becky were excited for the prospect, and they told Joe about Mrs. Fairchild. She seemed like a nice lady, and they were hopeful of meeting some other people at the tea.

The next evening while they were walking through the lobby to go to their rooms after supper, as the evening meal was called, Henry came into the lobby and called out to Joe. Joe turned to him and said, "Good evening, Mr. Bennett. May I present my fiancé, Miss Rebecca Simmons, and my sister, Kimberly."

Henry acknowledged both ladies and then looked at Joe. "We are headed to a meeting, and I was wondering if you would like to join us."

"What kind of meeting?"

"A railroad meeting," was Henry's reply.

"Sure, I would enjoy coming along and listening to what you have to say."

Joe said he would return momentarily and took Becky and Kim to their room. Becky said to be careful and to knock when he got back. When Joe returned downstairs, Henry motioned him outside to a waiting wagon hitched to two horses. Joe climbed up, and Henry drove the team of horses down the street. They took a road that led outside of the confines of Philadelphia's downtown district to the beginnings of farmland. In the total darkness, Joe realized that he might have made a mistake in coming as he had no sense of how to get back to the hotel and to Becky and Kim. He was beginning to get rather concerned when Henry pulled into a drive and up to a barn that clearly had light coming from behind the semi-closed doors.

Joe climbed down and so did Henry, who said, "In here are a bunch of us that run fugitive slaves to and from railroad stations. We talk about issues and plans here."

"You know, my sister, Kimberly, is already a committed abolitionist. She is going to be very jealous when she hears where I have been tonight."

"We have jobs for the ladies too. They get notes around to the different stations and move supplies around under the guise of correspondence and visits to neighbors. If you want, you can have your sister and your fiancé start to help out there as well. It sometimes is good to have new people help in that regard. Kind of a meet-your-neighbors disguise."

"I will speak to Rebecca and let you know."

"Come on then."

They went inside, and there was a man speaking on a raised platform of the barn. The barn was lit with candles, and lamps hung on hooks and nails all around. It was fascinating to Joe how people managed to do anything in this light. The room was filled with mostly young men—some were black men but most were white. All looked to be from about Joe's age up to about mid-twenties, but it was hard to tell. The man was speaking about the pressure from southern masters coming up north and filing in court under the fugitive act. How they had revised the workings of the railroad to ensure that no one person could attest to the location of fugitives on the "train", and therefore could avoid prosecution for their efforts. Then the man introduced Mr. Robert Purvis. Joe was amazed at his luck to get this close to their goal so quickly, and he smiled.

Henry leaned over and said, "You know him, from your family in North Carolina?"

"Not really. My father knew someone from his family is all. I was just hoping to get an introduction so I could ask the man to help me find employment."

"Well, we can arrange that tonight, I think."

"That'd be great."

"Excuse me, what did you just say? Is that some foreign language?"

"My apologies, we had many field hands back in Carolina, all free of course, but they had their own language, a short version of known words, I guess. I occasionally revert to their words in moments of excitement."

"Is that so? Exactly what were you trying to convey then?"

"I was trying to say that I am pleased to be able to make Mr. Purvis' acquaintance so quickly and certainly appreciate your assistance in making that happen."

"I see. There might be some value in that short version, in some circumstances."

Joe was glad he managed to explain his lapse in language. He turned his attention to the stage and tried to look like he wasn't relieved his explanation was believed. They listened to Mr. Purvis talk about horses being provided and wagons for use so that no one person would have to provide and wear down their horses for the conducting activities. Mr. Purvis spoke for about thirty minutes, and then they said they would pass along notices to various conductors tonight where they could. The crowd started to disperse, and Henry took Joe over to meet Mr. Purvis. Henry shook hands with a man and introduced him as Thomas Bingemton, who had been speaking with Mr. Purvis. Henry explained that Joe was wanting to be introduced, so Mr. Bingemton turned and touched the shoulder of Mr. Purvis. He turned, and Mr. Bingemton said, "Robert, may I present to you, Mr. Joseph Fitzgerald. Formerly of North Carolina. He has recently relocated to Philadelphia with his fiancé and sister."

"It is a pleasure to meet you, Mr. Purvis," Joe said.

"The pleasure is all mine, sir. Where in North Carolina are you from?"

"Most recently from Raleigh, sir. I was completing my studies at university there. My parents have passed, and I felt it was time to strike out with my inheritance and seek my fortunes."

"Ah, a fate similar to my own. I lost my father as well. I also gained an inheritance in the ordeal and found myself in Philadelphia. What did you study?"

"Mathematics."

"A great skill for a man to have."

"I hope so, sir. I was actually hoping you might have some knowledge of an opportunity I might seek. I need to secure a home for my fiancé and I—and address my sister's education."

"I am certain we can come up with something, and I am always ready to assist a kindred spirit. Why don't you come to see me on Monday, say ten?"

"That would be my honor."

Mr. Purvis pulled a card from his front pocket and gave it to Joe. Henry said they ought to be leaving, and he and Joe left the barn and made their way back to the city. On the way they discussed the conductors, how word got around, and if Joe was interested in helping out. He said he would consider it, but he was sure Rebecca and Kimberly would be interested in doing their part. Henry said he would pass the word along, and they would be contacted by one of the ladies, and then he left Joe back at Girard House.

Joe went directly to the girls' room and softly knocked. Becky answered and motioned him into the room. He relayed all the information about the meeting, including that he was introduced to Mr. Purvis, which Kim was very excited about. The girls were excited about the possibility of helping by traveling around and leaving notes for people, but Kim said, "Why can't we do more than just pass notes?"

"Kim, we have to take this slowly," Joe said, trying to calm Kim down.

"I never expected it to be so hard to do what I wanted. Well, at least we get to help."

Finally, Becky wondered how they would manage to navigate in a carriage. Joe explained that he could arrange for a carriage with a driver, and they would give addresses to that driver who would do all the navigating. They thought it was a great idea. When Joe replayed the moment he almost messed everything up by saying 'that's great'. Both Becky and Kim gave him a reproachful look but laughed. They all agreed to be more diligent in their conversations.

That Friday, Becky and Kim went to tea at Mrs. Fairchild's home. After the short ride from the hotel to her house in the fashionable district of Philadelphia by hired carriage, Becky knew that they had arrived at one of the society matrons' homes. They were shown by a maid to the sunny room where several ladies were gathered around a few tables. Mrs. Fairchild rose from her seat and greeted Kim and Becky and then introduced them around to the other ladies. The girls were asked all kinds of questions about where they came from and about Joe. Becky and Kim both kept to the story, giving just enough details to please everyone but being discrete and a bit vague as well. When Kim was asked what her plans were, she replied, "Well, my brother has indulged me, and I had been doing some studying with a tutor back home. I hope to continue that while adding to my education with music and art. And, of course, soon to have my own household to run and a family."

"Well, with Joseph's inheritance and your means, I am certain you will make a good match. Perhaps I could assist in introducing you in a few years to the eligible appropriate men?" Mrs. Fairchild said.

"That would be so helpful, Mrs. Fairchild. Joseph and I so want to make sure Kimberly is well taken care of with a fine gentleman. I fear that with our move here, even after a few years, we will need some guidance to ensure this," Becky said wanting to get this help. What no one understood, least of all Mrs. Fairchild, was she only wanted it for a week.

"Oh, dear, I am sure I can help you both. We should start, of course, by introducing you and your fiancé around very soon, and naturally, you will want to invite some of the right people to your nuptials."

"Thank you, Mrs. Fairchild."

The girls managed to get through the tea without any glaring issues but were happy to be returning to the hotel. They laughed about the ritual of the tea party and the gossiping the ladies did about those that Becky suspected were not there. When they arrived at the hotel, Joe had not returned, but the desk attendant indicated they had some correspondence that had been dropped off. Becky took it, and the girls went upstairs to inspect what had arrived with only Becky's name on the first letter.

What they found in the first letter was an introduction from Mrs. Bingemton to the Ladies in Support of the Railroad. This group of ladies, she said in the letter, provided correspondence and supplies to the various conductors on the railroad and their families. It requested that she and her sister make introductions and visits to three ladies and deliver the included packages to them. Kim was thrilled that they were finally going to be able to help in the underground railroad, even if it wasn't directly with Mr. Purvis. When Joe came back from a visit to the bank, he found the girls, and they showed him what they had received.

"I want to meet Mr. Purvis and be more active in the railroad," Kim moaned as she sat down on the bed.

"Kim, we've come to understand, ladies don't do that kind of activity in this time period. We don't do the daring things here. We bring the letters and supplies and have tea parties," Becky said, laughing at the end at what she was implying.

"I know you wanted to come here and make daring runs through the countryside with fugitive slaves, but, Kim, that's not just a cultural thing. Also, it's dangerous. I realized that last night—what a danger we're in here. I got into a wagon last night, in the dark, and I rode out of town with a virtual stranger. I had no way to contact you guys back here, and with no street lights or even street signs, I had no way to know where I was," Joe said, a little impassioned.

"I know, I just didn't think it would be like this. I mean I read about women and their roles in this time, but I guess I didn't believe all women were like that. I mean there had to be a first woman that did things, right, or we wouldn't be where we are in our present."

"That's true, but the thing is, we can't be that first. It will draw way too much attention to us. You're going to have be content delivering notes and supplies—oh and going to tea parties!"

"Thanks a lot, Joe!" Kim said, but she was smiling.

"So, what are you supposed to do with these letters and supplies? I mean you can't just call Mrs. Bingemton up and tell her you'll do it, right?" Joe asked.

"I suppose we should send her a letter back," Becky said.

"With what?" Kim asked.

"I believe we'll need writing supplies," Becky said.

They made a trip to the general store down the block and came back with a writing set. Becky and Kim prepared their notes to send to the ladies to schedule a visit next week, and Joe went to the desk to see if they could deliver the correspondence for them.

That night, Joe again left the girls after supper to attend a meeting. This was a more formal meeting that included some older gentlemen, and the discussion was both planning and strategy. It seemed that with the new fugitive act, an owner from the south could simply claim a man his slave, and no court appearance, nor rebuttal, need be provided. They were all concerned and trying to come up with funds to assist a black man, named Anthony Burns. Mr. Burns had apparently stowed away on a merchant ship bound for Philadelphia and had been living and working here. He was named as a slave by a Mr. Suttle from Virginia, and the hearing was set for Monday. The group had procured representation for Mr. Burns, but the more radical aspects of the abolitionist movement in Philadelphia was plotting to storm the courthouse and free Mr. Burns. Mr. Purvis and another man, Mr. Still, were trying to calm down the radicals in the group and prevent a confrontation with the military, who had been called out by President Fillmore to protect the courthouse. When the hat was passed around as funds were collected for the representation for Mr. Burns, Joe put a considerable amount of money in the hat. Mr. Purvis later found Joe and asked if they could move their planned meeting on Monday to Tuesday so he could attend the trial, and Joe agreed.

Joe, Kim, and Becky attended a party on Saturday evening, via an invitation from Mrs. Fairchild, and on Sunday, they went for a stroll. Monday, as the trial was getting underway, Becky and Kim left in their hired carriage to visit the first of their three ladies assigned from the note they got on Friday. The first home they visited was located at the west end of Philadelphia proper, near the Schuylkill River. A large Victorian mansion, the home of Mr. and Mrs. William Kettering, was surrounded by a tall iron fence and had a large, very deep front porch. The girls hired carriage took them up to the door, and the driver assisted the girls down. They were greeted by a young lady in a pale-yellow dress who announced herself as Annabelle Kettering. They were taken into a sunroom at the side of the house, and Mrs. Kettering rose to greet the girls. As they enjoyed tea, Becky said, "You have a very lovely home, Mrs. Kettering."

"Thank you so much. It is always nice to entertain new residents of our great city—and especially those of the Ladies for the Support of the Railroad."

"Unfortunately, we cannot stay long. We do have other appointments today. We have brought you a package, however."

Becky slid the package across the table toward Mrs. Kettering and smiled. Mrs. Kettering took the package and walked over to the table against the wall and placed it there. She came back to where the girls were sitting and said, "Yes, we do try to make these visits short, to avoid any gossip or such, don't we? Thank you so much for your visit. I do hope to see you again soon."

Mrs. Kettering walked the girls to her door, and the carriage driver assisted them back into the carriage. The girls made two other visits that day, both receiving their packages and politely conversing for a few short minutes with the girls. One house was similar to the Kettering house, but the other was quite a drive and was instead a large farmhouse. The girls commented about the difference between the people of the town and those out of town and how smoothly it seemed the women were passing money and information around to assist the railroad in moving escaped slaves. It was no wonder it went on for so long, Kim commented as they took the rather long ride back from the farmhouse to the hotel.

There was quite a commotion going on in the streets when they got close to the hotel. The girls wondered what was going on, but the driver insisted on not stopping until he had the ladies safely back at the hotel, and they couldn't make out what all the shouting was about. When they got to the hotel, the desk manager was standing in the lobby and came to them immediately when they entered, "Ladies, you should not be outside today. It is not safe without your fiancé. There is such chaos in the streets because of that fugitive trial!"

"My goodness, what has happened?" Becky asked.

"Oh, well, first thing this morning, a group of men, some black some white, tried to storm the courthouse building to free Mr. Burns. They were repelled by the military that President Fillmore had assigned to protect the building, but apparently, a guard was shot. Then the trial started, and Mr. Burns must have decided to end the chaos and identified Mr. Suttle as his owner. The military then marched Mr. Burns to a waiting ship in the harbor to take him away, and the crowds got out of control. They were waving banners about it being a kidnapping. You should wait here for Mr. Fitzgerald to return."

"We will do that. Thank you for the information, sir," Becky said.

The girls then went up to their room and waited for Joe.

8

WHILE THE GIRLS WERE waiting in their room after hearing there was a scuffle in town today, Joe was being processed into the jail. He couldn't believe this had happened. He was standing there, with Henry, watching the parade of men carrying signs about this being a kidnapping and several with abolitionist call to action. There were men lining parts of the street in what appeared to be uniforms, but Joe wasn't positive. He didn't want to ask Henry in case that was the standard for something in this time period. That would blow their story and cause all kinds of issues. One of those soldiers came across the street toward where Joe was standing when there was a break in the parade crowd and pushed the men in the front of the group standing there, saying they had to stay back from the street or they would be arrested.

When the pushing started, the men in front tried to push back against the officer, and several more officers appeared from somewhere, Joe wasn't sure. He was starting to get the feeling he shouldn't be here and was looking around for a way to break away from the crowd and get off the street, when all of sudden pushing started from everywhere, and someone grabbed for the officer's rifle. It escalated quickly as more officers arrived. The men just in front of Joe started surging forward and one of the stocky officers shoved him hard. He went flying toward Joe and Joe reached out to keep the man and himself from tumbling the ground. The man turned to thank Joe, but was yanked away from the group by a tall officer. An officer then grabbed Joe's arm and said, "You are under arrest sir, for rioting and insurrection."

"Wait a minute, I was peacefully observing the goings on here. I was not engaged in any rioting!" Joe declared as the officer tried to pull him toward the street.

"Were you or were you not, part of this group protesting the proceedings to return Mr. Burns to his owner?" the officer asked.

"No, Sir. I was simply called to the street by the noise and was standing at the back of this crowd to observe," Joe protested.

"Well, you are coming with us and you can tell that story to the judge," the officer said, as a wagon had pulled up and the officers were loading several offenders into the back.

Joe's hands were tied behind his back quickly and he was hoisted up into the cart. He looked out to the crowd and spied Henry trying to make his way off the street. Joe called to him to get word to his fiancé as the wagon pulled away.

The five offenders were roughly pulled out of the wagon when they arrived at the courthouse. Each man was brought in front a large, high wooden counter with an officer sitting behind it in full dress uniform. When Joe was presented to the commander, he was asked his name, and present address. Joe gave them his name and said because he and his sister and fiancé had just arrived in Philadelphia they were staying at Girard House on Chestnut Street. The commander at the counter asked why he was involved in this riot and Joe replied he was not. He was wrongfully brought in because the officer shoved someone against him. The commander stared down at Joe and said he could save that for his defense.

Joe was untied and walked into another section of the courthouse that had cells against one wall. A cell door was opened and Joe was pushed into the cell. It had two cots, a sink and two chairs. *This is the worst possible thing that could ever have happened,* Joe thought as he heard the door behind him close. Joe sat down on the right-side cot and leaned over, resting his elbows on his knees and putting his head in his hands. *Now what? He thought. How am I going to get out of this and get back to Becky and Kim?*

Joe sat there for a long time, trying to come up with a solution. No solution came. He didn't even know how he was going to get word to Becky. He wasn't sure Henry heard him as he was taken away. He laid down on the cot and wished he had never agreed to this trip.

Back at the hotel, when supper time arrived, and they still had heard nothing nor seen Joe, Becky began to get worried. So did Kim. They went downstairs and inquired about whether or not the chaos had settled down, and someone seated in the lobby said that it appeared it soon would be, but there had been several arrests. The desk manager encouraged Becky and Kim to stay in the hotel, and they agreed and went to the dining room for their meal. They sat in the lobby that evening and didn't hear a thing until just before they were planning to go up to their room, when Henry came into the lobby. He went to the desk and asked for Joseph Fitzgerald's fiancé. The manager brought Henry to where Becky and Kim were sitting and introduced him.

After the manager walked away, Henry said, "I regret that I am the one to have to tell you this, but Mr. Fitzgerald was arrested today."

"What?" Becky asked.

"It seems he was rather caught up in a crowd that was surging toward the courthouse when they brought Mr. Burns out, and when the scuffle started, Mr. Fitzgerald ended up being pulled out by an officer and taken with some others to the station. He is being held there."

"Mr. Bennett, what are we to do? I have virtually no experience with this," Becky said.

"Miss Simmons, I will do what I can, but unfortunately, I do not have the funds to get him released. I was going to reach out to Mr. Purvis for some assistance, but I felt it was only right to inform you first."

"Thank you, Mr. Bennett, I appreciate you coming here first. Perhaps you could reach out to Mr. Purvis and see if he could meet us here tomorrow morning to assist us?"

"I will go there right now."

"Thank you."

The girls went upstairs, and both paced the room. When they realized there really wasn't anything they could do that evening, they both tried to sleep.

Meanwhile, at the jail five blocks away, Joe was having a terrible evening. He paced back and forth in the cell or sat with his head in his hands for what seemed like hours. The officer brought him a plate with some sort of meat swimming in gravy and mashed potatoes to eat for dinner, but Joe barely touched it. At some point after the plate was taken away, the officer left and then arrived back at Joe's cell with a man in tow. The man was pushed into the cell and the cell door locked again. Joe thought at that moment that things couldn't get much worse. Now he had to contend with a man he didn't know, didn't know what he was arrested for. Joe was barely keeping his thoughts straight and now he had to keep up the charade of being part of this society that he knew very little about. This was terrible.

The man sitting on the chair said, "What is your name?"

"Joseph," Joe replied. "Yours?"

"David. David Herold."

"You get caught in that public fray over Mr. Burns?" Joe asked.

"Yes. Came here to make sure that slave got returned, and I got snapped up by the military and brought here."

"I was just trying to see what all the fuss was about."

"That ain't right."

"No, it sure ain't."

"You one of those abolitionist Quakers?"

"Not a Quaker. Not sure about the abolitionist part."

"What do you mean by that?"

"Well, David, I seem to be reviewing my beliefs since coming to Philadelphia from North Carolina."

The two talked for several hours. They decided at some point to debate the merits and failings of slavery and switched sides once or twice. It was a long night, but Joe appreciated the distraction. As he waited to see how he was going to get out of this situation, he hoped that somehow Becky and Kim had found out where he was and were planning something or at least that they knew. He decided this David Herold was probably ok, and if possibly he changed one mind on slavery, he could say he made a difference on this trip. At any rate, he couldn't wait to tell Becky and Kim about it.

Joe spent the night staring up at the ceiling of his cell. He didn't know what to expect would happen now. He had no experience with jail period, let alone in another time. He wasn't read any rights; he didn't get asked if he wanted a lawyer. Joe felt so out his element, he was confused, scared and couldn't collect his thoughts into anything like a plan of action. His last thought as he finally drifted off to sleep was that he hoped Becky was thinking clearer and she had a plan. If he ever saw her again.

In the morning, the girls went downstairs for breakfast and found Henry in the lobby with a man that Kim whispered to Becky as they descended the stairs was Mr. Purvis. They walked up to the two men, and Henry said, "Miss Simmons and Miss Fitzgerald, may I present Mr. Robert Purvis."

"I apologize for our having to meet under these circumstances, ladies, but it is a pleasure," Mr. Purvis said.

"The pleasure is ours, Mr. Purvis," Becky replied.

"Shall we go to the dining room to talk?" Henry asked.

They agreed and went into the dining room. Once seated, the girls ordered some tea and pastries, and the men ordered coffee. Becky then asked what Mr. Purvis understood about Joe's arrest and what was to be done about it today.

"Well, I have discovered today that his charges include disorderly conduct, resisting the military's efforts to control the crowd, and aiding a fugitive slave," Mr. Purvis said.

"How can that be? I do not believe he was ever in direct contact with this Mr. Burns, was he?" Becky asked.

"No, he was not, but this is going to mean there will be a trial," Henry said.

"Does he have to stay in jail until this trial?" Kim asked, getting more than a little concerned.

"Yes, young lady. He will have to stay in jail. However, I believe I can get the trial set for a few days from now, and we should be able to get him cleared of these charges," Mr. Purvis said, trying to calm Kim down.

"Can we see him?" Becky asked.

"I believe we can arrange that. I propose you ladies finish your breakfast and prepare yourselves, and Mr. Bennett and I will return shortly. We will then escort you to the courthouse where we can arrange a visit for you both," Mr. Purvis said as he got up from the table.

Kim and Becky finished their breakfast and returned to their room to freshen up. Henry was waiting in the lobby when they came downstairs, and they left the hotel. At the police station, Mr. Purvis asked to see Joe. They were brought to a room and told to wait. A few minutes later, a guard brought Joe to the room. Becky rushed to him and hugged him. Kim hugged him too. They all sat down at a table with Mr. Purvis and Henry.

"Mr. Still has provided me with the name of a lawyer to represent you. His name is Mr. Jacob Cartwright. He will be asking for the case to be moved up later today. We are asking for the violation of the fugitive act to be removed. Having just moved to Philadelphia, and being the only provider for your sister and fiancé, we can show you could not have had time to involve yourself in fugitive protective actions and had no contact with nor knowledge of Mr. Burns' case. You were simply caught on the street by a mob," Mr. Purvis said.

"What about the other charges?" Kim asked.

"Those will probably carry a fine," Mr. Purvis replied.

"Joseph, can I access the accounts at the Merchant's Exchange?" Becky asked.

"I suspect they will allow that, from you or Kimberly. Mr. Purvis, would it be too much trouble to ask you to assist Rebecca in procuring the funds for Mr. Cartwright and the possible fines?" Joe asked.

"I would be happy to help. We can go to the bank directly after this visit. If that is acceptable to you, Miss Simmons?"

"It is, and thank you again for all the assistance you have provided to us, Mr. Purvis," Becky said.

"I am sincerely sorry this is your first impression of Philadelphia. It usually is a much more welcoming place."

"We thought so too until yesterday," Kim said.

The guard took Joe back to the cell, and the girls left with Mr. Purvis. Henry left them at the front steps of the courthouse, saying he had some railroad business to finish. The ride over to the bank was quiet. When they arrived at the bank, a man came out from an office and greeted Mr. Purvis. Mr. Purvis explained the girls' situation, and the man said he would be glad to assist them. He took Becky to his office, and she asked that the vault box be brought to her. When she had the box, she took several of the gold bars out and asked the manager to convert them to banknotes for her. The man left to return the vault box and get her banknotes. When their business had been concluded, they left the bank, and Mr. Purvis returned the girls to the hotel.

When the girls got into their room, Becky turned from the door and Kim said, "I'm really scared now, Becky. What have I done? Joe is in jail, and we are stranded here in eighteen fifty-three."

"I'm scared too. And I feel so helpless. I hate that we're in a time when women can't do anything themselves. I've had to keep reminding myself when we talk to people, men especially, that we are either in the care of our fathers or our husbands here. There's almost nothing we can do to save Joe but play along with Mr. Purvis. And what if this lawyer can't get

Joe's charges removed or if it takes so long that we don't have money to pay the fine?"

"How much money do we have left?"

"Thankfully, there are still eight or nine gold bars in the box held in the vault. I exchanged three today for banknotes so that we have money to pay to stay here and eat, and some so we can pay this lawyer and whatever the fine is. It was more banknotes than I expected, but I haven't seen a bill from here. Joe took care of everything. I'm going to ask the desk manager when we go down for dinner about our bill and make sure I know what's going on so we don't get caught."

"I'm trying to remember how long we said we could stay here before it starts to move our nineteen seventies timeline so far forward that we aren't back by Monday. Do you remember?"

"It is about nine days. But there's nothing we can do about that now. We have to stay as long as it takes to get Joe out of jail."

"I wasn't thinking about leaving, it's just that it will be a mess back home if we have to be here longer. Maybe Joe can figure out a way to send us back to the time we need to be back?"

"I don't know. There was something in the math about after so much time, the elapsed time in the present couldn't be rolled back or we would be there twice or something. We're just going to have to figure that out once we figure out how to get Joe out."

Kim and Becky had been pacing back and forth in the room, and finally, they sat down. That didn't help much. Kim announced that she thought dinner would start soon in the dining room, so they checked their hair, smoothed their skirts, and went downstairs.

Back at the jail, Joe was pacing also. David had a meeting with someone he knew from town, so Joe was alone with his thoughts. This Mr. Cartwright that Mr. Purvis had found had come to see Joe and they talked about when he arrived in town and who could verify where he had been. Joe relayed the name of the desk manager at the hotel, the bank manager and shipyard manager to Mr. Cartwright. Mr. Cartwright thought the testimony from the shipyard manager and the hotel manager would be most helpful. That was good news to Joe. However, when they talked about what could happen if Joe was convicted, that was when Joe really panicked. It seemed the penalty for violating the fugitive slave act was pretty harsh. Joe might be hanged if he was found guilty.

Joe stopped pacing when David was returned to the cell and their dinner trays were brought in. Some type of stew and a large chunk of bread was to be the meal today. Joe sat down and started eating, and realized that he should somehow get word to Becky for her and Kim to return to their present in the machine if it didn't look like he was going to get out of these charges.

When the girls arrived downstairs, the desk manager called Becky over.

"Yes?" Becky said as she stood at the counter.

"You have several correspondences that were dropped off today while you were out. Also, I heard about the changes to the charges for Mr. Fitzgerald. Are you both alright?"

"Well, it is quite distressing. However, our good friend Mr. Purvis is working to rectify the matter with a lawyer friend of his. Apparently, Mr. Fitzgerald was simply caught up by the mob and mistaken for someone more involved. Mr. Purvis thinks this will soon be resolved. However, while Mr. Fitzgerald is away, I am afraid I will need to attend to our charges here. Could you possibly provide me some details on the rate and when payments should be made?"

"Oh, Miss Simmons, we can certainly wait for Mr. Fitzgerald to return and settle up with him then. We wouldn't think of making this any worse for you and his sister."

"Mr. Wilson, that is very nice of you to be so understanding of the fear and anxiety this is causing Kimberly and myself, but I must insist that you at least share the rate and such with me. You see, Mr. Fitzgerald and I were considering the purchase of a house, and well, perhaps I will need to move forward with that in his absence if this takes too long and, as you understand, I do not have the faintest idea of the costs of staying here."

"I see. We certainly hope you will stay until Mr. Fitzgerald is released, but we can, of course, supply you with an accounting of your stay to date. Would that be helpful?"

"Yes, Mr. Wilson, it would be helpful. That way I can confer with Mr. Fitzgerald, and he can direct me as to when to address our housing situation. Can you prepare that while Miss Fitzgerald and I are at dinner?"

"Yes, of course."

"Thank you, and the correspondence?"

"Here you are."

Mr. Wilson, the desk manager, handed Becky the two packages and two letters. Becky and Kim went into the dining room and had dinner. The letters they received were from the Ladies in Support of the Railroad. They included a package to be delivered and a request to pick up some supplies at the general store to deliver to another address. When they had finished dinner, Becky and Kim went directly upstairs and prepared their notes. Becky went down to the desk and asked the manager to send those on and was given the accounting for the room. She took that back up and looked it over. Relieved, she told Kim, "Well, apparently I shouldn't have been worried about the money. With a room rate of two dollars a night and barely anything for the meals we have had here, money isn't going to be the problem."

"That's good. Now, all we have to worry about is Joe."

"I think you and I need to go get some new clothes, Kim. We likely will be here longer than we expected, and with all these invitations and things, we're going to need it. I asked Mrs. Fairchild where to go for clothing, and she directed me to a place that was one block from here. I suggest we distract ourselves while we wait to hear what's going on in court this afternoon by ordering some new clothes."

"I don't see how that's going to help, but if you want to, let's go."

The girls went downstairs and out of the hotel. They entered the clothing store and introduced themselves to the owner. Explaining they were there at the recommendation of Mrs. Fairchild, the owner welcomed Kim and Becky into the store and began a process to make them several new dresses, hats, and other items. Mrs. Owens, the store owner, suggested two more evening gowns as she measured the girls and made fabric selections. She said the dresses would be delivered to the hotel the next day.

Back at the hotel, Henry was waiting in the lobby. He rose from his chair when the girls entered and went directly to Becky.

"Miss Simmons, good afternoon. I was asked by Mr. Purvis to deliver this to you."

"Thank you, Mr. Bennett. Good afternoon to you as well."

"Mr. Purvis asked that if you have any questions, to please send those on to him."

"Thank you," Becky replied.

"Well, good day to you, Miss Simmons and Miss Fitzgerald."

"Good day," both girls replied as Henry left the hotel. The girls went out to the courtyard and requested tea, and Becky opened the letter. Mr. Purvis indicated that the judge had not accepted the argument the charges should just be dropped, so there would have to be a trial. It was set to begin on Monday. That was four days away. That would be on day seven of their trip. Kim said she was worried they would end up having to be here past the nine days, but they agreed, there was nothing they could do about it now. Becky indicated that she wanted to arrange to see Joe again, and they went to prepare a note to send to Mr. Purvis asking if he could arrange it for them. When they had delivered the note to the desk manager, they both felt more than a little tired and asked for a supper tray to be sent to their room and retired for the night.

The next morning, Becky felt a little more comfortable when they went downstairs. The desk manager greeted her and Kim and provided them a note that had just arrived. It was from Mr. Purvis, who indicated that he would be making arrangements for the two of them to visit Joe each day at eleven in the morning. He said he would be by each day to pick the ladies up and take them over to the jail so he could also speak to Joe. Becky was glad he had been able to arrange this, and after breakfast, she and Kim prepared to go on their visits for the Ladies in Support of the Railroad. They had the desk manager hire them a carriage for the afternoon, and they went to a general store before heading to their first visit.

On the way back to town, Kim commented that she didn't like the timid way all the women appeared in public, while having such resolve at home. She noticed on the visits today that while they were standing with these women, they were managing children, households, and workers on their property. It seemed strange that they settled with their position behind the men.

"I've noticed that too. Look at Mrs. Fairchild. She's this force to be reckoned with in society. You don't get anywhere in this town without her knowledge and approval. But she's still someone's husband. I'm glad we live when and where we do, Kim."

While all this was going on, Joe sat, again with his head in hands after hearing the judge pronounce he would not drop the charges. He said it was time this community understood they could not defy the fugitive slave act. Apparently, Joe and the others were to be an example. Joe couldn't believe what was happening. He had resolved as he was being brought back to his cell that he would send Kim and Becky back. He had to keep them safe and the only way to do that was to send them back. He figured he was going to be convicted now — now that the judge had decided to make an example of him. *This couldn't be any worse!* Joe thought.

He didn't touch his supper and when David tried to engage him in conversation that night, Joe just said he wasn't up for talking tonight and rolled over on his cot and pretended to sleep.

Meanwhile, Kim didn't want to spend another night dining in the hotel, so the girls went down to the City Tavern for supper that night after their visits. Just before they left for supper, the dresses were delivered. The next morning, Mr. Purvis arrived at the hotel at ten forty-five to pick up the girls.

"Good morning, Miss Simmons and Miss Fitzgerald. I see you received my note?"

"Yes, thank you, Mr. Purvis. It was so kind of you to arrange these visits for us to see Joseph. I have become simply distraught thinking of what he must be going through," Becky replied.

"We will set this right. There is no need for you to worry so."

The girls were helped into the carriage, and they went the few blocks to the jail. Again, they were brought to a room, and again, Joe was brought in to see them. He exchanged words with Mr. Purvis and discussed details of the trial next week, and then Mr. Purvis left to confer with the lawyer in Joe's case. When he left, Joe asked the girls, "How are you both doing? Is everything ok? Are you getting food and everything you need?"

"Yes, Joe, we're doing ok. Mr. Purvis took us to the bank, and I exchanged three bars for banknotes. I confirmed the rate on the rooms, and I know the money is going to be ok. Kim and I got several new dresses since we have to be here longer, and we keep getting invitations from Mrs. Fairchild and the railroad ladies. We're ok. How are you? I'm so worried about you being stuck in here!"

"It's ok. I have a cellmate; his name is David Herold. He's a southerner. Believes in slavery. We've had some spirited discussions. I think I might be changing his mind, actually."

"We've been very busy with the Ladies in Support of the Railroad. We've gone on four or five visits, delivered packages, and even took supplies yesterday."

"I'm glad you're getting to help, Kim. Now if we can just get me out of here."

"So, with the trial on Monday, we will be at day seven. As long as this trial is quick, we can be back where we belong before day nine," Becky said.

"I think you should just go back to the machine today and go back to Choate," Joe said, looking Becky right in the eyes as he said it.

"What are you saying? We are absolutely not leaving here without you!" Becky practically yelled back at him.

"Becky, you have to. It's the only way I can protect you both. I'm not sure this is going to turn out well for me."

"Joe, we can't leave you here," Kim said, "plus, Mr. Purvis thinks this lawyer will be able to convince the judge. He said the lawyer met with the shipyard manager yesterday and was going to the hotel today to talk to Mr. Wilson."

"Yeah. The lawyer thinks this should be easy to prove since we've only been in town for a few days. He's said he was going to get affidavits from the desk manager at the hotel, the shipyard manager, and the bank manager. He said these people will prove when I got to town and how I didn't have time to get involved with Mr. Burns. But you weren't there for the hearing. That judge wants to make an example out of me and the others."

"We have to stay strong Joe. The lawyer and Mr. Purvis will get you out of this!" Kim said.

"I think so too, Joe. We have to have faith in them and that the truth will change the judge's mind. Did the lawyer say anything else when you met with him?" Becky asked.

"He asked if there was anyone else that might be able to testify on my behalf, but I can't think of anyone else. Can you?"

"I don't know anyone else, other than Mrs. Fairchild. Maybe I'll speak to her. We're having tea with her later today at the City Tavern."

"Be careful. The society madam might not think highly of you if she knows you've hitched your wagon to an outlaw."

"Joe, this is not funny, and Mrs. Fairchild is a nice lady," Kim said.

"Sorry, sis, just trying to find the humor in here somewhere."

"What did you say your cellmate's name was?" Becky asked.

"David Herold. Why?"

"That name sounds so familiar, that's all."

Just then Mr. Purvis re-entered the room. He informed them that one of his colleagues was going to testify since he was introduced to Joe right before the riots and could attest to Joe's lack of involvement in any abolitionist activities. Joe thanked him for his help and for being so kind to his fiancé and sister. The guard came in and said Joe had to go for his midday meal. They departed, and Mr. Purvis returned the girls to the hotel, saying he would see them the next day. Becky again thanked him for his assistance, and they said goodbye.

That afternoon at tea, Becky relayed the status of Joe's case to Mrs. Fairchild.

"My dear, this must be so distressing for you. For both of you really. Dear Kimberly, you lost your parents, and now this," Mrs. Fairchild said.

"Yes, Mrs. Fairchild, it has been difficult, but Kimberly and I are keeping a stiff upper lip," Becky said.

"Thank you, Mrs. Fairchild, for your kind words," Kimberly added.

"What can I do?" Mrs. Fairchild asked.

"I'm not certain there is anything you can do. Today when we met with Mr. Fitzgerald, he said the lawyer was asking several people for an affidavit attesting to when we arrived in town. With so few correspondence here, it is a short list," Becky said.

"Well, I can certainly provide such an affidavit as I met you nearly on your date of arrival, at this very establishment!"

"That is very kind of you, Mrs. Fairchild. I would not want to burden you or create any problem for you by offering your support to us, however," Becky added.

"Nonsense. The authorities do not have a right to just arrest whomever they wish. I ask, was this not what this country was founded on? Who should I contact regarding this?"

"Well, I am not acquainted with Mr. Fitzgerald's attorney, ma'am, but Mr. Robert Purvis has been providing us much support and aid, and the lawyer's name is Mr. Cartwright," Becky replied.

"I will send Mr. Purvis a note expressing my intent to provide aid and request that he get this attorney to me with this affidavit this very afternoon. To think that one of our newest citizens of Philadelphia is being so abused. I just will not have it. I will be speaking to Mr. Fairchild as well to see what aid he can provide."

"I simply do not know how to thank you, Mrs. Fairchild. You are truly the most gracious of women, and we are so blessed to have found you. Our moving here could not have been anything but fate to come into contact with you," Becky said.

"You are such a dear, Miss Simmons. I have decided at this moment, I am completely taking you under my wing, it is decided, and you too, Kimberly. We should review your education plan as soon as this dreaded trial is completed next week."

"Thank you, Mrs. Fairchild," Kim added.

While the girls were having tea with Mrs. Fairchild, and plotting the future of Kimberly and the marriage of Joe and Becky, Joe was returned to his cell for midday meals. He sat with David and ate the cold fare while they talked more. David was currently trying to convince Joe on the merits of slavery and the predestined nature of the white race. Unfortunately, for each argument David made, Joe had a counterargument that seemed to impact David much more than the arguments for it were impacting Joe. At each counterargument, David would say that he hadn't thought the point through as far as Joe had or at least that Joe had made a good point. Joe found the discussion lively and challenging as he couldn't possibly bring up anything about the civil war, Lincoln, or anything that came after the war as those events had not taken place yet. He missed Becky and Kim, and he was secretly very worried about the situation he found himself in. The talks with David just temporarily took his mind off it. At night, when everything was quiet in the jail, Joe worried that he would never get home, and what would become of Becky and Kim if he didn't get out of this mess. He wanted to talk to Ken, for Ken would surely know what to do. If only.

The next day, when Mr. Purvis came to escort Becky and Kim to the jail, he reported that he had a meeting that morning with Mr. and Mrs. Fairchild, and a second attorney was going to be working on Joe's case. He also mentioned that Mr. Fairchild was going to testify to his intent to hire Joe for his bank, and Mrs. Fairchild had already reviewed her affidavit and would be signing it later that day. The girls were pleased with these advancements and the way Mrs. Fairchild was quickly becoming their champion. They relayed all this information to Joe, who was a little less worried while they were all together and with the good news that they brought.

9

THE REST OF THE week was marked by visits to the jail, luncheons with Mrs. Fairchild, and several more trips to homes for the Ladies in Support of the Railroad. Mr. Purvis came on Monday morning to escort the girls to the courthouse for the beginning of the trial. There they found Mr. and Mrs. Fairchild. Mrs. Fairchild insisted on the girls sitting with her and told Mr. Purvis she and her husband would escort the girls for the remainder of the trial.

The first day of the trial there was a litany of people who testified that Joe was directly involved with the group that wanted to break Mr. Burns out of jail. There were guards from the military and people that neither Kim nor Becky had ever seen that testified that they knew Joe was involved and had helped plan it. One person, in particular, that Becky whispered to Kim she had seen in the tavern that first day when Joe was meeting Henry, she remembered and wondered about.

It was a long day, and when the judge announced they would be in recess until tomorrow, the lawyer for the state said that he had many more witnesses to get through. Kim groaned as she worried that tomorrow was day eight of their trip and one more day closer to the point where they would be missed back in their present. At supper that night with Mr. and Mrs. Fairchild, Becky asked if there was nothing that could be done to prevent the parade of witnesses that were clearly lying from taking the stand. Mr. Fairchild wondered if an argument could be made against this, and he left in the middle of the meal to go and confer with the attorneys. He returned an hour later and was scolded by Mrs. Fairchild, "Dear, where have you been? The girls are ready to expire here from waiting for you. Poor little Miss Fitzgerald is ready to drop right into her dessert, she is so taxed from the day we have all had."

"My apologies, ladies, I just wanted to be sure that the attorneys prepared a motion for tomorrow to stop the parade, as Miss Simmons so eloquently put it, and move this trial along."

"Thank you, Mr. Fairchild. We do not want to seem ungrateful for all you have done for us," Becky said, trying not to seem argumentative to Mrs. Fairchild.

"No, Mrs. Fairchild is correct. I have kept you all waiting far too long. Let us get you ladies back to your lodging for the night."

They all proceeded to the carriage, and the Fairchilds left the girls at the hotel entrance. The next day, the lawyer Mr. Fairchild brought in for the case did make a motion to stop the parade of witnesses, and the judge agreed with his argument. This made the other side rather upset, and they asked for a continuance to plan their strategy. The judge, thankfully, said no, that if the state had no more witnesses, then it was time for the defense to start their arguments. Joe's lawyer questioned the shipyard manager, the desk manager at the hotel, and the bank manager. They all reported when they first met Joe and how they were aware they had just come to town. Mr. Fairchild also testified that he heard about Mr. Fitzgerald's arrival to town from his wife and that he intended to hire Mr. Fitzgerald for his bank, and if that wasn't trust in his character, he didn't know what was. The only other witness they had was going to be Mr. Purvis, who was not in the courtroom that day. So, they had to leave the courthouse and wait until the next day to hopefully learn Joe's fate.

That night, while Joe sat awake worrying about tomorrow being the ninth day and how he couldn't possibly get them from the courthouse to the skiff and to the island to get back in the machine with so much notoriety, and how they would get away without him if he was convicted. Kim and Becky were awake a few blocks away, worrying too. He wondered if maybe he should send Becky and Kim back in the machine to get Ken. He wondered if anything could save him from jail, and he wished he hadn't agreed to this trip. The girls paced and talked until well into the night about how they were going to get out of town and back to the machine if Joe was freed, and if not, what they were going to do. As usual, after many hours of back and forth, Kim, the insightful one of the group, said, "I don't know why we are pacing and worrying and carrying on. It's going to be what it's going to be. We can't leave without Joe, so we have to just stay here and hope we can come up with a way to lessen the impact back home."

"You're right. We can worry all night, but it isn't going to change the decision. We have to stay here for Joe—no matter how long that is. Let's try to get some sleep."

When the girls were assisted up into the carriage, Mrs. Fairchild exclaimed, "My goodness, did neither of you sleep a wink last night? You poor dear girls. You have no need to worry. No matter what happens today, Mr. Fairchild and I will watch over you and protect you."

"Mrs. Fairchild, you are the kindest woman I know," Kim said.

"Thank you, dear, but I mean it. You have nothing to worry about. Besides, Mr. Fairchild told me just this morning that he has a business acquaintance that knows the President. If this judge does not rule in Mr. Fitzgerald's favor today, we are going to go straight to the President of the United States to repair this injustice!"

"Where is Mr. Fairchild this morning?" Becky asked.

"He went on ahead to the courthouse to confer with the attorneys."

Mr. Purvis testified to his introduction with Joe via another business associate and how Joe had asked him about Mr. Burns' case because he knew nothing of it and was concerned for his sister and fiancé's safety. Mr. Purvis also stated that all the witnesses for the state were known slave owners and those that were in business to track down fugitive slaves, and he had some documentation to prove that. He said this was a purposeful effort to make an example of Mr. Fitzgerald to punish Philadelphia for its Quaker heritage and abolition background.

Once the day had concluded with closing statements and arguments, the judge announced he would render his verdict soon and dismissed the courtroom. As Kim and Becky left the courthouse, escorted by Mr. and Mrs. Fairchild, Kim asked, "How long will the judge take?"

"They can take as much time as they want. I am afraid all we can do now is await his return," Mr. Fairchild replied.

"I concur. Unfortunately, all we can do now is wait," Mrs. Fairchild added.

The Fairchilds tried to get Kim and Becky to join them for supper, but the girls said they were exhausted from the trial. They agreed to meet them the next day for dinner at the City Tavern.

Kim and Becky went directly to their room. Becky was beside herself. This was the end of day nine of their trip, and any more delay would mean they would likely get back to Choate after Tuesday. They wouldn't be in class, and they wouldn't be in the dorm. She explained this when Kim asked her what she was pacing about.

"I don't know what we can do. Are Joe's notes about the time-lapse calculations here?" Kim asked.

"I think they're in his room."

"You could ask the desk manager to let you in there. I'm sure he would if you asked, and then maybe you can look at those papers and see if there is anything that can be done."

"That's a good idea actually. I never really looked at the calculations, so maybe there is something we can do."

"If not, then what?"

"Well, we can't leave, so I guess that's all we can do."

Kim said she was going to wait in their room, and Becky went downstairs. The desk manager did let her into Joe's room, and she found the papers in the desk. She took them to the girls' room and asked the desk manager to send up a supper tray. The girls stayed in that night, and Becky worked on the calculations as Kim read.

The next morning, at breakfast, Kim asked, "So, did you figure something out with the calculations?"

"I think we can fudge the time a little bit, but I have to have Joe check this. It's frustrating because I feel so helpless."

"Yeah, I know. I wish we hadn't done this trip. I'm thinking it might have been a mistake."

"No, Kim, you shouldn't be doubting what we've done. Think about it. We accomplished what you wanted, right?"

"We have brought all the supplies and notes and money to the different houses. I just wish I could do more, and I really wish Joe hadn't been arrested."

"On that, we can agree."

As they finished breakfast and headed back upstairs, Mr. Purvis entered the hotel.

"Oh, good, you are both right here. Good morning, Miss Simmons and Miss Fitzgerald," he said.

"Good morning, Mr. Purvis. Do you have news about Joseph?" Becky asked.

"No, I am sorry to say. I stopped off at Mr. Cartwright's office, and he has not heard from the judge yet this morning. Actually, I am here to see if the two of you might be able to assist me today."

"We will try, Mr. Purvis. What can we do for you?"

"Perhaps we can go out to the courtyard and discuss it?"

"Certainly."

The three of them went out to the courtyard. They sat at a wrought iron table and chairs in the sunny part of the courtyard. Kim wondered what they could possibly do for this man that had given them so much help. She was actually excited.

"Ladies, I am in need of your special escort for a few travelers. I know this is much to ask of you while you await Mr. Fitzgerald's fate, but I have no one else available today."

"Mr. Purvis, are these railroad travelers?" Kim asked.

"Yes, they are," he replied.

"Where and when? I believe we would both enjoy the distraction today," Becky said.

"I have an address here, where the travelers will be awaiting your arrival. You will receive their destination when you pick them up."

Becky took the piece of paper from Mr. Purvis and put it in her lap. Then she asked, "Is this address far from here?"

"An hour or so out of town by carriage. Also, you will need a covered carriage for this trip, I think. The sun will be out in force today, and you would not want to keep young Miss Fitzgerald out in that all afternoon."

"We have rented livery from the stable down the street. Do you know if they have covered carriages there?" Becky asked.

"I believe they do," he replied.

"We will have to send a note to Mrs. Fairchild, Rebecca, as we likely will not be back from this trip in time to meet them for dinner," Kim mentioned.

"Oh, if you have plans, perhaps I can find someone else," Mr. Purvis said, holding his hand up.

"It is no problem, Mr. Purvis. The Fairchilds have become quite fond of Kimberly and feel a bit paternal towards us both. They were only trying to waylay our fears. We can certainly meet them for supper tomorrow," Becky said.

"Then it is settled. I so appreciate your assistance, Miss Simmons and Miss Fitzgerald," Mr. Purvis said as he rose from his chair.

The girls stood up as well, and Kim added, "Thank you, Mr. Purvis, for this chance to be helpful to the railroad."

They left Mr. Purvis in the lobby to go to their room. There, Becky drafted a note to the Fairchilds, and they returned to the lobby.

"Mr. Wilson, could you please deliver this note to Mr. and Mrs. Fairchild on 7th Street?"

"Certainly, Miss Simmons, I will have it sent over directly," Mr. Wilson, the desk manager replied.

"Also, Miss Fitzgerald and I require a carriage for the remainder of the day, but an enclosed carriage please as we are going out of town a bit to visit a new acquaintance. Can you please send someone down to the livery and arrange that for us?"

"I would be happy to do that. I believe the livery requires a payment of three dollars for the day for an enclosed carriage."

Becky put three banknotes on the counter for Mr. Wilson as she said, "Here you are. Miss Fitzgerald and I will be waiting here in the lobby."

"Very good. I will send someone down there immediately."

"Thank you, Mr. Wilson."

Mr. Wilson came up to the girls a short time later and informed them the carriage had arrived. He assisted them into the carriage and then asked Becky where they wanted to go.

"I have an address here," she said as she handed Mr. Wilson the paper Mr. Purvis had given her earlier. Mr. Wilson handed the paper to the driver and asked if he knew the way. He did, and they left on their journey.

The day was getting rather warm, and the girls were wondering how much longer it would be when the driver turned onto a road leading up to a farm. The driver helped the girls down and waited as they went up to the door.

"Good afternoon. My name is Miss Rebecca Simmons. This is my fiancé's sister, Miss Kimberly Fitzgerald. We were sent by Mr. Purvis," Becky said to the woman that opened the door.

"Oh, do come in. I apologize, but those of us at the railroad stops are very careful about new people. My name is Anna Jorgens," she said as she led them into a sitting room.

"It's a pleasure to meet you, Mrs. Jorgens," Kim said.

"Would you like some lemonade?" Mrs. Jorgens asked the girls.

"That would be lovely, thank you," Becky said.

Mrs. Jorgens went to get the lemonade as the girls sat in the cooler sitting room.

"Whew, it's hot out. It has been fun to dress this way, but not today," Kim whispered to Becky. Becky laughed a little and nodded in agreement. Mrs. Jorgens came back with the glasses and handed one to each of the girls. Just then three young children came into the sitting room.

"Children, are you done with your letters?" Mrs. Jorgens asked them.

"We are, Mother," the oldest replied.

"Then out with you. Go do your chores," their mother said. The children left, and Becky asked, "Where are our travelers?"

"They are in the barn. When you have finished your drinks, I will go and get them. Best be on your way right away though so you can get back to town before nightfall," Mrs. Jorgens replied.

When the girls were finished, Mrs. Jorgens took the glasses and motioned for the girls to follow her. They went out into the yard and waited as she left to get the travelers. Out of the barn came a young lady, holding a bundle that appeared to be a baby and carrying a bundled-up pack on her back. Behind her was a young boy, no more than three or four years old. They walked up to the girls, and Mrs. Jorgens introduced the young lady to Kim and Becky, "This is Ruby and her boy, Jerimiah."

Becky held out her hand, and the young lady tentatively grasped it. Becky said, "It is a pleasure to meet you, Ruby. My name is Miss Simmons, and this is Miss Fitzgerald."

She smiled but kept looking around the yard.

"We best be off," Becky said, "Do you have the address for the next station we are headed to?"

Mrs. Jorgens handed Becky a small slip of paper with some information on it. They turned and went to the carriage. Becky handed the note to the driver, and they left.

"What is your baby's name, Ruby?" Kim asked.

"Her name is Evangeline."

"That's a lovely name."

"Thank you, Miss."

"Call me Kimberly, please."

"Oh, no, Miss, I must'n do that."

"You most certainly can. We are going to be friends, are we not? If I am to call you Ruby, I insist you call me Kimberly."

She smiled at Kim but didn't say anything, so Kim added, "Have you or Jerimiah eaten today?"

"No, Miss, I mean, Kimberly. We been traveling most of the night."

"Well, all we have is some bread and cheese and this canteen of water, but you and Jerimiah are welcome to it."

Kim handed Ruby the basket and the canteen and sat back while Ruby and her boy ate like they hadn't eaten in weeks. As they finished, Becky said, "Oh, I almost forgot. Mrs. Jorgens gave me this small bottle of milk from her cow. She said it was for your baby."

Becky handed Ruby the small bottle that had a rubber-like end on it. Ruby smiled and put the bottle to the baby's mouth. She slurped it loudly, and Kim laughed, saying, "Looks like Evangeline was hungry too."

They traveled north for over an hour. Most of the time, Ruby and her children rested. At some point, she opened her eyes and looked at Becky as she asked, "Why are you doing this? Helping me?"

"Well, Ruby, we do not abide slavery. We think it is wrong and against the Lord's will. We are just two young ladies ourselves, so this is all we can do to help correct that wrong."

"You take much risk. You could get caught, then something bad could happen to you too."

"Perhaps, but we feel it is worth the risk."

"What do you get out of it?"

"Whatever do you mean?"

"Do you get money or something?" Then she looked around suspiciously like she expected to be pounced on at any moment.

Becky reached out and put her hand on Ruby's as she said, "You do not have to worry. We have no plans to take you back to wherever it is you came from. We are taking you north. You have to go farther north so the fugitive catchers will not find you. The place we are taking you to will let you rest for a day or two, and then they will help you get farther north. And as far as why we do it? That's simple. We want Jerimiah and Evangeline to grow up free and safe. That is all."

"Bless you, Miss."

Kim smiled as she listened to what Becky said. She wanted to ask Ruby all kinds of questions, but she figured that one, that wasn't allowed on the railroad, and two, she doubted Ruby would even know where she came from.

After about another hour, they arrived at their destination. They all disembarked from the carriage, and the owner of the farm said they would be in the house in a special room at the back. Ruby turned to the girls and thanked them. They were walking away when little Jerimiah ran back and reached out to Kim. She bent down and wrapped her arms around him as he hugged her and said, "I know you're an angel, and you saved us. Thank you." Then he hugged Becky and ran back to his mother. The girls returned to the carriage and told the driver to take them back to the hotel. It was nearly two in the afternoon when they started their journey back to town. Kim asked how long it would take, and the driver said they should be back at the hotel by supper.

Kim and Becky were very tired when they arrived at the hotel just after six that night. Mr. Wilson greeted them and offered a supper tray, which they accepted. They ate and prepared for bed.

"That was interesting, wasn't it?" Becky asked.

"Yes, Ruby was so worried that we were going to take her back or turn her in or something. I felt so bad for her. I hope they make it somewhere safe."

"Me too. You know what else? This has totally distracted us from worrying about Joe!"

"I hope he isn't worried that we didn't visit him today."

"Gosh, I didn't even think of that. We're going to have to go over there first thing tomorrow."

"Will they just let us in?"

"I think so, now. I mean, I am his fiancé."

"That's so funny. When we first got here, every time someone said that I almost laughed."

"Yeah, just barely sixteen years old and engaged. My grandmother would be so proud!"

They laughed. Then Kim asked what Mrs. Fairchild had to say in her note.

"That she was glad we had a distraction today, and they would see us promptly tomorrow for dinner unless the judge came back with a notification."

"What did you tell her?"

"I told her we were invited for a visit with some new friends, we would have to respectfully reschedule our dinner, and that we hoped they didn't mind the change too much. I said that we needed an all-day distraction."

"Good idea. I don't know if the Fairchilds are involved with the railroad."

They blew out the candles at that point and slept a tired, deep sleep.

10

THE NEXT MORNING, BOTH Kim and Becky felt better, but they were getting very worried. They had breakfast, and while they ate, they requested a carriage to take them to the courthouse. When they arrived, the desk clerk did not want to allow them to visit Joe. Fortunately, Mr. Cartwright arrived to check on Joe's status, and he cleared the way for them to visit.

"Where were you yesterday? I was expecting a visit and didn't see you," Joe asked as he hugged first Becky and then Kim.

"We were asked to do a favor for Mr. Purvis and didn't have time to get word to you," Becky replied as they all sat down.

"I am going over to the courthouse to see if the judge is ready to rule or if he will be at some point today. I must say that I am very concerned about how long this is taking," Mr. Cartwright said. "I will be back over as soon as I have made some determination on the judge's temperament."

They said their goodbyes to Mr. Cartwright and then Joe leaned across the table and asked, "So, what were you doing for Mr. Purvis?"

"We were assisting with the railroad," Kim said proudly.

"What does that mean?" Joe asked.

"Perhaps we should discuss that later," Becky replied before she added, "should we be worried about the judge taking so long?"

"I don't know. Cartwright is worried because he thinks this means the judge is going to rule for the state. Mr. Purvis thinks it means he's trying to formulate his statement so it doesn't incite more trouble."

"Well, I like Mr. Purvis's answer better than Mr. Cartwright's," Kim said.

"Me too," Joe added.

"Hey, tell Joe about your calculation thing, Becky," Kim said.

"What is she talking about?" Joe asked, looking at Becky.

"First, Kim, remember, language is more formal here. Second, I was looking over the time-lapse calculation, and I think there might be a way to fudge the return calculations to buy us some more time on the trip home," Becky said, excitedly.

"Really, how?" Joe asked.

Becky explained the variable that if shifted and programmed a bit differently might restore at least some of their time on the return trip in the machine.

"That's good news since we're at day eleven or twelve, right?" Joe asked.

"Yeah," Kim said.

"Listen, if this doesn't go well, I think you should go back in the machine—maybe get Ken or Mr. Brewster and come back here. I think you'd be ok to come back as long as you programmed the return here to be just after you left," Joe said, looking seriously at Becky.

"No. We're not leaving here without you. I just have a bad feeling about doing that, Joe, and we can't just leave you here," Becky said adamantly.

Just then Mr. Cartwright returned. He said he had seen the judge and asked him about his progress. The judge had indicated that he had been unable to spend good time on the review of the testimony, but he was locking himself in his office that afternoon. He would have a ruling by tomorrow.

"He said he hated you sitting here waiting, and he was not going to make you wait any longer," Mr. Cartwright said with a smile on his face.

"That certainly is good news!" Becky said. "Do you think, Mr. Cartwright, this means he might be leaning toward my brother's side?"

"I hope so," Mr. Cartwright answered.

"What should we do to prepare?" Becky asked.

"Well, we will need to pay the fines, as I expect that will be in the ruling."

"And what do you we owe you for your services?" Joe asked.

"Well, I don't usually ask for money from my clients unless I win."

"If you win, what will we owe you?" Becky asked.

"I think twenty-five dollars ought to be sufficient."

"I will endeavor to have that with us tomorrow in the hopes that this will be over then!" Becky proclaimed.

The guard came at that moment to return Joe to his cell. They asked if he needed anything, and he asked for a change of clothing. Becky said she would get it over to him that afternoon. They all left after the guard took Joe away.

"Thank you, Mr. Cartwright, for assisting us in this visit. I appreciate it," Becky said.

"You are very welcome. If you like, I can escort you to the hotel and wait while you gather what Mr. Fitzgerald has requested, and I can bring it back over here for you."

"That would be wonderful, thank you."

They left and went back to the hotel. Mr. Cartwright waited while Becky and Kim gathered items for Joe, and then he left to return to the jail. The girls went to the courtyard and requested tea.

A short time later, the girls walked down to the City Tavern and went upstairs to the dining room and located Mr. and Mrs. Fairchild. Mr. Fairchild rose from his chair and seated the girls before he sat back down.

"How was your visit yesterday?" Mrs. Fairchild asked.

"It was lovely, Mrs. Fairchild, thank you for asking," Becky replied.

"We had a lovely visit with a lady and her children that Mr. Purvis introduced us to," Kim added.

"That is just lovely. It is nice that you are meeting people here, but be sure they are the right people. You do not want to get labeled incorrectly, you know," Mr. Fairchild said.

Dinner was served, and they all ate. During dinner, Mr. Fairchild asked if they heard any news about Joe, and Becky replied they had been to the jail that morning, and she went on to describe what Mr. Cartwright had told them from the judge.

"That is very good news that the judge believes he will have his ruling tomorrow. I know you have been on pins and needles waiting to find out your fate," Mr. Fairchild said.

"Well, ladies, now that we are just about finished with our meal, I must confess that Mr. Fairchild and I have a greater purpose behind inviting you to this meal. We want you to consider gathering your things from the hotel and coming to stay with us," Mrs. Fairchild said, looking directly at Becky.

"Why, Mrs. Fairchild, that is so kind of you to offer. I do not know what to say," Becky replied.

"Then you must agree. I see no reason for you to while away the hours in that hotel, and dear, I know we do not speak of such things, but at some point, the money might run out, and where will you and Mr. Fitzgerald's dear sister be?"

"Well, Mrs. Fairchild, we are doing quite well in terms of our finances. As you know, Joseph did receive an inheritance when his parents passed away. Kimberly and I are living a quiet life in the hotel, and our expenses are minimal," Becky replied.

"That is all well and good, but living in a hotel cannot be the life you imagined—and certainly not the life that Mr. Fitzgerald or even his parents planned for dear Miss Fitzgerald."

"Perhaps, but I would prefer to make this decision after I have spoken to Mr. Fitzgerald, and it appears we will at least know the ruling tomorrow, so it might not even be necessary," Becky answered.

"That is sound reasoning, Mrs. Fairchild," Mr. Fairchild said to his wife.

"I will relent to your wisdom, Mr. Fairchild, but, Miss Simmons, if the ruling does not go in Mr. Fitzgerald's favor, we will need to sit down tomorrow and plan. You do see the need for that, do you not?"

"Yes, Mrs. Fairchild, that is so wise of you to be thinking ahead, and so kind and thoughtful and generous of you to consider taking us in like this," Becky said.

"Then we will dine here again tomorrow to finalize plans."

"Mr. Fairchild, I wonder if I could prey upon your generous nature and request that you accompany me to the bank next door. Mr. Cartwright suggested I be prepared tomorrow to pay fines and his fees so that if the judge does rule in our favor, Joseph could be released," Becky asked.

"Of course, my dear. If we are done here, I can escort you there right now," Mr. Fairchild replied as he rose from his seat.

They walked to the bank for Becky to again retrieve a gold bar and exchange it for banknotes. Then Mr. Fairchild returned Becky to the City Tavern where they retrieved Kim and Mrs. Fairchild for the carriage ride back to the hotel.

When they were in their room, Kim asked, "Why were you so against going to the Fairchilds'?"

"Because there we can no more get to the machine, nor help with the railroad, and I didn't want to make it harder for us than it already is."

"You're right. But will we have money if Joe ends up in jail longer than tomorrow?"

"I think we'd be ok for a little while, but I'm really hoping he's released tomorrow."

"I can't spend this whole afternoon cooped up in this room. Can we go for a walk or something?"

"Yes, let's go for a stroll."

They walked for a bit, then returned to the hotel. They had supper, and then the next day, just as they were finishing breakfast, Mr. Purvis came into the hotel and said he had heard from Mr. Cartwright, and he was there to escort them to the courthouse. They waited in the courthouse for nearly an hour, but finally, a clerk alerted Mr. Cartwright that the judge was ready to rule. They all filed into the courtroom and waited.

Thankfully, the judge ruled in Joe's favor. The judge dropped the charges of aiding a fugitive slave, and he was only bound to pay the fines on the disorderly conduct. Becky and Kim wanted to dance and yell, but they controlled their emotions. Becky went with Mr. Cartwright and paid the fines and then gave the money to Mr. Cartwright that they owed him. They waited about thirty minutes more, and Joe was released. Mrs. Fairchild insisted that they all gather for dinner, and there was nothing Becky could say to convince her they couldn't. When the fine was paid, and Joe was released, they all rode back to the hotel in the Fairchild carriage.

Joe was still reeling from being in jail and his subsequent release, but he recognized that he needed to appease Mr. and Mrs. Fairchild, so he agreed to the meal after he had a chance to bathe and clean himself up. They all met at the City Tavern and had what Joe said was his first warm meal in a week. When the dessert was served, Joe and Mr. Fairchild went down to the bar where Mr. Fairchild regaled the guests with the tale of Mr. Fitzgerald's daring and his battle with the slave-owning monsters. Joe still wasn't very comfortable with the spotlight, but he suffered through this celebration until finally saying that he wanted to spend time with his sister and his fiancé to reassure them both.

Safely back at the hotel, Joe first thanked the hotel manager for his testimony. He settled the bill and went upstairs with the girls. As soon as they were behind closed doors, Kim ran to Joe and hugged him, "Joe,

I'm so sorry. I'm sorry I made us go on this trip, and I'm sorry you had to go through this, and I promise I will do anything to make it up to you."

"It's ok, Kim. I'm ok."

"Yes, but I had no idea you didn't even have hot food. I can't believe for the past week I didn't even ask what was happening in that jail. I feel terrible. And now we're here days longer than we were supposed to be, and who knows what's happening back at Choate right now. It's all my fault."

"Kim, you had no way of knowing, and we had no way to plan for what happened here. That's the biggest problem with traveling through time. We can't plan. Remember in Dallas how we changed our minds several times on how to get the notice out about Lee Harvey Oswald? We just don't know," Joe said, trying to reassure Kim.

"Joe's right. Kim, we can plan all we want, but when we go to some other time, we just don't know what's going to happen."

"I know, but I'm sorry anyway."

"Well, let's hold that for the time being and figure out how we're going to be able to get out of here," Becky suggested.

"Can't we just go, right now?" Kim asked.

"No. I agreed to meet with Mr. Fairchild in the morning about a job. I think it would be best to do that. And then to calm things down, I will tell him I wanted to spend the rest of the week taking care of the two of you, starting with a picnic. After the meeting, I can go to the bank and retrieve what's left of the bag of gold, and then I will come here and collect you two. We need to somehow avoid suspicion and get the clothing out of here and maybe ask the manager to prepare a picnic basket and then go to the shipyard and get the skiff. Then we can get to the machine and get out of here tomorrow," Joe explained.

"That sounds like a good plan. I wonder what they will all think when we are suddenly gone?" Becky asked.

"Maybe you should write some notes to Mrs. And Mr. Fairchild? Maybe tell them something like we decided to not settle here because of what happened, and we left to find a new place," Kim said hopefully.

"That's a great idea. Let's write the notes right now, and we can ask the bank manager to deliver them," Becky said.

"Will he do that?" Kim asked.

"I saw him the other day tell someone that he could deliver something for them. I'm pretty sure the person was a bank customer, so I think so."

"While you're writing the notes, I will look over the calculation changes you suggested, Becky, and see how much I can fudge the time for our return to get us back with the least amount of fuss," Joe added.

Notes written, calculations made, they went to supper in the hotel and retired early. The next day, Joe went to his meeting with Mr. Fairchild, and the girls requested the picnic basket from the desk manager. They also asked for a trunk to be procured for their belongings as they were looking for more permanent housing now. The desk manager did as they asked, and the girls had their things packed in no time. They asked the desk manager to deliver the trunk to the shipyard that afternoon. Then they all left the hotel, and Joe stopped at the bank to retrieve their gold.

They paid the shipyard manager for holding the skiff longer and loaded the picnic basket and the trunk onto it. Luckily, the shipyard manager was not around when they loaded up the trunk. He was asked to hold it there for them, again, using the permanent housing story. He might wonder what happened to that trunk, but Kim wasn't worried. Joe rowed the skiff to the island, and they took their trunk to the machine. Becky and Kim pulled all the clothing out of the trunk and loaded it into the machine, while Joe transferred the calculations to the machine.

"Whew, I'm glad to be back into my own clothes!" Becky said once she had changed.

"I don't know. I was kind of liking the dressing-up part of this trip," Kim said.

"Yeah, but in my own clothes, I don't feel so restricted. I just felt like girls couldn't do anything for themselves here. I'll be glad to get back to the time we belong in."

"Kim, are you disappointed about not being able to help the fugitives?" Joe asked.

"Well, we did make a bunch of trips for the ladies' group, and on one of them, we actually gave one of the railroad travelers a ride in our carriage. It was a young mother and her two children. So, we did help—a lot I think," Kim pondered.

"What happened to your cellmate? I forgot to ask you," Becky asked.

"Oh, he was released the second day of my trial. He had some family member that arrived from Virginia or somewhere that paid his fine."

"What was his name again?"

"David Herold. You're usually way better with names, Becky."

"Yeah, well this was kind of a hectic week for me. My boyfriend, or fiancé or whatever, was in jail, and we could barely take care of ourselves."

"True."

Just as the machine fired up, Becky exclaimed, "I know who he is. Joe, you spent the week in jail with one of the people in on the plot to assassinate Lincoln and the others!"

11

THE MORNING AFTER JOE, Becky, and Kim arrived in Philadelphia, 1853, Ken rose from a fitful sleep and headed off to class. He was wrestling with the reaction he had been getting from Mary lately. She didn't seem to be moving in the direction he wanted—which was to admit that her break-up plan to save him from some terrible fate was a bad idea. No matter what he did to comfort her, or help support her or bring her more information to learn that she was not in the kind of danger she thought, it didn't seem to change her mind one bit.

As classes ended for the day, he made a decision. He was going to Wellesley that afternoon to confront Mary about his disappointment and either get her to change her mind or end things. As he drove to Wellesley from Cambridge, he planned what he was going to say. He pondered what Mary's reaction would be, and he went back and forth on whether he was going to be strong enough to hold his ground. Needless to say, he was troubled when he arrived in front of Mary's dorm.

He went up the stairs and asked at the desk for Mary to be called. When no one answered the phone in her dorm room, he turned away from the desk and nearly bumped into Mary's roommate, Ashley.

"I'm so sorry, Ashley. I wasn't paying any attention. Are you ok?" Ken said to her, and he reached out to keep her from falling down.

"Yeah, I'm ok. I guess I wasn't really paying much attention either." She laughed.

"Do you happen to know where I might be able to find Mary?"

"You mean you didn't come all this way to bump into me?"

"Not really," he said and laughed.

"She's in class for another twenty or thirty minutes. Want to wait over here in the lobby? I can bring down some soda and snacks and wait with you if you want?"

"If you're not busy, that'd be great."

She left but returned in about ten minutes carrying two cans of soda and a bag of chips. They sat down in the lobby area on some couches, and she handed him a can and the bag.

"Hope this will do. It's all I have upstairs right now."

"This is great. I haven't eaten all day. Left as soon as my classes were over."

"Did Mary know you were coming? She was talking about doing a museum walk tomorrow and getting together with some friends here tonight."

"No, she didn't know I was coming. I just felt like I needed to clear the air a bit with her, so I just got in the car and drove over here."

"I see."

"What is it? You seem like there's something you want to say."

"Well, I mean, I know I don't know you very well, except for these visits you make over here lately, but I do think I know Mary pretty well now. And it's just, well, I don't understand why you keep hanging on like this."

"What do you mean?"

"She's pretty determined. I mean, once she's decided something, it seems like her mind is made up."

"Yeah"—he kind of laughed, "that's Mary."

"I don't mean it in a bad way or anything. But she's told me she's made up her mind, that you and she can't be together."

"She's said that, has she?"

"I mean, it's been a while since we talked about it, so I guess it's possible she's changed her mind, but if not, why are you wasting your time? I like her, and we get along great, but I feel like she's just stringing you along to be able to say she has someone and that's not really fair to you."

"That's not the Mary I know. I mean I doubt she would string anyone along. It's just that she's worried that what happened to her grandmother is going to happen to her someday, and she thinks holding me at arm's length is going to keep me safe somehow."

"Yeah, she's said that. But I've also seen her tell other guys that try to ask her out that she sort of has someone at another school, and sometimes she talks to the girls from the dorm here about you in a kind of possessive way. But then she won't just agree to take you back, right?"

"Maybe."

"I'm not trying to rain on your parade or anything. You just seem like a really nice guy, and maybe you can do better. You probably deserve better anyway."

Just then Mary walked into the dorm with several other girls. She didn't notice Ashley and Ken sitting in the lobby, so Ashley called out to her. She walked over to where they were sitting and sat down next to Ashley.

"What are you doing here, Ken?"

"Well, I wanted to surprise you, but maybe I'm the one surprised, huh? Don't you want to see me?"

"It's not that, it's just I wasn't expecting to see you. You said you would call Saturday morning, is all."

"Maybe I came to see Ashley?"

Ashley laughed but stood up as she said, "No, no way you are putting me in the middle of this. Keep the bag of chips if you want, Ken. I'm getting out of here though. You two figure this out."

With that, Ashley walked over to the stairs to go up to the room, leaving Mary and Ken sitting on opposite couches in the lobby. After a few minutes of silence between them, while Ken finished his soda, he looked at Mary and said, "Maybe we should go somewhere and talk."

"Ok," Mary said a bit hesitantly, "do you want to drive somewhere or walk and talk?"

"Walk and talk is fine."

They left the dorm and walked toward town. Ken asked her how her week had been and how much homework she had this weekend. She answered that classes were good, and she had a paper to write. She asked about his week, and he replied that he had a project to finish up. After a few more minutes, Ken said, "I didn't come here to ask about your week. And apparently, you have some plans tonight and tomorrow, so maybe I'll just get to the point."

"I don't have plans."

"That's not what Ashley thinks."

"Well, maybe she doesn't know everything."

"Mary, there's no need to get angry at Ashley. She just mentioned that she thought you had plans when I bumped into her in the lobby of your dorm. She said a lot of things actually."

"Like what?"

"Listen, I came here today because I've really been struggling lately. I do whatever you ask, I'm considerate of your time, I call, I send you notes and flowers, I spend time with you, and all the time you put me off with the maybe a little more time excuse. I guess I came here today to ask you if it's ever going to change."

"Ken, I'm not sure what you mean. I mean, you said you'd give me time. That was all I was asking for. I don't understand why now it's some sort of problem."

"The thing is, Mary, I don't think it's going to matter how much time I give you or what I do to convince you. You aren't going to ever come to me and say, 'Hey, Ken, I'm ready, let's be boyfriend and girlfriend again' are you?"

"I don't know."

"Is there something I'm not doing that you need or something I'm doing that you don't like?"

"No, it's none of that. You've been very understanding and helpful and supportive. All things I need from a friend. I'm just still dealing with this. I don't understand why you can't give me the time?"

"Here's the thing, though, Mary, nothing is changing. We are stuck here where you get a great friend, and I work my butt off trying to convince you it's going to be ok, and I get nothing."

"What do you mean you get nothing?"

"I mean, what I have wanted, and I think, what I have been very clear about from the first time I came here to talk to you, was that I want us to be together again. I don't think this is as big a deal as you're making it."

"Not a big deal? I might have cancer!"

With that Mary turned and started walking back toward campus. Ken followed and let her walk ahead for a block or two, and then he caught up to her and grabbed her to stop her from crossing a street. He pulled her toward a park bench, and they sat down.

"I know this scares the life out of you. I know your grandmother died a horrible death because the doctors didn't recognize, test, or believe her. I know you don't want that to happen to you. I don't want it to happen to you either. But you know you have the marker. All you need to do is keep on top of the research developments, find a good doctor that will listen to you, and I guarantee, what happened to your grandmother is not going to happen to you. It's that simple, Mary."

"I don't think it's simple at all."

"Well, it is. And furthermore, I think I've had enough of being the friend you get to lean on, while you move through your life in this depression, taking advantage of the fact that I care about you. When two people care about each other, love each other, they try to give to each other. You're not giving anything to this relationship."

Mary started to cry and put her head down. She said tearfully, "What are you saying? You don't want to even be my friend anymore?"

"I do want to be your friend. I want to say to the world that you are the woman I love and spend my life with you. But, Mary, I think I've decided that if you don't feel the same way about me, the way I feel about you, then it's not about what I want anymore. It's about what is good for me."

"And I'm not good for you anymore?"

"Not like this."

"I don't even know what to say," she said with her head down and tears falling into her lap.

"You could say yes. Yes, you are ready to let me fully back into your life and act like you love me again. We will face whatever this cancer thing is going to be together. You could do that."

"So, this is an ultimatum? Say yes or say goodbye?"

"I don't want it to be. But, yes, I guess it is. You can't ask me to continue to be strung along while you drift through your life as a victim to this possible cancer."

"I don't want to lose you again," Mary said, beginning to sob.

"Then don't."

"You're acting like we're talking about where to go for dinner. Isn't this making you even a little upset? You don't care about me at all do you?"

"Of course, I care, Mary. I love you. But love is not a one-way street. And right now, I feel like one of us has to stay calm."

"I can't believe you're doing this to me. You can't make me choose right now, right here in the park, if I'm ready to be your girlfriend or ready to never see you again."

"I could say the same thing to you, Mary. I can't believe you're stringing me along, using me as the sometimes boyfriend, when it's convenient to say you have a boyfriend, never calling me, always waiting for me to call you."

"I'm not doing that!"

"Yes, Mary, you are. Your roommate told me she's seen you do it."

"You believe her over me?"

"What she says makes perfect sense. It's how I feel when I'm with you."

"How can you say that?"

"Because I haven't felt like your boyfriend, really, since before last summer. Make a decision."

"I can't."

"Then I guess you already have."

Ken waited for her to say something else, but she didn't. He handed her a handkerchief he had in his pocket. He waited for a couple more minutes, and then he said, "Do you want me to walk you back to your dorm?"

"No."

"I can't just leave you here."

"You're leaving me, what difference does it make where it is?"

"First, I'm not like that, and you should know that. And second, you left me first remember? That day at Choate when you said we should see other people?" Ken was getting angry now, and he hated the idea that she was going to spend the rest of her life thinking he left her, when this was actually her doing.

"I meant, if we're over, then I'm not your responsibility anymore. You can leave me here. I know the way back to my dorm."

"Fine. If that's the way you want to play this."

"No! This is not how I want to play this!"

"Goodbye, Mary. I wish you all the best. And you should know that I will always love you."

He turned and walked away from her. He couldn't look at her again for fear of changing his mind. He didn't want to do this, but he knew there was no other way. She wasn't ever going to let go of the crazy idea that she was saving him and everyone else by not really living her life. When he got back to his car, he had calmed down some, but he went in and asked for Ashley. She came down the stairs and looked confused when she saw only him.

"Listen. Mary is sitting at that park just this side of town. She didn't want me to walk her back here. You might want to go and get her. I don't want her out there alone. Also, is there a phone I can use here?"

"What happened?"

"Well, I told her I was done being held at arm's length, and she still couldn't do it. She couldn't let go of this crazy notion that her life was basically already over, and she was going to die a slow painful death by cancer. So, we broke up, probably for good."

"But you still want to make sure she's ok and gets home safe? Doesn't sound like your feelings have changed."

"Well, they haven't. I still love her. I just know that I can't keep going like this with me doing all the work and her just sleepwalking through her life."

"Yeah, you're probably right. I'm sorry."

"Thanks. So, is there a phone?"

"Yeah, sure, right over here."

Ashley walked Ken over to the desk and told the person at the desk that he needed to use the phone. He called Deb. He briefly told her what happened and asked if she didn't have plans, could she meet him at the apartment in the city. He was leaving Wellesley. She said she would do it, and then she called Uncle Darrick. He and Aunt Alicia were packing to leave for the week for business and a little pleasure. He said it was fine if they came to the apartment though, and he would let the doorman know and said he'd leave them some money. He asked what the visit was about, and Deb told him. He said he would call later in the weekend to speak to Ken, and they said goodbye.

It took Ken a bit longer to get to the city than he planned. But by the time he got close, there was some end of day and Friday traffic. Luckily, most of the traffic was headed out of town, while he was headed in. When he got to the apartment, he heard Deb talking to Ryan in the kitchen. He went in there and said, "Hey, sorry I'm so late, the traffic picked up."

"We figured that's what kept you. Listen, if you'd rather be here with just Deb, I can head out. I just didn't want her sitting here alone waiting for you," Ryan said as Ken sat down.

"No, stay. You might as well hear this first-hand, and I'd rather have some people around tonight if that's ok?"

"Sure. Did you eat?"

"Not yet, but let's talk for a few, and then we can decide where to go for dinner. I think I'd like to get out of here for a little bit."

"Why don't you start at the beginning then," Deb said.

Ken proceeded to tell them about his frustration over the past couple of weeks and how he had finally decided it was time to confront the situation. He told them how he'd driven to Wellesley, waited for Mary to get done with classes, and then all about their conversation. They listened intently and didn't interrupt while he replayed the whole conversation with Mary, and how she had gotten upset and didn't even want him to walk her back to campus. Then it was quiet for a few minutes.

Deb was first to react. "How do you feel now?"

"I don't know. I little shell shocked but strangely relieved. Does that sound normal?"

"I'd say so," Ryan said. "After all she put you through the last couple of months? I'm sorry I didn't say something sooner, but man, it sure seemed like she was stringing you along."

"That's what her roommate Ashley said too."

"What do you mean?" Deb asked.

"When I first got there and Ashley was waiting with me, she said that she thought Mary was stringing me along. Like she was happy to tell people she had a boyfriend when it suited her. But to me, it seems like she's so caught up in this 'poor me' thing about the cancer that she doesn't even want to be happy."

"I'm not sure she feels that way, exactly, but where you are concerned, she's seemed content to wallow in this not quite together state. I have noticed that," Deb reflected.

"You can't be with someone that isn't going to give you anything. I mean a relationship, especially a lifelong one, should be give and take," Ryan said.

"That is totally where I was coming from when I went to talk to her. She just didn't see it that way at all. All she said over and over was why couldn't I give her the time she needed," Ken said as he got up from the table to get something to drink.

"So now what?" Deb asked.

"Now, I try to get on with my life I guess," Ken said as he sat back down.

"What if she calls you, later, and needs your help or wants to talk or changes her mind?" Deb asked.

"If she needed help, I'm sure I would help her. I mean, that's the way Dad taught me to behave. All that other stuff, talking or changing her mind, I'm not sure," Ken said somewhat resignedly.

"It's hard to believe after everything you've been through that you're ready to just end it, that's all," Deb said, reaching for Ryan's hand.

He added as he reassured her, "Sometimes you just know. You know when it's right, and you know when it's not."

"Yeah, that's right. I just woke up today, and I knew that if it was going to be this way, I had to let her go," Ken said. "So, I'm hungry. How about you two?"

They all got up and left the apartment to find something for dinner. It was after eight at night, but it was New York. They decided on an Italian place near the apartment and were nearly the only people in there. They laughed and talked about school, the dig that Deb was interviewing for in a few weeks to participate in the next summer, and how Ryan was preparing for a business internship. He wanted to do what Darrick did for a living, but this internship was not in a financial place. Ken said he was going to speak to Darrick and see if he could help Ryan arrange something at his office.

They stayed up late talking and playing some card games. The boys tried to teach Deb to play poker but that was a lost cause. They finally went to bed after midnight.

The next day, while Joe, Becky, and Kim were just beginning their adventures and during the day Joe was arrested, Ken, Deb, and Ryan decided to go on the trip from Battery Park to the Statue of Liberty and Ellis Island. Playing tourist was kind of fun, they decided, and they spent the day down by Battery Park.

While they were on the ferry returning from Ellis Island, Deb asked Ken, "What about the fact that Thomas and Mr. Brewster knew you were still with Mary in the future? I mean you showed up at the hospital, remember?"

"I've been wondering about that. I've actually had a few conversations with Joe about it this fall on phone. See, that was part of why I always felt confident I could convince her to change her mind. The fact that we were still together in the future gave me hope. But what if that's not really what our future is going to be? Joe says that once you know about something that happens in the future, you naturally change it a little bit. You tweak it and make it into something different. That's the scientific theory."

"We've talked about this a few times, but we've really focused on the idea that if you know your future you lose all hope. That's pretty interesting. You mean that since you know that in the future, you're going to the hospital to see what Mary is doing, you're changing the course of your timeline as you get to that event?" Ryan asked.

"Kind of. Joe says there's a theory that if you have knowledge of a future event, it will never happen exactly as it did when you found out about that event in the first place. Also, Joe says that Mary pronouncing that she was going to change her future and prevent me from having to deal with any of this means that she's going to make choices all along the timeline that will change all kinds of things and get us to a completely different end on that day I was supposed to go to the hospital. He says that's part of the scientific theory about time travel, and why going to the future is so hard to imagine. Once you know, you change it." Ken replied.

"So, making that trip and finding out about Mary having that marker has already changed things. This sounds like just one more reason for me to regret that trip." Deb lamented.

"Don't feel bad, Deb. I'm sure—as sure and as absolute as Mary thinks sometimes—she would have gotten us to the point where it ended, with or without confirmation she has that marker. She is so afraid of dying from this that at least where we were concerned, she'd already stopped living."

Ryan added, "Man, that's just pitiful. She's so afraid of what might happen that she's making it come true now."

"Yeah, self-fulfilling prophesy," Ken said.

The ferry had landed, and they were disembarking with the crowd of people that had made the trip to Ellis Island when Ryan announced, "Man, am I hungry!" He looked at both Deb and Ken and added, "Am I the only one?"

"No, I'm starving too. It feels like I've been living on the edge of a cliff and am finally over it, and now I realize how hungry and tired I am," Ken said.

"Well, then, let's find something to eat for you two starving guys!" Deb said, laughing.

At the end of Battery Park, there were several food carts. They selected a hot dog cart and ordered dogs and drinks and then sat on a bench and ate. They watched television and ate some pizza that night, but the next morning, Ryan left early to go to church with his parents. Ken and Deb went to church on the other side of the park and walked back through the park afterward.

"Was it too weird that the pastor was preaching about relationships today?" Deb asked.

"Yeah, I spent the first couple of minutes wondering if he could just tell what was going on in my head."

"Are you still struggling with your decision?"

"I don't know. I don't think so. I mean, I love her still, but it just isn't working for me, and although I hate to admit this, I want a different kind of relationship than the one she was offering. She just wanted me to always do what she wanted, follow her feelings and perspective, and I want something better."

"Like something where there are mutual respect and a desire to continue to do things for them after the honeymoon is over?"

"Yeah, like the pastor said, it's work, but it's work born from love and a desire to give to another person no matter what state you're in, what kind of day you've had, or what issues you're facing."

"Maybe Mary should have listened to this sermon."

"Maybe."

They walked a few more minutes, then Ken said, "Let's forget about this for the rest of today, can we? I need to not deal with this anymore!"

"Sure. Want to get some lunch before we head out?"

"Sounds good. How about that Chinese place next to Schwartz?"

"Sounds good."

They ate and went back to the apartment and packed up. Ken drove Deb back to her dorm, and then he left for Harvard. When Deb got to her room, her roommate Kathy was just heading out.

"Do you want to go to the library? I have a huge test tomorrow to study for," Kathy asked.

"Yeah, can you give me five so I can unpack quickly and gather up my books?" Deb replied.

"Sure. Oh, wait a minute! You have like five messages from Mary. She started calling late Friday night and a bunch of times yesterday. You better call her before we go," Kathy remembered, and she handed Deb a pile of notes from when Mary called.

"Maybe I better meet you at the library then. This is going to be a long call. Ken and Mary broke up on Friday night."

"Is that why you went home for the weekend?"

"Yeah. Spent the weekend with Kenny and Ryan, consoling Kenny. Well, not really. He actually seems ok with this. It's been hard for him for a long time. It's sad, but maybe for the best."

"Maybe not, if Mary has been calling all weekend."

"Yeah, maybe not. I'll unpack and call her, and then I'll meet you at the library. Where do you think you'll be?"

"In the science section."

"Ok, see you soon."

Kathy left, and Deb finished unpacking her clothes. She was going to have to do some laundry soon. She had a pile overflowing her laundry basket in the closet. She was about to pick up the phone when it rang. She answered, "Hello?"

"Is that you, Deb?"

Deb could barely understand what was being said, there was so much sobbing going on, so she said, "Excuse me? I can't understand you."

Deb heard someone blowing their nose and then the phone being picked back up.

"It's me, Mary."

"Oh, I'm so sorry, Mary. I could barely understand you. I just got back and got all your messages and was just about to call you."

"Where have you been all weekend?"

"I was at home."

"I called you and called you. I didn't think to call the apartment."

"Sorry about that."

"Ken came over here Friday. It was awful. He said he felt like I was never going to change my mind and never be his girlfriend again, and he didn't want to do it anymore, and he barely acted like it was bothering him at all. Then Ashley told him that she thought I was stringing him along, and he deserved better. Then he said I had to make a decision. He gave me an ultimatum, and I had to decide right there in that moment in the park, and I couldn't say anything and he left."

"I'm not sure you're making much sense right now, Mary. Why was Ashley involved in the conversation? It sure doesn't sound like Ken to give an ultimatum either."

"Ken talked to Ashley before I got back to the dorm from classes. That's when she told him she thought I was stringing him along. Later, late Friday night, she told me she felt sorry for Ken and maybe he deserved better than what I was willing to give him. I don't know if she said that to Ken but probably."

"I see now."

"He was so cold, like no emotions at all. Why would he do that?"

"Maybe because he's been dealing with this for a long time, and he just doesn't have any emotions left?"

"What do you mean?"

"Well, Mary, you kind of were stringing him along ever since he showed up the first time and told you he would just be your friend and help and support you until you were ready to accept him back in your life fully. You were fine with it then, but it's been months, and no matter what he's done, you can't even see that he might have been right."

"That's not fair. I'm dealing with this the best I know how."

"That is probably true, but, Mary, you've got tunnel vision now. You can only see that you're going to die this terrible death and you have to save him from whatever that was going to mean. You said that last spring at Choate."

"I still love him."

"I know you do. I also know he still loves you."

"Then why can't we keep going the way we were?"

"Because, Mary, that was all you taking and all Ken giving. And that isn't good for either of you."

"He called it a one-way street. But I do things for him! It's not true that all I was doing was taking while he gave."

"When was the last time you called him? Even called him back when he called you first? When was the last time you wrote him a letter? Or visited him at Harvard?"

"I don't know. But I do those things."

"No, Mary, you used to do those things, last year—when we were at Choate and he was at Harvard. You called him almost every day, you wrote him notes all the time, and you went to see him as much as you could."

"I'm dealing with cancer you know."

"Yeah, I know. We all know. You wear it like a suit of armor to keep everyone away from you. Here's the thing. Joe has told us the scientific theory about time travel. That when you go into the future and find out something and come back. Now you know it, and the mere fact that you know it, changes it. So, you see, your future is not set in stone."

"First of all, we're talking about my genetics, not the clothes I pick out to wear each day. And secondly, remember when we were dealing with your parents' death and you couldn't change that, and we decided it was because you couldn't change when you died. When the Lord was ready to call you up, there's no changing that."

"I know we're talking about genetics and not clothes. But the point is still the same. You know you have the genetics. All you have to do is prepare. Find the right doctors and work through it. That's all we have all been saying to you for months. And, yes, with the right doctors and right treatment, you can change the outcome of this. That is, if you even get cancer."

"I'm kind of tired of everyone trying to tell me this same thing over and over again. The right doctors, the right treatments. Blah, blah, blah."

"You know what I think the problem is, Mary? I think you're settled into being this victim, and you want everyone to cater to you. You don't want a friend or a boyfriend. You want everyone to do whatever for you, whenever you need it. And you know what I'm tired of? You acting like you're practically dead from this cancer already. You have the marker that says you might get cancer. You don't have cancer!" Deb was practically screaming into the phone.

Mary didn't say anything for a long time. Then she said, "So this is how it's going to be, huh? I can't believe today, of all days, when I'm dealing with losing Ken, that you decide to yell at me because I'm not doing what you want."

"Mary, I'm not trying to tell you to do what I want. I'm just asking that you wake up and look at this more objectively and see that you are pushing away your boyfriend, your best friend, your roommate, and who knows who else."

She was quiet for a long time.

"Mary, are you still there?" Deb asked.

"Yes, I'm still here. Listen, if I think about this, like you asked, will you talk to Ken for me?"

"Mary, if you want to try to work this out with Ken, you need to think about it, talk to your pastor some more, maybe talk to Thomas or another doctor, and then *you* call Ken. I'm not getting in the middle of this. Ken is trying to be ok. I'm not going to mess that up. I want to be your friend, but I'm done tiptoeing around your moping, ok?"

"You sure don't seem like you want to be my friend today."

"I'm sorry you feel that way. Mary, I am your friend. Sometimes your friend needs to tell you that you're full of it, and it's time to get up and change your situation."

"I guess. Bye."

"Bye, Mary."

Deb walked over to the library and found Kathy. They sat and studied, and when they were at dinner later, Deb told Kathy what was going on. Kathy agreed with Deb, which made her feel better. When they got back to the dorm, Deb tried to call Kim, but she wasn't around. Then she tried Joe, and he wasn't around. She was starting to get a bit worried, and she called Ken. He said there was probably something going on at school, and he would try Joe again tomorrow. He also reported that Uncle Darrick had called him, and they talked for a bit. Ken and Deb agreed to talk on Monday after they tried Kim and Joe again.

12

KEN WASN'T SURE WHY he wasn't overly upset about the conversation he had with Mary over the weekend, but when he woke up, he had to admit, he felt calmer than he had in months. Classes were better, and by the time he got back to his dorm from classes, he had decided that this must be how it was supposed to turn out. As he walked into his room, he laughed to himself, thinking *look at this, now I'm believing there is a plan.* He looked at his bulletin board and saw he had four messages. He pulled them off and realized they were all from Mr. Brewster. He picked up the phone immediately and called Mr. Brewster's house.

"Hello," Mr. Brewster said.

"Mr. Brewster, it's Ken. I'm sorry, I was in class. What's up?"

"Ken, I don't know how to tell you this, but the kids went on a trip in the machine."

"They what?"

"They went to 1853, and they're not back yet. I'm getting worried. They were supposed to be back earlier today, even yesterday, and we have to be back in class tomorrow."

"Was it just Kim and Joe?"

"No, Becky is with them."

"What do Becky's parents think she's doing this weekend?"

"I believe they said that her parents think she is with Joe on Long Island."

"Holy crap! It's not just that Joe and Kim disregarded the rules, they brought Becky into it, and now we have to manage her parents too?"

"I think, Ken, we might want to focus on dealing with today. You can certainly take us all to task after we address the obvious issue, that the kids might not be back in time for classes tomorrow."

"Ok, you're right. What do you think we should do?"

"Well, first of all, I think we need to come up with a plan for all three of them to not be in classes tomorrow. That will require parental intervention. Then at least we have some leeway."

"I'm going to call Deb. One of us will call you right back, is that ok? I think she will be better at coming up with a plan than me since I'm still so agitated."

"Ok. Talk with you soon."

"Bye."

Ken hung up and then immediately dialed Deb's room at NYU.

"Deb?"

"No, this is Kathy, her roommate."

"Oh, hi, Kathy. This is Ken. Is she around?"

"Yeah, she's down the hall. Do you need me to run and get her?"

"Yes, please."

"Ok, I'm setting the phone down. Be right back."

Ken waited for what seemed like an hour and then, "Hi, Ken, what's up?" Deb said.

"Is Kathy still there?"

"No, she was just leaving to go to the library, Why?"

"I don't want anyone to hear this. Mr. Brewster just called me. Joe, Kim, and Becky went on a little trip in the machine, and they're not back yet."

"Oh my gosh. I knew they had a long weekend off, and I left messages for both Joe and Kim yesterday. I didn't think much of that."

"Well, they apparently decided to go to 1853 and aren't back, and we need a plan."

"Well, they had a few days off from classes, so what's the immediate problem?"

"If they aren't back by tonight, then they will miss their classes tomorrow."

"Ok, so we have to come with some reason for them not to be there and get some excuse to the school, right?"

"Yeah, but how are we going to explain this to Becky's parents? Or to Aunt Alicia or Darrick?"

"Let me think a minute."

"Think fast."

"Oh, I know, Becky's parents are out of the country. That's probably why they aren't crazy about not hearing from her. So, we need to get someone to cover for all three of them."

"You want to call Aunt Alicia or Darrick?"

"I hate to say this, but I think Uncle Darrick is the better choice. I think he will at least listen to us."

"They're out of town too, remember?"

"Yeah, but he's just hanging out today because Aunt Alicia is at that conference or whatever."

"Ok. I'm packing a few things and arranging for notes in class, and then I'm leaving to come and get you. You call Darrick and see what you can do, and before you do that, call Mr. Brewster back and tell him we are on our way."

"Where are we going to stay?"

"I'll get a hotel for us. Can you miss class for the next couple of days if we do this?"

"Yeah, I'll arrange things while I wait for you."

"Ok, see you soon."

"Bye."

They hung up and Deb called Mr. Brewster and told him their plan. He agreed and said he would be waiting for them at his house. Then Deb called Uncle Darrick.

"Hello?"

"Uncle Darrick, it's Deb."

"Are you ok?"

"Kind of. I need your help, but first I need to ask that you keep a totally open mind and hear me out. Can you do that?"

"You're scaring me, Deb. How about you start, and I will try to keep an open mind."

"Ok. So, this is going to sound crazy, but that first year we were at Choate, when you and Aunt Alicia first started dating, remember? Well, we went exploring in an old building around Halloween, and Joe found this notebook with all kinds of math formulas in it and a prototype of a small machine. He had befriended Mr. Brewster, that science teacher we've talked about. They figured out the formula and the machine prototype, and it turns out it was a formula for bending time and a time machine."

Deb paused, and Uncle Darrick didn't say anything. "Are you still with me?"

"Yes, I'm listening. Getting nervous, but I'm listening."

"Well, we built the machine, and we tested it, and then we started using it. First, we tried to change something that would bring our parents back, then we had to fix something Joe did in the machine, then we helped Mr. Brewster with something, and then late last year, Mr. Brewster went forward to find out if Mary was going to get what her grandmother had."

"Is that what the big secret was last summer? And why she broke up with Ken?"

"Yeah. Anyway, the problem is that Joe, Kim, and Becky went in the machine at the end of classes last week."

"Where did they go?"

"Well, Mr. Brewster told us they went to 1853."

"What?"

"Yeah, so that isn't the problem—well, at least, I don't think it's the problem. The problem is they aren't back yet. Classes start again for them tomorrow."

"Ok. Let me get this straight. You all figured out a huge scientific unknown, that no one else could figure out, and started traveling through time, and now Joe, Becky, and Kim are potentially lost somewhere?"

"Well, they have the machine there, where they are, so as long as they can get to it and there's nothing wrong with it, they can get back."

"That's not helping, Deb."

"Sorry."

"What do you need from me?"

"Well, I guess the kids all said they were going out to the Hampton house, so I was hoping you could call Choate and tell them something and give us a day so the kids don't have issues with that. And maybe we might have to get a message to Becky's parents to reassure them that Becky is with us."

When Uncle Darrick didn't answer right away, Deb started to worry. "Uncle Darrick, are you still there?"

"Sorry, yes, I'm here. Listen, I'll call the school, and if you give me a number, I will call Becky's parents, but I'm flying home today and coming to get you, and we are going to Choate, ok."

"Ken's actually on his way here, and we're heading over there this afternoon."

"Ken's involved in this too?"

"We all are, Uncle Darrick. And Mary knows, and Ryan knows, and Mr. Brewster's son, Thomas, knows."

"I see. Well, I'm still flying home, and I guess I'll meet you at Choate."

"What are going to tell Aunt Alicia?"

"I don't like the idea of lying to her, Deb. Any more than I like the idea that you all have kept something from us for nearly three years now."

"I know you're mad, and you probably should be, but can we hold all of that until we know that Joe, Kim, and Becky are safe?"

"Yes, we can hold it, but you and Ken have some explaining to do."

"Ok."

"Give me a number for Becky's parents then."

"It might be best to call her dad's office. They are in Europe now. You know Becky's dad is an ambassador now, right?"

"Yes, I knew that."

Deb gave Uncle Darrick the numbers, and they hung up. She packed a few things, called Ryan and told him what was going on, and arranged for her absence from classes for maybe the rest of the week. Ryan insisted on going with her, so he also arranged to be gone and then came to her room to wait for Ken. On the drive to Choate, Ken relayed everything he heard from Mr. Brewster, and Deb did the same. They talked about Uncle Darrick and how to handle explaining anything else to him and tried to come up with ideas on how to fix this if the machine never made it back.

Ken, Deb, and Ryan arrived at Mr. Brewster's house around five that night. They sat down at his kitchen table, and Deb said, "Mr. Brewster, you better start from the beginning and tell us everything you know."

"Joe and Becky came to me last fall and wanted to discuss the time-elapsed calculation. Becky had a brilliant idea that the variable we were missing was the amount of time the machine traveled and how that might play into the elapsed time in the present and wherever the machine went. So, we worked on it for several weekends and found she was right. We know now that the farther the machine travels, the disparity in time elapse increases."

"That's interesting, Mr. Brewster, but what does that have to do with this trip?" Ryan asked.

"Just after the kids got back to school from Christmas break, they all came to me and wanted to discuss the particulars for traveling to the eighteen hundreds. Apparently, Kim had it in her head that she needed to help out with the underground railroad. She had landed on this from her studies of the Civil War and reading *Little Women*. I think Joe and Becky were hoping I would come up with something to deter her, but she said she was tired of waiting until she was older to make her mark on the world—and particularly, in her family. She felt left out of everything last year, thought that everyone was doing something great, and she was going to be left in the background. I suggested they bring you all in, and she was first to protest, saying that Ken would try to stop them, and Deb would want to run everything. Joe said he understood, and that was that. They researched everything and decided to go to Philadelphia in eighteen fifty-three to see if they could meet up with a Robert Purvis, who was active in the abolition movement and a big part of the underground railroad in the area."

"What did they do for money and clothes, and where were they planning on staying?" Deb asked.

"You would have been surprised and very pleased, Deb. They did a considerable amount of planning and research. They got time-appropriate clothing from the theater department, and they found a hotel that was in place when they were going, and they even managed to get money to have while they were there."

"But, Mr. Brewster, you can't just walk into a hotel and hand over a few fifties from nineteen seventy-seven and expect people to not question it," Ryan said.

"They took gold bars and went to a bank and had them changed to local currency."

"That was a good idea," Deb replied.

"Ok, so back to the point. How long were they planning to be gone?" Ken asked, trying to redirect them.

"They knew they had nine days in the past before they would not be back by today," Mr. Brewster replied. "They left Wednesday after classes ended."

"And we have no way to communicate with them, and no way to know what is going on with them," Ken added.

"Well, that is correct," Mr. Brewster said, forlornly.

"I hate to be the one that brings this up, but what do we do if they don't come back?" Ryan asked.

"Well, we have the original plans for the machine, and we have the current program, don't we, Mr. Brewster?" Ken asked.

"Yes, we have all that. Plus, Joe, Becky, and I have completed all the documentation on the machine, the formula, and the programming. Why do you ask, Ken?"

"In case we have to quickly build a machine and go after them, right?" Deb asked.

"Yeah, well, if one of you has a better idea, I'm all ears," Ken said, looking around the table.

"Again, I hate to be the damper in the room, but remember when Deb and I went back to Cambridge to stop Joe? We couldn't use two machines very well," Ryan added.

"Let's talk about that. What exactly happened with the machines on that trip?" Ken said.

"Well, part of the problem was that Joe and I were having symptoms of being in the same space and time, but we found that the machine couldn't be powered up at the same time, and in fact, when they were both in the same space and time, the second machine couldn't be programmed to return to the correct present date and time. Isn't that right, Mr. Brewster?" Deb said.

"Yes, but in this case, both machines would be coming back to the same present, so I don't know if that would present a problem."

"We ended up having no issues after the first machine, the one Joe was in, had completely left. So, if we have to do this, we just don't start up the second machine until we know the first one left," Ryan added.

"But wait a minute, wasn't the issue really that both Ryan and I, and Joe, used the same machine last year. If we build a whole new machine, will any of that even happen?" Deb added, excitedly.

"You're right, Deb. This would be a whole new machine." Mr. Brewster smiled.

"Ok. Let me get this straight. On that trip to Cambridge, you, Deb, and Ryan went back in the same machine we have been using to the same location as the other machine," Ken started.

"No, we didn't go to the exact same location. Joe went to Fresh Pond in the Highlands, Ken, and we went to the backyard behind ours—the one that was vacant three years ago," Deb interrupted.

"Ok, so you took the same machine, but it was a different trip from a different starting date and time, and you went back to the neighbor's yard, a different place, and waited for Joe. Then you had to wait for Joe to start his version of the machine, but yours wouldn't take the correct programming. Where was it trying to send you?" Ken said.

"It was trying to send us to Joe's return date and time, the spring before we went to your graduation," Ryan said.

"What did you do?"

"That's when I went looking for Joe and found that he hadn't made it to his machine, that he'd passed out. I got him into his machine and got him out of there, but when he pushed the start button, I was standing at the window of the machine, and the force of the machine threw me. I blacked out, and when I came to, I went back and got Deb strapped in, and the machine took the settings and we left," Ryan explained.

"I'm going to have words with you, Deb, after this over. You never told me any of these details. But, for now, what you're saying is that the mere fact that the machine was there twice did not allow the second machine to take another destination, right?" Ken said sternly.

"That's right. But Deb is correct. If we build a second machine, it shouldn't have the same signature to the time-space continuum, so you shouldn't have any of these issues," Mr. Brewster jumped in to calm Ken down.

"And, since none of us existed in eighteen fifty-three, we shouldn't have any of the other issues," Deb concluded.

"I think we better get busy on another machine then. In case we have to go after them," Ryan said.

"The only problem with this plan, is the first time it took us about two months to build that machine. Do we even have any supplies to get that done?" Ken asked.

"I have some things in the barn, but not enough to build a replica of the first machine," Mr. Brewster said, thinking aloud.

"Does it have to look exactly the same? I mean, part of it has to work the same to create the energy and the magnetic field, but does the vessel have to be the same?" Ryan asked no one in particular.

"I suppose it doesn't have to look exactly the same. I mean we did use a bunch of parts you had in the barn, so the cockpit or whatever was based on the parts we had," Ken thought aloud.

"That's right, Ken. It wouldn't have to be the same exact shape. It would just need to be able to generate the energy for the magnetic field," Mr. Brewster added.

"Should we go see what parts we have then?" Deb asked.

They all got up and walked over to the barn. Ryan turned the lights on, and they looked around.

"Looks like we depleted the machine parts quite a bit, Mr. Brewster. The only substantial piece of metal in this barn now is your old car and the sheets to fabricate your missing panels and stuff," Ken said as he looked around.

"What about that old shed we landed the machine in a few times last year? Anything in there we could use?" Ryan asked.

"Well, whatever is in there, hasn't been in use in years, so I imagine if it went missing, no one would notice. I can't remember the last time the caretakers even used it," Mr. Brewster said.

"Got any flashlights? We should get started right away in case we have to do this," Ken said.

"Yes, in the kitchen."

Mr. Brewster left to get some flashlights, and Ken asked if Deb would mind staying at Mr. Brewster's house since Darrick was due to land soon and would be here within the hour or so. She agreed. Ken and Ryan left to see what they could find in the shed, and Deb and Mr. Brewster sat waiting for Uncle Darrick to arrive.

Ryan and Ken made it to the shed without anyone on campus noticing them. They didn't turn their flashlights on until they got behind the shed and opened the doors. Inside were some old tractors, but against the wall were several metal drums that were empty and had the tops off and an old hopper for storing fertilizer or something. It was pretty big, and Ken said it should work. They had no way to move them, but they figured that they could come back in the early morning and get them over to Mr. Brewster's house and start working. They headed back to Mr. Brewster's house.

Just before Ken and Ryan got back, there was a knock on the door. Mr. Brewster opened the door, and Uncle Darrick introduced himself. They came into the kitchen, and Uncle Darrick gave Deb a quick hug and sat down.

"Did you reach Becky's parents?" Deb asked.

"No, but I did speak to an assistant of her father's and told them we had chartered a boat for a couple of days trip and had an issue and wouldn't be back in time for classes tomorrow. The assistant told me he would contact the school and inform them that Becky would be out a few more days and excuse her. I did the same for Joe and Kim. What are you doing about classes?" Uncle Darrick asked.

"I've arranged to be out and left messages for the professors. I told them I had a family issue and got several people to take notes for me, so I should be fine," Deb replied.

Just then, the boys returned. Ryan and Ken greeted Uncle Darrick, and they talked about the plan. Uncle Darrick wasn't happy about the idea of more time-hopping, as he called it, but he recognized that if Joe, Becky, and Kim didn't return on their own, there was no other choice. Ken, Deb, Ryan, and Uncle Darrick left to go to the hotel, and Mr. Brewster agreed to call them if the kids returned.

The next morning, Mr. Brewster went out to leave a note in case the kids returned during the day while he was teaching classes, and when he opened the door, he was shocked to see the machine back in the barn. He ran back into the house and called Ken right away. When he told Ken that the machine was back, Ken said he would drive over immediately and try to head them off before going to class. Ryan heard all this and said he would go with Ken. They drove over, and Ken dropped Ryan off at the girls' dorm, and he drove over to the boys' dorm. Ryan was able to stop Becky and Kim from leaving the dorm to go to breakfast, and Ken found Joe on the road to the dining hall. He swung back around and grabbed Ryan and the girls, and they all drove back to the hotel.

They got breakfast at the hotel, and Uncle Darrick joined them. Ken suggested they wait until they were at the barn to discuss what happened, so they would only need to tell the tale one time. Mr. Brewster arranged for a substitute teacher but had to coordinate that. He told Ken he would meet them at the barn around ten. When they got to the barn, Uncle Darrick asked Joe to show him the machine. They were inside it when Mr. Brewster arrived. When the tour was finished, they all sat at the table, and Ken said, "Someone please tell us what happened."

"I want to do this. It was all my idea," Kim said.

"Ok, Kim, go ahead," Ken replied.

"Can I start from when we arrived in Philadelphia, or do you need to know about the planning?"

"Mr. Brewster filled us in on most of the planning while we were waiting for you. Start when you got to Philadelphia," Ken answered.

"So, we landed the machine on a small island that was used part of the year by a family for grazing. It was empty when we got there. We rowed a small boat down to the port and stored it with a harbor guy, and then we checked into the hotel. We exchanged some of the gold for banknotes and stored the rest of the gold at the Merchants Bank, and while we were at lunch the first day, Joe met someone that knew Robert Purvis. We also met this nice lady, Mrs. Fairchild. Over the next few days, Joe spent time with the men working on the underground railroad, and Becky and I got involved with the women in support of the railroad—an organization of women that moved supplies and notes and sometimes helped move the fugitives. It was going well until the day there was a trial for a man named Mr. Burns. He was claimed by some man from the south as a fugitive slave. The crowds were pretty big, and the President called in the military to keep the peace, and Joe was there, watching, and got tangled up in something and was arrested."

"What did you do, Joe?" Deb asked.

"I was just standing there watching the crowd carrying signs that said this was kidnapping and the fugitive slave act was bad and talking with people and then someone near me got hit by someone that was there for the trial and was in support of slavery. The guy fell kind of on me, and I pushed back at him to keep him standing up. Then a military guy saw what was going on and came over and just arrested all three of us. That was it," Joe said.

"Joe sat in jail for four days waiting for the trial and everything. I mean it was eighteen fifty-three, so things moved slower. Anyway, he was acquitted, and as soon as we could, we left and got back to the machine and back here last night," Kim finished.

"What made you decide to go there and at that time?" Uncle Darrick asked.

"Well, I wanted to help with the underground railroad. I wanted to know that I had done something good. I wanted to fit into the family," Kim replied, starting to tear up.

"You do fit in the family, Kimmy. You fit perfectly in our family as the thoughtful, insightful one. You don't have anything to prove," Ken said as he went over and hugged her.

"You don't understand, Kenny. You've always been this star. Star athlete, star student, star boyfriend. Deb is this super smart historian, Joe has the computers and this time machine, and what do I have? Art and girl scouts. I wanted to be a part of this, and I wanted to plan, research, lead, and do something great."

"Kim, you've always been a part of this," Deb said.

"Not really. You planned everything, and last year, I was not even on some of the trips."

"But that doesn't mean you haven't been part of this, part of our family," Ken added.

"I don't understand what's going on here, yet, but, Kim, you're a very important part of this family. Unfortunately, as the youngest, you are going to look up and see your siblings getting to milestones before you, and that simply makes it sooner they get to do things. It doesn't mean you never will," Uncle Darrick said.

"I agree with your uncle. I would also add, Kim, the advantage of being youngest, is you get to learn from your siblings. That means there's a good chance you will do something greater than all their accomplishments," Mr. Brewster added.

Kim sniffed loudly and wiped her eyes. She looked around and smiled a little. Then Ken said, "Is there anything else? I mean besides Joe getting arrested and sitting in jail for four days? Did anything else happen?"

"We got to meet Mr. Purvis. And we got to take a fugitive slave and her two kids from one place to another," Kim said, brightening up.

"Tell us about that," Deb said.

"Well, Mr. Purvis came to the hotel the day after Joe was arrested and met with Becky and me, and he took us to see Joe at the jail, helped Becky get some more money, and took us to the court hearings. He's a very nice man. He's part black, on his mother's side, and he identified more with his black heritage. He married a black woman, and they had children. He had a business in Philadelphia, and he was the organizer of the underground railroad there, I think."

"So, you accomplished what you wanted to on this trip, didn't you?" Deb asked.

"Yes, except for Joe getting arrested."

"Becky, do you want to add anything?" Mr. Brewster asked.

"It was strange to me, the differences in culture. I mean I've read all about it in history, but it was different to experience it. The formality of the language, the fact that everyone goes by miss or ma'am or mr. was kind of weird. Oh, and the fact that I could barely do anything on my own. Everywhere, it was all about my fiancé doing things for me. Girls had almost no rights," Becky replied.

"Who, as if I don't already know, was your fiancé?" Ken asked, looking at Joe.

Joe smiled and turned red. "Yes, that was part of our planning. We decided that the only way we could be there alone was for me to be the head of the household and Becky my fiancé. It worked. No one even blinked at a sixteen-year-old being engaged or responsible for his sister and fiancé. The thing I thought was strange was how trusting everyone was. I mean, we didn't pay for the hotel or put anything down to secure it. The guy at the harbor waited a day for me to pay him to store the boat. There are no ID rules in eighteen fifty-three either, so it was simple to just walk into town and announce ourselves."

"How did you manage to get gold here? Or how did you get gold at all?" Uncle Darrick asked.

"I called the bank here and told them I wanted to keep some of my money in gold, and they said no problem. I went to the bank and picked up a case full of little gold bars. The bank in eighteen fifty-three didn't even blink at that. Said that's how everyone moved money from town to town and just exchanged a few bars at a time into banknotes, and we were fine," Joe replied.

"Is there any left?" Ryan asked.

"Yeah, sure, we have about half of it left. It's in my dorm room."

"Ok, so it seems like everything turned out ok, except for the fact that you weren't back on time, and we needed to cover for you, so Uncle Darrick here called Becky's parents and the school. That's why we pulled you away from the dorms so quickly this morning. You aren't supposed to be there today. We'll have to make a show of returning you later today and call Becky's parents again and everything to smooth this over," Ken said, trying to clean things up.

"Kim, did Amy see you this morning or last night when you got back?" Deb asked.

"No. We decided because of how late it was that Kim would stay with me. We didn't get back here until about two this morning," Becky answered.

"That's actually good, if not many people saw any of you," Ken added.

"Joe, did you run the regular printouts from the machine when you got back?" Mr. Brewster asked.

"No, I fired them off when I was showing the machine to Uncle Darrick. I thought we might go over them later. I'm pretty wiped today."

"I'd like to see that," Uncle Darrick said.

"We could do it next weekend if you want to come back here," Joe said.

They agreed, and Uncle Darrick asked if he could use Mr. Brewster's phone to call Becky's parents. He went inside and called them. He then called Choate and told them Joe, Kim, and Becky would all be returning today and would be in classes tomorrow. Mr. Brewster returned to campus, and everyone else went to get some lunch. It was decided to return the kids after lunch, and then Uncle Darrick took Ryan and Deb back to NY while Ken returned to Harvard. Just before they all left, Uncle Darrick pulled Ken aside and asked, "So, how are you doing after the break up? I meant to call you more while I was away, but it was a bit chaotic with your aunt. As you can imagine. Are you doing ok?"

"Yeah, before all of this happened, I was thinking yesterday that I was calmer and happier than I had been in months. What does that say about it all?"

"It says that perhaps this was how it was meant to be, I suppose."

"I guess so. I mean, I miss her still, but it just feels so much better to not be stressing every day about trying to prove myself. Do you think that's what that means, that it was meant to be? Maybe we weren't meant to be together forever."

"I totally understand what you mean. And, yes, maybe this was how it was meant to turn out. If you need to talk, at all, about anything, give me a call, ok? It might be a good idea if you all decided to come home soon on the weekend, so we can spend some time together."

"I'd like that."

During the ride back to New York, Ryan and Deb kept Uncle Darrick entertained with tales of classes and activities, and he kept them entertained talking about all the things that Aunt Alicia was getting involved in at Vogue. They dropped Ryan off, and Uncle Darrick asked Deb if she would like to get some dinner. She agreed, mostly because she didn't want cafeteria food. She knew he had many more questions, and she wasn't sure she wanted to face that, but she wanted to face the cafeteria less. They found a little pizza place near NYU and sat down.

"I've been trying to piece together everything you've all told me in the last twenty-four hours with the timeline of what I know, and I have to say, I have a lot of questions," he said just after they placed their dinner order.

"I expected you to have some questions. I'm just not sure dinner is going to be enough time."

"No, probably not, but how about if I start, and then we can decide how many more of these conversations we need to have."

"Ok. What do you want to know?"

"How about you start with telling when and in what order these trips took place."

"Well, in the spring of my junior year we made the first trips. After Joe and Ken finished building the machine and putting the programming in place, they tested it by first starting it up, and then Mr. Brewster made the first trip. He went back to Iowa just before his father left for the war and talked to him."

"What war?"

"World War II. Mr. Brewster's father married his mother, and they had a wedding night and then he left for training. He was killed on Normandy beach during the first day of the invasion, so Mr. Brewster never knew his father. I researched details so he dressed appropriately and stuff, Kim helped determine where to land the machine, and Joe programmed it. Then a couple of weeks later, we all went in the machine to try to stop our parents from being killed."

"How did you do that?"

"Well, I was communicating with Mr. Davis and determined that the point they met was at the Kennedy assassination, so we went to Dallas, and we alerted the newspapers and left a note for the secret service, and they arrested Lee Harvey Oswald and stopped the assassination."

"What are you talking about? Kennedy was killed by sniper in early December of nineteen sixty-three."

"Actually, originally, he was killed in Dallas at the parade supposedly by Lee Harvey Oswald. I mean there were all kinds of theories about there being other shooters and about the government or mafia being involved, but that was when Mr. Davis and Dad originally met. I thought if I could change that moment in time, I could change the course of our parents' lives and stop their accident. Lee Oswald was arrested for trying to assassinate someone else a week prior and for threatening to kill Kennedy, but he wasn't there the day of the parade. Whatever was going to happen that day, him not being there, and our alerting the newspaper and the secret service, stopped it, but they, whomever they were, simply regrouped and did it a few weeks later, back in Texas, with a sniper in a car."

"Was Johnson implicated in the first timeline?"

"No, but he was in the second, and as a result, he didn't win his second term, like he did in the original timeline. He left Washington under the scandal of being brought in for questioning by congress."

"So that means, that before you went into the time machine, the Presidents all were different?"

"Some were, but mostly it's on the same track. What I realized after we made that trip was a few things, but one was that what I wanted to change was a pivotal moment in my Dad's life, and what I ended up doing was changing a bunch of people's lives. It was a ripple affect across many years. The timelines converge with the election this year with Jimmy Carter."

"Wow. So, there were other trips, right?"

"Yes. When we made that trip to stop the assassination, and we got back, we did change our parents' lives, but not in a good way. They ended up dying months earlier than they had. It really upset Joe. He thought that his life was never going to work out unless our parents were here, and he thought he had unlocked the key to making that happen. So, after that Dallas trip, Ken said we shouldn't use the machine again. Joe so desperately wanted our parents back that he went back in the machine alone. He went back just a couple of years and met our father, telling him about the machine and everything."

"What did your father say to that?"

"He believed him. I mean Joe brought all kinds of printouts and data and the formula, and Dad believed him, but, of course, Mom didn't. See she was with Joe that whole day at Harvard's campus, so naturally, she couldn't wrap her mind around the time travel idea and was convinced the whole thing was Joe having issues. She took him to therapy, and she and my Dad fought constantly. They ended up separating, and then they both died anyway."

"When was this?"

"Right before Ken's graduation. Remember when Joe wasn't with us for dinner and Ken was so bothered? And then when Joe came with me to get loaded up for the summer, and he had that big cut on his forehead? That's when he did that trip."

"And that was why he was so quiet most of the summer—and why you and Ken were angry with him?"

"Yes."

"Is that all of the trips?"

"No, the next year, when I was a senior and Ken was at Harvard, we decided to help Mr. Brewster. In our original timeline, Mr. Brewster was a caretaker at Choate, not a science teacher. He befriended Joe because of a love of math and science and because they both lost someone. Mr. Brewster's wife was killed while they were in Las Vegas. He was involved in the testing of the nuclear weapons. She was hit by a car on the way home from a retirement dinner and was killed."

"What did she do?"

"She was a teacher. So, Ryan and Joe and I decided we needed to try to help Mr. Brewster, and we used the machine to go back at nineteen fifty-seven and tried to prevent that car accident."

"But if you couldn't stop your parents, what made you think you could stop this?"

"I decided that the plan to fix our parents was too elaborate, and this was going to be simple. I know, it sounds crazy, but I was also dealing with the loss of my parents and was questioning God's role in my life and, really, we all were doing that. Anyway, we decided that even if we changed her death and they got to be together longer or they at least got back here for his teaching interview, it would be better. So, we went to Las Vegas, and Kim and I met Mrs. Brewster and stopped her from being in that accident."

"Wow, where is she now? I didn't meet her."

"Well, she didn't die in that accident, but she died about ten years later after she had their son and Mr. Brewster had become a teacher. It worked for him. Well, sort of. He still lost his wife, but his life is so much better."

"I guess so."

"Well, that boosted my confidence, and Ryan and I went back to Cambridge to try to stop Joe from talking to my father. We did that because Kim was so upset, and Ken was so upset about our parents' splitting up, and I just didn't like the idea of my parents dying alone and not together."

"And that trip worked?"

"Sort of. We did stop Joe, and we put most of our parents' timeline back to normal, but it was a disaster anyway."

"How so?"

The pizza arrived at that moment, and they ate some while Deb thought about how to tell Uncle Darrick about what happened in Cambridge.

"Are you going to tell me what happened on yours and Ryan's trip?"

"Yeah."

"How's the pizza, by the way?"

"Good. I wanted to have a few pieces while they were hot. So, on the trip Ryan and I made, we ran up against several laws of physics. First, you can't be in the same space and time more than once. Joe started having some weird physical symptoms when he went back there, and when we both were there, it was way worse. Also, there is some issue, that I don't understand actually, with the machine being in the same place more than once."

"Like we talked about last night. That's why Ken wanted to build another whole machine, right?"

"Yeah. Even though the machine isn't a live being, it has some sort of energy signature, and it couldn't operate properly when there was a second copy of it."

"I feel like this was much more dangerous than you are letting on here, Deb."

"Well, it was probably. I mean, Joe and Mr. Brewster explained that there are some universal truths, like gravity and relativity, and the universe will not allow more energy to exist than is supposed to. So, when Joe and I were both back in Cambridge, where we already existed, the universe was trying to reconcile that. Joe passed out on the way back to the machine he was supposed to be in, and Ryan had to get him into it and fire it up, but then Joe had to push the button to start it up. Ryan was standing close trying to get Joe to push the button, and he got thrown and hit his head. I was unconscious for the trip back with Ryan, and it took me about an hour to wake up. I was weak for about a day afterward. That's how dangerous it was."

"And when was this?"

"Last year."

"Wait a minute, why didn't Ryan have any issues? If you all only went a couple of years back in time, didn't he exist then too?"

"He did, but Joe says he didn't have issues because he didn't exist in that space, like geography, and time. When it comes to the second version of a person, there is a link to actual physical locations, not just simply that you go to a year where you were already alive."

"Oh, so I could go back to when I was eighteen, but as long as I wasn't near where I was at that date and time, it would be ok. But if I got close to, say, the Hampton house, I would have the same issues."

"Yeah. I don't know if Joe, Mr. Brewster, and Becky have figured out how small the unit is, but yeah, that's basically it."

"Is that all your trips?"

"No, there was one more last year. It was right at the end of the year, and that time Mr. Brewster and his son, Thomas, went forward."

"What for?"

"Remember when Mary's grandmother passed away? Mary found out from the doctors that the cancer that her grandmother died from was kind of hereditary. She was worried she would get it and it would mean Ken would have to take care of a woman wasting away, and so she wanted to go forward and find out if she was going to get breast cancer."

"And that's why she broke up with Ken right before the end of the year?"

"Yeah. We found out she does have the marker for the cancer, and she wanted to save Ken."

"What marker?"

"Thomas said that they developed a test where you could find out if you had a marker showing if you had a predisposition to get cancer. It didn't mean you definitely have the cancer, but she didn't really see it that way."

"Why did Thomas and Mr. Brewster make that trip?"

"Because of the space and time issue. We figured that Ryan and I, Joe and Becky, and Kim had a pretty good chance of existing near New York. Mr. Brewster felt this was better because he thought he was not very likely to be in New York."

"And that's all the trips?"

"Until this one by Joe, Becky, and Kim."

"Finish your pizza while I think a bit."

Deb ate several more pieces of pizza while Uncle Darrick thought about what she had told him. After a few minutes, Uncle Darrick said, "So six trips?"

"Well, seven if you count the one Joe, Becky, and Kim just went on."

"I'm finding this hard to believe, quite frankly. I mean, a fifteen-year-old solves a math problem, which unlocks the secrets of time travel, and the seven of you kids embark on seven trips in this machine, and until this trip, no one knew what you were doing?"

"Yeah, I guess. I mean until this one, none of the trips lasted more than a couple of days. It's complicated, but there is this calculation that shows how time progresses during this present and while the machine is traveling. Time moves slower here in the present, so you can be gone a few days and only have a day elapse here in the present."

"And that matters?"

"Well, yes. We did most of the trips in the machine on the weekend. No one missed classes or was even noted as missing."

"And Joe figured this all out?"

"Well, he had help from Mr. Brewster, I mean Mr. Brewster is a brilliant scientist, but yeah, it was mostly Joe that figured out the formula, programmed the machine, and understood the science of this."

"And now he makes computers that can fit on a desk and created a new programming language that will revolutionize the business world."

"That's ironic, isn't it? He was the one two years ago that was the most lost and was sure he would never amount to much."

"Ironic is an understatement. It's getting pretty late. I should get you back to the dorm."

"Yeah, I better get back."

"Can I come and take you to dinner Friday or something? I'm sure I'm going to have more questions."

"That would be ok. Aren't you coming back to Choate on Saturday to talk through what happened on this last trip?"

"Yeah, but I think I might want to talk more with you first."

"Sure, that's fine."

They left the pizza parlor after Uncle Darrick paid the waitress. He drove up to her dorm and let Deb out. The next day, she and Ryan talked over what Deb told Uncle Darrick and were sitting in her dorm lobby after classes when her roommate found her and said that Ken had called twice and that someone named Becky had just called.

13

DEB AND RYAN WENT to her room, and she called Ken first. He wasn't in his room, so she left a message and then called the girls' dorm at Choate and asked for Becky. After a couple of minutes, Becky picked up the receiver and said, "Hello?"

"Hi, Becky, it's Deb, calling you back."

"Oh, hi, Deb. Thanks for calling. I have a real problem."

"What's going on? Are you guys ok?"

"Well, I just had history class and was shocked by the lesson we were working on, and so I came back here and looked this up in several books. We really messed up history with this trip!"

"Tell me what you think you did."

"Well, in my old history class, and the timeline I still remember, Lincoln was assassinated in a theater by John Wilkes Booth. The reconstruction of the south was a complete disaster, and there were what were called Jim Crow Laws and discrimination and it went on for years. In the sixties, a movement started, and President Johnson signed an anti-discrimination law, and we desegregated schools and neighborhoods, and it started to get better."

"That's not how I remember it all."

"Exactly."

"What did you all do when you were in Philadelphia?"

"Well, Kim and I helped the underground railroad, but all we did was take notes and supplies and things. Oh, one time we helped a lady with her two kids get from one stop to another. But otherwise, we didn't do much of anything except wait for Joe to get out of jail."

"Oh, yeah, I remember Kim mentioning she helped a lady and her two kids."

"She's pretty proud of that, I think."

"So that doesn't sound like an issue. What do you think happened?"

"while Joe was in jail, his cellmate was David Herold."

"Who's he?"

"In my original timeline, he is one of the conspirators that helped in the assassination of Lincoln. See they were going to assassinate Lincoln and everyone in the line of succession to create chaos, so the south could swoop in and take over Washington. But Joe talked to him for days and apparently changed his mind about a lot of things. He then changed the minds of Booth and the others, and they only attempted to kidnap Lincoln, but Mrs. Lincoln saved the day. She beat John Wilkes Booth with her umbrella, and they went home after the play they saw."

"So how did not assassinating Lincoln change what you knew? I mean, he kept the country from blaming the south for the war and helped them rebuild and gave the freed slaves citizenship and voting rights during his second term in office."

"Yes, but the problem is that the time he spent trying to move the country forward, and accepting the south, gave the southerners time to plot and plan. That's how Jefferson Davis became president after Lincoln. You know this part, right? Davis then spent his one term in office trying to undermine everything Lincoln did, and we started having battles again in cities all over the Midwest and even Virginia. And that brought on the next president, John Brown, who put down all the rebellion with the army and then put southerners in jail and confiscated land. That brought on the next two presidents, who put in all the discriminatory laws that Jimmy Carter was promising to remove in his campaign. It's why my father says that he thinks Carter won because everyone is finally ready to end the discrimination for good in this country!"

"And that's not how it happened in the original timeline?"

"No. In fact, there's no mention of Martin Luther King in the history books anymore. He led marches and civil disobedience activities and gave a famous speech in Washington. None of that happened in this new timeline."

"Wow."

"Yeah. All Joe did was talk to a guy in a jail cell."

"And he shifted the course of history."

"Yeah. Now the question is, what do we do?"

"What do you mean, what do we do?"

"Well, we have to fix this. We have to put things back to the way they were."

"Listen, you and Joe and Kim cannot go back there and try to change things back. When Ryan and I did this in Cambridge, it was a disaster. Remember? You almost had to take me to the hospital. Promise me you and Joe won't do this."

"I wasn't actually meaning the three of us jump back into the machine. I just mean that we have to figure this out and find a way to fix what we did."

"As long as you promise me you won't go back to the same place and time, I promise we can discuss it this weekend."

"That's fair."

"Ok, so let's table this until Saturday then, ok? But you should write down everything you remember from your original timeline in terms of what happened, who the people were, and any dates you can remember."

"Ok, but why?"

"Just to be sure you remember, so we can figure out what all changed, and if we're going to fix it, how we're going to do so."

"Ok, yeah. I have to go meet some kids from speech class. We have a group speech to finish."

"I have some homework I'm trying to finish too. Remember, you promised, don't do anything until Saturday, right?"

"Yeah, I promise."

"Ok, bye."

They hung up, and Ryan asked what in the world was going on. Deb got interrupted from answering because her room phone rang.

"Hello."

"Hey, Deb, it's Ken."

"Oh, hi. What were you calling for?"

"Well, I wanted to make sure you got back ok and see what you were thinking of all of this today."

"I just got off the phone with Becky actually. I was thinking about all the questions Uncle Darrick asked last night over pizza, but then I got that other call, and I was about to go over it with Ryan."

"What did she have to say that rattled you so much? I can hear it in your voice without even seeing your face."

"She told me that she thinks they completely changed history."

"Oh, is that all?"

"I'm not kidding."

"Sorry. What did she say, exactly?"

"She said that Joe spent a few days in jail talking to a man named David Herold. He supposedly was part of an original plot to assassinate President Lincoln with another man named John Wilkes Booth. Booth shot the President at the theater where the kidnapping attempt took place where Mrs. Lincoln hit the guy repeatedly for trying to pull Lincoln out of their carriage after the play. The newspapers made a big fuss over a wife protecting her husband and made Lincoln look weak for a while. Anyway, Becky says that's not how history is supposed to play out and that the fact that we have such strict segregation laws on the books still is because of what they did."

"Great! Here we go again, making a muck of things with that machine. Sometimes I wish we had never found that formula and started all of this!"

"I might be starting to agree with you. I mean we've talked about it, how you can change history without realizing it by such simple things. In this case, Joe talking to some guy about the evils of slavery changed his mind, which changed someone else's mind and changed the Presidents for the next hundred years."

"And let me guess, she wants to fix it, right?"

"That's what she said, but I got her to promise they wouldn't do anything silly and would not go back in the machine where they could meet themselves until we all talked on Saturday."

"They can't go back to the same place. Not only would that mean they might meet themselves, but even if they don't do that, they would be in the same space and time as another version of themselves. You all told me that was bad—really bad."

"Yeah, it was bad. I doubt they will do anything silly. I'm just not sure what we can do. Even the machine had issues when it was somewhere twice."

"Yeah, we've talked about that. Even though this whole weekend has turned into a blur me."

"If we have to fix this, someone other than the three of them has to go back there and stop Joe from getting into trouble."

"Shouldn't we just leave things alone? I mean, I don't know about you, but I've learned that we have to take life as it comes. The good and the bad. The only good thing that has come out of that machine is that we're all closer. Otherwise, maybe it was a crutch to help us deal with our parents' deaths, but we can't cheat death, and we can't substantially change a person's life, but we can sure mess things up."

"You know, if Becky is right about the changes they brought about, they did change peoples' lives. A lot. But I get what you're saying. We do have to look at the good and bad and consider them lessons for life. You can't really enjoy the good, if you don't learn from the bad, right?"

"I'm thinking so. And in my case, knowing what's in store for you doesn't help either."

"Yeah. Speaking of that, how are you doing?"

"Considering we had a crisis right after the breakup, I guess I'm ok. It's weird, but I feel calmer than I have in months. Darrick said something to me last night, that maybe this is how it's supposed to be. I don't know. I miss Mary a lot, but she's so hung up on one possible future that she's missing out on the present, and I can't win that race. I can't prove to her that I'll love her no matter what until we reach the end, and then I've spent my life trying to live up to something and never enjoyed a moment of it while it was happening."

"No way to count your blessings in that scenario. It makes me sad that you won't be together, but I get what you mean."

"Well, don't let this end your friendship with her. If you want to be friends with her, I'm ok with it."

"I'm not sure how I feel about that actually. And before I got a chance to think that through, this came up."

"Yeah, the crisis. Well, hey, let's talk tomorrow, ok? I've got a test to study for, but I'll do some thinking on how we might be able to fix what they did. Maybe you can try to come up with something too?"

"I'll try. Sounds good. I'll call you tomorrow after my classes."

"Great, bye."

"Bye."

Deb looked at Ryan as he said, "I got the gist of it. So, Joe talked to some guy, and they basically re-wrote history from the civil war on?"

"It seems that way."

"We're not thinking of trying to go back there to stop this are we?"

"I certainly don't want to try that again. I don't think Ken does either, but we're going to talk it over this weekend I guess."

"I'll see what I can come up with too. How about dinner, I'm starved?"

"Me too, surprisingly."

They left to have some dinner and then finished studying in their respective rooms that night.

The next day, as Deb was walking back to the dorm after class, Ryan ran up to her and said, "I've been looking all over for you. I think I have a way to fix what Joe, Becky, and Kim did without having the machine issues."

"Oh yeah, and what is your plan?"

"We build another machine."

"How is that going to help?"

"Well, if it's another machine, it will have a different energy signature and won't have to wait until after the other machine left to come back to the correct present. Ken and I can go back and find Joe before he gets arrested and stop him."

"Do you think that will work?"

"I think so. I mean, we'll have to ask Mr. Brewster and Joe, but I think it will work."

"Well, I mean, if it works, that will solve one of the problems, right?"

"What's the other problem?"

"Well, the two people in one place and time problem?"

"If Ken and I go, there would be no issue with the same person in the same place issue, dear."

"Why do you need to go with Ken?"

"Because as great as you are, and I mean great, girls were not looked at the same way in the eighteen hundreds remember? Becky said that she could barely function without Joe speaking for her. I think it would just be easier if Ken and I go."

"Maybe. It's not up to just you and I anyway."

"Well, let's at least float the idea to Ken and the others. Would that be ok?"

"Sure."

The next day, Uncle Darrick showed up and took Deb out for dinner again. This time Ryan came with them. They ended up at a small Chinese place near Washington Square, and as they waited for food to arrive, Uncle Darrick dove right back into the discussion of the machine and the time-traveling, "I have a few more questions, Deb. But before I ask them, I'd like to hear what you think you've all learned from the time-traveling you've done."

"I'm not sure where to start. Is there something you're thinking that we should have learned?" Deb asked.

"No, I'm just wondering what a small group of very smart teens came up with after seven trips in the machine."

"I can tell you that what I've learned is that the machine is powerful but dangerous," Ryan said.

"What do you mean by that?" Uncle Darrick asked.

"Well, we've seen that we can change things, change lives and history. Deb spent forty-five minutes with Mr. Brewster's wife and kept her from being in a car accident. They had a child, and Mr. Brewster became a teacher after working on the nuclear weapons testing in Las Vegas. We shifted the lives of Deb's parents as well. But there is a danger too. A danger that you might make a change you're not aware of or change something and make it worse," Ryan answered.

"I think I learned that every moment is special. Some tiny thing can happen today that seems inconsequential, but it has the power to change your life. I mean look at what Ryan said. I talked to Mrs. Brewster about nothing important and changed her life. But I also researched and found that our departure sparked a renewed conspiracy theory in Las Vegas that the testing was like a beacon for aliens. People started getting closer to testing. Someone actually died trying to break in and be close to where the testing was being done. The military went after them and someone was shot. So, you never know. On that trip, we saved Mrs. Brewster, but someone else died that likely wouldn't have if they hadn't seen the flash of light we made when the machine started up," Deb said, somewhat solemnly.

"I see things differently now, I think. I look at my relationships differently, like with Deb and Joe, and even my parents. I look at them as more important. Events can change, like Deb said, so what really matters is the relationships. It's made me way more patient with my mother, I think," Ryan said.

"It's strengthened my faith too. I mean, we did find this way to change things, go to a place and change events and history, but there is always a force underlying everything. This force of God that steers our lives, guards us. If you listen, and you allow yourself to see His presence in events, people, and relationships you know this," Deb added.

"Guards you how?" Ryan asked.

"Well, when we first started, we were looking for a way to bring our parents back. It never fixed that, but nothing worse happened either. I think we were being protected from our grief getting so much worse that we couldn't handle it. Kept us close so we could help each other. It's also, after several tries, taught me that we might be able to shift some things, but when God calls one of us, there isn't anything we can do, even with this powerful tool."

"It makes me very happy that you four are so close. It was always my hope to have a house full of kids. I'm so glad I get to be a part of this family," Uncle Darrick said.

"Yeah, I've learned that you have to trust your family implicitly, even if you don't understand what they're going through or don't agree with them. You have to stand with them," Deb said.

"I've learned a lot about science and math too," Ryan added, laughing.

"Yeah, first hand, we learned that the theories are correct, there is a finite amount of energy in the universe, and if you use a time machine and go somewhere where you already exist, the universe will work to eliminate that extra energy," Deb added, then after a moment, she added, "I've learned a lot about myself too, I think. I mean, where my strength comes from, what I value, and how much my parents gave me."

"What about when you kept secret the trips to fix what Joe did and the trip forward last spring to find out about Mary?" Uncle Darrick asked.

"Well, just like the trips in the machine can have unintended consequences, the best intentions can have unintended consequences too. I learned that even the best intentions don't give you a pass. The ends do not always justify the means. You have to think about the long-range impact of what you do and say, not just the immediate goal," Deb replied.

"Does that mean you regret those trips?" Uncle Darrick followed up.

"I'm not sure. I wanted to fix what Joe did to our parents. It hurt my heart to think that my parents died apart and weren't together in the end. It just felt so wrong. Maybe I used Kim's grief and Ken's struggles as an excuse, and what I really wanted to accomplish was to make me feel better. But, no, I don't think I regret doing it. Maybe I just wish I could have handled it differently," Deb attempted to explain.

"What about the trip for Mary's future?" Uncle Darrick asked.

"I don't know. I might have regretted that trip right away. I remember thinking during the first night that Mr. Brewster and Thomas were gone about the theories of knowing what your future holds. How you stop living your life because you know what's coming and also about self-fulfilling prophecies. I was afraid then, that regardless of what we learned, Mary was going to take it as a pronouncement that she was dying a terrible death. And that's what happened. Unfortunately, along the way, it also hurt Ken."

"But he told me earlier this week that he was calmer than he had been in months. Perhaps it didn't hurt him as much as you thought?" Uncle Darrick pondered.

"I think he's been hurting and getting over that relationship since she first broke up with him right before the end of the year. That's why it doesn't bother him as much now," Ryan added.

"True, Ryan. He's been processing this loss for some time now. But have you thought that perhaps they weren't meant to be together beyond last spring," Uncle Darrick reflected out loud?

They were just about finished eating, and Deb asked, "Are there other questions you have? I mean, you said you might have some more."

"I might want to reserve my questions until tomorrow," Uncle Darrick answered.

"Well, then maybe we should bring you up to speed on what's happened," Ryan said.

"What do you mean?" Uncle Darrick asked.

"Becky called me the day after we all got back to our respective homes and told me that she discovered that they really changed something with this trip. Something that she thinks got worse," Deb said.

"I don't feel any different," Uncle Darrick replied.

"Well, you wouldn't because you weren't in the machine. Although you were aware of the trip while it was happening, you never had any idea of what changed because we were so focused on the issue, not what our memories of any one historical event was. Your reality just shifts. Those in the machine always remember the old and new timeline, and those that are aware of the trip, but not in the machine, hold the old and new timeline for a very short time. But then they also start to forget the old timeline, and the new history takes over," Ryan explained.

"I see. What do they think they changed?" Uncle Darrick asked.

"While Joe was in jail in eighteen fifty-three, he shared a cell with a man named David Herold. David Herold was part of the original plot to kill Lincoln. Joe talked to this guy and convinced him that slavery was bad, the premise for the war was bad, and the south had to relent on slavery. That trickled into this guy's timeline, and he convinced his friend, John Wilkes Booth, not to shoot the president. Mr. Booth instead tried to kidnap the president to force a better treaty for the south at the end of the war, but Mrs. Lincoln beat him off with her umbrella. This changed Lincoln's second term—actually, gave him a second term—which changed all the presidents after that and created a new timeline where racial tension escalated into the segregation laws we know today. There was a civil rights movement in the old timeline, and laws changed in the sixties to prevent discrimination and segregation. We don't have any of that now," Deb summarized from her conversations with Becky.

"Becky understands a completely different twentieth century, doesn't she?" Uncle Darrick asked.

"Yes. And it's all because Joe spent a few days talking with a guy in a jail cell," Deb answered.

"Does she know a whole different set of presidents and events?" Uncle Darrick asked.

"She knows both the old and new timelines because she was in the machine. We don't remember any of the old because we weren't with them," Ryan reiterated.

"Wow, that's so hard to grasp. That a whole different history sprung out a few conversations," Uncle Darrick thought out loud.

"Yeah, and Becky wants to try to come up with a solution to set it back to what she knows of the original timeline," Deb added.

"How would you do that?" Uncle Darrick asked.

"Well, the easiest way is to go back to where they were and stop Joe from being arrested so he doesn't spend any time with this guy, and hopefully, it totally resets things," Ryan said.

"But we're going to discuss all that tomorrow when we're all together," Deb said.

"Does Ken know about this?" Uncle Darrick asked.

"Yeah, he's aware," Ryan replied.

"Ok, well are you both done eating? I was thinking perhaps it would be easier if you both came back to the apartment. We can then leave first thing to grab Ken and go out to Choate," Uncle Darrick said as he paid the waitress for their dinner.

They agreed and all went to spend the night at the apartment. Aunt Alicia was not due back until a week later as she had to fly directly from the conference she was at to Paris for a fashion event. *That was fortunate,* Deb thought as she drifted off to sleep, as they didn't need to tell anybody else about this machine.

14

AS THEY DIGESTED ALL that Joe, Becky, and Kim told them about their trip, what the machine printouts showed, and all the documentation that Becky had done about the old and new timelines, the barn was quiet except for the occasional bird chirping in the rafters. Around the table were Mr. Brewster, Uncle Darrick, Ken, Deb, Ryan, Joe, Becky, and Kim.

After what seemed like hours, Kim said, "I feel bad for all the people that died and were hurt by the changes we created. All I wanted to do was help and do some good for slaves."

Ken, who always jumped to his baby sister's defense, replied, "Kim, no one thinks you did something wrong here. We know you were just trying to find a way to be helpful to others."

"I wanted to fit into this family."

"I thought we covered this the other day, Kim?" Uncle Darrick asked.

"I mean, we did cover it, but I still probably feel the same way. All my brothers and my sister are doing great things, and then there's me. Little baby sister, Kim. I wanted to do something that would make everyone proud of me."

"Oh, Kim. You are such an important part of this family. Who keeps us honest with each other? Who picks just the right moment to ground us with one of your insightful thoughts or ideas?" Deb said, smiling at her sister.

"And, by the way, you have navigated every single trip we've made with this machine. You picked the places, remember?" Joe said.

"It's not the same, and you all know it. I wanted to be something great like all of you," Kim said as she looked down at her lap.

Ken walked over and put his arm around Kim and whispered in her ear, "Kimmy, without you, none of us would be together. You're the glue that holds this family together. And some day, very soon, you are going to change the world with your sensitive, smart soul."

Kim smiled up at Ken as Mr. Brewster added, "Kim, as the youngest in my family, I know exactly what you mean. As your siblings grow up and move on to their adult lives and start to accomplish things, you want so much to belong and be where they are. You have to remember, they had to grow up to get to those accomplishments—and you do too. Also, you have the best set of cheerleaders for when you get to your accomplishments. Who could ask for anything more?"

"Yeah. Kim, I promise I will be there for every gallery opening of your artwork, every speaking engagement you ever have, or whatever thing you do that the world takes notice of," Joe said, "'cause you're the only reason I made it through that first press conference. You smiling up at me at that podium was the only thing that kept me from stuttering and running away."

Kim smiled at Joe as she asked, "I never knew I did that, why didn't you tell me?"

"I don't know. But I'm learning that we should be good to our family. You never know what might happen."

"Ok, but what about the people we hurt by this trip? What are we going to do? I mean, we have to fix it, right?" Kim asked, looking around the table.

"Back to business then?" Mr. Brewster asked.

"Yes, I'm better now," Kim replied.

"Then, let's hear from Ryan because he thinks he came up with something," Deb said.

"Ok, so as I see it," Ryan started," we have two issues. First, we can't have anyone meet themselves. That means that Joe, Becky, and Kim can't go back to change back what they altered. Second, we don't want to send anyone else there and force them to stay until after the first machine leaves. We learned this lesson when Deb and I went back to Cambridge last year to stop Joe. We couldn't get the machine to take off until Joe's had left because the machine somehow knew of the other version's existence and would not return us to the correct presence."

"Yes, we haven't been able to explain that. In fact, we have no good theories why an inanimate object can't exist in the same space and time, so the only answer can be the energy the machine creates to move through time. That has to be why one version of the machine must be gone for the other version to start to move." Joe added.

"What if it were a completely different machine? Joe, would that change the signature of the new machine and thereby allow it to return to the correct present even if the other machine was still there?" Ryan asked.

"But would the energy signature created in the exact same way in the new machine have a different signature? I know we talked about this last week when we thought we were going to have to build a machine to rescue Joe, Becky, and Kim, but when I thought about it later, I wasn't sure it would work," Ken asked.

"This might be a dumb question, but how can we even tell what the machine's energy signature is?" Deb asked.

"Let's start with Deb's question since that seems to be a basis for the others. In nuclear science, there is an energy signature created by the destruction of particles when fission occurs. It's measured by a spectrometer, and it's looking for the radioisotopes. However, I'm not certain you create any isotopes when you generate the energy field for the machine. That would mean a nuclear explosion is taking place, and we know that isn't how the machine works," Mr. Brewster explained.

"But doesn't the spectrometer measure other particles as well?" Becky asked.

"Yes, Becky, it does," Mr. Brewster answered.

"Could we build just the part of the machine that generates the energy and get one of those spectrometer things and measure both the original machine and the parts of the new machine and see?" Ryan asked.

"It's not quite that simple, Ryan. We can't just put the part of the machine that generates the magnetic field in the middle of this table and start it up. We have to give it some parameters and boundaries. Otherwise, the whole barn would be inside the magnetic field and that would probably not turn out too well," Joe said.

"Couldn't we build some kind of box and mount the parts that generate the field, like the machine has without the whole machine being built to test this out?" Ken asked.

"Yes, that should provide adequate means for a test," Mr. Brewster said while he rubbed his chin as he often did when he was thinking.

"What about this spectrometer? How do we get one of those, Mr. Brewster?" Kim asked.

"Well, we can make one of those as well. It can be contained in a couple of boxes. But we likely will have to dismantle the machine and put it on a smaller box, perhaps inside plexiglass or something to run the test," Mr. Brewster explained.

"So, are we doing this?" Ryan asked.

"I think we can do this. I probably have most of what we need here in this barn," Mr. Brewster said.

"There's a bunch of old metal in the shed where we have brought the machine back to a few times. Can we use some of that, Mr. Brewster?" Becky asked.

"We might need it," Joe replied.

"We can't exactly lug a bunch of metal around campus though. How do you propose to get it over here?" Ken asked.

"The pastor at my church has an old flatbed truck. I'll give him a call and ask if I can borrow it. We can wait until just after dark and go over there and see what we can use," Mr. Brewster replied as he stood up to go into the house to make the call. "While I do that, Joe, why don't you, Ken, and Ryan see about dismantling the parts of the machine we will need, and let's try to construct some tables to set this all on here in the barn."

The kids started to get up from the table, and when Uncle Darrick didn't move, but just looked around at them, Deb asked, "Are you ok, Uncle Darrick?"

"Just amazed, is all."

"About what?"

"All of you. You just come up with solutions to this big problem and go to work. It's amazing to watch."

"Want to help?" Joe asked.

"Sure, what can I do?"

"We're going to need two tables, probably about six feet long and about four or five feet wide. We're going to need some boards for that. Mr. Brewster keeps the wood up the stairs there in the loft of the barn. Can you and Ryan maybe go up there and see what you can find?" Joe asked.

"Sure," Uncle Darrick replied as he stood up.

For a short period of time, there was a bit of a flurry going on in the barn. Ken and Mr. Brewster left to get the truck, while Ryan, Joe, and Uncle Darrick built two large tables to set the field generating parts of the machine on. They built a separate table to put the spectrometer on as well. When Ken and Mr. Brewster got back, they also had several large sheets of plexiglass that the church had in their basement. The pastor was excited to get them out of the way after Ken explained they were doing some experiments at Mr. Brewster's house. So, all that afternoon, they worked to set up the tables, the plexiglass, and got the machine dismantled enough to have the field generating parts off. Deb and Uncle Darrick left late in the afternoon to go and get pizza to bring back to the barn, and while they were away, Ken and Joe started constructing the second field generating parts.

After they all ate and cleaned up from dinner, Ken and Mr. Brewster took the flatbed truck over to the shed and pulled a bunch of metal and old parts and put them on the flatbed. They brought it all back to the barn and unloaded it. Deb noted at that point that it was getting late, and Joe, Becky, and Kim needed to get back to the dorms. As they walked toward campus, Ken, Deb, Ryan, and Uncle Darrick decided to stay in town, and they headed off to the hotel for the night.

On Sunday, after church, they all gathered again at the barn. Kim and Becky worked on homework because they had assignments to finish, but Ryan, Ken, and Joe worked with Mr. Brewster and Uncle Darrick on the final steps to dismantle and prepare the machine's field generating parts for the testing. They also built the spectrometer and cut and prepared the box of plexiglass to put around the machine's parts. While that was going on, Deb was reviewing the notes that Becky and Kim had written up of all the details of their trip. She occasionally asked the girls questions and took some more notes.

When they took a break for lunch, Deb went with Mr. Brewster to prepare sandwiches for everyone, and they sat around the table in the barn and ate. Deb said she thought she had a plan for when and how to intercept Joe.

"What's the plan?" Ryan asked.

"Well, as you suggested, Ryan, I think it would be a good idea for you and Ken to make this trip. You will have the least problems getting around and talking to people as Becky has noted that women didn't generally have that freedom and were thought very forward if they tried."

"That was the part that caused us trouble when Joe was in jail. We had to get Mr. Purvis and the Fairchilds to help with everything. I wasn't even going to be able to get money from the bank if Mr. Purvis hadn't gone with us and explained the situation to the bank manager," Becky explained.

"Remember, this was before the suffrage movement and before almost all of the women's rights changes. Women were still under a man's protection—either their father's or their husband's," Deb added.

"Yeah, it was also very formal. Everyone was miss or ma'am or sir and full formal names and stuff," Kim said, curling up her nose.

"Ok, so Ryan and I will go. What else is in your plan, Deb?" Ken asked.

"I think it would be wise to land the other machine near the first one, but then you'll need to get to Philadelphia. Joe, was there any other boat or anything on that island?"

"There was another boat, but it was smaller, more like a canoe, and I knew I couldn't manage Becky and Kim and our stuff in that. They had long dresses on and everything."

"It should be fine for Ken and Ryan, though, right?"

"Sure. But I think they're going to need to land a little north of the harbor where we left our boat. There just isn't a place they can row up to there, but a little north, there was a place where there seemed to be a walkway to the water."

"I can draw that on the map we made, if you want?" Kim said.

"That would be really helpful, Kim," Ryan replied.

"I think it will be best if you plan to arrive the morning of the demonstration. Then make your way to just outside the hotel where they stayed and pull Joe aside before he leaves with Henry Bennett. Then, once you have explained to Joe why you're there and keep him from that demonstration, then you, Ken, and Ryan can just come back. Joe, Becky, and Kim can do what they went to do—help the fugitive slaves—and they can be back here the night they arrived back here. Joe, I think it's best to not redo your present return any more than you have to."

"I agree," Joe said.

"That would give us time to help that nice lady and her kids, wouldn't it?" Kim asked.

"Yes, I know you really wanted to help some people, Kim, and I think this solves the real problem, correcting the history of Lincoln, and the other people and presidents, while allowing you to finish what you planned," Deb replied.

Kim got up and went over to Deb and hugged her. She whispered into her ear, "Thank you."

"All of this works, so long as our test here shows that a new machine will have a different energy signature to the original. And, of course, we'll have to build a whole new machine," Ryan said, trying to temper Kim's excitement in case they couldn't figure the machine issue out.

With that, they all got back to work. Deb was finalizing some notes at the table when Kim walked over to her from where she had been working on homework.

"Are you mad at me?" Kim asked.

"No, Kimmy, I'm not mad. I know you were trying to help people, and I know you just want to fit in, but, honey, you'll always fit in this family. We need you."

"I just wanted to do something great."

"I know. But I also know that your greatest accomplishment is yet to come. Please stop worrying about this, Kim. You have your whole life to find your place and make your mark."

"It's really hard being the youngest."

"I bet it is. But here's the thing. You guys went into the machine, did what you thought was right, and tried to help people, but something happened. You impacted hundreds of people's lives. And probably not always for the good. We have to finally learn this lesson about the machine. It's powerful and dangerous. And I'm learning that just because we can, it doesn't really mean we should."

"I don't understand why it seems to turn out like this every time we use the machine."

"I know. The only trip that worked out was the one where you and I talked to Mrs. Brewster."

"Every other time, we made it worse, not better."

"Yeah. I'm starting to realize that you have to take the loss, the bad, with the good. I think we might not even be able to see the good without the bad. The other day, Uncle Darrick asked me what we learned from the machine. I was thinking a lot about that lately. Losing our parents, Mr. Brewster losing his wife to cancer, Mary's grandmother, they're all things we wish we didn't have to go through, but I wonder, would we appreciate the days we got to play on the beach, or your party in the city for your birthday, or the cool things you made us all these past years for our birthdays, without those bad things?"

"Maybe God plans it that way. Maybe we have the bad so we can count our blessings when they happen."

"Yeah, maybe. I think it might be more though. I think we need the bad to learn not just to appreciate the good but to learn about ourselves, our place in the family, and in the world."

"I wish Mom was here right now."

"Me too, Kim, me too. Remember how she smiled so big when one of us did something? Got an "A" on a test, learned to play the violin, or scored a touchdown in the game. That look... that's why I tried so hard. I wanted to see her proud of me."

"I think she is proud of us, Deb. I think she sees what we're doing."

"Yeah?"

"Right now, she has that look. We're all here, working together, solving a problem. She has that look."

"See, Kimmy, you already made your mark on this world. Our family needs you."

"Thanks."

At about that moment, Becky announced that she had to go meet some kids from her history class for a presentation they had to finish. Joe announced that he had some homework to finish, and Uncle Darrick chimed in saying that the college kids probably needed to get back as well. They cleaned up the barn and made plans for Joe to work with Mr. Brewster to build another version of the machine's field generating parts during that week. Ken said he would be back the next weekend, and Uncle Darrick said he'd also like to be there, so he would get Ryan and Deb and meet everyone out there. They agreed to meet the next Saturday morning as everyone departed to head back.

As Mr. Brewster closed up the barn and headed back to his house, he heard his phone ringing. He rushed into the kitchen and lifted up the receiver and said, "Hello?"

"Hi, Dad. It's Thomas. How're you doing?"

"Oh, I'm fine, Thomas. How are you and Brittany doing?"

"We're doing ok. You sound winded. Did I catch you at a bad time?"

"No, no. I was just heading in from the barn."

"Working on that old car again?"

"No, the kids were all here. We're working on something with the machine."

"What's going on?"

"Well, it's a long story. The short version is that Joe, Becky, and Kim went on a trip and inadvertently caused a pretty big shift in history. The kids want to correct that, but given what happened when they tried to correct Joe's mess a year ago from that other trip, they are exploring some options to avoid the universal truths they continue to run up against."

"What truths?"

"Well, finite energy in the universe, a space and time continuum that will not allow you to be the same space twice, nothing too tough!"

"That sounds pretty tough, Dad. But, with Joe on the case, maybe not."

"This time it appears Ryan is going to be the brilliant mind. He has come up with an idea that might work."

"What idea was that?"

"Well, we are testing the energy signature of the machine to see if we can create a separate signature. Then we can manage having the machine in the same place twice."

"Why does the universe care about an inanimate object?"

"It's the energy, not the metal, I think."

"I guess so. So how are your students this semester?"

"Good, good. And how is your residency going?"

"It's tough. Long hours and grueling work, but I love it."

"Well, that's good."

"So, listen, Dad, Brittany and I were thinking about driving out for a visit. Would that be ok?"

"Of course! I love having you here, and having Brittany is a bonus. When were you thinking of coming out?"

"Well, next weekend if that's ok? We discovered that we have both Saturday and Sunday off from our respective work."

"Well, sure. But the kids will all be here next weekend. Would that be a problem?"

"Not at all. I would love to see what they're coming up with."

"Ok, then I guess I'll see you next weekend."

"Sounds good, Dad. We're going to leave Friday after work so we should be there around eight or eight-thirty Friday night."

"Drive careful then, and I'll see you Friday night."

Mr. Brewster went to sleep that night happy. The kids were all there, and they were working on something, and his son was coming for a visit. He looked over at the picture of his wife holding Thomas as a baby and said, "You'd be so proud of him, dear. He's going to be a doctor and change the world!" As he drifted off to sleep, he had a bit of an epiphany. They didn't need two machines, did they.

15

ALL THAT WEEK, JOE and Mr. Brewster worked on creating new parts for the field generation process of the machine. Becky and Kim spent the week closer to campus due to class projects—and because their absences over the past two weekends when they made the trip, along with this past weekend that they spent in Mr. Brewster's barn, were beginning to raise some questions. Mr. Brewster proposed to Joe that rather than build a whole new machine, if the test proved that the energy signature was different between the two sets of parts, they could simply strap on the new parts to the original machine and use it for Ryan and Ken's trip. Joe thought it was a good idea and would definitely save time, however, he wasn't sure that the test was going to show different energy signatures. They had decided to build the new set of parts exactly as the old ones were built in an effort to ensure the test was valid.

The next Saturday morning, they were all gathered in the barn again. Everyone was excited to see Thomas and Brittany. They introduced them both to Uncle Darrick and visited for a while. Finally, Thomas asked, "I may be way out of line, but does Mr. Reynolds know what's going on here? I mean, does he know about what you and we have done?"

"Yes, we told him. Well, we had to tell him when Joe, Kim, and Becky didn't get back on time a couple of weeks ago from the trip they made in the machine. We needed a guardian to cover for them with Choate," Deb explained.

"I see."

"I'm over the shock of it all, Thomas, but still a little amazed at what you all have done. I understand you made a trip in that thing as well?" Uncle Darrick said.

"Yes, with my dad last spring. It was quite an adventure."

"I bet."

"I was shocked too, when Thomas told me, Mr. Reynolds, but for some reason, it settled in ok—and pretty quickly. I'm not certain why that is, but I seem to trust and believe them all," Brittany added.

"Anyway, on to the business of today," Uncle Darrick said.

Joe outlined the idea that Mr. Brewster came up with, and they discussed the actual test they were going to conduct. When everyone was ready, Joe started up the old field generation parts, and Mr. Brewster manned the spectrometer. They let the field generation begin and get to the point that it would require the entry of the navigational data. Mr. Brewster recorded the energy signature in both photo and numerical values. Then, they shut down the first set of parts and did the same thing to the new set of parts.

As they sat back down at the table, Uncle Darrick was the first to speak, "Wow, that was really cool to watch, Joe. I'm amazed at all you've done here!"

"Thanks, but it wasn't just me. This was actually Ryan's idea, and everyone helped—even you."

"I don't know how much I helped, but I meant all of you. Working together and figuring this all out."

"Well, let's have a look at the data, shall we?" Mr. Brewster said as he brought the photos and numerical listings over to the table.

"It looks obvious to me. They're definitely different. But, maybe, Mr. Brewster, you should explain what we're looking at," Ken said.

"Well, the photos are actually the exposed film of the spectrometer showing the distribution of light waves from each of the field generators. They are definitely different in their patterns. The numerical listings are a little less obviously different, but they are different, nonetheless. I would say that means the two generators do, in fact, create different energy signatures. Joe?"

"I agree. This was a great test."

"What about what Mr. Brewster suggested? Can we simply put the new parts onto the machine and use it then?" Ryan asked.

"I think so," Joe replied. "I think it would be good to do some testing once the new parts are on, but I don't see why it wouldn't work."

"Let's get started then, shall we?" Mr. Brewster asked.

Uncle Darrick, Joe, Ken, and Ryan started dismantling the test setup. Becky and Deb took the spectrometer and placed it on a side table so that it would not be damaged in all the work, and Mr. Brewster set aside all the testing materials. They had the plexiglass stored near the old car and the table moved that had the old field generator pretty quickly. They then spent the afternoon putting the new parts onto the machine.

While the building was going on, Deb sat at the table confirming details with Becky and Kim as Thomas and Brittany sat listening. When they had finished with the mapping, the navigational data, and reviewing the clothing that Deb had gotten a hold of in New York City that week, Brittany said, "However did you figure out what clothing to get and all this detail?"

"Research. Lots of research," Deb said.

"Yeah, Becky and I spent a couple of days at the library looking all this up. The places, the hotel, the maps, and the people. We plotted out our story and went over it so we wouldn't draw too much attention. We even looked at how people talked and everything," Kim added, excitedly.

"It must have been a great adventure, getting to immerse yourselves into another culture. It's not just reading history, it's living it," Brittany commented.

"That was the fun part, but the hard part was kind of knowing my place as a lady. I almost slipped up a few times. And it got so frustrating when Joe was in jail that no one would just deal with me. I wanted to shout that I had a brain too!" Becky said.

"I guess, we should be glad for the advancements we have in our time, shouldn't we?" Brittany said to no one in particular.

At that point, the building was all done, and the noise stopped. They all agreed to spend the evening away from the barn. Joe, Becky, and Kim went to the school activities at the main hall, Uncle Darrick, Ken, Ryan, and Deb went to have dinner in town, and Mr. Brewster, Thomas, and Brittany went inside to enjoy a family dinner. They agreed to meet the next morning for Ryan and Ken to make their trip.

When Joe, Becky, and Kim got to the main hall, they seemed to be surrounded by friends. "What were you doing all day?" and "Where have you been?" seemed to be all they heard for a few minutes. Joe took charge and said, "Listen, Ken, Deb, and Ryan came into town, and we spent the day with them. That's all. We did some shopping, had lunch, and went to the park and just ran around a bit. It's the first pretty warm day this spring, and they surprised us."

Everyone seemed to accept that, so Amy dragged Kim off to the game table where they were signed up to play some games, while Joe and Becky went to the ping pong table where they were playing matches with their friends.

Meanwhile, Uncle Darrick, Ken, Deb, and Ryan went to the Italian place in town. After they ordered food, Uncle Darrick said, "Ok, it's just the grown-ups now. Ken, tell me how you're doing?"

"Getting busy with studying and preparations for midterms next week."

"I don't think that's what he meant," Deb laughed and punched Ken in the shoulder.

"I know. I'm just not sure what to say. I feel kind of foolish at this point."

"Why foolish?" Uncle Darrick said.

"Well, I spent all last summer aggravated at everyone for keeping a secret, then all fall and into the winter break trying to convince Mary that she was wrong about all of this. I feel foolish 'cause I wasted so much time."

"You loved her, right? That's not wasting time," Ryan offered. "I mean you had to find out if it was for real, right?"

"I guess. But all along I kept telling myself and all of you that 'that's how Mary is, when she makes a decision, she sticks with it.' And never once did I look myself in the eye and say, if that's true, why are you wasting time on this."

"I know she still really loves you. She just has made this decision that she won't waiver on. She somehow believes that loving you means she has to push you away or keep you at arm's length to save you," Deb said, somewhat sorrowfully.

"I spent all this time gathering all this information. I mean, Deb, my research rivaled anything you've done, I think. I had Thomas come to Wellesley and talk with her and did all that, and nothing I said or did or asked her to read made any difference. And then it started to feel like she liked having me come around and treat her with kid gloves and wait on her and give her everything she asked for. It became so one-sided."

"Ken, I know you love her, but you can't live your life with someone that is going to do nothing but take from you and never give you anything," Ryan said emphatically.

"Ryan's right, Ken. Relationships are hard at best, and they require a level of commitment that surpasses anything else I've ever encountered. It's true that sometimes one person may need a lot of attention, a lot of care, but that shouldn't be the rule. You don't want to keep score, or anything, about how much time one of you got to be cared for and treated special, but at the end of the day, everyone has to have a sense of fairness, and when you're feeling like this, that it's so one-sided, you have to evaluate whether or not it's right for you," Uncle Darrick offered.

"Well, that's what I did, and I decided if she wasn't going to be involved in our relationship, if it was going to be so one-sided, then maybe I needed to let her go."

"And now?" Deb asked.

"And now, I'm just enjoying the fact that I'm not worked up all the time and trying to come up with that thing that will break through to her or chasing my tail."

"It helps that we had this little crisis, didn't it?" Ryan asked.

"You bet it did. Gave me something to focus on. And I know, Ryan, your plan was part of it."

The food arrived, and they all ate and laughed and talked about school and what Aunt Alicia was up to. After dinner, they decided to walk through town. Deb took that opportunity to check in with Uncle Darrick. "So, Uncle Darrick, you've been hit with a lot in the last week. How are you doing?"

"Where to start?" he started to reply and then stopped for a minute. "First, let me say that today, Brittany commented about how it was shocking when she heard from Thomas about the time-traveling but then strangely easy to accept, and I guess that sums some of this up for me. It was shocking, but it feels like it didn't take long for it to just seem like something else you all were involved in. I don't know, maybe it was watching you all solve these problems. What happened, what did they change, how to fix it, the energy signature, the testing and everything. Everything seems like a bit of a whirlwind."

"You did take a lot of information in at a very fast pace," Ken added.

"Yes. But in some ways, I'm not at all surprised. You kids have amazed me since I first met you. Granted, you were a little timid when you first showed up at the Hampton house, but I could tell right away that you were all bright, resourceful, and supportive of each other. That came through loud and clear the last two weekends."

"You said Friday night you had some more questions. I didn't hear any of those today," Deb prodded.

"Well, I asked what you had learned because I was wondering what made you abandon trying to get your parents back."

"It didn't work. We kept making it worse. First, by speeding up the date when they died, then when Joe went back on his own, he caused them to separate and die alone but right after one another," Ken said, solemnly.

"But it seemed to work for Mr. Brewster," Uncle Darrick offered as they reached their hotel.

They sat down in the lobby as Deb said, "I've struggled with this quite a bit since last year. I visited with the reverend at the church near Choate a few times, too. What I've come up with is that we can change a lot of things with the time machine. We can shift presidents, events, and people's lives. But what we can't change is when God calls you to heaven. When that part of your plan is set, there isn't anything you can do. Mrs. Brewster was an unintended casualty of a man trying to end his life. When we took her off that road, we took her out of that situation. Her intended end was going to be from that cancer. So, when we changed her timeline, we set it to the correct path. I don't know, maybe correct isn't the right word. I think it's possible for someone to be caught up in someone else's timeline and have their life end unintentionally, but the original plan, God's plan is set in terms of your ending and that maybe is what makes it correct. In our parents' case, all we did was change the circumstances of their deaths with our time travel. Even Joe couldn't change the situation when he simply went to our father and told him we could time travel. We can shift our path, we can leave the path God intended for us, but the end is not really in our control unless we speed it up—like that man that killed himself and took Mrs. Brewster in the original timeline."

"I see. I have to be honest, I'm not sure I buy into that. But I haven't been to church in a decade," Uncle Darrick said.

"Yeah, I didn't buy into it either in the beginning. I mean, I went to church every single weekend, nearly my whole life. Grandpa wouldn't have it any other way, but I questioned it. I mean, I buy into the free will ideas and that I have some control over where I go and how I look at things, but it really is the only explanation that works, Darrick," Ken added.

"Why haven't any of you tried to just go meet people you've read about or famous people from history?" Uncle Darrick asked.

"I'm sure it's because of the original motivation to save our parents and then everything that's happened. We never got around to considering that use of the machine. It's an interesting idea though, isn't it? You could meet all kinds of people and just talk to them. I would want to meet Margaret Mead. And maybe Joan of Arc or Marie Antoinette," Deb replied.

"Yeah, just talk, like Joe did with that guy David Herold. Imagine for a minute that you talked to Joan of Arc, and she decided not to lead the armies in France? I think if we've learned anything from this last trip, it's that anything innocent can change everything we know about history," Ken chided.

"What about something simpler, like your grandfather or someone like that?" Uncle Darrick asked.

"Who knows if that would work. Clearly, you have to be careful who you talk to and about what," Ryan said.

With that, they rose and decided it was time to get some sleep. The next morning, they all again gathered in the barn at Mr. Brewster's. Ryan and Ken changed into the period-appropriate clothing, and they stepped into the machine. The now-familiar wind and noise began, and then there was a flash of light and the machine was gone, leaving Deb and the others sitting around the table.

"If they accomplish the plan, they should be back here in three hours. I think I'm going to head to the library to get a paper started," Joe said.

"I'm going with you. I have a paper to work on too," Becky replied.

"What about you, Kim, do you have homework to finish up?" Deb asked.

'No, I finished all of mine already."

"Well, then why don't we go to the park and walk a bit?" Uncle Darrick asked.

"That sounds like a great idea!" Kim said.

With that, Joe and Becky left for the library, and Deb, Kim, and Uncle Darrick headed off to the park. Mr. Brewster, Thomas, and Brittany went inside so that they could pack up their things. They couldn't stay, and shortly after they finished packing, they said goodbye to Mr. Brewster and left. While Ryan and Ken were off on their time travel journey, Deb, Kim, and Uncle Darrick walked around the paths of the Wharton Brook State Park and then went into town for ice cream.

16

KEN WAS THE FIRST one out of his seat when the machine landed on the island that Joe had programmed for them. He looked out the small window and saw the other machine, sitting there amongst some brush. He looked back at Ryan as he said, "It is so strange being here in the same machine. I can see it sitting right over there."

"Yeah, that was weird when Deb and I went back to Cambridge. How in the world two versions of the same machine can be in the same place? The difference now, of course, is that we have different field generation parts. Hopefully, that works for this trip."

"I guess we'll find out when we get back here later and start ours up, won't we?"

"That's not funny. When it didn't work before, I had to get Joe out of there before Deb and I could leave. I don't want to spend any more time here than we need to."

"Agreed. Let's get going then."

They had to walk to the other side of the island to find a small boat they could use. It was moored up to a makeshift dock, and there was no one around, so they took it. They walked it back around to the other side and then headed down toward the same harbor where Joe stored their small boat. When they got close, Ryan pointed at a place where the river's edge became a shallow embankment with many trees nearby. They pulled up there, tied off the canoe, and walked up the embankment to the street level. They made their way down to the harbor and asked directions to the Girard House. After speaking to the same dock manager that was holding Joe's boat, they headed off toward the hotel where Joe, Becky, and Kim were staying.

It was just after breakfast when they arrived at the hotel. Ken asked the desk attendant if he could speak with Mr. Joseph Fitzgerald. The desk manager said that Mr. Fitzgerald, his fiancé, and his sister had just gone up to their room. He rang for the busboy who presented himself. The manager asked the young man to go to Mr. Fitzgerald's room and tell him he had a guest. He then looked at Ken and asked, "What name should we give Mr. Fitzgerald?"

"I am Mr. Kenneth Fitzgerald. Mr. Fitzgerald's cousin. I've come to join him and his sister in business here."

"Oh, I see. Well, then, Davey, go up and tell Mr. Fitzgerald that his cousin, Mr. Fitzgerald is here."

The busboy went up, and when Joe opened the door, he indicated that his cousin was downstairs. The news surprised Joe, but he recovered quickly and said he would be right down. He then went to Becky and Kim's room and told them what had happened. They all prepared to go downstairs, not certain what they would find and more than a little anxious. Kim even whispered as they were about to go down the stairs that she hoped it wasn't some long-lost relative or they might be in real trouble.

Joe grinned, but then he looked a little alarmed when he saw Ken and Ryan in the lobby. Kim rushed at Ken and hugged him. He lifted her up and said, "My goodness you have grown, my little cousin, Kimberly. It's been far too long since I have set eyes on you!"

Kim laughed a little, and they finished greeting one another. Ryan asked if there was somewhere they could go to talk, and Becky suggested the courtyard behind the hotel. They walked out there and thankfully found it empty. They sat at a wrought iron table and chairs.

"What are you doing here?" Joe asked.

"Please don't say you came to stop us, Kenny. We're helping the fugitive slaves!" Kim said, rather adamantly. Becky reached over and put her hand on Kim's arm and held her other hand up to indicate that Kim should be quiet. Kim looked down and said nothing more.

"Listen, we didn't come here to bring you back. We came to keep Joe from doing something today," Ryan said quietly.

"What are you talking about?" Joe asked.

"Joe, when you get back from this trip, we find out that you were arrested later today for being too close to some protests about a fugitive slave," Ken said.

"What?" Becky asked, incredulously.

"Joe goes to see what the fuss is about with some new friend he's made, and he gets jostled around and ends up getting arrested. You spend the next four or five days in jail. Where you share a cell with David Herold."

"Who is he?" Kim asked.

"He is an old friend of John Wilkes Booth," Ryan replied.

"Oh, my goodness. Joe, he was part of the plot to kill Lincoln!" Becky exclaimed in a whisper.

"Exactly. And while Joe is hold up in that cell, he and his cellmate David spend hours talking about slavery and the south, and good old Joe here turns David into an abolitionist. That changes the history and has a profound impact on civil rights," Ryan added.

"Joe, you can't go near that protest today," Ken said.

"How bad is it?" Becky asked.

"Well, there is institutionalized racism that is accepted in society, and it's pretty bad. If you really want to help the fugitive slaves and help people of this time, you can't go to that protest today," Ken said.

"But do we have to leave?" Kim asked, "We have several appointments this week to help the ladies' group that Becky and I are involved in."

"You don't have to leave. In fact, you should stay until you've been here nine or ten days, like you were on the original trip so you don't mess up things when you get back. We've already covered for you for returning late Monday night and missing school on Tuesday," Ken said.

"So, we can stay here and help the fugitives?" Kim asked hopefully.

"Wait a minute, when did we leave here in the timeline you guys know? We need to know that so we know when to leave," Joe said, with a concerned look on his face.

"You got back early Tuesday morning—like 2 am. Does that help?" Ryan said.

"I'll need to work out the calculations, but we'll figure it out."

"One other thing, while you were in jail, Becky did something with your calculations that set the departure time, so you'll need to get whatever paperwork you have and look that over," Ryan added.

"What did I do?" Becky asked.

"You changed something about the variables related to how far in time you traveled. That gave you leeway to stay another day. Also, Kim told us that you left the day after Joe was released. If we count that out, he was in jail and through the trial in eight days. That means if you can fix the calculations, you can stay for nine more days, counting today," Ryan said.

Ken pulled a couple of folded up pieces of notebook paper out of his jacket pocket and handed them to Joe. "These are notes of Deb's. It should give you all the information you need to be sure you change the calculations and come back at the right time."

"Ok, we'll look at it this afternoon," Joe said.

"What about my question? Does this mean you're not going to want us to go back now?" Kim asked pleadingly.

"Yeah, you can stay, Kim. In fact, it will be better if you do. Ryan and I are going to head back right away, but you guys can stay here."

"Did you want to see a little of Philadelphia or anything before you leave?" Becky asked.

"I don't think that's a good idea. The idea today is for you all to stay out of the fray," Ryan said.

"Well, we did get an invitation to go to the Fairchilds' for luncheon. Perhaps we should do that, and then Joe wouldn't be where he was supposed to be," Becky mused.

"That's a great idea. Now, Ryan and I are going to head back."

They all got up and walked back through the lobby. Ken understood that he was leaving them to be here for a few more days, so he made a show of saying goodbye and reflecting that he would be returning in a week or so, once he concluded his business in Virginia. The desk manager seemed to be paying some attention and nodded to Ken and Ryan as they left. Becky had gone up right away and prepared a note to be sent to Mrs. Fairchild. She asked the desk manager right after Ken and Ryan left to get it delivered to Mrs. Fairchild.

Ken and Ryan walked back to the harbor, made their way to the embankment, and retrieved their little boat. They rowed back to the island, returned the boat to where they found it, and made their way to the machine. They set the programming to return them to the barn and fired it up. As the noise started, Ryan held up both of his hands with his fingers crossed, as he said, "Well, here goes nothing... Hope this works!"

A few seconds later, the machine powered down, and they opened the door. There, at the table, sat Mr. Brewster, Joe, Becky, Deb, Kim, and

Uncle Darrick. The boys sat down, and Ken asked, "Did it work? Did we fix things?"

"Well, I don't think Joe was arrested, if that's what you mean. At least it doesn't seem like he was," Becky said.

"That and all the history we changed," Ryan added.

"It appears so. I mean I still have a memory of the adjusted timeline, and the history books don't have any of the newly adjusted timeline yet. However, if the pattern holds true, we should wake up tomorrow with no memory of the old timeline that Joe, Becky, and Kim originally adjusted, and the books should all be changed, but I'm not sure what Ken and Ryan are going to remember. Or, for that matter, what Joe, Becky, and Kim will remember," Deb commented.

"Well, if the process of the other trips holds true, Becky, Kim, and I will have a memory of the first timeline, the adjusted, and the new, corrected one from today for a day or so. The rest of you should only know the adjusted and this new timeline," Joe thought aloud.

"I don't know about you, Ken, but confession time, I don't know history well enough to remember any of the old or new facts!" Ryan said.

"I don't understand. I have a vague memory of what you told me was your original timeline of history, I know what the history should be, that you say is the adjusted timeline, and you're saying that tomorrow I will have some intermingled memories of a new timeline. How is that possible?" Uncle Darrick asked.

"It's a part of time travel that we don't really understand, Uncle Darrick. See the people that travel and the people that help the planning of the travel, seem to have the old timeline and the new for a short period, and then the old timeline starts to fade away after a day or so. People that didn't know about the time travel, like when Ken didn't know that we went to Cambridge last year, they only know the new timeline from when they wake up the day we return. So, no one outside of this room, and Thomas and Brittany, will know that there was a different timeline at all. The one that they now know is the only one they will know. You didn't travel in the machine, so you only know the timeline we messed up and the one that we corrected with Ryan and Ken's trip. But, by tomorrow or the next day, you will start to lose any memories of the messed-up timeline and only know the new, corrected one," Deb tried to explain.

"But Becky, Kim, and I retain most of the memories of all three for some period of time," Joe added.

"Because you made the original trip?" Uncle Darrick asked.

"Yes."

"Will our correction completely reset everything?" Ryan asked.

"We'll have to wait to see," Becky said.

"That's nerve-wracking, isn't it?" Uncle Darrick asked.

"Yes!" Joe and Deb answered.

"Let's hope so," Ken said, "but now it's late on Sunday, and we need to get everyone back where they belong."

"Agreed," Mr. Brewster said. "We could all use a few days of normal, I think."

With that, Joe ran the printouts from the machine, and they all prepared to leave. Ken drove Joe, Becky, and Kim back to campus, and Uncle Darrick left with Ryan and Deb to get back to New York.

On the drive back, Uncle Darrick asked many questions about the idea of meeting people and how to prevent changing too much. Deb and Ryan answered him as best they could, but Deb was beginning to think Uncle Darrick's questions were hitting closer and closer to home. She said something to Ryan that night while they studied in her room, and he suggested that they wait until mid-terms were over to bring this up with Uncle Darrick. Deb agreed and forgot about it in preparation for tests.

Deb noted when they got home that night that she had several messages from Mary, but she was so far behind on preparing for mid-terms because of the flurry of events at Choate that she didn't even call Mary back until the end of that week.

The next day, Deb woke up and first thing, went to her neighbor's room because she had a US history class. She asked to look at her textbook and went directly the chapters on the Civil War. She scanned through it all and saw that it was as Becky said the original timeline was. She ran back to her room and called the girls' dorm at Choate and asked for Becky.

When Becky got to the phone, Deb said, "Sorry to call in the morning, but I just checked a textbook on history and everything seems to match what you told me. What do you think?"

"It mostly looks right. I think. It seems like I recall one or two things that are different. The abolitionists from Philadelphia were more open about their opposition to slavery sooner, and they actually refused to support the fugitive slave act as of late 1853. It seems to have changed Lincoln's mind about the purpose of the war sooner because of the pleadings from influential people from Philadelphia, like Mr. Purvis and the Fairchilds. But everything else happened as it was supposed to. The assassination, reconstruction, and the presidents are all back to the original timeline," Becky answered.

17

WHILE ALL THE ACTIVITY was going on with the Fitzgeralds and their friends over two weeks, Mary was still reeling from Ken saying goodbye. She struggled to make it to classes and barely completed homework. She told her parents she just wasn't feeling well. She couldn't bring herself to tell them she and Ken broke up for good. While Ken was off in the machine over the weekend, Mary was lying in bed. She didn't get up to eat or anything.

Ashley found her that way when she got back from the library Saturday. She'd left for breakfast, which Mary said she wasn't hungry for, and told her she would be at the library until after lunch. She found Mary in the same place.

"Mary, what are you doing? Or more specifically, what are you not doing today that you should be doing?" Ashley asked.

"I don't feel good. I just want to lie here all day. Is that such a big deal?"

"It's not a big deal, if you were really sick. You've barely been out of that bed to attend class and do homework for almost two weeks now. And who knows how long it's been since you actually showered and brushed your teeth. It's getting pathetic."

"You don't understand."

"I may not know what's it like to have a terrific guy begging me to take him back for months, but I sure understand one important thing that you can't seem to see at all."

"And what's that?"

"You have convinced yourself that you're going to die from cancer, and you've already stopped living in anticipation of that event."

"That's not entirely true!"

"Oh yes, it is. Don't you see? Ken has brought you all kinds of research and all kinds of resources that show that the medical field is making huge strides in breast cancer research. And, I might add, he's made a more than convincing argument that you can't live your life under a blanket waiting for some possible bad thing to happen to you. I know it's scary thinking that you might have what your grandmother had. But, Mary, you know it might happen. You can see the right doctors and get checkups and get diagnosed early enough where you have a chance your grandmother never had."

"It's not that simple."

"Yes, Mary, it is. And how is this any different from when you talked to the other floor girls about preparing for tests and acing classes. Do you even remember what you said? The more you know in the beginning of what is expected, the more you can prepare. Just pace yourself, do the preparation, and it will be fine."

"This is not the same."

"Why not? If you know in the beginning there is a chance you have cancer, prepare. Read, see doctors, get tests, and be prepared."

"You sound just like Ken."

"Well, I always liked him. Now I know why. He's smart, like me."

"Very funny."

"I say, enough of all of this. Get your behind out of bed, take a shower, and call Ken and see if there is some way to win him back. Stop waiting in misery for this mystical future calamity."

"I'm afraid."

"Yeah, I believe that. But you do understand, don't you, that some of your fear is facing this without Ken. You pushed him away, and now you're facing all this uncertainty alone."

"I did all that pushing so he wouldn't have to take care of me or watch me get sick."

"That's a load of baloney. He loves you, and I know for a fact that he doesn't care if you might get sick. He didn't care what the future held as long as he was with you, and you threw that away."

"I wanted him to have a better life."

"You just wanted to be the center of attention, is what I think. I'm done dancing around this, Mary. You treated Ken badly. He was always doing exactly what you wanted and giving you anything you asked. That's not a loving relationship, that's a selfish one. You were being selfish!"

"No, I wasn't!"

"Yes, you were!"

With that Ashley stormed out of the room, leaving Mary with her thoughts. Mary lay there for probably another hour thinking about what Ashley, Deb, Ken, Thomas, and Brittany had said to her over the past few months. She began to see that perhaps they had all been right. She got out of bed, took a shower, and sat down to finish her homework while she pondered it all a little more. By the time she was finished, she had decided that Ashley and Deb probably were right, and she had handled this badly. Just as she was about to go and call Deb, Ashley returned.

"You're up. What's the occasion?"

"I thought about what you said, and I decided you might be a little right."

"Only a little right?"

Mary tentatively smiled a little as she said, "Well, maybe a little more than a little right."

"Finally! How about leaving this room for dinner?"

"Yeah, I could use some normal food, I guess."

Mary got up, put shoes on, and they left to go to the dining hall to get dinner. As they walked, they talked more.

"So, what changed your mind? I mean, I don't think I said anything different or magical or anything?"

"I don't know. I'm miserable, that's for sure. I thought my feelings were about the fact that I might end up sick and not get to do all the things I want to do, but it's probably more about the fact that I've ruined my life already by pushing Ken away, being terrible to my friends, and basically putting my life on pause."

"Well, they say the first step is acknowledgment, so you've taken the first step. Now, to analyze what you did, what you were feeling, and what made you do the things you did. Then we figure out how to fix what you did and change your process so you don't make the same mistakes."

"Your classwork, miss future psychologist, is paying off."

"Not funny."

"Sorry."

"Well, then, start talking, sister."

They walked into the dining hall, got food, and found a table before Mary started talking.

"I was scared. Really, really scared, and I didn't want Ken to see me as sick as my grandma was. It was the worst thing I've had to do so far in my life. Seeing my grandmother shocked me. She was so thin, looked so pale, and had all kinds of tubes and lines and stuff connected to her. And then when I heard that I could maybe get this cancer, I freaked out. I didn't want to end up looking like that."

"Mary, I know it was scary seeing her like that. I've been through the same kind of scenario. My grandfather got sick when he was in the nursing home, and they took him to the hospital in an ambulance. He was hooked up to a ventilator and all kinds of things. It was pretty awful seeing him like that. But, you know, that image does fade with time."

"I hope so. Every time I close my eyes, I see that, and then I imagine it being me in that bed, and I'm instantly scared to death."

"Yeah, that would be scary."

"If that was my fate, I needed to push everyone away. That way no one would see me like that. I mean, I imagined my hair all stringy and my skin looking all splotchy and wrinkled and not wearing anything good, just a terrible hospital gown."

"Oh, Mary. You got so immobilized by fear, you pushed friends and Ken away because you were afraid you were going to lose your looks?"

"Not just that, but yes. I mean, all I've ever heard from everyone is 'look at how pretty she is', and 'you got all the best qualities of both of your parents', and everyone always pushing me toward this standard of being the most pretty, the most popular, and the most wanted."

"I don't know what to say to that. I mean, you're smart and funny and kind to everyone. Why would you be so worked up about being pretty?"

"It's bad, isn't it? I mean my being so vain?'

"It's not terrible, but wow, you lost Ken over worrying about him thinking less of you for not being pretty anymore?"

"It didn't start that way. It started with my simply wanting to save him from having to take care of a sick woman. You don't understand. He's lost his parents; he's had to take care of his siblings. He's had enough. I mean, I couldn't imagine being something he has to deal with instead of simply living life with."

"You know, we've all faced our share of tragedy. You lost your grandmother, I've lost all my grandparents, so we all face loss. Ken's had his share, but that doesn't mean he needs to be insulated now. Plus, how much he faces isn't up to you, it's up to him."

Mary stopped talking at that point to think a bit, and they finished eating and took their trays to the conveyer belt. They left the cafeteria as Ashley said, "So, we know why you did what you did, you were trying to save Ken and others from having to face troubles, although I don't see taking care of someone you care about as trouble. Then you get caught up in your image of yourself as the pretty girl. The question now is, what did you learn?"

"What do you mean, what did I learn?"

"Well, you seem to have acknowledged two main issues with your response to this event and bad news. You push away people that you care about and do not allow them to help you. Also, you look at your material side too much when you worry more about your looks and how you will be perceived rather than looking at the real issue or what's important. That's what happened, and those are the behaviors you need to look at changing. How you respond to bad events and bad news. You can't really start to change until you learn anything from it."

"This feels like a test."

"It's not a test, Mary, but it is a critical part of change. You have to recognize that the way you deal with something isn't working for you to be able to change it."

"Clearly, I ruined relationships with the way I reacted."

"What about the pushing you did? You messed things up with Deb and even with friends here."

"Yeah, I suppose." They finished the walk to the dorm in silence. When they got back to the room, Mary sat down on her bed and Ashley turned her desk chair around to face her. Ashley leaned toward Mary to get her attention. When Mary looked up, Ashley said, "Suppose isn't going to help you change anything. You know that, right?"

Mary stood up and started pacing, getting frustrated with Ashley's pushing, "What do you want me to say? I just got to a point where I see it differently today. Let me get used to that before I have to admit guilt or whatever."

"Ok, ok." Ashley sat back in her chair. She chuckled a little and sighed.

"Seriously, thanks, Ashley." Mary smiled at Ashley and sat back down.

"For what?"

"Kicking my butt, a little, and opening my eyes."

"Oh, then you're welcome."

They laughed, and as they did, some of the girls from the floor stopped by and asked if Ashley and Mary wanted to go to a movie. They said yes and headed out.

Mary woke up the next day feeling much better. She went to church and then tried to call Deb. She didn't reach anyone and tried again early in the afternoon. Deb's roommate said Deb had been gone all weekend. Mary left a message. In fact, Mary left messages on Sunday, Monday, and Tuesday, and Deb didn't return her call until Thursday. After they greeted one another, Deb said, "Sorry about not getting back to you. I've been busy with midterms all week."

"Oh, my midterms aren't until next week."

"Does that mean your break is a week later?"

"Yeah."

"What are your plans for break?"

"Well, I had hoped to see you, but if our breaks aren't the same, I guess I'll just go home."

"Sorry."

"Is Ken's break the same as yours?"

"Yeah, but he's going on a business trip with Mr. Davis for the whole week, so he's not going be around."

"I see. I feel so out of touch with everybody and everything."

"Mary, Ken told me what happened. I'm really sorry."

"I really screwed things up, huh?"

"I tried to call you a few times, when it first happened. You didn't answer or call back then. I figured you were mad at me, too."

"No, Deb, I wasn't mad at you. I wasn't mad at Ken either. I really let this all get way out of hand."

"So why didn't you call me back three weeks ago?"

"I was pushing everyone away. I know it was wrong, but I couldn't stop myself."

"What changed?"

"Ashley kind of gut-punched me last weekend, and I guess I had some kind of breakthrough or something. That's what she said anyway, and she's going to be a therapist."

"What did she say?"

"She said a lot of things."

"No, I mean to change your mind."

"She asked me why I was bothering to do anything since I was already acting like I was dying from cancer."

"And that snapped you out of it?"

"Yeah."

"And now what do you think?"

"That I messed up my friendships and my relationship with Ken."

"Well, you didn't ruin your friendship with me, Mary. I was always your friend. I just couldn't reach you."

"I know. It's been a long road, but I think I'm heading home now."

"That's an interesting way to look at it, I guess."

"So, what have you been up to?"

"Nothing much, classes and studying."

"How's Ken?"

"Mary, I'm your friend, but now that you two have broken up, I can't tell you about what I know of his life, any more than I can tell you what he's feeling or saying to me. It wouldn't be right."

"Deb, I miss him. I know I hurt him, and I know I probably deserve this because of the way I acted. Besides pushing people away because I was scared, I was petrified that I would get cancer, and then I would start to get ugly and pale and have stringy hair and blotchy skin. I didn't want Ken to see me like that."

"I can't believe you!"

"What do you mean?"

"First of all, pushing people away when you probably need them the most, when you're scared or need help, is kind of stupid. Second, it's pretty petty of you to think that the only thing Ken cared about was how pretty you are."

"You're right."

"Then I guess Ashley is right, you did have a breakthrough."

"I want to make it up to you. Can I?"

"Of course, we will still be friends. Don't be ridiculous. You can act stupid, and I'll still like you."

"Do you think I can make it up to Ken?"

"Mary, I'm not sure about that."

"Is he already seeing someone else?"

"No. but that isn't the point. You strung him along for months and kept denying him when he was trying so hard to win you back. I'm not sure there's a chance to fix that now."

They talked for a few more minutes, and then Deb said she had to go—she had one more test in the morning, and she had to study.

When they hung up, Mary thought a long time and decided she had to try. She picked up the phone again and called Ken at Harvard. Ken's roommate said that Ken was at the library. Mary left a message. Ken didn't call back, and now after talking to Deb, Mary knew he was leaving on Friday for break. She called the New York apartment and got Deb. She said that Ken was out with Uncle Darrick but she would leave a message. Ken didn't call her, but she had decided she would not give up.

On Thursday, Mary was done with her tests and told her parents she was going to see Deb. She showed up at the New York apartment just as Deb and Ryan were walking up to the entrance to the building.

"Hi, you two," Mary said.

"Hi, Mary," Ryan replied.

"Hi, why didn't you tell me you were coming to New York?" Deb asked.

"I just decided to come. Is it ok?"

"Of course. Why aren't you at school though?" Deb asked.

"My tests got done this morning."

"How did your tests go?" Ryan asked.

"Ok, I guess. I haven't exactly been fully with it this semester, so who knows how this will turn out."

"I'm sure you'll do fine," Deb said, "you always do."

"Did I interrupt plans you had?" Mary asked.

"No, actually, I was just getting Deb home as I have something I have to do with my parents tonight," Ryan said.

Ryan said goodbye to Deb and then to Mary, and he left. The girls went upstairs. They talked most of the afternoon about classes, friends, Ryan, Joe, Becky, and Kim, and, of course, Ken. At some point, Aunt Alicia came home and had all kinds of clothes brought up to the apartment. The girls spent a couple of hours going through clothes, with both Deb and Mary trying things on and laughing. Aunt Alicia said they could keep their favorites, and the girls were ecstatic. When Uncle Darrick got home, they sat down and had dinner, and Aunt Alicia suggested Mary stay the night.

Secretly, Mary was hoping that she would be invited to stay. She was hoping Deb and she would have something to do that would keep her there until Ken got home later on Friday. The next morning, Deb and Mary went to do a little shopping, but Deb told Mary she and Ryan had already made some plans. Mary wrote Ken a long note and left it in his room and then prepared to head home by mid-afternoon. She was upset about not being able to stick around until Ken came home, but the more she thought about it, the more she thought this might be better. He might not like the surprise, and the note would give him an idea of her intentions and time to think.

Ken got home and everyone was out. Deb had left a note too, but hers was on the kitchen table. Ken had some dinner and sat down to go through his notes from the business meetings he and Mr. Davis had been at all week, when he saw the note from Mary. He read it, started pacing around the apartment, sat down, read it again, and then abandoned his notes and turned the television on. He was sitting there in front of the TV when Deb got home.

"What're you doing?" Deb asked him.

"Thinking. How was your night?"

"Great. Ryan and I went to a show."

"Great. So, have anything to tell me?"

"What do you mean?"

"When was Mary here?"

"Oh, that. Mary showed up here yesterday after her midterms were over. She hung out with me, we got some new clothes from Aunt Alicia, and then we had dinner here. We had some fantastic pork chops. I really like the things the new cook makes. Mary left this afternoon."

"Did you know she left me a long letter?"

"No, she didn't tell me anything about that."

"Well, she did. She said she was wrong, she treated me badly and pushed everyone away, and she was worried about how she was going to look to me if she was sick."

"I know. She told me all of that last Thursday when I called her back."

"Why didn't you tell me?"

"Well, I thought it best for her to tell you what she wanted when she was ready. Plus, you've said you're better now, so I didn't think you'd even want to hear from her. I mean you've been pretty clear lately you think this is for the best and you're happier now."

"Yeah, I guess. I don't know what to think about it now. Hey, did you tell her about the trip Joe, Becky, and Kim made? Or the one Ryan and I made?"

"No. We didn't talk about the time machine at all. So, what are you going to do about the note?"

"I'm not sure. Do you think she really changed or is this just a way to keep me hanging on for her cause she's lonely?"

"She seems different to me. Like she realizes she did something stupid and wants to fix it, but I don't know. I don't think she's just lonely though."

"Man, I was just this past week thinking I was going to be able to get past this, and I was going to get over her and move on. Now what am I supposed to do?"

"Do you want to get over her?"

"I'm pretty darn confused, that's for sure. I mean, not too long ago all I wanted to do was get things back to where they were with her. Then I was so frustrated and wanted nothing more than to be out of what I saw as a bad situation, where I was giving and giving and giving and all she was doing was taking. Then I thought I finally had gotten to a calm place, and now, she sends this letter."

"Do you still love her?"

"I do. I can't help it, but I do. I have to ask you; do you think Mary is vain or selfish or anything like that?"

"I don't think she's vain, I just think she puts too much emphasis on how she looks and what that means in terms of people's opinion of her. I think she's acted selfishly with this cancer thing, but I'm not sure that I blame her. I mean, you find out you have the marker for a cancer that has no cure yet after watching your grandmother die a terrible, painful death, I'd be a little bit 'poor me'."

"Yeah, I get that, but you don't think she's generally selfish or overly focused on herself, do you?"

"No. I think she gets weird when you talk about her faith, and this thing with her being so focused on people judging her by her looks is bad, but she's a good, kind, giving person."

"What do you mean weird about her faith?"

"Well, you know, she's sure she's right about it, and everyone else is wrong."

"Oh, well, yeah, she did come off that way in the past didn't she."

"Yeah."

"Thanks for telling me about your conversations with her, and thanks for letting me bounce this off you."

"Any time, my big brother. We're here for each other, right?"

They said goodnight and headed off to their rooms. Deb went right to sleep, but Ken sat there thinking and rereading Mary's note a few more times. The next day they checked in with Joe and Kim and hung out with Ryan. On Sunday, they all headed back to their respective schools.

18

TWO WEEKS LATER, KEN picked up Joe and Kim from Choate and drove them to the Hampton house for their spring break. Deb and Ryan went out as well, to celebrate the Easter weekend with everyone. Aunt Alicia and Uncle Darrick arrived on Saturday morning, and Kim convinced them to color Easter eggs. They had a lot of fun and later went out on the boat that Uncle Darrick had purchased the week before. They sailed around looking at houses and people gathering for the weekend. The dinner was a bit more casual as Uncle Darrick and Aunt Alicia prepared to head back into to the city for another big party. Ryan decided to spend the rest of the weekend with them too.

They decided to watch movies and sat down in the family room with their popcorn and snacks. As the movie started, Deb asked, "So, how are things at Choate?"

"Going well, I'd say," Joe replied.

"No lingering issues from your trip?" Ken asked.

"None."

"That's good. Hey, did you hear, we set a sales record on the new personal computer models last month?"

"Yeah, Mr. Davis called me this past week to tell me. I think the new design, with the integrated monitor to the machine, was a great idea. Plus, now that we have a couple of different models, the business sales might pick up, don't you think?"

"I hope so. The sales team is excited about it."

"What were you and Mr. Davis doing out of town during your break?" Kim asked.

"Well, we met with some investors and some engineers. I had this idea for a way to put a telescope into orbit on a satellite and point it out into space and then send the data back to Earth. We could look out farther in space than we can currently travel in any one person's lifetime and learn things to someday make that travel easier. We were meeting to discuss it and determine if it was a viable idea."

"And, do you?" Joe asked.

"Yeah, that was the conclusion of the meeting. We're going to be exploring different designs this summer."

"Who's doing the programming for the transmission of the data back to Earth?" Joe asked.

"We haven't discussed that part. I figured I would ask you about it, though."

"I'd love a chance to work on that. It would be totally cool," Joe said excitedly.

"I'll report back to Mr. Davis that you're on board. We'll probably meet right after school is out this year."

"Well, now we know what Joe's doing this summer. How about you, Kim, have you been planning anything with Amy or your other friends?" Deb asked.

"Amy's parents are taking me on a trip to Ireland this summer for about two weeks, right after school is out. After that, though, I don't have a plan," Kim said.

"I have an idea. I saw this in the museum last week when I was there for a class. They're running a summer art program, and I think you might love it," Deb said.

'At the museum?"

"No, at the Art Institute school attached to the museum. It's an eight-week program that starts in late June. You get to learn about landscape painting, portrait painting, photography, sculpture, and printing. It sounds like a lot of fun."

"That would be a lot of fun, but how would I get there? You're going on that dig, right? And Ken and Joe will be going to the office."

"We'd figure out a schedule so someone was there to take you and pick you up, Kim," Ken said.

"Let's talk to Aunt Alicia and Uncle Darrick about it tomorrow," Deb said.

"What are you doing all summer, Ryan, with Deb off in the desert?" Joe asked.

"My grandfather has set up an internship for me in North Carolina at his friend's architecture office. So, I'll be down there all summer."

"Your phone bills are going to be ridiculous!" Joe said.

"Are you two going to be able to handle being apart that long?" Kim asked.

"Well, Kim, both Deb and I want to be sure to get ready for our lives after college, and this is the best way to do it, we think. We get to try out the careers we think we want to do right now and determine if they're a good fit. I won't like it, but we have to do it, and we can talk every day. So, like Joe said, our phone bills are going to be really high," Ryan replied to Kim.

They all laughed and got back to watching the movies.

The next day after hunting down the Easter eggs, they all had a great dinner and prepared for Ken, Deb, and Ryan to head back to school. All that week, Kim and Joe played on the beach, talked to their friends, and went sailing with Uncle Darrick. It was a relaxing week, but they were ready to head back to school. After Uncle Darrick had dropped off the kids, he headed back to the city and called Deb to see if she could meet him. He had also called Ken, who had agreed to drive into the city.

The three of them met at a little Italian restaurant and ordered pizza. While they waited for their food, Deb asked, "Uncle Darrick, what are we here for? I mean, is everything ok with you and Aunt Alicia?"

"Your Aunt is fine. I just wanted to talk to you both about something I've been thinking about."

After a few more minutes of silence, Ken said, "We're all ears, Darrick. What's up?"

"I've been doing a lot of thinking since the weekend when all the time travel happened," Uncle Darrick started, "I want to discuss something related with the two of you. I know I've spoken to you both about my difficult relationship with my parents, and my father, in particular. I regret much about my actions and words and have always wished for the opportunity to go back and correct those mistakes. I'd like to use the time machine you all have developed to do that."

Deb was the first to react, "Uncle Darrick, I know it seems like the machine would be the answer to your prayers, but you have to believe me when I say that just because you can use the machine for this, it doesn't mean you should. Sometimes correcting one mistake makes other mistakes happen."

"Yeah, Darrick, Deb's right. Remember when we told you about our trips? How we wanted to fix our parents' deaths and just made it worse? We made the accident happen sooner, we made them separate and die apart, we really messed it up," Ken added.

"I'm not asking to save my father from a death that was certain. I'm simply asking for the chance to repair our relationship sooner, so I can have more time with him in the end. The two are not at all the same."

"You're right about that, they're not the same situation at all, but look at this last trip. All Joe had to do was talk to someone, and they totally changed the course of history. That could happen to you," Deb implored him.

"How could speaking to my father a year before I did, change history?"

"Ok, so you might not change US history by doing that, but you could change the history of your life. What if doing this means you don't meet Aunt Alicia, for example?" Ken asked.

"How could talking to my father mean I don't meet your aunt?"

"Look, let's say you go back, a year before you heard from your mother that you needed to see your father because of his health issues. Let's say you show up at the Hampton house a year earlier and knock on the door, and your mother is excited, and you patch things with both of them and spend the next year doing things with them and seeing them. Then along comes the day when you would have met Aunt Alicia, and you're not there because you're with your parents doing something," Deb explained.

"I see what you're saying, but I met your aunt after both of my parents had died. I'm not talking about trying to save them, just spend more time with them."

"Yes, but, Darrick, spending more time with them might change the trajectory of your life, and you might not be where you were when you met Aunt Alicia. What if seeing your parents means you go into politics like your father did? Then you wouldn't even have the same job. What we're trying to explain is that small, even tiny changes, like eating in a restaurant and seeing a beautiful woman that you strike up a conversation with, and your whole life goes off in a new direction. Trust me, it could happen. I mean, it did happen, right? You met our aunt and struck up a conversation and ended up married to her with four kids. We changed the course of history for President Kennedy and nearly killed his wife in the process. All from a little note Deb wrote that we snuck into the secret service workroom," Ken said, trying a new approach to get Uncle Darrick to understand.

"Isn't there a way to protect myself from this? This is important to me. I didn't realize how important it was for me to fix this until I learned about time travel from you all. This seems like fate somehow. I met your aunt, you are part of my life now, and you all accomplished this astounding feat of science and technology."

"Protect yourself? Darrick, the problem with the time machine and going to another place and time and changing something, is that we have no way to know what you're going to change until you get out of the machine," Ken tried to explain.

"Plus, we don't know why, but the new memories created by the actions of time-traveling, don't seep into your thoughts for about twenty-four hours, remember. You might think things are ok, and then you wake up a day later and find that some critical thing has changed," Deb added.

"I can't believe after all you've researched and done, that you haven't thought of how to protect some event or thought or whatever from getting too overwritten by the actions of the time travel," Uncle Darrick mused.

"Well, let's think about this. I mean, you're right. We have figured out a lot of questions and solved a lot of problems with our time travel. Why can't we figure this out?" Deb thought out loud.

"What about the note you guys left in the barn for Mr. Brewster about where Mary was when you moved forward? Would something like that work?" Ken asked Deb.

"You mean, like we would have Uncle Darrick carry something in his wallet or something that would say, no matter what on this day, be here to meet your future wife?"

"Yeah, but a note in the wallet might not work."

"Yes, it would. I've written myself notes and left them in my wallet for years. To remind me of events, or people that I met, or whatever," Uncle Darrick said.

"I think we should involve Joe and Mr. Brewster in this proposal," Deb said.

"Yeah, probably. They can tell us if this is a good plan or not, but what are we saying we're going to do?" Ken asked.

"I think," Deb replied, "we're suggesting that we send Uncle Darrick back in the machine to a time before he reconciled with his father to start that process earlier. But, to ensure he still meets Aunt Alicia, and we get to the point we are in his future from this time-traveling trip, we're going to have Uncle Darrick write a note now, to carry in his wallet all that time from his time travel to when he meets Aunt Alicia."

"When can we do this? Next weekend?" Uncle Darrick asked, excitedly.

"Not so fast. We have to research where to land the machine, what date you're going to, and plan for when Ken and I can be with you to do this. It has to be some time when you definitely aren't going to be where your parents are, or you'll have issues. Also, we made a serious promise to one another a year ago that we would never have anyone in the machine alone on a trip. The risks are too high. Someone will have to go with you."

"I'll go with you, and I'll stay close to the machine," Ken said.

"Won't I have to be there for a long time though?" Uncle Darrick asked.

"No, you have to be there long enough to reconcile. You would leave then, and it would create a change in your then-present self and all events that come after in your life. At least, that's how I think it will work. We'll have to talk to Joe and Mr. Brewster about that. But, if I'm right, you would only need to be there for a few hours," Deb said.

They finished eating by this point and got up to leave. Ken said goodbye on the street after they agreed that Deb would call Joe the next day and discuss this with him. Uncle Darrick was going to figure out Aunt Alicia's schedule and let them know when she might be off doing something for the magazine and give them an opportunity for the trip.

The next day when Deb talked to Joe in the afternoon, he seemed excited about the possibility of using the machine and said he would talk to Mr. Brewster. Deb had alerted Ryan to the plans, and he agreed with Deb, about the note and the time required, but they agreed to wait on Joe and Mr. Brewster's evaluation. Joe called back on Thursday and said that they agreed with Deb's assessment of the note in the wallet to ensure Uncle Darrick showed up to meet Aunt Alicia and determined that he would only need to be in the other time long enough to reconcile and should leave before the end of that day—whatever day it was. That would ensure he would not run into himself the next day. Mr. Brewster pointed out while discussing the situation with Joe that it was actually a risk for Uncle Darrick to remain longer than one day, as when he got up the next day, his past self would have a memory of the reconciliation and would probably rush to see his parents, and then they would meet.

Later that evening, Deb called Uncle Darrick.

"Hello, this is Darrick."

"Hi, Uncle Darrick, it's Deb."

"Oh, hello. Michael didn't specify it was you."

"That's ok."

"Is everything alright?"

"Oh, yeah, everything's fine. I've talked to Joe, and he talked to Mr. Brewster, and I just wanted to update you."

"Great. What did they think of your plans?"

"They said the note would work, and that you only need to be in the old time for a day and can't stay any longer as your other self in that time would likely show up the next day, and you can't be in the same space and time."

"I hadn't thought of that, but I'm sure if I wake up that next day and realize that we've reconciled, I will want to go directly to see my father."

"That's why you can't stay more than one day. If your other self shows up near where you are, the universe tries to reconcile that there are two of you there. It will start to erase the you that traveled there."

"How do you know that?"

"Remember, we found this out when Joe traveled to Cambridge and when Ryan and I went there to fix what he did last year. It was a disaster. I think we told you about it."

"You did. I remember now, you almost died."

"Not exactly, but yeah. So only one day for your travels. That means you would be gone about four or so hours. That is what Joe calculated with all their understanding of elapsed time and distance or time away from your present you traveled and how long you'd be there."

"Ok."

"So, we need to draft the note you're going to put in your wallet before you go, and you need to pick the date and stuff so we can make sure you have on appropriate clothing. You know, if you go a decade earlier, you might need different clothing."

"Well, I thought the note should just say to be sure to be in the right place on the date I met your aunt. Does it need something else?"

"Didn't you meet her at a party? I would think the note should say that you need to be at that party on that date."

"Ok."

"All we need to do now is pick the day you and Ken are going and figure out where to land the machine."

"Your aunt is going to be at a location starting next Saturday morning. We could all drive over to Choate Saturday morning and go then if everyone is ready."

"That would be good, so long as we can find a good place to land the machine. I will work with Kim and Joe to figure that out."

"Thanks, Deb. I appreciate you all understanding my desire to do this."

"You mean the world to all of us. We want to try to make you happy, and we know how much you wish you could change things with your father. We totally understand. It's that desire to fix things that started all of this. I just hope you don't come to regret this."

"I don't see how I can."

"I've got to run, study session. I'll let you know what Joe and Kim come up with."

"Have a good week. Talk to you soon."

"Bye."

After the study session and talking to Ryan, Deb called both Kim and Joe and relayed to them what the plan was. She asked Joe and Kim to research a good landing place and gave them the date Uncle Darrick gave her for the destination of the machine. The next day she relayed all of this to Ken, and they decided to proceed with the plan for the next Saturday.

19

IN ORDER TO NOT raise any suspicions with Aunt Alicia, who was leaving for a photoshoot somewhere in the city, Deb and Ryan didn't come over to the New York apartment until early Saturday morning. They drove over to Choate and went directly to Mr. Brewster's house. Ken had already arrived and had assisted Joe and Becky in loading the navigational data into the machine, preparing the machine for the trip. Because they had decided to only go about eight years back into history, they didn't need different clothing, and both Uncle Darrick and Ken opted for casual clothes for the trip.

Joe spent some time trying to prepare Uncle Darrick for the machine's noise and how his body would likely react. He also had spent much of the time while they waited for the others preparing Ken for what might happen if the other Uncle Darrick managed to get into their space and time.

Ken assisted Uncle Darrick in getting situated in the machine and seat belted for the trip. Then he announced to the others outside that they were ready to start up the machine. The noise started, then the wind and bright light, and then the machine was gone.

"Well, hopefully, everything goes well," Mr. Brewster commented.

"I have to say, that I have a bad feeling about this," Deb commented.

"What do you mean?" Kim asked.

"Well, I don't really know, Kim, I just have a bad feeling that Uncle Darrick is going to accomplish what he wants to and repair his relationship with his father, but that things will be altered somehow here when he gets back."

"The big problem with that is, we might not know what the issue is until tomorrow when we wake up," Joe said.

"What do you think might happen?" Kim asked again, getting a little agitated.

"I don't know. I'm just worried that doing this might change his timeline so much that he doesn't meet Aunt Alicia or something and our whole present will be impacted."

"That would be awful!"

"Wasn't that why he wrote himself a note? It is supposed to ensure he would be at the location on the right date to meet your aunt?" Becky asked.

"That was the plan. But what if changing things with his father, changes him a little bit, and he no longer has any interest in our aunt?" Deb asked out loud.

"Then we'll just have to fix it, like we've had to fix details of the other trips," Kim said with some conviction.

"In any case, we won't know what happened until they get back. What's everyone up to today?" Ryan asked.

"I have a girl scout thing that I really need to get back for," Kim said as she prepared to leave.

"I'll go with you. I have a huge paper I need to work on," Becky said.

"Me too!" Joe added.

"Ok, so, Mr. Brewster, how about you?" Ryan asked.

"I have some papers to grade, but you two can stay here and work on your homework if you have some."

"That sounds great. I've got a lot of reading to catch up on," Deb said.

So, Joe, Becky, and Kim headed back to campus, and Deb and Ryan went into the house with Mr. Brewster. They all tried to focus on their tasks while they waited for Ken and Uncle Darrick to return.

"Wow, that was loud and bright!" Uncle Darrick declared as the machine came to a stop.

"Yeah, but you get used to it," Ken added.

"I feel a little queasy."

"That is pretty normal. But Joe said you need to be alert to other physical changes while we're here. It might be an indication that your other self has wandered into the space and time with us. If you start to get headaches or the queasiness returns or gets worse, or you get dizzy or anything, you need to use this walkie-talkie and get my attention, ok?"

"I will. Now what?"

"I'm just going to check to see if anyone is out here."

Ken looked out the window and didn't see anyone, so he opened the door to the machine, and they stepped out. The machine was well hidden actually. The landing they made put them in the middle of a large weed and brush area behind an old factory near the port. They were about half a mile from the Hampton house. Ken asked Uncle Darrick to confirm he had the note in his wallet, which he did, and then he said he was going to head into town and get something to eat but would be back near the machine in about half an hour. They made sure the walkies were working, and Ken headed in one direction while Uncle Darrick walked the other way, toward his family home.

Uncle Darrick arrived at the house and hesitated. He was suddenly unsure whether this was a good idea. As he paced back and forth at the base of the circle drive in front of the house, his mother must have seen him from a window as she came running out the front door.

"Darrick, what are you doing? My goodness, how have you been? I'm so glad to see you!"

"Hello, Mother."

"Well."

"I was trying to build up the courage to come to the front door. I guess."

"Your father asks about you regularly. I've not told him we speak every few weeks, as you requested, but he's been asking for you."

"Is he well?"

"He's beginning to have some difficulties with the diabetes."

"Is that why he's asking for me?"

"No, I think because it's harder for him to get around, he's had many hours to think. I think he may regret some of the heated discussions the two of you had."

"It seems I regret them as well, or I wouldn't be here."

"Might it be prudent of you to come inside then and speak to him?"

"Yes, I've found my footing."

"It's no wonder you two have such difficulty. You're cut from the same cloth."

They walked together into the house, and his mother led him to his father's office. He looked around as they went, remembering all the times he was in this house as a child and that mid-century modern design his mother always decorated in. When his mother opened the office door, his father was sitting at his desk, with a newspaper in front of him. He didn't look out to see who had entered. His mother slowly backed out of the room, leaving Darrick standing there. After more than a few minutes, Darrick finally said, "Father."

His father did put the paper down when Darrick spoke. He had a look of surprise and a fleeting look of happiness upon seeing his son, but then he scowled a bit.

"I don't mean to interrupt your paper, Father, but I wanted to speak with you."

"Sit down then. It hurts my neck to look up at you this way."

Darrick sat down as he said, "How have you been?"

"I'm sure your mother has told you; my health is failing. I've had to stop working and turned over running of the company to the board and the newly elected president."

"I read about it in the paper."

"That should have been your job, you know."

"Father, I didn't come here to rehash old arguments. I don't know how to make you understand that although I appreciate everything you've given me, and I know it all comes from your work in politics and that company, I wanted neither of those things for my life's work. You chose your career path, why are you denying me my choice?"

"Perhaps some of the things I've said to you throughout your young adulthood were too demanding or too strong. I only wanted to give you a future. And, truth be told, I wanted a legacy."

"I was hired on as a founding member of the investment firm three months ago. Did you know that?"

"Yes, the news was delivered to me at a dinner party. Not by you, but by some near stranger."

"Yes, Father, we've been estranged for a long time. I wish I could take some of this back, but I can't. What I was hoping for, was a chance to change the future for both of us."

"In what way?"

"Well, I would like to be a part of your life. I would like you to be a part of my life. I'd like to forgive you for the things you've said, and I'd like you to forgive me for the things I said."

When his father didn't reply right away, Darrick said, "Is that too much to ask?"

"You just want to let go of everything we've said to one another? You don't want to blame me for your childhood, your troubles getting along with people? Trying to run your life?"

"Yes, I want to just let that go. Actually, what I would like is a chance to get to know you. Not as a child views his father, but as one man getting to know another man. I want to see you in another light entirely. I'm hoping you might want to get to know the man I've become."

"I would like that as well."

Darrick stood and held out his hand to his father, "So, what was said in the past is over, we move forward from this moment?"

His father struggled to stand, and when he had finally accomplished it, he held out his hand and they shook, smiling at one another.

They spent the next hour or so talking and getting caught up on what Darrick had been doing and what was going on with his father's health. Darrick's mother came in and announced that lunch was ready. The three of them ate on the back patio and enjoyed food and conversation. After lunch, Darrick announced that he had to meet someone in town and get back to the city, but that he would return the next day. He was smiling as walked up to Ken and the machine. Ken grinned back at him and asked how it went. Darrick relayed the conversation and how happy the day made him. He commented about how it was only possible thanks to the kids' remarkable discovery and effort. They got back into the machine, and Ken started it up. The noise, wind, and bright light started, and in a flash, they were back in the barn at Mr. Brewster's.

Everyone was waiting for them to return, so when Ken and Uncle Darrick stepped out of the machine, they were all there. Joe was first to react, "How did you like time-traveling, Uncle Darrick?"

"It was pretty amazing, Joe. Not sure if I would ever get used to the noise and light, but it was amazing."

"Did you see your father?" Kim asked.

"Yes. I was surprisingly nervous, but we talked and agreed to make amends, and it worked out exactly as you all planned."

"Does anyone feel anything from this trip? I mean do any of you feel like something has changed?" Mr. Brewster asked.

206

They all agreed that nothing felt different, but Joe pointed out that they might not notice anything until tomorrow. They were preparing to leave the barn when Kim grabbed Uncle Darrick's hand and said, "Uncle Darrick, where is your wedding ring?"

"I don't have a wedding ring."

They stopped and looked stunned.

"What do you mean you don't have a ring?" Deb asked.

"Well, that's strange because why would my ring be missing, and why did I say that?"

"I think we have a problem," Becky said.

"What's going on?" Uncle Darrick asked, getting more agitated.

"Something must have changed that made you and Aunt Alicia not marry, but until we get the new memories, we won't know what that is," Joe said.

"Is there any way to verify any of this?" Uncle Darrick asked.

"We could go to the library and look up the announcement, right? That was in the papers, wasn't it?" Kim said.

They piled into both Ken's and Uncle Darrick's cars and went to the library on campus. Deb, Becky, and Kim started pouring through microfilm but could find no record of the wedding that should have taken place the previous spring. Uncle Darrick was pacing and getting more and more upset. Finally, he stopped and looked at Deb, "This is what you meant isn't it? I have to choose between reconciling with my father or having a life with Alicia?"

"We don't know anything yet. Until the new memories seep into our consciousness, we won't know."

"This is terrible."

"Let's not panic. We can't really do anything about it tonight. Maybe it would be better if we stayed in town tonight, and then tomorrow, we can decide what we need to do to fix this," Ken said, trying to calm everyone down.

They agreed with the plan, and Ken drove Joe, Becky, and Kim back to campus and then met Uncle Darrick, Deb, and Ryan at a diner near the hotel. They all agreed to not ponder on what happened and wait and see how they all remembered things in the morning.

Deb realized the minute she opened her eyes what had happened. Uncle Darrick and Aunt Alicia had met, and had been together, right up until the night that Aunt Alicia and Ken argued about the will and trust fund. That had started a string of arguments for Uncle Darrick and Aunt Alicia that culminated in their break up just before school started last year. When they all met for breakfast, they collectively remembered the arguments and break up.

"What are we going to do?" Deb asked no one in particular.

"Well, let's start with what the arguments were about, maybe that will give us a clue. Darrick, what did you and Alicia argue about?" Ryan asked.

"Family. I was so angry at her for the way she treated Ken that I couldn't control what I said. All I could think of was my issue with my father and how I nearly lost him, and nothing I said would convince her to manage that situation any differently. When she told me about the will and the circumstances of your parents' deaths, I encouraged her to involve you in the meetings, Ken. I thought at your age, you should be involved, and she disagreed. We settled it then, but when she got so fired about the will and you going to the lawyers, it came back up again, and I just couldn't separate the two situations, and we argued all the time. In the end, I said I couldn't be with her if that was how she was going to act. I was terrible to her."

"Yikes, that's bad," Ken said.

"Ok, well first thing, we should get over to campus and pick up Joe, Becky, and Kim and head over to the barn. Together, I'm sure we can come up with something," Deb said.

After they were all assembled at the table in the barn, Deb relayed everything that Uncle Darrick had shared with them and what she remembered. Kim and Joe agreed, that was their memory of what happened, and then Kim started to cry. Uncle Darrick went to her and hugged her, while Ken said, "We're going to figure this out. Kim, don't cry, I promise, we'll figure this out."

"Can we simply send one of us to go talk to Mr. Reynolds before this arguing starts and tell him he has to find a better way to address this or he loses her?" Becky asked.

"Yeah, can we do that?" Uncle Darrick asked.

"The problem is the space and time rule won't allow any of us to be in the same space and time as another version of ourselves. If we send someone to the Hampton house say, to talk to Uncle Darrick, we will be there already. That fight started when we were there for a school break," Joe pointed out.

"What about to my office in the city?" Uncle Darrick asked.

"I would be there," Ryan said.

"Me too," Becky added.

"What if you wrote a letter, and I delivered it to Mr. Reynold's office or to his home before you all get there for the break," Mr. Brewster offered.

"You can't go alone," Joe said, "We made a pinky promise, and like it or not, Mr. Brewster, it includes you. You're part of our family now."

"I could go with him. I'm sure I didn't go to the Hampton house that break," Ryan said.

"You could land the machine in the same place since we were behind an abandoned factory," Ken added.

"We could land, Mr. Brewster could walk to the house, give the note to Michael, and we could leave. We could go the day before the break starts, that way we can be sure no one is there, and just get back to the machine as soon as possible," Ryan suggested.

"Certainly, this plan would keep it as simple as possible and would be the least risk to the time and space issue," Becky commented.

"Ok, we have the coordinates, but we need some times and dates to program into the machine. Kim, how about you and Becky work on the dates part with that old calendar hanging over there, and, Deb, you can write the letter," Joe said, giving out instructions.

Becky and Kim hopped up and went to the calendar. Sure enough, it was from the correct year. They looked up the dates and came back to the table while Joe and Ken were documenting the programming points. Deb sat at the end of the table with several sheets of paper writing a letter to Uncle Darrick. Mr. Brewster left the barn and went to his house. He came back wearing a suit and bringing an envelope for Deb to put the letter in. They all waited while Deb completed her task, with the machine ready to go. When she finished, she folded the note and put it in the envelope, addressed it to Darrick Reynolds, and then handed it to Mr. Brewster.

They started the machine up, and after the noise, wind, and bright light, Ryan and Mr. Brewster were gone. Uncle Darrick was pacing around the barn. After a few laps, he returned to the desk and asked Joe, "How long will they be gone?"

"Well, the time elapse is based on how long they are gone, and how far in time they travel. It's a whole mathematical calculation. Do you want me to show you?"

"No, not really. I'd just like to know the answer."

Ken laughed. "Yeah, that's how we all feel when Joe starts talking math and formula and programming."

"They should be gone about an hour," Joe said, scowling at Ken.

They sat at the table and talked and waited. At some point in the waiting, Uncle Darrick asked, "Is there a bathroom in this barn?"

"No, but there's one inside. I'm sure Mr. Brewster won't mind. I'll show you," Ken said as he stood up.

The two of them left the barn and went inside. Ken waited a few minutes, and then he noticed the bright light and headed back to the barn. He figured Uncle Darrick would remember his way back. The machine was back, and Ryan said everything went fine. A few minutes later, Uncle Darrick walked back into the barn and looked around at all of them. Kim came running up to him and said, "It must have worked. Your ring is back!"

Uncle Darrick looked at his hand as he said, "That's amazing. I didn't even notice it. Suddenly, I have a ring on again. How is this possible?"

"Well, we won't know for sure that we put everything back to the way it was until we all get full memory of the changes, but we know for sure, you're married again!" Joe said.

"Are we sure you're married to our aunt?" Kim asked, still holding on to Uncle Darrick's hand.

"Yes, it must be with Alicia," he responded.

They sat around for a few more minutes when Ken noticed the time. "We had better get going. I don't know about Deb and Ryan, but I have some studying to do."

"I do too," Joe said.

They all gathered their things and prepared to leave. Uncle Darrick turned and held out his hand to Mr. Brewster. He took it as Uncle Darrick said, "Thank you. Not just for setting my life back on track, but for everything you've done for these kids. They mean a lot to me, and knowing they have you here is a comfort to me."

"They mean a lot to me too. And, I've learned at least as much from them as they've learned from me!"

"You said it! I've learned a lot from these geniuses!"

20

DEB AWOKE THE NEXT morning knowing that everything had worked out. She had a memory of the wedding when it was supposed to have happened, and everything seemed right with the world. It made her think of Ken and Mary, of course. Mary had left her at least four messages during the past weekend, and she wanted to talk to Ken before she called Mary back, so she tried to reach Ken during her break in the day. He wasn't there, so she was still waiting for him to call back when Ryan showed up at her dorm for dinner.

"Busy day today, huh?" he asked as they walked to the dining hall.

"Yeah, I had a meeting with Professor Henry about the dig this summer and then had to check in with my advisor for registration for next year."

"Oh, yeah, I do that tomorrow. So, what's the plan for the dig? When do you leave?"

"Looks like I will have a week before I have to report to the train station. All the workers are going by train out west for the dig."

"Ok, well, then I'll tell my grandfather that I will be down in North Carolina for my internship a week after our classes are over. I'm sure that'll be fine."

"Well, maybe you should check with Mr. Halbrook before you make plans so you don't start this internship off on the wrong foot."

"I have a call with him toward the end of the week, so I'll ask. Does that make you feel better?"

"Yes."

"Or is it that you want to be rid of me for that week?"

"Not at all! I just want it to go well for you."

"Don't look sad, I was teasing!"

"On to another subject then. You remember the wedding and everything, right?"

"Yeah, it all seems to fit to me. You?"

"Yeah, it all seems to fit the timeline I expected, it's just something seems a little off, and I can't describe what it is or anything."

"Maybe you should check with Ken and your uncle?"

"I tried to reach Ken a couple of times today. Mary called me like four times over the weekend, and I wanted to talk to him before I called her back. I'm just going to have to call her after dinner I think."

They went back to Deb's dorm room and were getting textbooks out to do homework when Deb's phone rang.

"Hello," she said when she picked up the receiver.

"Hi, Deb, it's Ken."

"Oh, hi."

"I saw that you called, what's up?"

"Well, I wanted to talk to you about a couple of things. First, did you wake up with the right memories of Uncle Darrick and Aunt Alicia?"

"Yeah, wedding last spring, everything seems ok to me. Why, do you remember something odd?"

"Not odd, it's just that something doesn't seem right. I can't put my finger on it yet, but I'm worried."

"Well, I'll admit when I got up this morning and I remembered the wedding, I kind of stopped thinking about it to focus on classes. I mean we only have a few weeks until finals."

"Yeah, me too, but then later in the day, I started to have this weird feeling something was still wrong."

"I'll try to think it through tomorrow and take some notes. I have a kind of busy day tomorrow, and on Wednesday I'm going in to the city to meet with Mr. Davis to talk over this summer. So, let's talk again Thursday. Is that ok?"

"Yeah, that works. I have a big test on Wednesday, so I'll be at the library most of the day and night tomorrow."

"You said a couple of things. What else is up?"

"Well, I got like four or five messages from Mary this past weekend, and I thought I better talk to you before I call her. She left some kind of urgent messages. Did you hear from her too?"

"She left me a couple of messages. Honesty, I didn't even think about calling her back. I know that sounds terrible, but I'm trying to move on.

I'm not sure I'm ready to just jump back into the same old routine, and I'm afraid that will happen."

"Ok, well, I'm going to call her and make sure she's ok and find out what's going on. Do you want me to call you afterward?"

"Not really. I mean, I can't imagine anything she has to say is going to change things for me. I don't believe she had some epiphany a few weeks ago and did a complete one-eighty, and I don't want to keep doing what we were doing. I guess I'm just trying to accept it for what it is."

"Have you forgotten that when Thomas and Mr. Brewster went forward, you were with Mary still?"

"I know. We've talked about this right? I was hoping that was significant, but probably it isn't since they went forward and now, we know and it's already changing. So, what they experienced on that trip, may not happen."

"Yeah, I know."

"Mr. Brewster also said that he would expect that if that is supposed to be our future, we'll find a way back to each other. I just don't think that's my future anymore."

"I'm so sorry."

"I know. But you were just trying to be her friend and help her when she asked. We can't regret what happened. Like our parents' dying, we have to learn from it and move on."

"I know that in my head. It's just sometimes my heart doesn't like it and wants to forget."

"I hear that."

"I'm going to call her though."

"I think you should. She's still your friend, and I wouldn't want what happened between her and me to change that."

"You're a great big brother. Did I ever tell you that?"

"Not really."

"Well, you are. I'm really glad you're my brother."

"Thanks. I'm glad you're my sister."

"Ok, I'll talk to you Thursday. Good luck in your meeting with Mr. Davis."

"Thanks, good luck on your big test."

"Bye."

After they hung up, Deb called Mary. She wasn't in so Deb left a message. Much later that night, after Deb had gone to bed, the phone rang. She sprang out of bed to grab the phone so it didn't wake up her roommate.

"Hello," Deb whispered.

"Hi, Deb, it's Mary."

"Oh, hi. I didn't expect to hear from you tonight. Hold on while I walk out into the hall."

"Sorry to call so late, but I was worried when I didn't hear from you and really needed to talk to you."

"It's ok. I just didn't want to wake up my roommate, Kathy."

"Where were you all weekend?"

"We went to Choate to see Joe, Kim, and Mr. Brewster."

"Oh, how is everyone?"

"Good."

"Aren't you going to see everyone in a few weeks when school is out? Why the urgency to go this past weekend?"

"Well, it wasn't an urgency. Uncle Darrick had a weekend when he was going to be free because Aunt Alicia was busy with work, and he asked a while ago if we wanted to do this. Ken and I thought it was a good idea because we're kind of scattering this summer, so we went over there and hung out. That's all."

"What do you mean scattering?"

"Well, I'm going with one of my classes on a dig that will be going on all summer long, Ken's going to be traveling with Mr. Davis all summer. Joe is going to be spending a few weeks with Becky and her family, and then he's going to be at the MIT lab for part of the summer and working on some project with Ken. We're just busy and wanted to spend some time together."

"Was Ryan with you?"

"Of course."

"Oh."

"What's wrong, Mary?"

"Well, I called all those times because I was hoping you had some news about Ken. I called him too, but he didn't answer. Now I know why."

"Well, I want to help you, Mary, but remember, I'm not going to let you put me in the middle. What you say to me is private, and what he says to me is private."

"I know you said that. I'm not trying to get you to tell me what he's telling you. I was just hoping what I wrote got through to him."

"I heard that you wrote him a note when you were with me at the beginning of your break. Ken told me."

"He did?"

"Yeah."

"So, what should I be thinking then? If he told you but didn't call me back?"

"I don't know what to tell you, Mary. He's busy with classes and planning for his summer, but I doubt that would hold him back if he was ready to try to work things out with you. I can tell you that he probably doesn't believe you suddenly changed so dramatically after all these months."

"Didn't you tell him I've changed?"

"I did tell him you seemed very different when you were here at your spring break. But, come on, you have to know that we all recognize that when you've made up your mind, you've made up your mind. Maybe he just doubts that's changed."

"How can I convince him if he won't talk to me?"

"I don't have a good answer for that."

"This is impossible! I've changed! Really I have!"

"It's just sudden. You can't expect him to just set everything aside that he's been feeling just because you had an epiphany."

"Wow, it seems like no one believes me, and no one recognizes this is news at all."

"Don't get me wrong, Mary, I think this is great news. I knew eventually you'd figure out you can't spend your life waiting for some illness to come. I'm maybe a little jealous that Ashley was the one that got through to you because I think I've been saying these things to you since Thomas and Mr. Brewster got back last spring."

"I know. I'm sorry. All I can say is that I wasn't ready to hear it or maybe that I needed to wallow for a while and sort it all out."

"I get that. I think anyone would feel that way if they found a way to see into their future and didn't like what they saw."

"Yeah, but now I can't seem to fix things."

"I don't know, Mary. Mr. Brewster says because you know what may be coming, that knowledge means your future changed. It won't be like it was when they traveled and saw you. The knowledge changes your timeline."

"What do you mean?"

"Well, the way he explained it, when we went back in time, we changed something that already happened, but it impacted the timeline we knew and put it into a new timeline. The same is true when they went forward. When they came back and shared the results with you, it started a change to your timeline. Your future cannot be what they saw."

"I think I understand. I don't think I like that at all."

"What do you mean?"

"I was calling all weekend to ask about what Ken might be thinking and to get your help."

"Oh, and you think because your future changed, that means your future with Ken changes?"

"It already has changed. We aren't together."

"I know."

"I really messed up, Deb. I pushed him away and treated him so badly. Just saying it makes me feel like such a terrible person. I kept promising him I would be open-minded, while all the while I knew I wasn't being that way. I just didn't want to be totally alone."

"Mary, I don't mean to sound mean, but you were alone because you pushed everyone away."

"You're right."

"It wasn't fair how you were treating Ken."

"I know. Which is why I need your help."

"I don't know what I can do to help you with this, Mary."

"Well, first, can you tell me why he hasn't called me back? I mean you have probably talked to him and know that I called him too this weekend."

"I did talk to him today about something else. He mentioned that you had called and left him a message. He's very busy this week though, like I already said."

"How is he doing?"

"He's ok, Mary. I mean I think he feels sad that it's over with you, but he's ready to move on."

"But, Deb, I don't want him to move on. I want to work this out with him. I want him back in my life. Actually, I've realized that I need him."

"And you don't think too much has happened or been said at this point to allow you two to work things out?"

"I love him. I know he loved me once. If we feel that way about each other, how can it be too much for us to work through?"

"What if he just needs time. You know, like you needed time?"

"If he won't even talk to me, how can I convince him though?"

"It was ok for you to hold him at arm's length to sort this mess out, but he can't have any time? Mary, it would seem you are still being a little selfish."

"Deb, don't say that. I'm not being selfish! I'm fighting for our relationship! Don't you have any advice on how I can reach him?"

"I can't speak for him, Mary. Actually, I won't speak for him in this. You and I are friends. I don't want to lose your friendship. But as far as Ken is concerned, I can't interfere here."

"Will you talk to him for me if I ask you to?"

"I don't want to go through that again."

"Not even if I ask you to talk to him?"

"I'm not sure he's going to listen to me. But I'll try to talk to him. You've got to understand though, Mary, that I'm not going to constantly bug him or go back to him any time you've decided you aren't brave enough to talk to him."

"It's not that I'm not brave enough to talk to him. I just was hoping to hear where his head was at where our relationship is. I guess I was hoping you might introduce the idea to him of talking to me, and he might call me. I'm sorry I asked. I don't know why you're being this way, Deb."

"I just want us to be friends and for me not to be in the middle of whatever is happening with you and Ken. I did that when you asked me to use the machine, and it turned out horribly."

"If you don't want to help me, then don't."

"I want to help you, Mary. I would just rather support you than reveal secrets to you and try to intercede on your behalf with Ken. If you guys are going to work this out, you have to do that without me in the middle. Ok?"

"Ok."

"I'm going to be talking to him on Thursday. I'll tell him only that you've had a huge change of heart and left messages for him because you'd like a chance to apologize and talk with him. Is that ok?"

"That would be great."

"Ok. I'll call you Thursday night then, ok?"

"Sure, thanks, Deb."

"I've got to get some sleep now, Mary. It's after midnight. I've got an eight o'clock class tomorrow."

"Ok. Talk to you Thursday."

"Bye."

Deb went back into her room and hung up the phone. Kathy asked, "Who was that?"

"Sorry. I didn't mean to wake you; it was Mary, my friend from Choate."

"Are you sure you're friends? I mean it sounded like she was badgering you to do something you didn't want to do."

"She said she's had some sort of epiphany, but then she went right back to doing what she does, thinking of only herself. I don't know why it took me so long to see how selfish she is sometimes. I mean, we are friends, well we were best friends, but that side of her really has a way of pushing me away from her."

"I consider you one of my friends, Deb, and I don't think it's right to ask a friend to do something they don't want to do. Plus, if what she wants is for you to pave the way for her to get back with your brother, that just seems childish. I mean, are we in junior high or something? Can you pass a note to the boy I like?"

"She knows Ken and I are close. We've had issues in the past with her being jealous of my relationship with Ken. Then she goes and asks me to do what made her mad a year ago."

"Doesn't seem like much of an epiphany to me."

"Me either. But I gave my word that I would say something to Ken, and that's what I'm going to do."

"I don't think the honor thing applies when you're bullied into doing something."

Deb laughed and said goodnight to Kathy, and the next day at the library when she was studying, she told Ryan about the late-night call and all that Mary had said to her. Ryan agreed with Kathy that it didn't sound like much of an epiphany to him either. He added that he thought

Mary's desire to get back with Ken was really about her not wanting to be alone. Then as he was getting up to go work in the computer lab, he kissed her and cautioned her not to push too hard on Ken. It needed to be left between them to decide if they wanted to work this out.

21

LATE AFTERNOON ON THURSDAY, Deb was just getting back from hanging out with Ryan when Ken called.

"Hello."

"Hi, Deb, it's Ken. How did your test go?"

"I think it went well. It was a test in my English class. How did your meeting go with Mr. Davis?"

"Great, we have at least three trips planned for the summer schedule. We have an interesting project coming up for a new couple of products actually."

"Oh really. What kind of projects?"

"Well, one is an advancement for the computers we have started—it's a disc that can store programs and data and be used by the computers. It was something that the MIT team suggested, and we took that idea back to the design team, and they came up with it. It's going to look like a small record and be held in a plastic kind of sleeve that gets inserted into a slot in the computer and read by the computer. We've already talked to Joe about the process to read the disc, and he put together a rough plan for the programming to make them readable, and the MIT team is working on a way to put data on the discs. It's really cool."

"Sounds like it."

"We're meeting with some companies that we might use to team up with for sub-contracting the production of these discs."

"Sounds cool."

"And the other idea that one of the design team came up with while we were in talks on the digital storage of data was to develop a camera that stores the pictures digitally and can be moved to these discs and a computer. We have meetings planned with several companies to develop the cases and the electronic parts, and we're going do the testing and final assembly."

"You're going to be busy this summer then, huh?"

"Yeah."

"Did you have time to go over the changes since Uncle Darrick made his trip?"

"Yeah. I didn't come up with anything though. How about you?"

"Not really. I was going to call Aunt Alicia tonight and just talk to her and see if I get a sense of what's going on."

"Ok, when're you going to do that?"

"Right after we're done, I think."

"Well, why don't you go do that and call me back. I'll be in my room for a bit finishing up a paper."

"Ok, I'll call you right back."

They hung up and Deb called Aunt Alicia. She was home already from work, which Deb was wondering about, but they talked and Deb mentioned the times she had gone to work with Aunt Alicia and how much she liked that, and Aunt Alicia suggested she do that during the week she was home before the trip west. Deb asked her how work was going, and it was then that Deb discovered what was different. Aunt Alicia had previously been promoted to the Trend Editor, but now, it seemed, she was struggling to manage work with all the planning and gatherings for Uncle Darrick and his job. They talked for quite a bit when Deb finally got up the courage to ask, "So, Aunt Alicia, I don't want this to sound bad or for you to think I'm not really proud of what you do, but I thought you wanted more from your career. Didn't you want to become an editor or something? I could have sworn we talked about that one of the days I was with you at work."

"Well, I might have said something like that, and I was working on that, but once I met Darrick, I wanted to be with him, and he is very important as the founding head of his investment firm, and he has many social events to attend and host, and that takes a lot of my time."

"It's great that you support him, but I wonder if he knows about this dream of yours?"

"Oh, I don't know that we ever talked about it actually."

"Maybe you should."

"Maybe someday."

"Well, I better get back to my studying. I just really wanted to see how you were."

"Thanks so much for calling, Deb. You take care, and we'll be there to pick you and your things up in two weeks."

"Great, thanks."

They hung up, and she immediately called Ken back and told him what she discovered.

"I can't believe it. Did it sound like she was giving up her career for Darrick because she wanted to or because he asked her or somehow expected her to?"

"It seemed like she was different. Not nearly as confident, and you know, a little pushy how she was where work was concerned. I guess the word I'm looking for is timid. She seemed like she had no self-esteem."

"What I don't understand is how this can happen when all that we did was have Darrick visit his father a year or so earlier than he did before. How could that have some an impact on our Aunt?"

"I don't know. I need to think this through some more and maybe call Mr. Brewster or talk to Joe."

"I think that's a great idea."

"Anyway, I have to work on a paper so I have to go, ok?"

"Sure. Let me know when you talk to them."

"Bye."

The next day, just before she met Ryan for lunch, Deb called and left a message for Mr. Brewster. He called her back later in the day when his classes were finished. After she explained her call with Aunt Alicia she paused, hoping Mr. Brewster had some insight. As the seconds ticked by, she began to wonder.

"I don't know what to think about this, Deb," Mr. Brewster finally said.

"I don't understand how Uncle Darrick seeing his father a year before he had seen him and reconciling while his father was not yet sick changed Aunt Alicia's drive at work?"

"Did they meet at the same time?"

"Yes, the whole point to the note you delivered was to tell Uncle Darrick to not put his history with his parents on Aunt Alicia. I said that he needed to understand her side, and her history too and some of the things he's said to me about how he feels about her. In this timeline, his father invested everything in the company Uncle Darrick had helped start. He has a much more prominent role because of all the investment by his father, and I don't know. I don't know how that alone could have done what it did to Aunt Alicia. Unless maybe something else changed that we don't see?"

"It might be something he conveyed to your aunt because of his change in circumstances at his company. Either purposefully because he changed slightly from the adjusted timeline and his reconciliation with his father or something he subtly conveyed to her. That is the only thing I can think, Deb."

"She talked like it was just expected that she would do these social things for him. Uncle Darrick said that because of their reconciliation, and his father's investment in the firm, he's a partner in charge. In the old timeline, he became a partner after they were together. Do you think that might have something to do with it?"

"That might be the right track, Deb. Did your uncle ever mention the role his mother played in his father's career? It's possible that your uncle just inadvertently expected your aunt to play a similar role, and he ended up not supporting your aunt as much because he had that year to become closer with and take on some of the family traits from his parents."

"I had a class last semester about sociology that discussed family dynamics, and we talked about the roles, how they change over time, and how they get conveyed to the younger generations and adapted as cultures adapt. I wonder if Uncle Darrick just assumed Aunt Alicia would play the role his mother played. Maybe he doesn't even realize he isn't being supportive to her."

"That could be it. I'm sure his renewed relationship with his parents changed him, even if it was just a small amount, in that year he had with them."

"I guess I need to talk to him now."

"Yes, and you're going to have to approach that delicately."

"Yeah. I certainly don't want him to regret his trip in the machine, but I think it is now changing my aunt, and she will likely be looking at a lifetime of regrets if he doesn't act on this situation quickly."

"Did she seem unhappy, your aunt?"

"I don't know if I would say unhappy. She just seemed to talk about her job and her life in a way that made me think she felt she was missing something. Maybe this is all because I know how she was in the old timeline. Do you think I'm attributing my feelings onto this situation, Mr. Brewster?"

"Perhaps the better way to handle this is to speak again with your aunt. Be a little more direct and just ask her if she feels she's missing something. Then talk to your uncle. What if she wanted this life? You don't want to create a different problem between them and be the seed of resentment and regret."

"You're right about that. I want her to be happy, and I want our new family to be happy."

"Sounds like a plan then."

"Thanks for talking with me, Mr. Brewster. I hope I didn't interrupt your day too much."

"Not at all. I already miss having you all here. If you need to talk over anything, you can count on me, Deb."

"Thanks. You can count on us too, you know."

"See, it's like we're all family, and families help each other."

"It's not like we're family, Mr. Brewster. Everything you've done for Joe and all of us. You are part of our family now."

"I feel the same way."

"I hope Thomas doesn't mind sharing you!"

"He actually gets a kick out of all of us. And he loves thinking he's inherited brothers and sisters. He doesn't mind at all."

"Well, that's good. I need to get going. It was great talking to you."

"Good luck on the dig this summer. Keep in touch, dear."

"I will. Bye."

With that, they hung up, and Deb sat there trying to plan how to speak to her aunt. After playing out several possible ways to start this conversation in her mind, she finally came to one that sounded at least plausible and smiled as she picked up the phone to call her aunt.

"Hello?" Aunt Alicia said as she picked up the phone in the New York apartment.

"Hi, Aunt Alicia, it's Deb. Did I catch you at a bad time?"

"Not at all. I just finished putting away the groceries I got on the way home from work. Is something the matter?"

"Not really. I just wanted to talk to you."

"Didn't we talk yesterday? Is something going on with your sister or brothers?"

"No."

"Well, I can tell something's bothering you. How about you tell me?"

"Well, I've been thinking a lot this week about the dig this summer."

"Is something worrying you about it?"

"Well, not about the dig specifically. It's just I've been thinking about school, my career dreams, and Ryan."

"Oh really."

"Yes. Can I ask you something, maybe this is too personal, so you can tell me no, if you want to? But, did you ever wonder if there would be a conflict between your desire for a career and desire for a good marriage?"

"Oh, I don't know if I ever gave it a lot of thought, Deb. Is Ryan pressuring you to give up your studies and career to be his wife?"

"No, no, we haven't talked about this at all. Just me thinking. Did you and Uncle Darrick ever talk about this before you got married?"

"Well, I don't remember a conversation about my career with Darrick, but there was one moment, right after we were engaged, when he said I would need to start attending things for his business."

"Really? Did you have an argument?"

"No, why do you think we'd have an argument over that?"

"Well, to be honest, Aunt Alicia, I always thought your career in the fashion industry was very important to you. You once told me it was something you used to do all the time. Draw designs and pour over magazines when you were younger. I would think, if you felt that strongly about your career, you might be angry at the thought of him wanting to make your career second fiddle to his."

"Well, it was always important to me. You're right. I wanted to open my own fashion house. But, Deb, you know I love him, and I want to support him, so it wasn't as hard as I thought it would be to give up some of the potential for my career to ensure his was where he wanted it to be. And, he had already attained the pinnacle of his career, so it made sense for me to let my career play second fiddle."

"I never knew you wanted to design your own clothes. That is the coolest idea. You have such a good eye for fashion—and especially what works on what body type. I love it when you helped me pick clothes from the room."

"Well, you know, maybe someday."

"That's what I mean. I mean what I've been thinking about. Why should I give up my lifelong dreams because I want to be married and have a family? Why is it always the female that has to sacrifice her dreams when there is a marriage?"

"To begin with, you're much younger than I am. I think the culture is changing, and it's becoming much more acceptable for women to have a career nowadays. Further, I think every woman has to decide for herself what the primary focus of her life is going to be. I'm not sure you can have dueling priorities of career and family. But I also think it matters when you get together with the man you marry. Like in your case, you and Ryan are together at a very young age. Your careers will be starting at the same time. Perhaps when you do it that way, like in your parent's case, there can be a balance between the two careers."

"Maybe. Do you regret your choice?"

"No. Well, I guess to be fair, some days I'm more confident in that 'no' than other days."

"Do you think, if it continues like that, where some days you're happy with your choice and some days you're not, you'll get to a point where you resent him and his career success?"

"I certainly hope not."

"Me too."

"I guess, as I think about this as we talk, I would suggest you have a more sincere discussion with Ryan. Put it in the context of the changes taking place with the women's movements and see where you both are. Maybe this won't even be an issue for the two of you."

"Yeah, maybe you're right. I guess I'll have a talk with Ryan about this."

"I think that's a good idea. Anything else?"

"No, that was it. Have a good evening."

"You, too. I'll see you in two weeks, ok?"

"Yeah."

They hung up, and Deb realized she had arranged to meet some friends for dinner, and she was going to be late. She rushed off to the place they were meeting, thinking about what her aunt said, and she hurried to the neighborhood restaurant. Later that night, she called Ken and went over all the conversations she had. He agreed with the plan for Deb to try to talk to Uncle Darrick. Ken said he thought this might all come off better if Deb had this discussion without anyone else helping. Deb said she would call Uncle Darrick the next day, and when she did, she arranged to meet him on Friday for lunch.

When Deb sat down at the table, Uncle Darrick smiled and asked, "So to what do I owe the honor of this lunch date?"

"I just wanted to talk with you, after the fix effort on your trip and see how you were doing?"

"Great actually. Things couldn't be better with your aunt and me."

"Really?"

"Yes. You seem very nervous. Why don't you just come out with it? Is there something about my trip and the fix to the trip you're concerned about?"

"Well, to be honest, there is something I'm worried about."

They ordered some food, and after the waiter left with the menus, Darrick looked at Deb expectantly.

"You don't remember that she had a different job prior to your trip?"

"Not really. Well, now that you mention it, I do have some vague memories of her traveling a lot and being busy a lot. I think you better start at the beginning and just give me all the gritty details, dear. We only have an hour."

"Ok, in the old timeline, prior to your trip, Aunt Alicia interviewed for the trend editor position, and she got it. She traveled a lot and had new responsibilities and loved her job. Do you remember that?"

"Vaguely."

"You do remember that in this new timeline after you had your reconciliation with your parents, she isn't that editor. She's in the same job she was and is home every night, working to be sure your parties are planned and things."

"Yes, I know what she does for me. I'm very grateful for her support, and she's an amazing host and planner. Everyone loves her."

"Really?"

"Of course. You know your aunt is wonderful with social events, and she's beautiful and funny, and she has brought me to a whole new level in the New York financial scene."

"Uncle Darrick? Do you hear yourself?"

"What are you talking about?"

"She has dreams, you know. She told me this week that she always wanted to open her own fashion house and design clothing. She'd be fantastic at it. She's got such an eye for trends and how any piece of clothing will work or not work on any body type."

"I'm not trying to be obtuse here. What are you trying to say to me? I get the sense you're actually mad at me. After everything you've done to help me with my father, I certainly don't want you to be angry with me."

"Here's the thing. I know you and Aunt Alicia are from a different generation. The generation that still believes that the wife supports the husband and doesn't have a career, but when you first met Aunt Alicia, she was this vibrant, driven woman. She doesn't seem that way anymore, and quite frankly, she told me earlier this week she doesn't always feel confident that she's happy with her choice to give up her career dreams."

"She did?"

"Yes. You have a wife that is great at something, and she's given it up to plan parties."

"When you say it like that, it seems like I'm thoughtless and heartless. How could her career life and our marriage be adjusted so much by my simply reconciling with my father?"

"I'm not sure, but I think it's because when you reconnected, you sort of re-established the general dynamics of your family. Your mother did all those things for your father's career, didn't she?"

"Yes, for many years. Then when he was well established, she started doing her own thing, but it was much later in their lives."

"Did she ever talk about having to start her career so late?"

"Not really, but I do remember one time when he wanted to go to some event, and she had something else planned, and he started pouting, and she retorted that he would have to wait on her now after she waited so many years."

"See what I mean?"

"I'm starting to."

"I also asked Aunt Alicia if you two ever talked about this. You know, before you got married."

"What did she say?"

"She said no, but that she remembered a time when you said she would need to help you on some things now that you were engaged."

"Wow, I've been a king-sized chauvinist, haven't I?"

"Maybe a little one." Deb laughed and then continued, "I'm not trying to blame you, but clearly the extra year you had with your father, his backing your business, and all the time you spent with them just reinforced the norms they took for granted. I don't think you did any of this purposefully. I think it became second nature to you."

"And so, the child becomes the parent?"

"Not really. I just wanted this to work out for you, and I was surprised that it had this negative effect on her. Listen, I'm not saying you did anything terrible. I just think you need to ask her what she wants."

"The good news is a man can change. When something is pointed out to me, I hope I can look at it objectively and decide whether or not I want to change."

"I guess I can't ask for anything more."

"I'm going to leave work early and meet my wife when she gets home and have a long conversation. That way, I can make sure my happiness at solving my relationship with my father won't negatively impact anyone."

"I think that's a great idea!"

"How's your lunch?"

"This was great. Way better than cafeteria food. But it looks like our hour is just about up. I don't have class this afternoon, but you clearly have a job to return to."

"Yes, I do. And I have an executive meeting to run."

"Then you better get back to it."

"I'll walk back to the office, it's just around the corner. Michael is here today because I had a meeting across town this morning. I'll have him drive you back to campus."

"That'd be great."

They got up, Uncle Darrick paid for lunch, and they left. Deb got in the car with Michael, and Uncle Darrick started down the street. Deb felt torn by the conversation. In some respects, it went better than she expected, and she was happy that Uncle Darrick understood and wanted to be sure Aunt Alicia had a chance to make up her mind. But in other respects, she felt he was feeling accused or something, and maybe she should not have said anything at all or approached it differently. She hoped the conversation they were about to have would improve the situation for her aunt, but at the same time, she wondered if it would just start them down a path they couldn't recover from. She also still wondered if it was her desires that were being projected onto her aunt. Hopefully, their conversation didn't start any trouble or cause any more issues.

22

THAT EVENING, ALICIA ARRIVED home and was surprised when she entered the apartment and saw lights on. She walked around looking for what all was left on and entered the formal dining room to find Darrick standing near a chair pulled out. There were candles lit and food on the table.

"What's all this about?" she asked.

"It has been pointed out to me that I might have been neglecting my wife's needs of late, and I wanted to make a grand gesture to ask for her forgiveness."

She smiled at him and laughed a little as she asked, "What exactly do you think you did, and who, pray tell, pointed it out to you?"

"A little bird did the pointing, and what I did was presume and expect and not take any of my wife's dreams and desires into account."

"You look a lot like my husband, but what have to done to him?"

"Come and sit down. We'll enjoy some food and talk."

The food Darrick had brought home and put on the table was delicious, and she said so. They talked while they ate, and then he brought her to the living room overlooking the park, turned down the lights, and sat with her. They continued talking for hours. She told Darrick about her childhood dreams, how she wanted to design clothing, and how she came to work at Vogue Magazine. They talked about generational expectations and how they didn't want their lives to be set by any mold and about women's rights and many other topics. When it felt like they talked about everything there was, she looked up at him. He then said what he wanted to say to her all evening.

"If what you want is to open your own fashion house, why don't you do it?"

"Money. It takes a large investment to do that."

"Then I think tomorrow you should resign from the magazine."

"What!"

"I have an investor interested in backing your venture, and I would like to call him tomorrow and set up a time for you to meet with him. The firm will also be entering into a venture capital deal if you'll allow me to do that for you. That way you will have everything you need to put together a collection."

"Darrick, when did you do all this?"

"This afternoon."

"Really?"

"Yes, really. I never meant to expect or outright ask you to give up your dreams for mine. I love your ambition, your drive, and your willingness to take a big risk. I want nothing more than to help make that happen for you."

"I really love you. You know that don't you?"

"I really love you too. And I'm really sorry."

"Don't be silly. You don't have to apologize."

"Yes, I do."

"I guess I'm going to have to get a bird feeder."

"Why a bird feeder?"

"I owe a little bird a great deal of thanks for making my husband look around a bit and change his way of thinking."

"Very funny!"

While all this was going on, Deb was filling Ryan in on her lunch with Uncle Darrick. They both were wondering when he was going to do whatever he was going to do with Aunt Alicia, but as they were talking about that, Deb's phone rang.

"Hello?"

"Hi, Deb. It's Mary."

"Oh, hi, Mary. How're you doing?"

"Ok. I was hoping I could ask one more time for your help with Ken."

"Mary, I'm sorry. I've been busy this week, and I haven't had a chance to talk to Ken yet."

"Oh, is that why I still haven't heard from him? I thought it was because you said what you were going to say, and it didn't change his mind."

"I don't know if what I say is going to change his mind, but I promised you I would tell him you wanted to speak to him. That you had this epiphany, and he might want to hear what you have to say. I have thought about it, and I asked you to do that for him when he was trying to reach you, so I need to be ok with doing it for you. And I promise I will do it as soon as we get off the phone, so I don't forget again."

"Is there any chance I can ask you to plead a bit more on my behalf with him?"

"Mary, I agreed to open this door and tell him that you wanted to speak to him. I can't step in the middle of this and fix it for you. You're going to have to do that on your own."

"I'm sorry, I'm just so anxious, and I wish I knew how he was going to react. You will call me and let me know that, right? How he reacts to what you say to him?"

"I will. Now, let me go call him, and I will call you back."

"Ok, bye."

As she hung up with Mary, Ryan said, "Are you sure you want to do this? I mean, one, it doesn't sound like she's really changed at all. I guess maybe we've changed this year, but she seems a little selfish. And I know I wouldn't respond well to someone trying to pave the way for a girl to get back with me if I was in Ken's shoes."

"I promised her. And, although I agree with you, I think Ken still might have feelings for her, and if nothing else, this will give him a chance to either finish it with her or decide he still wants her. Like I said to Mary, I did this for Ken during the past year, I need to do the same for her. Just ask him to hear her out, that's all I'm going to do."

With that, she dialed the number for Ken, and when he answered, she said, "Hi, Ken, it's Deb."

"Hey. How did your lunch go with Darrick?"

"In some ways it went way better than I expected, in other ways, I'm not sure. I felt a little like I was butting in on their lives. At first, he didn't think he'd done anything to Aunt Alicia, but then as we talked, he realized he might have set expectations with her without even saying anything, and he felt bad about that. He said he was going to fix it. He didn't elaborate on that."

"Well, leave it to you to know the exact way to approach this and work it out. Great job, sis!"

"Thanks, but we'll have to wait and see if it works. I just don't want Uncle Darrick to have a good thing from the machine trip only to make things worse for Aunt Alicia."

"I know, I get it."

"Anyway, that isn't really why I called you."

"Oh yeah, what's up?"

"Well, remember last week when we talked about Mary calling me, and you said she'd called you too? Well, I did talk to her, and she was calling me to apologize and to talk about the little epiphany she had about how she'd been acting and treating people and pushing people away."

"Oh yeah."

"And she asked me if I would talk to you because she called you to see if you would listen to her."

"What are we back in junior high now? She needs you to pass me a note to say I like you and make sure it's ok to tell me she likes me?"

"I know it sounds a little silly. I only promised to let you know why she had called you. Remember, you asked me to do this for you once. But, if you don't want to hear what she has to say, don't call her."

"But then you'll be mad at me or she won't be your friend anymore, and I'll feel guilty. Man, I hate this!"

"First of all, I won't be mad at you. I told her I was not going to intercede on her behalf or try to talk you into getting back together with her. Second, we talked about our friendship, and I told her it either goes on because of her and me or not. I don't want that to be because of you, so you don't have to feel guilty."

"I'm not sure that helps."

"Ken. Listen, I think despite everything, you might still have feelings for her. If that's true, maybe you should at least listen to what she has to say. Maybe it will make it clear for you once and for all."

"Maybe."

"What do you mean?"

"I don't know. I mean, I just was starting to see the light you know. I was getting to point where the future wasn't so dark, thinking she and I wouldn't be together. It was a long road. I don't know if I want to go back and do any of that over."

"I get it, Ken. I don't want you to be hurting again either. Let me ask you though, what if you talked to her and she had totally gotten over this possible cancer and just wanted to be happy, live her life, and totally forget what she knew might be coming in her future? What if the only way she could be happy was with you and making you happy? Would there be a chance you would want to try again with her?"

"I don't know."

"Maybe that's your answer then. I mean if you don't feel sure about any possibility you can work things out, maybe that means you shouldn't talk to her."

"Here's the thing, Deb. How will I know it won't just come back up or if she's really changed?"

"I think the answer is you don't."

"Yeah, and that's pretty darn scary."

"I know."

"I wish Mom and Dad were here."

"Yeah, at moments like this, I wish they were too."

"Really?"

"Yeah. It would be great to bring your troubles to Dad or Mom and just know they would have the answers or at least be right by your side while you figured it out."

"I wonder. I mean, we're a couple of years now further down the road. Do you really think they would have an answer or would they be wanting us to think for ourselves and figure some of life's little troubles out ourselves?"

"I don't know. I feel like I'll always need you and Joe and Kim. I'll always consider you my sounding board, my support. I think we got that from Mom and Dad. Why would they not be that for us if they were here?"

"I think they would be all those things. I just don't think they'd give us the answers all the time."

"You're probably right."

"Thanks."

"For what?"

"For being my sounding board and support."

"Right back at you!"

"Ok, I got to run. I'll think about what you said, ok?"

"Yeah. Bye."

Deb looked at Ryan after she hung up and said, "It's weird, but sometimes I miss my parents so much, and sometimes I'm glad we had to do this on our own. I know I owe the closeness I have with Ken, Joe, and Kim to my parents' accident. Is that bad?"

"No, sweetheart, I think that means you're moving forward, and although I never met your parents, I'm sure this is what they would want."

"You're the best boyfriend!"

"Don't you forget it! Now call Mary and get that over with. I want some ice cream!"

Deb called Mary back and told her that she talked to Ken, and he was going to think about whether he wanted to hear what she had to say. Mary pressed her for details, but Deb didn't budge. She just said that he wasn't sure he could trust that things changed. Then Deb and Ryan got ice cream.

After Mary talked to Deb, she sat on her bed for a long time. Ashley came in, looked at her sitting there, and said, "Not again!"

"No, I'm not wallowing. Just thinking."

"About what?"

"I just talked to Deb. She talked to Ken, and apparently, he's not sure he wants to talk to me because he doesn't believe I've changed."

"Do you blame him?"

"What do you mean by that?"

"You know what I mean. We talked about this. You treated him badly. If you want him back, you're going to have to work for it, darlin'. I've told you that. And I wouldn't be waiting around here for his sister to fight this battle for you."

"What are you suggesting?"

"You've got a car, right? Get in it tomorrow after class and drive to where he is and get down on your knees and beg him to forgive you. Profess your love for him and pray that he sees the light."

"And what if he doesn't?"

"Well, then you know you did everything you could to correct what you did wrong, and you try to learn from it."

"Thanks. You sure paint a sad picture there."

"Well, Mary, you have to face the fact that he might not want to listen, he might not believe you, and he might not want to try again. That's how life works. But none of that means you give up and stop trying."

"You're right."

The next day, Mary packed a bag before she went to class and put it in her car, and as soon as her classes were over, she got in her car and drove to Harvard. She tried Ken's room but he wasn't there. She sat in her car waiting in front of his dorm until he walked up with several guys carrying baseball equipment. She got out of her car and stood there. Ken saw her and left the guys he was with. He walked over to where she was in the parking lot in front of his building.

"Hi," Mary said, smiling as he walked up.

"Hi. What're you doing here?"

"I figured if Mohammad wouldn't come to the mountain, the mountain had best come to Mohammad."

"And am I Mohammad in this picture?"

"Yes."

"Hmm."

"I know I've been terrible to you, but will you give me just this one chance? Can I talk to you and tell you some things? You don't have to be ready to answer me, just listen."

"I guess I can do that."

They walked over to the quad area of campus and sat on a bench. Mary turned to Ken and started.

"Let me start by saying that I have been so very foolish. And I need to ask your forgiveness for all the things I said to you and all the things I've done to you this past year. I know you were trying your hardest to help me, and I didn't listen and actively ignored everything you said."

"Ok."

"I'm not done."

Smiling he said, "Sorry, go on."

"Here's the thing. When my grandmother died, I was shocked and scared, so very scared. When the doctor said it could be passed down, all I could think was my whole life had been planned, and now it was never going to happen. I was in a complete panic. I couldn't listen to anyone, couldn't see any reason, and all I could think was 'why me' and 'why isn't anyone just listening to me'. It felt like all anyone wanted to say was it won't be so bad, and we can plan for it. And it was all swirling around in my head every minute of every day."

"Why did you do it then? Why did you ask Deb to use the machine to find out your fate if you were so scared of it?"

"I don't know. At that time, I just wanted to know. It was a spot, a focus I couldn't let go of, and I just had to know."

"Mr. Brewster's right. Your course did change—pretty dramatically too."

"Yes, it did. I lost friends, I lost you, I lost almost everything."

"And then what happened?"

"One day, Ashley, who was the only one still trying to get through to me, yelled at me. She actually did yell at me. And she said something that finally seeped through. She said that I might as well go ahead and end it since I was not really living anyway," Mary stopped for moment and then shook her head. "No, it probably wasn't that harsh, but that's probably what I was thinking as I lay there after she left, and I guess I realized she was right, but then the thought of not doing any of the things I wanted to started to make me mad. I realized I didn't want to die. Not by my own hand, not slowly rotting away in that bed, and not because of some cancer."

"Wow."

"Yeah, wow. But here's the thing. The whole time, while you were trying to talk to me and being so nice and agreeing to just be friends and all that, I knew, somewhere deep down, I knew I needed you. I knew I couldn't do this without you. I felt really bad. I kept you hanging on like that because I needed you, and I didn't return the favor by being nice to you, nor acknowledge the fact that I needed you. It's no wonder you didn't want to talk to me."

"I just don't understand. If you needed me so much, why wasn't I able to get through to you? Why was it Ashley and not me?"

"I don't know. Maybe because all my fears were tied up with you. Maybe because I wasn't ready to hear it until the day she yelled at me. I don't know."

"You look a lot better, anyway."

"Thanks. I'm feeling better. I talked to Thomas, and he's looking for a specialist for me. I managed to finish my classes in an ok spot, even though I barely attended classes this semester."

"That's good. I'm glad Thomas is helping you."

"You sound like you have no interest in being with me anymore. Is that true? Have I done too much to hurt you?"

"I don't know, Mary."

"Well, I have more to say, is that ok?"

"Sure."

"So, here's the thing. I know I hurt you, and I know you're going to have a hard time trusting me. But if I make some promises to you, tell you how I want things to be and let you tell me how you want things to be between us, would you be willing to give us another chance?"

"I thought you said all I was going to have to do is listen?"

"You don't have to answer me today, right here. Just know that what I'm offering, is an equal relationship. Where I take care of you, and you take care of me. Where sometimes, I'm helping you, and sometimes, you're helping me."

"Ok."

"I also want you to know, that while I've been wallowing for months, I've missed you terribly. I miss the way your smile makes your eyes crinkle up, the way you wink at me when you tease me. The way your hair looks after you've been playing football, so much about you I miss every day. Most importantly, I want you to know how sorry I am."

"Ok."

"Is that all you're going to say, 'ok'?"

"I'm listening. Isn't that what I was supposed to be doing?"

"Yes."

"How about if I think about what you've said, and I call you soon to talk about it again, would that be ok?"

"Yes."

They got up and walked back to the dorm and to Mary's car. She turned as she got close to the car and said, "No matter what, I want you to know that I'm thankful every day that you came into my life, and you will always hold a large place in my heart."

He didn't know what to say to that, so he just stood there, looking at her.

"I will always love you, Ken Fitzgerald."

She got in her car then, and he stood there, watching her drive away.

23

BEFORE THEY KNEW IT, another school year was coming to a close. Ken and Deb arrived at the apartment at about the same time. Ken pulled up just as Uncle Darrick and Aunt Alicia were arriving with Deb and all her things. Michael was there, unloading, and after they had completed Deb's unloading, Michael assisted Ken with unloading his car. They decided a dinner out was in order and went to a neighborhood Chinese place and had fun eating and talking about school and their summer plans. Deb noticed that Aunt Alicia seemed livelier and more animated. She asked about it as they were leaving the restaurant.

"A lot has happened in the last two weeks while you were having finals. Your uncle and I had a long talk. He managed to locate and convince a very wealthy man to back my efforts to open my own fashion house. We should finish up the contract negotiations next week, and then I will be resigning from Vogue Magazine and opening up shop."

"Well, that's fantastic!" Deb exclaimed. "I can't wait until I have an occasion to wear the latest fashions from Alicia's Designs!"

"Oh, that's the name you think I should go with? I was contemplating AR House," Aunt Alicia said.

"Whatever the name is, I know it will be a huge success!"

"Deb, you've always been so good for my ego," she replied.

Later that evening, while Aunt Alicia was busy doing something in the other room, Deb took the opportunity to say, "It looks like we don't have to ask how your talk went with Aunt Alicia. She seems very happy."

"She does, doesn't she?" Uncle Darrick cryptically replied.

"What happened?"

"We talked—about many things—and I discovered I've managed to marry a remarkable woman, with an amazing capacity to adapt and change, who is very talented and has a fantastic business sense."

"Imagine that!" Ken added.

"And it was all thanks to a little, persistent bird that showed me the errors of my ways," Uncle Darrick said laughing as he kissed Deb on the top of the head.

"She does have the ability to make us think, I'll give you that," Ken added, winking at Deb.

Just then, Aunt Alicia returned to the family room where they were setting up a board game to play. She said, "What are you three laughing about?"

"The little, persistent bird steering all the men in the room to look at things differently," Ken said.

"Oh, yes, the little bird is here?" Aunt Alicia asked.

"Yes, dear, Deb is the little bird that pulled me out of meetings to have lunch with her a few weeks ago and pointed out that I might have been missing something."

"So, it's Deb I need to thank, is it? I thought as much."

"How about we get to the game? All this attention is starting to make me uncomfortable," Deb said, directing everyone to the table.

"What has she done for you, Ken?" Aunt Alicia asked.

"Opened my eyes to some possibilities I guess you'd say."

"Now who's being cryptic?" Uncle Darrick said, smiling, as he had lunch with Ken earlier that day and knew exactly what Ken was referring to. They had spent an hour discussing what Mary had said to Ken and Deb's role in that.

"Let's play!" Deb said, trying to steer the conversation away from the current subject, but they kept up the banter and laughs and had a great first day home.

At the end of that week, Joe and Kim needed to be picked up. Ken picked Deb up after being at the Fitzgerald and Davis offices, and the two of them drove to Choate to pick up Joe and Kim. Michael drove separately so he could cart all the belongings back to the New York apartment. After all the flurry of goodbyes to friends, they were in the car headed to the city when Kim said, "You guys aren't mad at us for the machine trip are you?"

"Kim, why would we be mad?" Deb asked.

"Maybe because we didn't tell you what we were doing, because we were gone so long, because we messed up so many people's lives through Joe's stay in jail, or that you had to rescue us?"

"Kim, although some of your list is true, and given what's happened with that machine, I guess it shouldn't make us mad when one of us tries to use it to help someone else. Remember we started all that with the desire to help Joe. I think we just need to sit down this coming week and talk about all we've experienced with the machine and decide its future. Is that fair?" Ken said.

"Yes, that's fair. I've been thinking a lot about the machine and what to do with it. A long talk is in order. I want you all involved in what we end up deciding," Joe added.

"Good. Now, tell us how finals went and how the year ended at Choate," Ken asked.

Deb looked over at Ken and rolled her eyes. Kim then started in on a lengthy description of all her activities of the last week. When she finally stopped to catch her breath, Ken asked if Joe was ready for his senior year.

"I guess so. I mean, it's going to get here whether I want it to or am ready for it or not, right?"

"You're so philosophical today, Joe!" Deb said, laughing.

"I mean, I'm glad it's here, it just feels a little weird. I've gotten used to being at Choate. It's going to be weird to not be there anymore."

"Did you hear from MIT yet?" Deb asked.

"No, I just submitted my test scores and had the letters sent. I mean, Mr. Brewster gathered the three letters I needed, and he mailed them yesterday. I hope to hear something by early this fall."

"I'm sure, after all you've done with them already, you're a shoo-in," Ken added.

"What has Becky decided?" Deb asked.

"She's going to apply to UMass, Harvard, and NYU."

"Why those schools?" Kim asked.

"Well, UMass 'cause it's closest to MIT, Harvard just because, and her parents went to NYU."

"What is she planning to study?" Deb asked.

"She wants to be a doctor."

"For kids, she told me," Kim said.

"An admirable career choice," Ken said.

They had arrived at the apartment, and moments later, so did Michael. They got everything unloaded and unpacked and had a pleasant family dinner and game night to celebrate the end of the school year. After everyone had gone to their rooms, Deb crept to Ken's door and knocked quietly.

"Come in."

"Hey, got a minute?"

"Sure, what's up?"

"Well, first I was wondering about your cryptic comment the other day. I know we haven't had time to discuss it, and it seems Mary left me a couple of messages today. Before I called her back, I wondered if the two were related."

"Yes, they probably are. Although I hope not."

"Well, do you want to talk about it? Or should I just leave you two alone on this?"

"She came to see me the Thursday before finals. She was just there in the parking lot in front of my dorm when me and some of the guys from the floor got back from playing a little ball to blow off some study steam. We talked. She apologized, talked about how scared she was and how lost she felt, and how she felt powerless to stop pushing everyone away. She also said that she needed me and knew that deep down the whole time. She said she loved me and wanted another chance."

"What did you say?"

"Not much. She seemed more like her old self but different somehow. She's been in a dark place for a long time, and maybe she's learned some things from that. I don't know."

"Now what?"

"Well, I asked her if I could think about it a bit, and she said that was ok. Then I was kind of busy this past week getting organized at the office and planned to call her tomorrow."

"Are you not going to the office tomorrow?"

"No."

"So, should I call her?"

"I'd rather you let me call her. Is that ok?"

"Sure. What are you going to say to her?"

"I'm really not sure. I mean, like you said, I probably still have feelings for her. I think I'll always love her. I just don't know. It's been a rollercoaster year, hasn't it?"

"They've all been that way, since Mom and Dad's accident."

"Yeah. Do you think it will always be that way?"

"I hope not. I guess as we're all growing up, I suppose things are going to be topsy-turvy. But it sure would be nice to not have so many crises to solve."

"Let me ask you, do you think the crisis in our lives steamed from the machine? Or was it our parents' or boarding school or something else?"

"Well, I mean, look at what's happened. We lost our parents, went to boarding school, you graduated, I graduated, we figured out the machine, went to Dallas, Las Vegas, Cambridge, Iowa, New York, and pre-Civil War era Philadelphia. You found Mary and lost her, I found Ryan, our Aunt got married, Joe found Becky. I mean, it's a big list."

"Yeah, when you list it all, I guess the crises haven't stopped for three years."

"Makes you wonder what's coming next, huh?"

"Not enough to use the machine to find out. I think we all learned our lessons when that little trip to discover Mary's fate happened."

"You know, the only two trips that really went ok are when Mr. Brewster went to Iowa and just talked to his father and when we went to keep his wife from that car accident. There have been issues with every single other trip."

"Makes you wonder, huh?"

"I guess. I'm getting tired. I think I'll get some sleep. I hope things work out the way you want with Mary. I'm sorry again about the machine trip and starting her down that dark path."

"I don't think any of us could have seen how that would go. And, if she had come to me with the request instead of you, I'm not sure I would have denied her either, so don't think for a minute that was all you."

"Goodnight."

The next morning over the kitchen table, Kim asked if they could spend the weekend at the Hampton house. She wanted a weekend out there before everyone got busy with their summer plans. Ken called Uncle Darrick and cleared it with him, and they packed up some things and left for the weekend. Before they left, Ken called Mary. When he said he wanted to talk some more, she said she would leave right away to come and see him. He said they had planned to go to the Hamptons and asked if she would like to come out. She agreed. Ken told them on the way Mary was coming out but probably wouldn't stay all weekend. Kim was thrilled they were talking again and said it was ok if she stayed the whole weekend.

They got out to the house by lunchtime. Mary arrived about an hour later. Deb and Kim decided they were going to look for shells. Kim wanted to make something for Deb to take on her dig trip. Joe walked into town to see about Uncle Darrick's boat so they could go out on the water on Saturday.

Mary and Ken walked out and sat on the terrace.

"It was good to hear from you. Thanks for letting me come out here."

"Mary, I don't want you to be nervous. I wanted to talk about what you said, and I'd like us to be able to talk like we used to."

"Ok. Maybe it would be helpful if you would share what you've been thinking?"

"Yeah. I suppose it is my turn."

"Unless you don't want to share."

"No. It's not that I don't want to share. This isn't really organized in any order, so it's just going to be a streaming thought. I hope that's ok."

"It's fine. I want to know what you think and how you've been feeling. I think you more than deserve a turn."

"Well, to begin with, I have some pretty strong feelings about the use of the machine to go forward and see what is in any of our futures. Clearly, the knowledge of what is to come is a double-edged sword. I don't think it matters if it's good news or bad, the mere fact that we know changes everything. I'm frankly a little surprised you wanted to do it, given how strong your faith is. Aren't you supposed to believe that your path is in God's hands? Anyway, clearly, we shouldn't know what is coming up. It makes us anxious and messes up everything."

"I was scared. I felt like I had to know."

"Yeah, I get it. I was scared for you. Although it didn't even occur to me to use the machine, but I was worried about what our future would be. It was pretty ingenious of Deb and you all to figure that out. But then when you did find out, you pushed hard—on me and Deb and everyone. It was so hard to want to help you and support you and have you unwilling to let me near you. It hurt. Really hurt. I was confused for a long time. What future can we possibly have when at the first sign of trouble you push me out of your life? Plus, you swore everyone to secrecy, so I had no idea what was causing it until I caught Joe on the phone. Sit in my shoes for a minute. You pushed me out of your life and wouldn't explain why."

Mary was crying now. She looked at Ken through her tears. "I'm so sorry. I don't know what else to say except that these were exceptional events."

"Everyone has exceptional events. Deb and I were just talking last night about all the upheaval we experienced in the last three years. This likely wouldn't be the last one we would have to face."

"I know you're right."

"Then when I figured it all out, I thought, this I can solve. This we can get through because we love each other and our souls reach for each other. That's what I felt the first time I showed up at Wellesley. And it didn't matter what I did, it wasn't enough for you. It was a constant stream of hurt. Every weekend I would get ready to come out to see you, and I would shore up to be ready to be hurt by your looks, your words, your rejection of my efforts. You were in a dark place, but, Mary, so was I."

Mary got down on her knees at that point and reached for his hands, "Please forgive me for doing that to you? Even if we don't ever get this right, I hope you can forgive me."

"Get up, Mary. This wasn't supposed to be a beat up on Mary session. I'm sorry."

"No, I think you need to say these things and tell me how it was for you."

"So, at Christmas, when I said I was done, I really thought that was the end. I realized I couldn't reach you. I finally accepted that we weren't going to get past this, and it was going to be the end of our relationship. I was miserable, but it seemed like the right choice. It was hard, but I got to a place where I had learned to accept it. And then you called Deb, and she told me you wanted to talk. You'd had an epiphany. That's what Deb said. She also said that maybe I still had feelings for you. I wasn't sure what to think about any of this new information. Then, walking back to my dorm, there you are. You seemed like the Mary I remember, but maybe a little wiser, a little more mature. You say you love me still and need me. I didn't know what to say to you then. I'm not sure I know now what to say."

"Why? Have you decided it's too late? Have I hurt you too much?"

"No, that's not what I meant. I'd already forgiven you. I just don't know how to start, how to move forward."

"But you want to?"

"Mary, you've been embedded in my heart for nearly three years now. I don't think there's anything too big that can't be forgiven in a relationship strong enough. I think I'm just coming to that conclusion right now, but there it is."

She smiled. "Maybe we could start over. I mean, a lot has happened in your life since this mess started, and some things have happened to me too. Maybe if we slowly get to know each other again, maybe that's how to move forward?"

"I think I should also say that I'm worried about the one-sided way our relationship was going last fall, and I need to go on record that I don't want that. If that's what you were hoping for, I have to say that I don't think I want any part of that."

"I'm most ashamed of that. I needed you so badly, and yet I could neither admit that to you nor bother to return the favor of all the attention you showered me with. I don't want that either. I know I'll have to prove that to you. Please give me a chance to."

Ken smiled at her and reached his hand out to her. She put her hand in his and smiled back at him.

Just then, Kim and Deb came up the stairs. Kim saw them holding hands, and she ran toward them. "Is it true? Have you two finally figured things out?"

"Well, Kim, we're working on it," Ken replied. "What have you found?"

"Deb and I decided that we would take some pictures tomorrow when we're out on the water, and I wanted to make her a collage frame to take with her on the dig trip. That way, no matter how far away she is, we'll be with her."

"What a great idea. If you have enough shells, you should make us all a frame," Ken said as he looked at his two sisters, realizing that how much he cared for his siblings.

"Are you staying, Mary?" Kim asked.

"I don't know, Kim."

"I'd like it if you did," Ken said.

"If it's ok with the rest of you that I invade your siblings' weekend," she hedged, giving them a way out if they wanted it.

"If Ken wants you to be here, then I think it would be good to have you with us, Mary. It's been a long time," Deb said, thinking that she was really glad her brother called her.

"Then it's settled."

"Let's go find Joe and see if the boat will be ready then," Ken said as he stood up. "And I'm hungry. Anybody else?"

They found Joe inside watching television. The boat would be ready in the morning, and they were expected by nine at the dock. He said he was hungry too, so they decided to walk into town and eat out since the cook had left for the day.

The next day, after an early breakfast, they went to the dock and got on the sailboat and headed out. They talked about everything. Kim mentioned to Mary that she'd helped the underground railroad, and Mary insisted she tell the tale of the long trip they had made earlier this spring. As they were disembarking much later in the afternoon, and Kim was finally finished with retelling their adventures, Ken suggested that they have a nice long talk tomorrow about some things.

The next day, they all walked down to the beach and set up blankets and things, and Ken put up an umbrella. They sat down, and he started.

"Clearly, with all that happened this year, we didn't have a chance to go over all we've done and learned with the machine. I've been thinking about it a lot and have come to some conclusions, but I want to hear what everyone else feels as well. As a family, we started this adventure, and it is as a family, we will decide how to move forward."

"It has been a busy year, hasn't it?" Kim said.

"What is it, exactly, that you're asking us to react to, Ken? I know we're talking about the machine, but is there something else?"

"The machine mostly, but I think there's a lot swirling around all the trips we made in the machine, and I think with some distance we can evaluate what we've learned and figure out a plan," Ken replied.

"I don't know if I get to be a part of this, but I'd like to say that going forward in time is a bad idea. Knowing what is coming on the road ahead changes you. It makes you either way too confident or way too anxious, depending on what you find there. And I think it takes all the magic out of our lives. If you know what's coming, there are no more surprises," Mary said, looking out at the ocean, "In the end, all it does is steal your time away. You're just waiting for whatever you know is already ahead in the road."

"Mr. Brewster pointed out to me, too, that the knowledge changes your timeline and path anyway. So, it never ends up being what you saw, so it's either going to be monumentally disappointing if the good thing doesn't happen or monumentally scary waiting for the scary thing," Deb added.

"The trips into the past haven't worked out much better. If we look at them honestly, we tried twice to bring our parents back, and both times it made it worse and then worse still. And boy did we mess things up when we went to eighteen fifty-three. A few days of conversations changed the whole course of history. We changed everything from the civil rights movement, the astronauts going to the moon, and the presidents of this country. Clearly, without knowing it, we have the power to change lives we will never know about," Joe said, solemnly.

"The only trip that really worked was when we went and saved Mrs. Brewster," Deb said.

"Mr. Brewster's trip to Iowa was ok too. But his father left the next morning and was killed at Normandy within weeks, so who knows if that might have backfired too if the circumstances were slightly different," Joe added.

"And don't forget the trouble we had when you, Deb, and Ryan went to Cambridge. It was scary when Ryan carried Deb out of the machine that day. She could have died. You all could have. I mean, Joe, you fell, and Ryan got thrown by the machine. It's a wonder you all made it back alive," Kim said and then visibly shivered.

"It's your machine really, Joe. Your discovery. What do you want to do with it?" Ken asked.

"If we've learned nothing, we certainly have learned it's a powerful tool. I was convinced after the Philadelphia trip that we can't let this get out. It would be so very dangerous if just anyone, or even worse, if multiple people started trying to move through time. And that isn't even considering what could happen if someone with evil intent got ahold of it," Joe replied.

"Have we considered where we started too?" Kim asked. "This all started with Joe wanting to use this discovery to get our parents back. To deal with his grief. We aren't in that place anymore, are we?"

"My beautiful, insightful little sister, as always," Ken said, hugging her, "you are absolutely right. We aren't those frightened kids dropped off at boarding school any longer. We're stronger, wiser, and together as we never would have been."

"I love the way we do things together, rely on each other, and help each other," Kim added.

"I love that too, Kim," Deb said.

"I was always so jealous of the four of you. Not just because I'm an only child, but because you were this unified force against the world, the four of you. Sometimes it seemed like you felt each other and knew what the other was thinking and what they needed. I'm still in awe of it," Mary said. She then looked around at each of them and added, "I want to thank you for supporting me last spring, but I need to apologize. I put you in a terrible position. Asking you to use the machine, then swearing you to secrecy only to then push you all away."

"Mary, we're just glad you've come back to us," Kim said.

"Me too."

"Me three," Joe added, laughing.

"So, anything else?" Ken asked.

"I just want to say, that I'm really grateful for all of you supporting me, way back at the beginning, when I was only thinking of myself. It's pretty amazing what we've learned, you know," Joe said.

"Joe, all the science and learning was you, man. I remember a day when my brother was troubled by the idea that he would never fit into this family and would never do anything remarkable. I hope you can look at all this and see your accomplishments. We might decide not to share them with the world here, but you did all that," Ken said a little excitedly. "You solved the mathematic formula that allows for bending time, you programmed a machine to hold us, and you figured out an energy-generating field to make that formula a real thing. It was dangerous, but you solved the space-time continuum theory. You actually took us to the past and to the future in that machine. It's wild that we did all that."

"Yeah, it sure was," Joe said, smiling at Ken. "But maybe you're right. Maybe we shouldn't share it with anyone."

"Does this mean we aren't going to use it either? Is that what you're getting at, Ken?" Kim asked.

"I don't know. That's part of what I wanted to talk about. I think we can all admit that there is more than a little bit of risk every time we step into that machine. We change history by talking to people, by interacting. We can do some good, but we can also do a lot of harm. I think what I'm getting at is the biggest question of all. Maybe even right back where we started. We were driven by our grief and our need to support Joe, but I think the question was always there. It was there when Mary pleaded with us not to mess with God's plan for our parents, and when Joe went to Cambridge; when Ryan and Deb went to Cambridge, when you all went to Las Vegas; when Mr. Brewster and Thomas went to New York, when you went to Philadelphia, and when Darrick went to New York. Just because we have this power to travel through time and try to change things, even if we think it's helping others, just because we can, does it follow that we should?" Ken said.

They all sat for a long time thinking about what Ken had said. Then Kim said, "It's a little funny, isn't it? We started all this when we felt lost and didn't know where home was anymore. I mean, Joe, isn't that what you were doing? Trying to get home? All the trips—and especially the really long trip to Philadelphia—weren't we always searching for something. Maybe it was home."

"Yeah, maybe, I mean, that makes some sense," Joe added.

"And look, here we are, home," Kim added.

"Wow, Kim," Deb said.

"It sure has been a long road to get here," Joe said.

"Yes, the long road home," Ken said. "You're absolutely right, Kim. Home is right here with all of you, and Uncle Darrick, Aunt Alicia, Ryan, and Becky. And someday some worthy guy that Kim chooses. Home is wherever our family is. It's funny it took time travel to get here."

"I think this might be the end of the machine too," Joe said. "Kim, I know you wanted to use it to help others, but we learned that didn't work out so well."

"Besides, Kim, you've already made your mark on this family—and given just a little more time, your mark on the world," Deb added.

"So, we're decided? No more machine?" Ken asked.

They all put their hands into a circle and said together, "No more machine."

They spent a little more time on the beach, and then Ken said they needed to get back to the city. Reluctantly, they packed up the blankets, balls, and umbrella and went up the stairs to the house.

Once back in the city, there was a flurry of activity, getting Deb ready to leave for her summer on the dig, Kim leaving to spend a few weeks with Amy and her family, and Joe heading first to see Becky and then on to MIT for a few weeks. Only Ken, Aunt Alicia, and Uncle Darrick would be there until the fourth of July holiday. Amy and her parents arrived on Thursday to pick Kim up, and on Friday, Michael left with Joe to head out to Becky's house. Friday night, Deb and Ryan went out for dinner and saw a show on Broadway. Ryan was flying to North Carolina with his parents on Monday, but they wanted to have this last night together. He stayed at the apartment, and on Saturday morning, they all went with Deb to the train station to meet the other classmates heading out for the dig.

24

AT FIRST, DEB MISSED her family terribly. She was surprised at the depth of longing she had each week when she spoke to Kim, Ken, and Joe. She got updates each week as to their activities and what cool things they were seeing on their summer vacations. She was a little jealous they were doing fun things while she was working in the hot sun, but in the end, all she thought was how much she wished she could be with them. Aunt Alicia left the magazine shortly after Deb left. She said she was pleasantly surprised by the reaction and was even called to the Editor-in-Chief's office to meet with Grace Mirabella. Aunt Alicia said that she was very helpful and offered to feature the first collection. It was an easy transition, but now she was busy drawing and working with a team of people to create the clothing for that first collection. She seemed excited but tired.

At the end of June, Deb was called off the field to take a phone call, and she was surprised when it was Uncle Darrick who was on the other end.

"Is everyone ok?" Deb asked.

"Yes, I'm sorry if I worried you. It's just that your aunt and I miss you terribly, and we wondered if you had any time off for the fourth?"

"I think we're going to take a three- or four-day break, but I don't think that's enough time for me to get back there by train and be back here when I need to."

"Actually, I was thinking we'd come out there. I spoke to Ken, and he's able to take a break, and your aunt told me last night she was a bit stir crazy and needed a break. Kim will be back. So, I'm thinking we'll fly out and get you and head over to Mount Rushmore. I hear they do a big thing for the holiday. We can try some new restaurants and swim in the hotel pool and relax. What do you think?"

"Sounds great."

"Unless you're enjoying the independence and don't want us to come?"

"No, I actually really miss everybody. But don't tell them. I don't want Ken to think I'm not brave enough to do this."

Uncle Darrick laughed. "Your secret's safe with me. And I miss you too. So does your aunt."

"Do I need to do anything?"

"No, I'll make all the arrangements. I'll go over the plan when we talk this Sunday. I'm sorry I pulled you away, I just wanted to make sure this was ok with you before I made hotel reservations and booked flights."

"Thanks. I can't wait to see you all."

"We can't wait to see you too. Now we both probably have things to get back to, don't we?"

"Yes, you're just probably enjoying an air-conditioned office, while I'm roasting in the sun."

"Think of the tan you'll have!"

"Bye, Uncle Darrick!"

"Bye, sweetie."

Two weeks later, they picked Deb up at the small dormitory they were all staying in for the dig, and they drove back to Mount Rushmore. Deb was surprised when Ryan bounded out of the car and ran and lifted her up in the air.

"You have a great tan, my wonderful girlfriend!"

"You don't. Haha."

"I'm working this summer, not playing in the sand."

"Very funny!"

They all laughed and talked on the way to the hotel. Kim went directly to the pool while Uncle Darrick checked them all in. They swam and found a place to eat, and then they swam again into the evening. Deb was happy to have her family here and so excited about Ryan being with them. She whispered to Uncle Darrick at the pool after dinner her thanks for the surprise. He smiled and said Ken had called Ryan to see if he could get free from work.

The next day they went to the parades and fireworks near Mount Rushmore and ate all kinds of food. There were food stands all over the place. They played carnival games, and that night, they swam some more.

Aunt Alicia brought some of her drawings along to show Deb, and they got them out after the fireworks. Deb marveled at the designs and said she loved them all and really wanted a few of them, and she was sure they all would be a big hit. Aunt Alicia commented on one of the designs Deb liked, saying that it was perfect for Deb and how she was the inspiration for the design.

Later that night, Ken, Deb, and Ryan sat by the pool after everyone else went up, and Deb asked Ken how things were with Mary.

"It's going well, I guess."

"What does that mean?" Deb asked.

"Well, I've been traveling a lot the last few weeks, and we haven't been able to spend a lot of time together, but we're taking it slow and just enjoying each other's company."

"What do we call her then? Your friend or your girlfriend?" Ryan teased.

"I think, for now, she's just a friend."

"Do you want it to be more?" Deb asked.

"I think I'm getting there. She has changed. I mean I think she'll always have a little selfish streak. Her parents spoiled her, and she's an only child. I don't think she does it on purpose anyway. We're different than we were at Choate."

"Of course, you're different. You're twenty years old now," Deb said.

"Yeah, and she's matured too. It's been hard on both of us, the last year."

"Did you ask her to come along on this trip?" Deb asked.

"No, she's working for her father this summer and didn't have the ability to take time off. He's not ready to accept us being together. I don't know for sure what she told them or if they believed what she told them, but he's also still adjusting to our being back together."

"What are you going to do to convince him?"

"I'm actually thinking about going to see them. I told Mary I would go to her next weekend. There's a concert she wanted to go see. So, I figured I would go earlier on Friday than expected and see if I can speak to her father."

"That's pretty brave of you, to face the lion in his den," Ryan said.

"It's not the first time, remember. I'm hoping it will get easier!"

The next day, they dropped Deb off back at the dormitory and then got themselves back to the airport for their flight. Later that night, as Deb lay in her bed in the dormitory, she looked out over the desert and thanked God for her family and the great weekend they'd planned for her. She whispered to her parents that if they were watching, they could rest easy knowing everyone was going to be ok, more than ok.

Kim was spending the rest of the summer at art classes in the city, and Joe was due home at the end of July. Deb returned home at the end of July, and they again had a weekend at the Hampton house before it was time to start getting ready for another school year. Ken had gone and talked to Mary's father again. It seemed to work wonders as he was now accepted by her parents.

The last weekend before Ken had to return to Harvard, Mary came into the city, and they spent the day together. They went to Battery Park and did a few tourist things. As they were taking the ferry back from Ellis Island late in the day, they watched the sun set over the buildings as they approached Battery Park. Ken stood behind Mary and put his arms around her. He whispered in her ear that he loved her. She turned and smiled at him and kissed him. She whispered she loved him too.

"Does this mean you're my girlfriend now?" he asked.

"I hope so."

"Good. It feels good."

"I guess it's been a long road home for us too."

"Yes, it has, Mary. It really has."

Ken was smiling when he returned from saying goodbye to Mary. Deb was in the kitchen when he came in.

"Well, you certainly look happy. Shouldn't you be frowning after a goodbye?" she asked playfully.

"No more frown."

"Oh yeah?"

"It's official. She's my girlfriend."

"Good."

"Yeah, good."

They laughed and then talked about what needed to be purchased for school. Although neither Deb, Ken nor even Joe needed much, Kim had grown probably three inches that summer, and she needed all new clothes. At thirteen years old, Aunt Alicia said she couldn't have anything too mature, but it was time for her to have some fun clothes too. The shopping spree was an all-day affair. Then all too soon it was time to take Deb back to NYU, and Ken left for Harvard. Two weeks later, Joe and Kim were taken to Choate. It would be Joe's final year there, and Kim was finishing junior high that year.

The visits continued. It seemed when they acknowledged the strength of their bond early that summer, they found they couldn't go more than a few weeks without seeing each other. So once a month, Deb and Ryan went out to Choate to do things with Joe, Becky, and Kim, and on a different weekend, Mary and Ken met there. They continued to meet with Mr. Brewster. He became a valuable resource for Ryan during that fall for the science class that Ryan had somehow landed in. However, on one of their first visits, they explained their thoughts and discussions about the machine. Mr. Brewster agreed that it was a power that wasn't ready to be shared and had many risks.

Later that fall, Joe decided to attend MIT and not Harvard as he had always planned. It seemed a better fit for what he wanted to accomplish, and frankly, he explained to Deb one weekend, he felt free to make a different choice now. She was thrilled. Becky had committed to go to Harvard. That meant they would be close and still close to Choate.

That Christmas break, Deb asked Kim how she felt about Joe's college choice, and she commented that it seemed right that he would end up in Cambridge and not at Harvard. Deb asked her about the next year when she would be the only one at Choate, and Kim replied, "There was always going to be a time when you were all gone, and I would still be in high school. I knew that. And now it doesn't seem so bad. You're all close enough that I can see you any time."

"That's true."

"I'm ready, I think."

"Of course, you are. I always knew you would be the most confident of us all, Kim."

"That's because I had the benefit of all of you around me for thirteen years."

And so, the year passed, Joe and Becky graduated, and Kim began a journey on her own at Choate.

25

KEN SAT AT HIS desk in the Fitzgerald offices after a long day of meetings on their latest product initiative. He wondered when Joe would complete the latest drawings and get them sent over. Joe, in his third year at MIT now, held patents on at least a dozen innovative designs. Ken smiled when he remembered that day long ago when Joe lamented that he would never find his place. He looked down and saw he had a message from Mary. He picked up the phone to call her.

"Hi, beautiful, what did you need?"

"Did you even think about waiting to see if it was me who answered the phone?"

"No," he replied and laughed.

"You're incorrigible, as usual."

"What did you need?"

"I wanted to be sure you have on your calendar the meetings we have this Saturday with the two banquet facilities and the florist. I don't want you to miss these appointments and leave me to make all of our marriage arrangements."

"I'll be there. I promise. How's the story coming?"

"Good. I think I finished all my research, so now I just have to sit down and draft it. Brad is anxious to get it in this issue, so hopefully, it writes itself tomorrow."

"I'm sure it'll be fabulous."

"You're so good for my ego. Have you heard from Deb?"

"Yes, she called ridiculously early this morning to say that she'd made it to the museum. Her research for her master's thesis is progressing."

"That's good news."

"Yeah."

"And how is Kim doing? Isn't her art show coming up in Boston?"

"Yes, it's in two weeks."

"Is everyone coming?"

"Of course. I think Deb is hoping to be done by then and home."

"Oh, I didn't realize she was only going to be in London for a couple of weeks."

"Actually, as I look at my calendar, Kim's show isn't for three weeks, and Deb comes home just before the show."

"I'm going to put all this in my calendar. Just in case you lose track."

"Very funny."

"Dinner tonight?"

"Yes, I'm starving. When're you done?"

"I can be done any time."

"Meet me at Benjamin's?"

"Sure, twenty minutes?"

"You got it."

That Saturday, as promised, Ken presented himself for meetings to determine where the wedding reception would be held next spring when he and Mary got married. After a very long day, with both Aunt Alicia and Mary's mother in tow, they made a decision. One more thing checked off.

The next Wednesday, as Ken was reviewing the latest drawings from his brother with the prototyping team, his secretary interrupted and said he had an urgent call.

"This is Ken Fitzgerald."

"Ken, it's Mr. Brewster."

"Hi, Mr. Brewster. How are you? Is something wrong? Is Kim ok?"

"Kim's fine. My apologies for interrupting your workday, but this is urgent."

"What's wrong? You sound really agitated."

"It's bad, Ken. You need to round everyone up and get here as fast as you can. I got home from class today and decided to tinker on the old car. The machine is gone."

Authors Notes

AS WITH ANY WORK of fiction, authors do take some license to use real information to assist in telling the story. I am guilty of this as well. However, I would like to take this moment to give credit where credit is due to those people, dates, accomplishments, and events.

Choate Rosemary Hall is an actual boarding preparatory school located in Wallingford, Connecticut. It was founded as Rosemary Hall for girls in 1890 by Mary Atwater Choate. Later a boys' school was added, the girls' school relocated and then returned to the original location. It became a co-ed school in the 1970s. President John F. Kennedy, and many other famous people, attended throughout its history. Several of the buildings named here are actual buildings at Choate. However, the inclusion of younger children Kim's age and various aspects of the schedule, buildings, and activities are my creation. You can learn more about this wonderful school at: www.choate.edu.

Time travel is theoretical. The theory of bending time has been in academia for many years. The idea that time is not a linear concept, but a plane that can be bent with magnetic fields and energy is widely recognized as a valid theory. What is known about two people being in the same space and time continuum and what one would know if you jumped forward in time are also mainstream academic theories. In this installment of Time Benders, the siblings and their friends travel again to the past. The idea that one can make a simple change in the past and have it trickle through many lives and events is also a big part of time travel theories. I have used this information to make assumptions and create the possibility that time travel can be accomplished, but to date, no machine has ever been created and no actual live tests have been documented of time travel.

Vogue magazine has been in production since 1892. It became the premier fashion magazine later in the 1960s. Grace Mirabella was in fact the editor of *Vogue* during the time period of this story. Several of the people and places mentioned related to *Vogue* are factual. However, Aunt Alicia being employed there and her activities are fictional.

The Wharton Brook State Park is an actual park near Wallingford, CT. This park opened August 1, 1919, and was the precursor to modern highway rest stops. It has evolved over the years and offers fishing, picnicking, swimming, and several footpaths. Unfortunately, in 2018, a small tornado transitioned into a microburst and caused extensive damage to the park, causing it to close for the rest of the year. It re-opened in January of 2019.

The Fugitive Slave Act of 1850 was actually the second such law passed by the less-than-100-year-old United States. They were intended to deter people from assisting fugitive slaves and to keep those free states from becoming safe havens for runaway slaves. The Fugitive Slave Act of 1850 was part of the measures from Henry Clay to compromise and prevent Southern states from secession. It denied those fugitive slaves the right to a jury trial, increased the fines for citizens who aided fugitive slaves, and put all matters regarding fugitive slaves in the hands of the federal commissioner. The backlash was swift with several states, including Wisconsin and Vermont, passing state laws in attempts to bypass this federal law. It is believed that several hundred slaves were returned south with the use of the Fugitive Slave Act of 1850, including several free black men that were labeled runaway slaves, who spent years in slavery after being born free.

The Quakers as abolitionists is a strange and complicated story. First and foremost, the Quaker religion did not abide enslaving any person and was fervently non-violent. However, many Quakers survived and flourished in the early part of the 1800s by trading with and for their southern neighbors, particularly those in Virginia. Several key people, some white, but many free black people, hailing from Philadelphia, did make notable contributions to the movement. Men such as William Lloyd Garrison, William Still, and Robert Purvis, and women, like Elizabeth Chandler, wrote and worked tirelessly to free slaves. In the early days of the country, organizations were founded on the idea that slavery was immoral.

The Pennsylvania Abolition Society was, in fact, founded in 1775. Later, in the early 1800s, free black men and others began to take a more aggressive stance toward abolition, proposing immediate but uncompensated release of all slaves. We credit William Lloyd Garrison as the first organized and public effort toward abolition in this country, however, the Quaker leaders spoke out against slavery as early as 1688.

The Underground Railroad is something we've all heard of. Nearly every American has read a story about Harriet Tubman. The first mention of the underground railroad was in 1831 when an enslaved man escaped to Ohio, and his former owner blamed the underground railroad. What is not widely known is that most slaves using the underground railroad escaped from border states like Kentucky, Virginia, and Maryland. Because capturing and returning runaway slaves was a very lucrative business, very few slaves escaped from the deep south using the underground railroad. Runaway slaves were moved from "station" to "station" by conductors with the stations being operated by stationmasters. The routes stretched west through Ohio, Indiana, and Iowa, while the eastern routes ran through Pennsylvania and up through New England to Canada. Most fugitive slaves had to move all the way to Canada because the Fugitive Slave Acts made it possible for them to be returned south at any point. Harriet Tubman was the most famous conductor. Escaping from a plantation in Maryland, she returned many times to assist family escape and may not have become a lifelong conductor if her husband, also a slave, hadn't remarried and refused to go with her. Another prominent player of the underground railroad was Fredrick Douglass, who aided hundreds of runaway slaves from his Rochester, New York home. John Brown, the leader of the rebellion at Harper's Ferry, was also a conductor. Several lesser-known conductors were John Parker, a foundry owner in Ohio, who rowed fugitive slaves across the Ohio River. Even wealthy people were active in the freeing of slaves; Gerrit Smith, who ran for President twice, once bought an entire family of slaves and immediately freed them. The railroad ceased operations in about 1863 during the Civil War.

Mr. Robert Purvis was born August 4, 1810, in Charleston, South Carolina. He was of mixed race. His father was a wealthy businessman from Europe, and his mother was a free black woman from Morocco. Robert and his brother chose to identify with their black ancestry because of a deep and abiding love of their black grandmother. After his parent's death, Robert moved to Philadelphia and married a black free woman. Robert Purvis was an active abolitionist. In 1833, he helped found the American Anti-Slavery Society and the Library Company of Colored People. From 1845–1850, he served as president of the Pennsylvania Anti-Slavery Society and also traveled to Britain to gain support for the movement.

The slave trial and insurrection of Mr. Burns actually did not occur in Philadelphia, nor did it occur in 1853. The trial of Anthony Burns, a fugitive slave from Virginia, occurred in Boston, Massachusetts, during the spring of 1854. Hired out in Richmond, Burns had saved money and stowed away on a ship to Boston, where he worked in a clothing store. A letter home to his brother unintentionally revealed his location, and when it was intercepted, Burns' owner, Charles F. Suttle, traveled north and claimed Burns under the Fugitive Slave Act of 1850. Members of the Boston Vigilance Committee, a group of antislavery activists who were committed to resisting the law, made an attempt to free Burns from custody. They stormed the courthouse and attempted to get inside to free him. The rescue effort was unsuccessful, and a guard was killed in the process. In the trial, Burns' lawyers argued that the Fugitive Slave Act was unconstitutional and that Burns was not actually the man whom Suttle claimed to own. Antislavery activists later purchased his freedom, and he became a minister, dying in Canada in 1862.

Louisa May Alcott is a famous novelist. Born in 1832 of transcendentalist parents, she spent most of her life in Concord, Massachusetts, growing up in the company of Ralph Waldo Emerson and Henry David Thoreau. She is most famous for her novel, Little Women—a tale somewhat based on her life of four young girls growing up. She wrote many stories under the pen name A.M. Barnard that were violent and lurid prior to this great novel. She never married. Her family is rumored to have assisted in the underground railroad, providing a safe haven for slaves. This is known only from letters of her mother to correspondences she had. Whether or not her family ever hosted a fugitive slave is not known for certain.

Other references to movies, dates, events in the book are occasionally adapted for use in the story and do not represent actual release dates or actual dates when certain events took place.

About the Author

JB Yanni, author of the Time Benders time travelling adventure science fiction series, ready with a smile at any time, and beach-lover. Surrounded by a boisterous but loving family, she began writing during her teens on newspapers and her high school yearbook. Always searching for creative outlets, JB painted, drew and created her whole life, but found writing novels later in life. A great collector of books, JB believes that a book can change you, move you and become a lifelong friend. Her favorite quote, "Reading is the sole means by which we slip, involuntarily, often helplessly, into another's skin, another's voice, another's soul," Joyce Carol Oates.

JB can usually be found with a book or her Kindle in her hands, reading, when she is not writing. Her motto - "In my utopia, books are free, and reading makes you thin!"

You can contact JB via Facebook - jb_yanni; twitter - @jb_yanni; email - jb@jbyanni.com